States of
Consciousness

States of
Consciousness

Charles T. Tart

E. P. Dutton & Co., Inc. | New York | 1975

LIBRARY OF CONGRESS CATALOGING IN PUBLICATION DATA

Tart, Charles T   1937-
    States of consciousness.

    Bibliography: p.
    Includes index.
    1. Consciousness. I. Title. [DNLM: 1. Con-
sciousness. BF311 T193s]
    BF311.T29 1975   153   75-5940

10 9 8 7 6 5 4 3 2

Published simultaneously in Canada by Clarke, Irwin & Company
Limited, Toronto and Vancouver
ISBN: 0-525-20970-0 (cloth)
0-525-47406-4 (paper)

Contents

Introduction

✿✿✿

This is a transitional book.

It is transitional, first, because our society is in the midst of many vital transitions. As this book shows, our ordinary or "normal" state of consciousness is a tool, a structure, a coping mechanism for dealing with a certain agreed-upon social reality—a consensus reality. As long as that consensus reality and the values and experiences behind it remain reasonably stable, we have a fairly good idea of what "normal" consciousness is for an individual and what "pathological" deviations from that norm are. Today, as many of the religious, moral, and emotional underpinnings of our civilization lose their guiding value for our most influential people, the concepts of normal and pathological begin to lose their meanings.

Because we have begun in recent years to question the foundations of our consensus reality and the value of our normal state of consciousness, some of us have tried to alter consciousness by experimenting with drugs, meditation, new kinds of psychotherapies, new religious systems. My own reading of history suggests that some of the experiences people have had in altered states of consciousness, generally called mystical experiences, have formed the underpinnings of all great religious systems and of the stable societies and consensus realities that were formed from them. Now we not only question our inherited social systems, we go directly to the sources, to altered states of consciousness, in our search for new values and realities. This is a very exciting, very dangerous, and very hopeful undertaking. We are in a social transition, and no one of us knows precisely where it is going. Yet we have, perhaps, a chance to understand our own transition and possibly to guide it—things no society in the past has been able to do.

This opportunity is granted us by science, particularly the young science of psychology. Instead of being blindly converted to ideologies created by the powerful experiences encountered in altered states of consciousness, or avoiding them because of fear, we may be able, through science, to gain a broader understanding of our own minds and of these forces and to exert some intelligent[1] guidance.

This book is transitional in a second way because psychology itself is entering a state of rapid transition. Once defined as the study of the *mind,* psychology made little headway as a science; it lacked the elegance, precision of understanding, and power of doing of the physical sciences. So it was redefined by many of its practitioners as the study of *behavior.* Overt behavior is easier to study than experience, and the examination of overt behavior has given us many useful tools for predicting and changing behavior.

Now I see psychology once again becoming a science of or the study of the mind. This trend seems undesirable to many of my older colleagues, but is welcomed by many younger psychologists and by most current students of psychology. We cannot shun the study of the nature of the human mind simply because it is difficult, and confine ourselves to the easier analysis of overt behavior. We are now developing many tools for more precise study of the mind.

Yet this second transition is unfinished. At the moment I am optimistic that a science of consciousness and states of conscious-

---

1 I use the word *intelligent* in a very broad sense and do not want to equate it with the strictly rational. Rationality is not some absolute, universally valid way of thinking, as we generally believe. Rational means "according to the rules"; but where do the rules come from? We now understand that there are many logics, many ways of being rational. Each logic has different assumptions behind its rules, and assumptions are arbitrary. You can assume whatever you wish. What kind of logic will enable you to survive in your particular society is a different matter: you must share most of the assumptions common in your society to fit in. It used to be "obvious," for example, that the world was flat, and people who disagreed with this could get in trouble.

ness will be developed within this decade. But I cannot be certain that this transition in contemporary psychology will definitely lead to a science of consciousness. The interest among younger psychologists and students is not simply a function of some linear progress in the psychological knowledge available to us; it is also a reflection of the transition in our society that has prompted our search for values. If there is a marked change in society, such as an authoritarian, repressive shift to buy security rather than to endure the stress of transition, the new science of consciousness may be aborted.

This book presents a new way of viewing states of consciousness—a systems approach. It is a way of looking at what people tell us about and how they behave in various altered states of consciousness that I have been slowly developing in a decade of research. I have worked out the major dimensions of this way of understanding to a point of great usefulness to myself, and I believe the method can be useful to others, as well. It is now clear to me that the need is great for some kind of paradigm to make sense of the vast mass of chaotic data in this field, and I offer this systems approach to others even though this approach is still in transition. It will take me another decade to think out all the ramifications of this approach, to begin the broad-scale experimental tests of its usefulness, to adequately fit all the extant and evolving literature into it. But I do not think we have time for such slow and orderly work if, given the first two transitions, we are to understand enough scientifically about states of consciousness to have some influence on the powerful transitions occurring in our society. Thus I present this systems approach now, even though it is unfinished, in the hope that it may lead us toward the understanding we need.

This book is transitional in still another sense; it represents a variety of personal transitions for me. One of these transitions is a professional one—from experimentalist to theoretician. I am not entirely comfortable with this change. My style has been to conduct small-scale experiments in various areas of the psychology of consciousness where I can stay personally involved with the factual data and not lose track of them in the course of pursuing intriguing abstractions. Yet the systems approach presented here has evolved in the course of that experimentation, and it seems so promising that I have chosen to deemphasize my immediate involvement in experimentation to look at the larger picture of the nature of states of consciousness. A forthcoming book, *Studies of States of Consciousness* [132], will collect some of that research for convenient reference. References to all of my research can be found in the Bibliography [61–139].

Another personal transition is that I have lately given more attention to direct experience of some of the phenomena associated with altered states of consciousness. While much of what I write about here is intellectual or theoretical knowledge based on reports from others and on the experimental literature, some of it comes directly from my own experience—enough so that the systems approach I describe clearly makes basic *experiential* sense to me, even though many of its ramifications are beyond the scope of my personal experience.

My personal experience of some of the phenomena associated with altered states of consciousness may be both advantageous and disadvantageous. In the early days of research with LSD (lysergic acid diethylamide), scientists often downgraded the work of a researcher who had *not* taken LSD himself on grounds that he did not really understand the phenomena he was researching. On the other hand, if he *had* taken LSD himself, his research was suspect on grounds that his judgment probably had been warped by his personal involvement. He was damned if he did and damned if he didn't. So I have tried to steer a middle course—not presenting a personal theory, but also not presenting ideas that have no experiential basis at all for me. Whether this is an advantage or disadvantage must be judged by the long-term usefulness of these ideas.

This book is addressed to everyone who is interested in states of consciousness, whether that interest is personal, professional, or both. Each of us lives in his ordinary state of consciousness, each of us experiences at least one altered state of consciousness (dreaming), and few of us are immune to the currents of social change that make us ask questions about the nature of our mental life. Understanding consciousness is not the exclusive task or desire of scientists or therapists. Because this is a subject of interest to all of us, I have tried to keep my writing straightforward and clear and to resist the temptation to talk in scientific jargon. I introduce only a few technical terms, usually where the common words we might use have acquired such a wide range of meaning that they are no longer clear.

This book is also addressed to practitioners and researchers who will see where this way of looking at consciousness is helpful and will refine and expand it, and who will also see where this way of looking at things is not helpful and does not fit their experience and so will alter it. I believe what is presented here will be useful to many of us now, but I hope that in a decade the progress made by others in the refinement and application of this approach will allow a far more definitive book to be written.

The book is organized into two sections. The first section, "States," describes my systems approach to states of consciousness, discusses some of its implications, and gives an overview of what we know about states of consciousness today. The second section, "Speculations," presents ideas that, while consistent with the systems approach, are not a necessary part of it and are more unorthodox.

My own thinking in evolving this systems approach has depended heavily on the contributions of many others. To name only the ones most prominent in my mind, I am indebted to Roberto Assagioli, John Bennett, Carlos Castaneda (and his teacher, Don Juan), Arthur Deikman, Sigmund Freud, David Galin, George Gurdjieff, Arthur Hastings, Ernest Hilgard, Carl Jung, Thomas Kuhn, John Lilly, Abraham Maslow, Harold McCurdy, Gardner Murphy, Claudio Naranjo, Maurice Nicoll, Robert Ornstein, Peter Ouspensky, Idries Shah, Ronald Shor, Tarthang Tulku, Andrew Weil, and my wife, Judy. I also wish to express my particular thanks to Helen Joan Crawford, Lois Dick, and Irene Segrest, who have done so much to aid me in my research.

Section I: States

I .

The Systems Approach to
States of Consciousness

✿✿✿

There is a great elegance in starting out from simple ideas, slowly building them up into connected patterns, and having a complex, interlocking theoretical structure emerge at the end. Following the weaving of such a pattern, step by step, can be highly stimulating. Unfortunately, it is easy to get bogged down in the details, especially when the pattern has gaps to be filled in, and to lose track of what the steps are all about and what they are leading toward. This chapter gives a brief overview of my systems approach to states of consciousness—a brief sketch map of the whole territory to provide a general orientation before we look at detail maps. I do not define terms much here or give detailed examples, as these are supplied in later chapters.

Our ordinary state of consciousness is not something natural or given, but a highly complex construction, a specialized tool for coping with our environment and the people in it, a tool that is useful for doing some things but not very useful, and even dangerous, for doing other things. As we look at consciousness closely, we see that it can be analyzed into many parts. Yet these parts function together in a pattern: they form a system. While the components of consciousness can be studied in isolation, they exist as parts of a complex system, consciousness, and can be fully understood only when we see this function in the overall system. Similarly, understanding the complexity of consciousness requires seeing it as a system and understanding the parts. For this reason, I refer to my approach to states of consciousness as a systems approach.

To understand the constructed system we call a state of consciousness, we begin with some theoretical postulates based on human experience. The first postulate is the existence of a basic awareness. Because some volitional control of the focus of awareness is possible, we generally refer to it as *attention/awareness*. We must also recognize the existence of *self-awareness*, the awareness of being aware.

Further basic postulates deal with *structures*, those relatively permanent structures/functions/subsystems of the mind/brain that act on information to transform it in various ways. Arithmetical skills, for example, constitute a (set of related) structure (s). The structures of particular interest to us are those that require some amount of attention/awareness to activate them. Attention/awareness acts as *psychological energy* in this sense. Most techniques for controlling the mind are ways of deploying attention/awareness energy and other kinds of energies so as to activate desired structures (traits, skills, attitudes) and deactivate undesired structures.

Psychological structures have individual characteristics that limit and shape the ways in which they can interact with one another. Thus the possibilities of any system built of psychological structures are shaped and limited both by the deployment of attention/awareness and other energies and by the characteristics of the structures comprising the system. The human biocomputer, in other words, has a large but limited number of possible modes of functioning.

Because we are creatures with a certain kind of body and nervous system, a large number of human potentials are in principle available to us. But each of us is born into a particular culture that selects and develops a small number of these potentials, rejects others, and is ignorant of many. The small number of experiential potentials selected by our culture, plus some random factors, constitute the structural elements from which our ordinary state of consciousness is constructed. We are at once the beneficiaries and the victims of our culture's particular selection. The possibility of tapping and developing latent potentials, which lie outside the cultural norm, by entering an altered state of consciousness, by temporarily *restructuring* consciousness, is the basis of the great interest in such states.

The terms *state of consciousness* and *altered state of consciousness* have come to be used too loosely, to mean whatever is on one's mind at the moment. The new term *discrete state of consciousness* (d-SoC) is proposed for greater precision. A d-SoC is a unique, dynamic pattern or configuration of psychological structures, an active system of psychological subsystems. Although the component structures/subsystems show some variation within a d-SoC, the overall pattern, the overall system properties remain recognizably the same. If, as you sit reading, you think, "I am dreaming," instead of "I am awake," you have changed a small cognitive element in your consciousness but not affected at all the basic pattern we call your waking state. In spite of subsystem variation and environmental variation, a d-SoC is stabilized by a number of processes so that it retains its identity and function. By analogy, an automobile remains an automobile whether on a road or in a garage (environment change), whether you change the brand of spark plugs or the color of the seat covers (internal variation).

Examples of d-SoCs are the ordinary waking state, nondreaming sleep, dreaming sleep, hypnosis, alcohol intoxication, marijuana intoxication, and meditative states.

A *discrete altered state of consciousness* (d-ASC) refers to a d-SoC that is different from some *baseline state of consciousness* (b-SoC). Usually the ordinary state is taken as the baseline state. A d-ASC is a new system with unique properties of its own, a restructuring of consciousness. *Altered* is intended as a purely descriptive term, carrying no values.

A d-SoC is stabilized by four kinds of processes: (1) *loading stabilization*—keeping attention/awareness and other psychological energies deployed in habitual, desired structures by loading the person's system heavily with appropriate tasks; (2) *negative feedback stabilization*—correcting the functioning of erring structures/subsystems when they deviate too far from the normal range that ensures stability; (3) *positive feedback stabilization*—strengthening activity and/or providing rewarding experiences when structures/subsystems are functioning within desired limits; and (4) *limiting stabilization*—restricting the range of functioning of structures/subsystems whose intense operation would destabilize the system.

In terms of current psychological knowledge, ten major subsystems (collections of related structures) that show important

variations over known d-ASCs need to be distinguished: (1)
Exteroception—sensing the external environment; (2) *Interoception*—sensing what the body is feeling and doing; (3) *Input-
Processing*—automated selecting and abstracting of sensory input
so we perceive only what is "important" by personal and cultural
(consensus reality) standards; (4) *Memory;* (5) *Subconscious*—
the classical Freudian unconscious plus many other psychological
processes that go on outside our ordinary d-SoC, but that may
become directly conscious in various d-ASCs; (6) *Emotions;* (7)
Evaluation and Decision-Making—our cognitive evaluating skills
and habits; (8) *Space/Time Sense*—the construction of *psychological* space and time and the placing of events within it; (9)
Sense of Identity—the quality added to experience that makes it
a personal experience instead of just information; and (10)
Motor Output—muscular and glandular outputs to the external
world and the body. These subsystems are not ultimates, but
convenient categories to organize current knowledge.

Our current knowledge of human consciousness and d-SoCs is
highly fragmented and chaotic. The main purpose of the systems
approach presented here is organizational: it allows us to relate
what were formerly disparate bits of data and supplies numerous
methodological consequences for guiding future research. It
makes the general prediction that the number of d-SoCs available to human beings is definitely limited, although we do not
yet know those limits. It further provides a paradigm for making
more specific predictions that will sharpen our knowledge about
the structures and subsystems that make up human consciousness.

There are enormously important individual differences in the
structure of d-SoCs. If we map the experiential space in which
two people function, one person may show two discrete, separated
clusters of experiential functioning (two d-SoCs), while the
other may show continuous functioning throughout both regions
and the connecting regions of experiential space. The first person
must make a special effort to travel from one region of experiential space (one d-SoC) to the other; the second makes no special
effort and does not experience the contrast of pattern and structure differences associated with the two regions (the two d-SoCs).
Thus what is a special *state* of consciousness for one person may
be an everyday experience for another. Great confusion results if
we do not watch for these differences: unfortunately, many

widely used experimental procedures are not sensitive to these important individual differences.

Induction of a d-ASC involves two basic operations that, if successful, lead to the d-ASC from the b-SoC. First, we apply *disrupting forces* to the b-SoC—psychological and/or physiological actions that disrupt the stabilization processes discussed above either by interfering with them or by withdrawing attention/ awareness energy or other kinds of energies from them. Because a d-SoC is a complex system, with multiple stabilization processes operating simultaneously, induction may not work. A psychedelic drug, for example, may not produce a d-ASC because psychological stabilization processes hold the b-SoC stable in spite of the disrupting action of the drug on a physiological level.

If induction is proceeding successfully, the disrupting forces push various structures/subsystems to their limits of stable functioning and then beyond, destroying the integrity of the system and disrupting the stability of the b-SoC as a system. Then, in the second part of the induction process, we apply *patterning forces* during this transitional, disorganized period—psychological and/or physiological actions that pattern structures/subsystems into a new system, the desired d-ASC. The new system, the d-ASC, must develop its own stabilization processes if it is to last.

Deinduction, return to the b-SoC, is the same process as induction. The d-ASC is disrupted, a transitional period occurs, and the b-SoC is reconstructed by patterning forces. The subject transits back to his customary region of experiential space.

Psychedelic drugs like marijuana or LSD do not have invariant psychological effects, even though much misguided research assumes they do. In the present approach, such drugs are disrupting and patterning forces whose effects occur in combination with other psychological factors, all mediated by the operating d-SoC. Consider the so-called reverse tolerance effect of marijuana that allows new users to consume very large quantities of the drug with no feeling of being stoned (in a d-ASC), but later to use much smaller quantities of marijuana to achieve the d-ASC. This is not paradoxical in the systems approach, even though it is paradoxical in the standard pharmacological approach. The physiological action of the marijuana is not sufficient to disrupt the ordinary d-SoC until additional psychological factors disrupt enough of the stabilization processes of the b-SoC to allow transition to the d-ASC. These additional psychological forces are usually "a little help from my friends," the instructions for deployment of attention/awareness energy given by experienced users who know what functioning in the d-ASC of marijuana intoxication is like. These instructions also serve as patterning forces to shape the d-ASC, to teach the new user how to employ the physiological effects of the drug to form a new system of consciousness.

This book also discusses methodological problems in research from the point of view of the systems approach: for example, the way in which experiential observations of consciousness and transitions from one d-SoC to another can be made and the shifts in research strategies that this approach calls for. The systems approach can also be applied within the ordinary d-SoC to deal with *identity states,* those rapid shifts in the central core of a person's identity and concerns that are overlooked for many reasons, and emotional states. Similarly the systems approach indicates that latent human potential can be developed and used in various d-ASCs, so that learning to shift into the d-ASC appropriate for dealing with a particular problem is part of psychological growth. At the opposite extreme, certain kinds of psychopathology, such as multiple personality, can be treated as d-ASCs.

One of the most important consequences of the systems approach is the deduction that we need to develop *state-specific sciences.* Insofar as a "normal" d-SoC is a semi-arbitrary way of structuring consciousness, a way that loses some human potentials while developing others, the sciences we have developed are one-state sciences. They are limited in important ways. Our ordinary sciences have been very successful in dealing with the physical world, but not very successful in dealing with particularly human psychological problems. If we apply scientific method to developing sciences within various d-ASCs, we can evolve sciences based on radically different perceptions, logics, and communications, and so gain new views complementary to our current ones.

The search for new views, new ways of coping, through the experience of d-ASCs is hardly limited to science. It is a major basis for our culture's romance with drugs, meditation, Eastern religions, and the like. But infatuation with a new view, a new d-SoC, tends to make us forget that *any* d-SoC is a limited construction. There is a price to be paid for everything we get. It is vital for us to develop sciences of this powerful, life-changing area of d-ASCs if we are to optimize benefits from the growing use of them and avoid the dangers of ignorant or superstitious tampering with the basic structure of consciousness.

2.

The Components of Consciousness:
Awareness, Energy, Structures

✿✿

People use the phrase *states of consciousness* to describe unusual alterations in the way consciousness functions. In this chapter we consider some of the experiences people use to judge what states they are in, in order to illustrate the complexity of experience. We then consider what basic concepts or components we need to make sense out of this variety of experiences.

I have often begun a lecture on states of consciousness by asking the audience the following question: "Is there anyone here right now who *seriously* believes that what you are experiencing, in this room, at this moment, may be something you are just dreaming? I don't mean picky, philosophical doubts about the ultimate nature of experience or anything like that. I'm asking whether anyone in any seriously *practical* way thinks this might be a dream you're experiencing now, rather than your ordinary state of consciousness?" How do you, dear reader, know that you are actually reading this book now, rather than just dreaming about it? Think about it before going on.

I have asked this question of many audiences, and I have only occasionally seen a hand go up. No one has stuck to defending this position. If you take this question to mean, "How do you know you're not dreaming now?" you probably take a quick internal scan of the content and quality of your experience and find that some specific elements of it, as well as the overall pattern of your experience, match those qualities you have come to associate with your ordinary waking consciousness, but do not match the qualities you have come to associate with being in a dreaming state of consciousness.

I ask this question in order to remind the reader of a basic datum underlying my approach to consciousness—that a person sometimes scans the pattern of his ongoing experience and classifies it as being one or another *state* of consciousness.

Many people make distinctions among only a few states of consciousness, since they experience only a few. Everyone, for example, probably distinguishes between his ordinary waking state, dreaming, and dreamless sleep. Some others may distinguish drunkenness as a fourth state of consciousness. Still others who have personally experimented with altered states may want to distinguish among drug-induced, meditative, and emotion-induced states.

Without yet attempting to define consciousness or states of consciousness more precisely, suppose we ask people who have personally experienced many states of consciousness how they make these distinctions. What do they look for in their experience that alerts them to the fact that they are in a different state of consciousness from their ordinary one? A few years ago I asked a group of graduate students who had had fairly wide experience with altered states, "What sorts of things in yourself do you check on if you want to decide what state of consciousness you're in at a given moment?" Table 2–1 presents a categorization of the kinds of answers they gave, a categorization in terms of the systems approach I am explaining as we go along. A wide variety of unusual experiences in perceptions of the world or of oneself, of changes in time, emotion, memory, sense of identity, cognitive processes, perception of the world, use of the body (motor output), and interaction with the world were mentioned.

If we ignore the categorization of the experiences listed in Table 2–1, we have an illustration of the current state of knowledge about states of consciousness—that people experience a wide variety of unusual things. While the experiencers imply that there are meaningful patterns in their experiences that they cluster together as "states," our current scientific knowledge about how this wide variety of things goes together is poor. To understand people's experiences in this area more adequately we

Table 2-1

EXPERIENTIAL CRITERIA FOR DETECTING AN
ALTERED STATE OF CONSCIOUSNESS

EXTEROCEPTION (sensing the external world)
Alteration in various sensory characteristics of the perceived world—
glowing lights at the edges of things, attenuation or accentuation
of visual depth

INTEROCEPTION (sensing the body)
Alteration in perceived body image—shape or size changes
Alteration in detectable physiological parameters—accelerated or
retarded heart rate, respiration rate, muscle tonus, tremor
Perception of special bodily feelings not normally present—feelings
of energy in the body, generally or specially localized, as in the
spine; change in quality of energy flow in the body, such as
intensity, focus vs. diffuseness

INPUT-PROCESSING (seeing *meaningful* stimuli)
Sensory excitement, involvement, sensuality
Enhanced or decreased sensory intensity
Alterations of dominance-interaction hierarchies of various sensory
modalities
Illusion, hallucination, perception of patterns and things otherwise
known to be unlikely to actually exist in the environment

EMOTIONS
Alteration in emotional response to stimuli—overreacting, under-
reacting, not reacting, reacting in an entirely different way
Extreme intensity of emotions

MEMORY
Changes in continuity of memory over time—either an implicit
feeling that continuity is present or an explicit checking of
memory that shows current experience to be consistent with continuous memories leading up to the present, with gaps suggesting
an altered state
Details. Checking fine details of perceived environment (external or internal) against memories of how they should be to
detect incongruities

TIME SENSE
Unusual feeling of here-and-nowness
Feeling of great slowing or speeding of time

Feeling of orientation to past and/or future, regardless of relation
to present
Feeling of archetypal quality to time; atemporal experience

SENSE OF IDENTITY
Sense of unusual identity, role
Alienation, detachment, perspective on usual identity or identities

EVALUATION AND COGNITIVE PROCESSING
Alteration in rate of thought
Alteration in quality of thought—sharpness, clarity
Alteration of rules of logic (compared with memory of usual rules)

MOTOR OUTPUT
Alteration in amount or quality of self-control
Change in the active body image, the way the body feels when in
motion, the proprioceptive feedback signals that guide actions
Restlessness, tremor, partial paralysis

INTERACTION WITH THE ENVIRONMENT*
Performance of unusual or impossible behaviors—incongruity of
consequences resulting from behavioral outputs, either immediate
or longer term
Change in anticipation of consequences of specific behaviors—either
prebehavioral or learned from observation of consequences
Change in voice quality
Change in feeling of degree of orientation to or contact with im-
mediate environment
Change in involvement with vs. detachment from environment
Change in communications with others—incongruities or altered
patterns, consensual validation or lack of it

---

* *This category represents the combined functioning of several subsystems.*

must develop conceptual frameworks, theoretical tools, that make
sense out of the experiences in some more basic way and that still
remain reasonably true to the experiences as reported.

We can now begin to look at a conceptual framework that I
have been developing for several years about the nature of consciousness, and particularly about the nature of *states* of consciousness. Although what we loosely call altered states of
consciousness are often vitually important in determining human
values and behavior, and although we are in the midst of a
cultural evolution (or decay, depending on your values) in
which experiences from altered states of consciousness play an

important part, our scientific knowledge of this area is still sparse. We have a few relationships, a small-scale theory here and there, but mainly assorted and unrelated observations and ideas. My *systems approach* attempts to give an overall picture of this area to guide future research in a useful fashion.

I call this framework for studying consciousness a *systems approach* because I take the position that consciousness, as we know it, is not a group of isolated psychological functions but a *system*—an interacting, dynamic configuration of psychological components that performs various functions in greatly changing environments. While knowledge of the nature of the components is useful, to understand fully any system we must also consider the environments with which it deals and the goals of its functioning. So in trying to understand human consciousness, we must get the feel of the whole system as it operates in its world, not just study isolated parts of it.

I emphasize a *psychological* approach to states of consciousness because that is the approach I know best, and I believe it is adequate for building a comprehensive science of consciousness. But because the approach deals with systems, it can be easily translated into behavioral or neurophysiological terms [52].

Let us now look at the basic elements of this systems approach, the basic postulates about what lies behind the phenomenal manifestations of experience. In the following chapters we will put these basic elements of awareness, energy, and structure together into the systems we call states of consciousness.

Awareness and Energy

We begin with a concept of some kind of basic *awareness*—an ability to know or sense or cognize or recognize that something is happening. This is a basic theoretical and experiential given. We do not know scientifically what its ultimate nature is,[1] but it is where we start from. I call this concept attention/awareness, to relate it to another basic given, which is that we have *some* ability to direct this awareness from one thing to another.

This basic attention/awareness is something we can both con-

---

[1] The reader may ask, "How can we study awareness or consciousness when we don't know what it basically is?" The answer is, "In the same way that physicists studied and still study gravity: they don't know what it is, but they can study what it does and how it relates to other things."

ceptualize and (to some extent) experience as distinct from the particular *content* of awareness at any time. I am aware of a plant beside me at this moment of writing and if I turn my head I am aware of a chair. The function of basic awareness remains in spite of various changes in its content.

A second basic theoretical and experiential given is the existence, at times, of an awareness of being aware, *self-awareness*. The degree of self-awareness varies from moment to moment. At one extreme, I can be very aware that at this moment I am aware that *I* am looking at the plant beside me. At the other extreme, I may be totally involved in looking at the plant, but not be aware of being aware of it. There is an experiential continuum at one end of which attention/awareness and the particular content of awareness are essentially merged,[2] and at the other end of which awareness of being aware exists in addition to the particular content of the awareness. In between are mixtures: at this moment of writing I am groping for clarity of the concept I want to express and trying out various phrases to see if they adequately express it. In low-intensity flashes, I have some awareness of what I am doing, but most of the time I am absorbed in this particular thought process. The lower end of the self-awareness continuum, relatively total absorption, is probably where we spend most of our lives, even though we like to credit ourselves with high self-awareness.

The relative rarity of self-awareness is a major contributor to neurotic qualities in behavior and to the classification of ordinary consciousness as illusion or waking dreaming by many spiritual systems, an idea explored in Chapter 19. The higher end of the continuum of self-awareness comes to us even more rarely, although it may be sought deliberately in certain kinds of meditative practices, such as the Buddhist vipassana meditation discussed in Chapter 7.

The ultimate degree of self-awareness, of separation of attention/awareness from content, that is possible in any final sense varies with one's theoretical position about the ultimate nature of the mind. If one adopts the conventional view that mental activity is a product of brain functioning, thus totally controlled by the electrical-structural activity of brain functioning, there is a definite limit to how far awareness can back off from particular

2 Something we can only know retrospectively.

content, since that awareness is a product of the structure and content of the individual brain. This is a psychological manifestation of the physical principle of relativity, discussed in Chapter 18. Although the feeling of being aware can have an objective quality, this conventional position holds that the objectivity is only relative, for the very function of awareness itself stems from and is shaped by the brain activity it is attempting to be aware of.

A more radical view, common to the spiritual psychologies [128], is that basic awareness is not just a property of the brain, but is (at least partially) something from outside the workings of the brain. Insofar as this is true, it is conceivable that most or all content associated with brain processes could potentially be stood back from so that the degree of separation between content and attention/awareness, the degree of self-awareness, is potentially much higher than in the conservative view.

Whichever ultimate view one takes, the psychologically important concept for studying consciousness is that the *degree* of experienced separation of attention/awareness from content varies considerably from moment to moment.

Attention/awareness can be volitionally directed to some extent. If I ask you to become aware of the sensations in your left knee now, you can do so. But few would claim anything like total ability to direct attention. If you are being burned by a flame, it is generally impossible to direct your attention/awareness to something else and not notice the pain at all, although this can be done by a few people in the ordinary d-SoC and by many more people in certain states of consciousness. Like the degree of separation of attention/awareness from content, the degree to which we can volitionally direct our attention/awareness also varies. Sometimes we can easily direct our thoughts according to a predetermined plan; at other times our minds wander with no regard at all for our plans.

Stimuli and structures attract or capture attention/awareness. When you are walking down the street, the sound and sight of an accident and a crowd suddenly gathering attract your attention to the incident. This attractive pull of stimuli and activated structures may outweigh volitional attempts to deploy attention/ awareness elsewhere. For example, you worry over and over about a particular problem and are told that you are wasting energy by going around in circles and should direct your attention elsewhere. But, in spite of your desire to do so, you may find it almost impossible.

The ease with which particular kinds of structures and contents capture attention/awareness varies with the state of consciousness and the personality structure of the individual. For example, things that are highly valued or are highly threatening capture attention much more easily than things that bore us. Indeed, we can partially define personality as those structures that habitually capture a person's attention/awareness. In some states of consciousness, attention/awareness is more forcibly captivated by stimuli than in others.

Attention/awareness constitutes the major energy of the mind, as we usually experience it. *Energy* is here used in its most abstract sense—the ability to do work, to make something happen. Attention/awareness is energy (1) in the sense that structures having no effect on consciousness at a given time can be activated if attended to; (2) in the sense that structures may draw attention/awareness energy automatically, habitually, as a function of personality structure, thus keeping a kind of low-level, automated attention in them all the time (these are our long-term desires, concerns, phobias, blindnesses) ; and (3) in the sense that attention/awareness energy may inhibit particular structures from functioning. The selective redistribution of attention/awareness energy to desired ends is a key aspect of innumerable systems that have been developed to control the mind.

The concept of psychological energy is usually looked upon with disfavor by psychologists because it is difficult to define clearly. Yet various kinds of psychological energies are direct experiential realities. I am, for example, full of energy for writing at this moment. When interrupted a minute ago, I resented having to divert this energy from writing to dealing with a different issue. Last night I was tired; I felt little energy available to do what I wished to do. Those who prefer to give priority to observations about the body and nervous system in their thinking would tell me that various chemicals in my bloodstream were responsible for these varied feelings. But "chemicals in my bloodstream" is a very intellectual, abstract concept to me, while the feelings of energy and of tiredness are direct experiences for me and most other people. So we must consider psychological energy in order to keep our theorizing close to experience.

I cannot deal in any detail with psychological energy at this stage of development of the systems approach, for we know little about it. Clearly, changing the focus of attention (as in trying to sense what is happening in your left knee) has effects: it starts, stops, and alters psychological processes. Also, attention/awareness is not the only form of psychological energy. Emotions, for example, constitute a very important kind of energy, different in quality from simple attention/awareness shifts, but interacting with attention/awareness as an energy. So while this book deals primarily with attention/awareness as psychological energy, the concept of psychological energy is much more complex and is one of the major areas to be developed in the future.

Note that the total amount of attention/awareness energy available to a person varies from time to time, but there may be some fixed upper limit on it for a particular day or other time period. Some days, we simply cannot concentrate well no matter how much we desire it; other days we seem able to focus clearly, to use lots of attention to accomplish things. We talk about exhausting our ability to pay attention, and it may be that the total amount of attention/awareness energy available is fixed for various time periods under ordinary conditions.

Structures

The mind, from which consciousness arises, consists of myriad structures. A psychological *structure* refers to a relatively stable organization of component parts that perform one or more related psychological functions.

We infer (from outside) the existence of a particular structure by observing that a certain kind of input information reliably results in specific transformed output information under typical conditions. For example, we ask someone, "How much is fourteen divided by seven?" and he answers, "Two." After repeating this process, with variations, we infer the existence of a special structure or related set of structures we can call arithmetical skills. Experientially, we infer (from inside) the existence of a particular structure when, given certain classes of experienced input information, we experience certain transformed classes of output/response information. Thus, when I overhear the question about fourteen divided by seven and observe that some part of me automatically responds with the correct answer, I infer an arithmetical skills structure as part of my own mind.

We hypothesize that structures generally continue to exist even when they are not active, since they operate again when appropriate activating information is present. I again know that fourteen divided by seven is two, even though I stopped thinking about it for a while.

The emphasis here is on the structure forming something that has a recognizable shape, pattern, function, and process that endure over time. Ordinarily we are interested in the structure's overall properties as a complete structure, as a structured system, rather than in the workings of its component parts. Insofar as any structure can be broken down into substructures and sub-substructures, finer analyses are possible ad infinitum. The arithmetical skill structure can be broken down into adding, subtracting, multiplying, or dividing substructures. Such microscopic analyses, however, may not always be relevant to an understanding of the properties of the overall system, such as the state of consciousness, that one is working with. The most obvious thing that characterizes an automobile *as a system* is its ability to move passengers along roads at high speed; a metallurgical analysis of its spark plugs is not relevant to an understanding of its primary functioning and nature. Our concern, then, is with the psychological structures that show functions useful to our understanding of consciousness. Such structures can be given names—sexual needs, social coping mechanisms, language abilities.

Note that some structures may be so complex that we are unable to recognize them as structures. We see only component parts and never understand how they all work together.

A psychological structure may vary in the intensity and/or the quality of its activity, both overall and in terms of its component parts, but still retain its basic patterns (gestalt qualities) and so remain recognizably the same. A car is usefully referred to as a car whether it is moving at five or twenty-five miles an hour, whether it is red or blue, whether the original spark plugs have been replaced by spark plugs of a different brand. We anticipate an understanding of a state of consciousness as a system here.

Some structures are essentially permanent. The important aspects of their functioning cannot be modified in any significant way; they are biological/physiological givens. They are the hardware of our mental system. To use an analogy from computer programming, they are fixed programs, functions built into the machinery of the nervous system.

Some structures are mainly or totally given by an individual's particular developmental history: they are created by, programmed by, learning, conditioning, and enculturation processes that the individual undergoes. This is the software of the human biocomputer. Because of the immense programmability of human beings, most of the structures that interest us, that we consider particularly *human*, are in this software category.

Permanent structures create limits on, and add qualities to, what can be done with programmable structures: the hardware puts some constraints on what the software can be. The physiological parameters constituting a human being place some limits on his particular mental experience and his possible range of programming.

Our interest is in relatively permanent structures,[3] ones that are around long enough for us conveniently to observe, experience and study. But all the theoretical ideas in this book should be applicable to structures that are not long-lasting, even though investigation may be more difficult.

Structures, for the outside investigator, are hypothesized explanatory entitites based on experiential, behavioral, or psychological data. They are also hypothesized explanatory concepts for each of us in looking at his own experience: I know that fourteen divided by two equals seven, but I do not experience the arithmetical skills *structure* directly; I only know that when I need that kind of knowledge, it appears and functions. Since I need not hold on consciously to that knowledge all the time, I readily believe or hypothesize that it is stored in some kind of structure, someplace "in" my mind.

Interaction of Structure and Attention/Awareness

Many structures function completely independently of attention/awareness. An example is any basic physiological structure

---

[3] I suspect that many of these relatively permanent psychological structures exist not just in the nervous system but as muscle and connective tissue sets in the body, and can be changed radically by such procedures as structural integration [54.]

such as the kidneys. We infer their integrity and nature as structures from other kinds of data, as we have no direct awareness of their functioning.[4] Such structures do not utilize attention/awareness as energy, but use other forms of physiological/psychological activating energy. Structures that cannot be observed by attention/awareness are of incidental interest to the study of consciousness, except for their indirect influence on other structures that are accessible to conscious awareness.

Some structures require a certain amount of attention/awareness energy in order to (1) be formed or created in the first place (software programming), (2) operate, (3) have their operation inhibited, (4) have their structure or operation modified, and/or (5) be destructured and dismantled. We call these *psychological structures* when it is important to distinguish them from structures in general. Many structures require attention/awareness energy for their initial formation. The attention originally required to learn arithmetical skills is an excellent example. Once the knowledge or structure we call arithmetical skills is formed, it is usually present only in inactive, latent form. An arithmetical question directs attention/awareness to that particular structure, and we experience arithmetical skills. If our original programming was not very thorough, a fairly obvious amount of attention/awareness energy is necessary to use this skill. Once the structure has become highly automated and overlearned, only a small amount of attention/awareness energy is needed to activate and run the structure. We solve basic arithmetic problems, for example, with little awareness of the process involved in so doing.

Note that while we have distinguished attention/awareness and structure for analytical convenience and in order to be true to certain experiential data, ordinarily we deal with *activated* mental structures. We acquire data about structures when the structures are functioning, utilizing attention/awareness energy or other kinds of psychological energies.

Although we postulate that attention/awareness energy is

4 We should be careful about a priori definitions that certain structures *must* be outside awareness. Data from the rapidly developing science of biofeedback, and traditional data from yoga and other spiritual disciplines, remind us that many processes long considered totally outside conscious awareness can be brought to conscious awareness with appropriate training.

capable of activating and altering psychological structures, is the fuel that makes many structures run, our experience is that affecting the operation of structures by the volitional deployment of attention/awareness energy is not always easy. Attempts to alter a structure's operation by attending to it in certain ways may have no effect or even a contrary effect to what we wish. Attempts to stop a certain structure from operating by trying to withhold attention energy from it may fail. The reasons for this are twofold.

First, if the structure is (at least partially) operating on energy other than attention/awareness, it may no longer be possible to change it with the amount of attention/awareness energy we are able to focus on it. Second, even if the structure still operates with attention/awareness energy, complete control of this energy may be beyond our conscious volition for one or both of the following reasons: (1) the energy flow through it may be so automatized and overlearned, so implicit, that we simply do not know how to affect it; and (2) the functioning structure may have vital (and often implicit or hidden) connections with our reward and punishment systems, so that there are secondary gains from the operation of the structure, despite our conscious complaints. Indeed, it seems clear that for ordinary people in ordinary states of consciousness, the amount of attention/awareness energy subject to conscious control and deployment is quite small compared with the relatively permanent investments of energy in certain basic structures composing the individual's personality and his adaptation to the consensus reality of his culture.

Since the amount of attention/awareness energy available at any particular time has a fixed upper limit, some decrement should be found when too many structures draw on this energy simultaneously. However, if the available attention/awareness energy is greater than the total being used, simultaneous activation of several structures incurs no decrement.

Once a structure has been formed and is operating, either in isolation or in interaction with other structures, the attention/awareness energy required for its operation can be automatically drawn on either intermittently or continuously. The personality and normal state of consciousness are operating in such a way that attention is repeatedly and automatically drawn to the particular structure. Personality can be partially defined as the set of interacting structures (traits) habitually activated by attention/awareness energy. Unless he develops the ability to deploy attention in an observational mode, the self-awareness mode, a person may not realize that his attention/awareness energy is being drawn to this structure.

There is a fluctuating but generally large drain on attention/awareness energy at all times by the multitude of automated, interacting structures whose operation constitutes personality, the normal state of consciousness. Because the basic structures composing this are activated most of a person's waking life, he perceives this activation not as a drain on attention/awareness energy, but simply as the natural state of things. He has become habituated to it. The most important data supporting this observation come from reports of the effects of meditation, a process that in many ways is a deliberate deployment of attention/awareness from its customary structures to nonordinary structures or to maintenance of a relatively pure, detached awareness. From these kinds of experiences it can be concluded that attention/awareness energy must be used to support the ordinary state of consciousness. Don Juan expounds this view to Carlos Castaneda [12] as the rationale for certain training exercises ("not doing") designed to disrupt the habitual deployment of attention/awareness energy into channels that maintain ("doing") ordinary consensus reality. And from experiences of apparent clarity, the automatized drain of attention/awareness energy into habitually activated structures is seen by meditators as blurring the clarity of basic awareness, so that ordinary consciousness appears hazy and dreamlike.

Interaction of Structures and Structures

Although the interaction of one psychological structure with another structure depends on activation of both structures by attention/awareness energy, this interaction is modified by an important limitation: that *individual structures have various kinds of properties* that limit and control their potential range of interaction with one another. Structures are not equipotent with respect to interacting with one another, but have important individual characteristics. You cannot see with your ears.

Information is fed into any structure in one or more ways and comes out of the structure in one or more ways.[5] We can say in general that for two structures to interact (1) they must have either a direct connection between them or some connections mediated by other structures, (2) their input and output information must be in the same code so information output from one makes sense to the input for the other, (3) the output signals of one structure must not be so weak that they are below the threshold for reception by the other structure, (4) the output signals of one structure must not be so strong that they overload the input of the other structure.

Now let us consider ways in which psychological structures may *not* interact. First, two structures may not interact because there is no direct or mediated connection between them. I have, for example, structures involved in moving the little finger of my left hand and sensing its motion, and I have structures involved in sensing my body temperature and telling me whether I have a fever or a chill. Although I am moving my little finger vigorously now, I can get no sense of having either a fever or a chill from that action. Those two structures seem to be totally unconnected.

Second, two structures may not interact if the codes of output and input information are incompatible. My body, for example, has learned to ride a bicycle. While I can sense that knowledge in my body, in the structure that mediates my experience of riding a bicycle when I actually am doing so, I cannot verbalize it in any adequate way. The nature of the knowledge encoded in that particular structure does not code into the kind of knowledge that constitutes my verbal structures.

Third, two structures may not interact if the output signal from one is too weak, below the threshold for affecting another. When I am angry with someone and arguing with him, there may, during the argument, be a still small voice in me telling me that I am acting foolishly, but I have little awareness of that still small voice, and it cannot affect the action of the structures involved in feeling angry and arguing.

---

[5] For complex structures, we should probably also distinguish among (1) inputs and outputs that we can be consciously aware of with suitable deployment of attention/awareness, (2) inputs and outputs that we cannot be consciously aware of but that we can make inferences about, and (3) inputs and outputs that are part of feedback control interconnections between structures, which we cannot be directly aware of. Further, we must allow for energy exchanges, as well as informational exchanges, between structures.

Fourth, two structures may not interact properly if the output signal from one overloads the other. I may be in severe pain during a medical procedure, for instance, and I know (another structure tells me) that if I could relax the pain would be lessened considerably; but the structures involved in relaxing are so overloaded by the intense pain that they cannot carry out their normal function.

Fifth, two structures may be unable to interact properly if the action of a third structure interferes with them. An example is a neurotic defense mechanism. Suppose, for instance, your employer constantly humiliates you. Suppose also that part of your personality structure has a strong respect for authority and a belief in yourself as a very calm person who is not easily angered. Now your boss is humiliating you, but instead of feeling angry (the natural consequence of the situation), you are polite and conciliatory, and do not feel the anger. A structure of your personality has suppressed certain possible interactions between other structures (but there may well be a hidden price paid for this suppression, like ulcers).

Now consider the case of smoother interaction between structures. Two structures may interact readily and smoothly with one another to form a composite structure, a system whose properties are additive properties of the individual structures, as well as gestalt properties unique to the combination. Or, two or more structures may interact with one another in such a way that the total system alters some of the properties of the individual structures to various degrees, producing a system with gestalt properties that are not simple additive properties of the individual structures. Unstable interactions may also occur between two or more structures that compete for energy, producing an unstable, shifting relationship in the composite system.

All these considerations about the interactional structures apply to both hardware (biologically given) and software (culturally programmed) structures. For example, two systems may not interact for a lack of connection in the sense that their basic neural paths, built into the hardware of the human being, do not allow such interaction. Or, two software structures may not interact for lack of connection because in the enculturation, the programming of the person, the appropriate connections were simply not created.

All the classical psychological defense mechanisms can be

viewed in these system terms as ways of controlling interaction patterns among perceptions and psychological structures.

Remember that in the real human being many structures usually interact simultaneously, with all the above-mentioned factors facilitating or inhibiting interaction to various degrees at various points in the total system formed.

Thus while the interaction of structures is affected by the way attention/awareness energy is deployed, it is also affected by the properties of individual structures. In computer terms, we are not totally general-purpose computers, capable of being programmed in just any arbitrary fashion. We are specialized: that is our strength, weakness, and humanness.

3.

Conservative and Radical
Views of the Mind

✿✿

An almost universal theory in Western scientific circles, sunk to the level of an implicit belief and thus controlling us effectively, is that awareness is a product of brain functioning. No brain functioning—no awareness, no consciousness. This is the conservative view of the mind. It is dangerous as an implicit belief for two reasons. First, many experiences in various altered states of consciousness are inconsistent with this theory, but implicit faith in the conservative view makes us liable to distort our perception of these phenomena. Second, parapsychological data suggest that awareness is at least partially outside brain functioning, a condition that leads to very different views of human nature. The radical view of the mind sees awareness as this something extra and postulates that physical reality can sometimes be directly affected by our belief systems. We must be openminded about the radical view to guard against maintaining too narrow and too culturally conditioned a view of the mind.

Although in general speech we tend to use the terms awareness and consciousness to mean basically the same thing, I use them here with somewhat different meanings. *Awareness* refers to the basic knowledge that something is happening, to perceiving or feeling or cognizing in its simplest form. *Consciousness* generally refers to awareness in a much more complex way; consciousness is awareness as modulated by the structure of the

mind. *Mind* refers to the totality of both inferable and potentially experienceable phenomena of which awareness and consciousness are components. These are not precise definitions
because the three key words—awareness, consciousness, and mind
—are not simple things. But they are realities, and we must deal
with them whether or not we can give them precise logical
definitions. Since logic is only one product of the total functioning of the mind, it is no wonder that we cannot arrive at a logical
definition of the mind or consciousness or awareness. The part
cannot define the whole.

Awareness and consciousness, then, can be seen as parts of a
continuum. I would use the word *awareness* to describe, for instance, my simple perception of the sound of a bird outside my
window as I write. I would use the word *consciousness* to indicate
the complex of operations that recognizes the sound as a bird call,
that identifies the species of bird, and that takes account of the
fact that the sound is coming in through my open window. So
consciousness refers to a rather complex system that includes
awareness as one of its basic ingredients, but is more complex
than simple awareness itself.

Few psychologists today would argue with the statement that
consciousness is awareness resulting from the brain's functioning.
But if you ask what is the basic nature of awareness, the simple
basic behind the more complex entity consciousness, you meet
the common assumption in Western culture generally and scientific culture in particular that awareness is a "product" of the
brain. When psychology was fond of chemical analogies, awareness was thought of as a sort of "secretion" by the brain.

I believe that seeing consciousness as a function of the brain is
sound, but I think that explicitly or implicitly assuming that
awareness is *only* a function of the brain, as accepted as that
theory is, can be a hindrance, for two reasons.

First, as psychology deals more and more with the phenomena
of altered states of consciousness, it will more and more have to
deal with phenomena that do not fit well in a conceptual scheme
that says awareness is only a product of the brain. Experiences of
apparently paranormal abilities like telepathy, of feeling that
one's mind leaves one's body, of mystical union with aspects of
the universe outside oneself, of supernormal knowledge directly
given in altered states, fit more comfortably into schemes that do
not assume that awareness is only a function of the brain. I have

nothing against *competent* attempts to fit such phenomena into our dominant Western scientific framework, but the attempts I have seen so far have been most inadequate and seem to work mainly by ignoring major aspects of these altered states phenomena. Thus the assumption that awareness is only a function of the brain, especially as it becomes implicit, tends to distort our view of real phenomena that happen in altered states. We dismiss their possible reality a priori. We cannot build a science when we start with such a selected view of the data.

The second reason for questioning this assumption is the existence of first-class scientific data to suggest that awareness may be something other than a product of the brain. I refer to excellent evidence of parapsychological phenomena like telepathy, evidence that shows that the mind can sometimes function in ways that are "impossible" in terms of our current, physical view of the world. I review our knowledge of the paranormal in *Studies of Psi* [131]. "Impossible" means only that these phenomena are para*conceptual,* that our conceptual schemes are inadequate because they exclude this part of reality. These same conceptual schemes underlie the belief that awareness is only a product of the brain, and if we question these conceptual schemes we question that assumption. This book is not the place for detailed argument, but I have discussed the subject at greater length in *Transpersonal Psychologies* [128], which reviews the impact of the spiritual psychologies on the evolving science of consciousness.

This view that awareness is only a function of the brain—the conservative or physicalistic view of the mind—is diagrammed in Figure 3-1. The brain (and nervous system and body) are depicted as a structure that has hardware qualities on the one hand and software qualities on the other. The hardware qualities are those inherent in the physical makeup of the brain itself, as dictated by the physical laws that govern reality. This dictation of limitation is shown as a one-way arrow from the physical world to the brain. The software qualities are the programmable aspects of the brain, the capacities for recording data and building up perception, evaluation, and action patterns in accordance with programming instructions given by the culture. The arrows of influence are two-way here, for even though the programming is largely done by the culture to the individual, occasionally the individual modifies some aspects of the culture. Awareness is shown as an emergent quality of the brain, and so awareness is

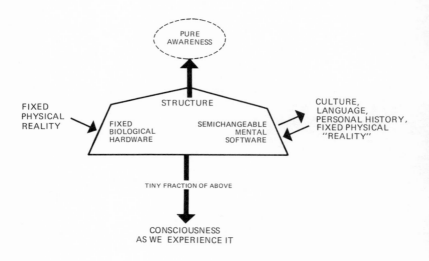

Figure 3–1.   Conservative view of the mind.

ultimately limited by the hardware and by particular software programs of the brain. Consciousness is the individual's experience of awareness diffused through a tiny fraction of the structure of the brain and nervous system.

The radical view of the mind is diagrammed in Figure 3–2. Two changes have been made to incorporate the radical view. First, awareness is shown as something that comes from outside the structure of the physical brain, as well as something influenced by the structure of the brain (thus giving consciousness) and the cultural programming. In religious terms, this is the idea of a soul or life/mind principle that uses (and is used by) the body. This is a most unpopular idea in scientific circles, but, as I have argued elsewhere [129], there is enough scientific evidence that consciousness is capable of temporarily existing in a way that seems independent of the physical body to warrant giving the idea serious consideration and doing some research on it.

The second change incorporated in the radical view is shown by the two-way arrow from the physical world to the hardware structure of the brain. The idea, held in many spiritual systems

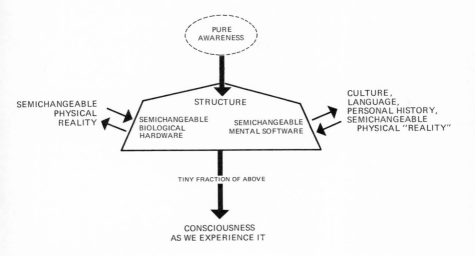

Figure 3–2. Radical view of the mind.

of thought that have dealt with altered states of consciousness, is that physical reality is not a completely fixed entity, but something that may actually be shaped in some fundamental manner by the individual's beliefs about it. I am not speaking here simply of *perceptions* of reality, but of the actual structure of reality. Pearce [49], for example, describes an experience as a youth where he accidentally entered an altered state of consciousness in which he knew he was impervious to pain or injury. In front of witnesses he ground out the tips of glowing cigarettes on his cheeks, palms, and eyelids. He felt no pain, and there was no sign of physical injury. The conventional view can easily account for the lack of pain: by control of the structures involved in sensing pain (nerve tracts and certain brain areas), pain would not be perceived. But a glowing cigarette tip has a temperature of about 1400° F, and his skin should have been severely burned, despite his state of consciousness. From the radical point of view, his beliefs about reality in the altered state actually altered the nature of physical reality.

To argue for or against the radical view of the mind would

take a book in itself, and this is not the one. (I recommend Pearce's book and my *Studies of Psi* [131] for data on paranormal phenomena.) I want to emphasize that the radical view of the mind, in various forms, is often reported as an *experience* from an altered state of consciousness. If we are going to study states of consciousness adequately, we shall have to confront the radical view, not automatically dismiss it as an illusion or a product of inferior brain functioning, but take it as data. I would personally prefer not to: I do not like the radical view that our belief systems may actually *alter* the nature of reality even though I can comfortably accept parapsychological data that show that reality is more complex than our current physical world-view believes. But we should stay open to that view and make a decision for or against its probability on scientific grounds, not simply because we have been trained to believe that there is an ultimate, immutable physical reality. Don Juan put it pithily: "To believe that the world is only as you think it is is stupid" [10].

I sympathize with the reader who finds himself rejecting the radical view of the mind. I suggest, however, that he honestly ask himself, "Have I rejected this view as a result of careful and extensive study of the evidence for and against it, or because I have been trained to do so and rewarded by social approval for doing so?"

4.

The Nature of Ordinary
Consciousness

✿✿✿

> If the doors of perception were cleansed every thing would
> appear to man as it is, infinite.
> For man has closed himself up, till he sees all things thro'
> narrow chinks of his cavern.
>
> William Blake, *The Marriage of*
> *Heaven and Hell* [31, p. 154]

The prejudice that our ordinary state of consciousness is natural or given is a major obstacle to understanding the nature of the mind and states of consciousness. Our perceptions of the world, others, and ourselves, as well as our reactions to (consciousness of) them, are semiarbitrary constructions. Although these constructions must have a minimal match to physical reality to allow survival, most of our lives are spent in *consensus reality*, that specially tailored and selectively perceived segment of reality constructed from the spectrum of human potential. We are simultaneously the beneficiaries and the victims of our culture. Seeing things according to consensus reality is good for holding a culture together, but a major obstacle to personal and scientific understanding of the mind.

A culture can be seen as a group which has selected certain human potentials as good and developed them, and rejected others as bad. Internally this means that certain possible experi-

ences are encouraged and others suppressed to construct a
"normal" state of consciousness that is effective in and helps
define the culture's particular consensus reality. The process of
enculturation begins in infancy, and by middle childhood the
individual has a basic membership in consensus reality. Possibilities for radical changes occur in adolescence, but even these
possibilities are partially shaped by the enculturation that has
already occurred. By adulthood the individual enjoys maximum
benefits from membership, but he is now maximally bound
within this consensus reality. A person's "simple" perception of
the world and of others is actually a complex process controlled
by many implicit factors.

One of the greatest problems in studying consciousness and
altered states of consciousness is an implicit prejudice that tends
to make us distort all sorts of information about states of consciousness. When you *know* you have a prejudice you are not
completely caught by it, for you can question whether the bias is
really useful and possibly try to change it or compensate for it.
But when a prejudice is implicit it controls you without your
knowledge and you have little chance to do anything about it.

The prejudice discussed in this chapter is the belief that our
ordinary state of consciousness is somehow natural. It is a very
deep-seated and implicit prejudice. I hope in this chapter to
convince you intellectually that it is not true. Intellectual conviction is a limited thing, however, and to *know* the relativity and
arbitrariness of your ordinary state of consciousness on a deeper
level is a much more difficult task.

Consciousness, not our sense organs, is really our "organ" of
perception, and one way to begin to see the arbitrariness of our
consciousness is to apply the assumption that ordinary consciousness is somehow natural or given to a perceptual situation. This
is done in Figure 4–1. A man is looking at a cat and believing
that the image of the real cat enters his eye and is, in effect,
faithfully reproduced on a screen in his mind, so that he sees the
cat *as it is*. This naive view of perception was rejected long ago
by psychologists, who have collected immense amounts of evidence to show that it is a ridiculously oversimplified, misleading,
and just plain wrong view of perception. Interestingly, these
same psychologists seldom apply their understanding of the complexity of perception to their own lives, and the person in the
street does so even less.

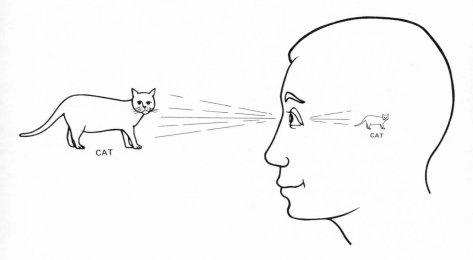

Figure 4–1.   Naive view of consciousness/perception.

While there are a great many simple perceptions we can very well agree on, there are many others, especially the more important ones in human life, on which there is really little agreement. I would bet that almost all adult, noninstitutionalized humans in our society would agree that this object in your hand is called a book, but as we define more complex things the bet gets riskier. If you go to a courtroom trial and listen to the testimony of several eyewitnesses, all of whom presumably had basically the same stimuli reaching their receptors, you may hear several different versions of reality. Or, if you discuss the meaning of current events with your acquaintances, you will find that there are many other points of view besides your own. Most of our interest is directed to complex, multifaceted social reality of this sort.

Most of us deal with this disagreement by simply assuming that those who disagree with us are wrong, that our own perceptions and consciousness are the standard of normality and rightness, and that other people cannot observe or think well and/or are lying, evil, or mentally ill.

A Sufi teaching story called "Bread and Jewels" [58, p. 113] illustrates this nicely:

A king once decided to give away a part of his wealth by disinterested charity. At the same time he wanted to watch what happened to it. So he called a baker whom he could trust and told him to bake two loaves of bread. In the first was to be baked a number of jewels, and in the other, nothing but flour and water.

These were to be given to the most and least pious people whom the baker could find.

The following morning two men presented themselves at the oven. One was dressed as a dervish and seemed most pious, though he was in reality a mere pretender. The other, who said nothing at all, reminded the baker of a man whom he did not like, by a coincidence of facial resemblance.

The baker gave the bread with the jewels in it to the man in the dervish robe, and the ordinary loaf to the second man.

As soon as he got his loaf the false dervish felt it and weighed it in his hand. He felt the jewels, and to him they seemed like lumps in the loaf, unblended flour. He weighed the bread in his hand and the weight of the jewels made it seem to him to be too heavy. He looked at the baker, and realized that he was not a man to trifle with. So he turned to the second man and said: "Why not exchange your loaf for mine? You look hungry, and this one is larger."

The second man, prepared to accept whatever befell, willingly exchanged loaves.

The king, who was watching through a crack in the bakehouse door, was surprised, but did not realize the relative merits of the two men.

The false dervish got the ordinary loaf. The king concluded that Fate had intervened to keep the dervish protected from wealth. The really good man found the jewels and was able to make good use of them. The king could not interpret this happening.

"I did what I was told to do," said the baker.

"You cannot tamper with Fate," said the king.

"How clever I was!" said the false dervish.

The king, the baker, and the false dervish all had their own views of what reality was. None of them was likely ever to correct his impression of this particular experience.

Consciousness, then, including perception, feeling, thinking, and acting, is a semiarbitrary construction. I emphasize *semi*-arbitrary because I make the assumption, common to our culture, that there are some fixed rules governing physical reality whose violation produces inevitable consequences. If someone walks off the edge of a tall cliff, I believe he will fall to the bottom and probably be killed, regardless of his beliefs about cliffs, gravity, or life and death. Thus people in cultures whose belief systems do not, to a fair degree, match physical reality, are not likely to survive long enough to argue with us. But once the minimal degree of coincidence with physical reality necessary to enable physical survival has been attained, the perception/consciousness of an action in the complex social reality that then exists may be very arbitrary indeed.

We must face the fact, now amply documented by the scientific evidence presented in any elementary psychology textbook, that perception can be highly selective. Simple images of things out there are not clearly projected onto a mental screen, where we simply see them as they are. The act of perceiving is a highly complex, automated *construction*. It is a selective category system, a decision-making system, preprogrammed with criteria of what is important to perceive. It frequently totally ignores things it has not been preprogrammed to believe are important.

Figure 4–2 shows a person with a set of categories programmed

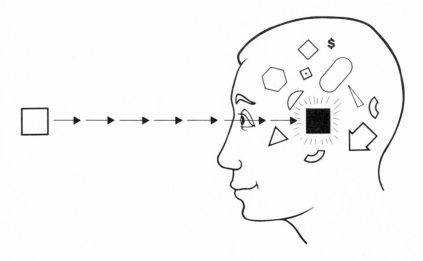

Figure 4–2. Consensus reality: fit.

in his mind, a selection of implicit criteria to recognize things that are "important." When stimulated by one of these things he is preprogrammed to perceive, he readily responds to it. More precisely, rather than saying he responds to *it*, which implies a good deal of directness in perception, we might say that it triggers a representation of itself in his mind, and he then responds to that representation. As long as it is a good representation of the actual stimulus object, he has a fairly accurate perception. Since he tends to pay more attention to the representations of things he sees than to the things themselves, however, he may think he perceives a stimulus object clearly when actually he is perceiving an incorrect representation.

This is where perception begins to be distorted by the perceiver's training and needs. Eskimos have been trained to distinguish seven or more kinds of snow. We do not see these different kinds of snow, even though they exist, for we do not need to make these distinctions. To us it is all snow. Our one internal representation of snow is triggered indiscriminately by any kind of actual snow. Similarly, for the paranoid person who needs to believe that others are responsible for his troubles, representations of threatening actions are easily triggered by all sorts of behaviors on the part of others. A detailed analysis of this is given in Chapter 19.

What happens when we are faced by the unknown, by things we have not been trained to see? Figure 4–3, using the same kind of analogy as the previous figure, depicts this. We may not see the stimulus at all: the information passes right through the mind without leaving a trace. Or we may see a distorted representation of the stimulus: some of the few features it has in common with known stimuli trigger representations of the known features, and that is what we perceive. We "sophisticated" Westerners do not believe in angels. If we actually confronted one, we might not be able to see it correctly. The triangle in its hands is a familiar figure, however, so we might perceive the triangle readily. In fact, we might see little but the triangle—maybe a triangle in the hands of a sweet old lady wearing a white robe.

Don Juan, the Yaqui man of knowledge, puts it quite succinctly: "I think you are only alert about things you know" [10].

I mentioned above the curious fact that psychologists, who know about the complexities of perception, almost never seem to

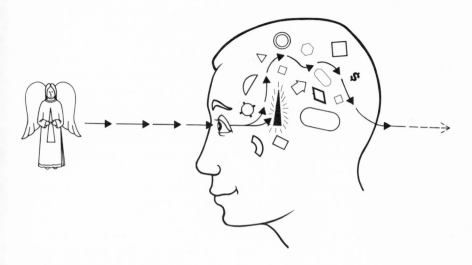

Figure 4-3. Consensus reality: nonfit, distortion.

apply this information to their own perceptions, Even though they study the often large and obvious distortions in other peoples' perceptions, they maintain an image of themselves as realistic perceivers. Some psychologists even argue that perception is actually quite realistic. But what does "realistic" mean?

We like to believe that it means perception of the real world, the physical world. But the world we spend most of our time perceiving is not just any segment of the physical world, but a highly socialized part of the physical world that has been built into cities, automobiles, television sets. So our perception may indeed be realistic, but it is so only with respect to a very tailored segment of reality, a *consensus* reality, a small selection of things we have agreed are "real" and "important." Thus, within our particular cultural framework, we can easily set up what seem to be excellent scientific experiments that will show that our perceptions are indeed realistic, in the sense that we agree with each other on these selected items from our consensus reality.

This is a way of saying that our perceptions are highly selective and filtered, that there is a major subsystem of consciousness, Input-Processing discussed at length later, that filters the outside world for us. If two people have similar filtering systems, as, for example, if they are from the same culture, they can agree on many things. But again, as Don Juan says, "I think you are only alert about things you know." If we want to develop a science to study consciousness, and want that science to go beyond our own cultural limitations, we must begin by recognizing the limitations and arbitrariness of much of our ordinary state of consciousness.

I have now mentioned several times that we believe certain things simply because we were trained to believe them. Let us now look at the training process by which our current "normal" or ordinary state of consciousness came about.

Enculturation

Figure 4–4 illustrates the concept of the *spectrum of human potential*. By the simple fact of being born human, having a certain type of body and nervous system, existing in the environmental conditions of the planet earth, a large (but certainly not infinite) number of potentials are *possible* for you. Because you are born into a *particular* culture, existing at a *particular* time and place on the surface of the planet, however, only a small (perhaps a very small) number of these potentials will ever be

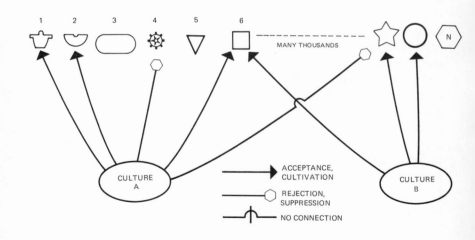

Figure 4–4.   Spectrum of human potentials.

realized and become *actualities*. We can think of a culture[1] as a group of people who, through various historical processes, have come to an agreement that certain human potentials they know of are "good," "holy," "natural," or whatever local word is used for positively valuing them, and should be developed. They are defined as the essence of being human. Other potentials, also known to the culture, are considered "bad," "evil," "unnatural." The culture actively inhibits the development of these potentials in its children, not always successfully. A large number of other human potentials are simply not known to that particular culture, and while some of them develop owing to accidental circumstances in a particular person's life, most do not develop for lack of stimulation. Some of these potentials remain latent, capable of being developed if circumstances are right in later life; others disappear completely through not being developed at an early, critical stage.

Most of us know how to do arithmetic, speak English, write a check, drive an automobile, and most of us know about things, like eating with our hands, which are repellent to us (naturally or through training?). Not many of us, though, were trained early in childhood to enter a d-ASC where we can be, for example, possessed by a friendly spirit that will teach us songs and dances, as is done by some cultures. Nor were most of us trained to gain control over our dreams and acquire spirit guides in those dreams who will teach us useful things, as the Senoi of Malaysia are [88 or 115, ch. 9]. Each of us is simultaneously the beneficiary of his cultural heritage and the victim and slave of his culture's narrowness. What I believe is worse is that few of us have any realization of this situation. Like almost all people in all cultures at all times, we think *our* local culture is the best and other peoples are uncivilized or savages.

Figure 4–4 shows two different cultures making different selections from and inhibitions of the spectrum of human potential. There is some overlap: all cultures, for example, develop a language of some sort and so use those particular human potentials. Many potentials are not selected by any culture.

We can change the labels in Figure 4–4 slightly and depict

1 For simplicity here, we will ignore subcultures and conflicts within a culture.

various possible experiences selected in either of two states of consciousness. Then we have the *spectrum of experiential potentials,* the possible kinds of experiences or modes of functioning of human consciousness. The two foci of selection are two states of consciousness. These may be two "normal" states of consciousness in two different cultures or, as discussed later, two states of consciousness that exist within a single individual. The fact that certain human potentials can be tapped in state of consciousness A that cannot be tapped in state of consciousness B is a major factor behind the current interest in altered states of consciousness.

Figure 4–4, then, indicates that in developing a "normal" state of consciousness, a particular culture selects certain human potentials and structures them into a functioning system. This is the process of *enculturation.* It begins in infancy, possibly even before birth: there has been speculation, for example, that the particular language sounds that penetrate the walls of the womb from outside before birth may begin shaping the potentials for sound production in the unborn baby.

Figure 4–5 summarizes the main stages of the enculturation process. The left-hand column represents the degree to which physical reality shapes the person and the degree to which the person can affect (via ordinary muscular means) physical reality. The right-hand column indicates the main sources of programming, the psychological influences on the person. The main stages are infancy, childhood, adolescence, adulthood, and senescence.

INFANCY

We tend to think of a newborn infant as a rather passive creature, capable of little mental activity, whose primary job is simple physical growth. Recent research, on the contrary, suggests that a person's innate learning capacity may be highest of all in infancy, for the infant has to learn to construct the consensus reality of his culture. This is an enormous job. The cultural environment, for instance, begins to affect the perceptual biases described in Chapter 8 as the Input-Processing subsystem. Most Westerners, for example, are better at making fine discriminations between horizontal lines and vertical lines than between lines that are slanted. At first this was thought to result from the

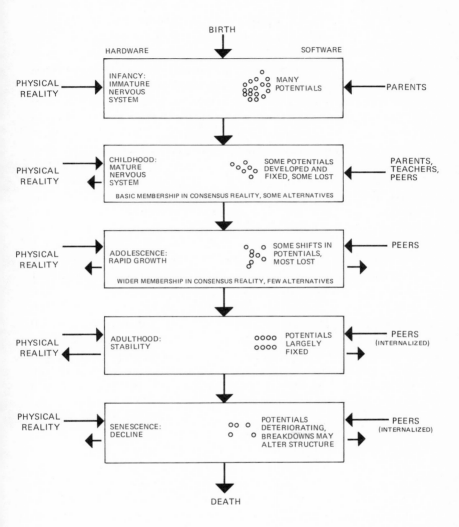

Figure 4–5. The enculturation process.

innate hardware properties (racial, genetic) of the eye and nervous system, but recent evidence shows that it is probably a cultural effect. Cree Indians, who as infants live in teepees where there are many slanted lines, can discriminate slanted lines as acutely as horizontal and vertical ones [2]. "Civilized" Westerners, on the other hand, grow up in environments where vertical and horizontal lines predominate. In more ways than we can even begin to think of, the enculturation process affects perception, and ultimately consciousness, even in infancy.

Note also that the structuring/programming of our consciousness that takes place in early infancy is probably the most persistent and most implicit of all our programming and learning, for at that time we have no other framework to compare it with. It is the only thing we have, and it is closely connected with our physical survival and our being loved and accepted. It gives us a loyalty and a bond to our culture's particular world-view that may be almost impossible for us to break, but again, one whose limitations we must be aware of if we are really to understand the workings of our minds. Another Sufi teaching story, "The Bird and the Egg" [58, p. 130], illustrates the power of this early programming:

> Once upon a time there was a bird which did not have the power of flight. Like a chicken, he walked about on the ground, although he knew that some birds did fly.
>
> It so happened that, through a combination of circumstances, the egg of a flying bird was incubated by this flightless one.
>
> In due time the chick came forth, still with the potentiality for flight which he had always had, even from the time he was in the egg.
>
> It spoke to its foster-parent, saying: "When will I fly?" And the landbound bird said: "Persist in your attempts to fly, just like the others."
>
> For he did not know how to take the fledgling for its lesson in flying: even how to topple it from the nest so that it might learn.
>
> And it is curious, in a way, that the young bird did not see this. His recognition of the situation was confused by the fact that he felt gratitude to the bird who had hatched him.
>
> "Without this service," he said to himself, "surely I would still be in the egg?"
>
> And, again, sometimes he said to himself: "Anyone who can hatch me, surely he can teach me to fly. It must be just a matter of time, or of my own unaided efforts, or of some great wisdom: yes, that is it. Suddenly one day I will be carried to the next stage by him who has brought me thus far."

CHILDHOOD

By the time an ordinary person reaches childhood, he has attained a basic membership in the consensus reality of his culture. A normal child has a pretty good idea of the dos and don'ts of his culture and behaves in a generally acceptable fashion. Many of the potentials present at the time of his birth are gone by now, but consensus reality has been formed from the few that have been cultivated.

One of the main ways in which consciousness is shaped to fit consensus reality is through the medium of language. The word for an object focuses a child's perception onto a specific thing considered important by the culture. Social approval for this kind of behavior gives words great power. As a child gradually grows in his mastery of language, the language structure and its effect on consciousness grow at an exponential rate. The tyranny of words is one of the most difficult things from which we must try to free ourselves.

A child's basic membership in consensus reality is not complete. The mind of the child can still do many strange (by adult standards) things. As Pearce [49, p. 56] comments:

> The child's mind is autistic, a rich texture of free synthesis, hallucinatory and unlimited. His mind can skip over syllogisms with ease, in a non-logical, dream-sequence kind of "knight's-move" continuum. He nevertheless shows a strong desire to participate in a world of others. Eventually his willingness for self-modification, necessary to win rapport with his world, is stronger than his desire for autonomy. Were it not, civilization would not be possible. That we succeed in moulding him to respond to our criteria shows the innate drive for communion and the flexibility of a young mind. It doesn't prove an essential and sanctified rightness of our own constructs.
>
> Maturity, or becoming reality adjusted, restricts and diminishes that "knight's-move" thinking, and tends to make pawns of us in the process. The kind of adult logic that results is dependent on the kinds of demands made on the young mind by parents and society.

It is precisely this kind of childish strangeness that both frustrates us adults when we try to deal with children and excites our envy when we realize children have a certain freedom we do not have.

ADOLESCENCE

Adolescence is a different stage from childhood, not just a continuation of it, because the influx of sexual energies at puberty allows considerable change in the ordinary consciousness of the child. For most adolescents this is a time of turmoil (at least in our culture) as they strive to adjust to bodily changes and to learn to satisfy their sexual needs within the mores of the culture.

For many there is a continuity with childhood, and after a transitional period of being difficult, the adolescent settles into a pattern of being a grown-up version of the child he was. For others a *conversion* of some sort occurs: the sexual and other energies unleashed at puberty become sublimated into a belief system that may be radically different from what they had as children. If this is traumatic or sudden, or if the belief system is radically at odds with that of the parents, we notice this conversion. If the sublimation of the energies is into a socially accepted pattern, we are not as likely to perceive it.

Conversion is a powerful psychological process that we do not understand well. It bears some similarity to the concept of a discrete state of consciousness (introduced later) but more basically refers to a psychological process of focusing, of giving great energy to selected structures, that may take place in any state of consciousness.

I do not believe that the conversion process is completely free to go wherever it will. By the time a person has reached adolescence (or later, if conversion takes place later), many human potentials he possessed at birth are, for lack of stimulation, simply no longer available. Of the latent potentials that still could be used, cultural selection and structuring have already made some more likely than others to be utilized in a conversion. Thus even the rebels in a society are in many ways not free: the direction that rebellion takes has already been strongly shaped by enculturation processes.

The adolescent is very much a member of the consensus reality of his culture: his ordinary state of consciousness is well adapted to fit into it, and he has a fair degree of control over his physical environment. For most "ordinary" adolescents, there are far fewer possibilities for unusual functions of consciousness than there were in childhood.

ADULTHOOD

Adults are full-fledged members of the consensus reality: they both maintain it through their interaction with their peers and are shaped by it and by parts of it. Adults are, as Don Juan taught, always talking to themselves about their ordinary things, keeping up a constant pattern of information flow in their minds along familiar routes. This strengthens and maintains their membership in the consensus reality and their use of their ordinary state of consciousness as a means for dealing with consensus reality.

Because of the power over physical reality given them by their consensus reality state of consciousness, adults are the most free; yet, because they are the most thoroughly indoctrinated in consensus reality, they are the most bound. They receive many rewards for participating in the consensus reality in an acceptable way, and they have an enormous number of external and internalized prohibitions that keep them from thinking and experiencing in ways not approved by the consensus reality. The Sufi teaching story, "Bayazid and the Selfish Man" [58, p. 180], shows how difficult it is for an adult to free himself from the power of ordinary consciousness and consensus reality, even when he believes he wants to:

> One day a man reproached Bayazid, the great mystic of the ninth century, saying that he had fasted and prayed and so on for thirty years and not found the joy which Bayazid described. Bayazid told him that he might continue for three hundred years and still not find it.
> "How is that?" asked the would-be illuminate.
> "Because your vanity is a barrier to you."
> "Tell me the remedy."
> "The remedy is one which you cannot take."
> "Tell me, nevertheless."
> Bayazid said: "You must go to the barber and have your (respectable) beard shaved. Remove all your clothes and put a girdle around yourself. Fill a nosebag with walnuts and suspend it from your neck. Go to the marketplace and call out: 'A walnut will I give to any boy who will strike me on the back of

the neck.' Then continue on to the justices' session so that they may see you."

"But I cannot do that; please tell me something else that would do as well."

"This is the first move, and the only one," said Bayazid, "but I had already told you that you would not do it; so you cannot be cured."

I stress the view that we are prisoners of our ordinary state of consciousness, victims of our consensus reality, because it is necessary to become aware of this if we are to have any hope of transcending it, of developing a science of the mind that is not culturally limited. Enormous benefits result from sharing in our consensus reality, but these benefits must not blind us to the limits of this reality.

SENESCENCE

The final stage in a person's life comes when he is too old to participate actively in the affairs of his culture. His mind may be so rigid by this time that it can do little but rerun the programs of consensus reality while his abilities diminish. If he is aware of other possibilities, he may find old age a way of freeing himself from cultural pressures and begin to explore his mind in a new way. There are cultural traditions, in India, for example, where a person who has fulfilled his main tasks in life is expected to devote his remaining years to exploring his own mind and searching out spiritual values. This is difficult to think about in the context of our own culture, however, for we have so over-valued youth and the active mode of life that we define older people as useless, a defining action that often affects those older people so that they believe it.

The Complexity of Consciousness

This chapter opened with a drawing showing the naiveté of the view that perception and consciousness are means of grasping physical reality. It ends with a drawing (Figure 4–6) that shows a truer and more complex view of perception (and, to some extent, of the consciousness behind it). In the center of the drawing are depicted various stimuli from others and from the physical world impinging on the individual. These stimuli pro-

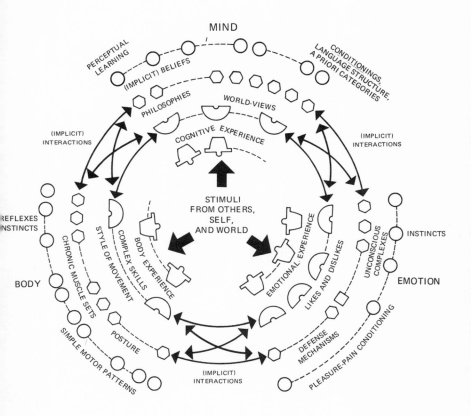

Figure 4-6. The complexity of perception.

duce effects that can be classified as mental, emotional, and bodily. The innermost reaction circle represents clearly conscious experiences. At this moment, as I write, I hear a pneumatic drill being used to break up the pavement outside my window. I mentally speculate about the air pressure used to operate such an interesting tool but note that it is distracting me; I emotionally dislike the disturbance of my writing; the muscles of my face and ears tighten a little, as if that will reduce the impact of the noxious sound on me.

While the three-part classification of effects provides a simplification, in reality the mental, emotional, and bodily responses to stimuli interact at both conscious and less than conscious levels. My mind notices the tension around my ear and interprets that as something wrong, which, as a minor emotional threat, aggravates the noxiousness of the sound, etc.

Immediately behind fully conscious experiences are easily experienceable phenomena, represented by the second circle. The mental effect of these phenomena relates to the individual's explicit belief system: I believe that noise is undesirable, but I am fascinated by the workings of machines. Their emotional effect relates to the things he readily knows he likes or dislikes: loud noises generally bother me and make me feel intruded upon. Their bodily effect relates to consciously usable skills and movements: I can relax my facial muscles. These phenomena affect the individual at a level that is not in the focus of consciousness, but that can be easily made conscious by paying attention.

These two levels are themselves affected and determined by a more implicit level of functioning, implicit in that the individual cannot identify its content simply by wanting to and paying attention. Where did I get the idea that noise is an intrusion? Why am I fascinated by the workings of machines? I do not know. I might be able to find out by prolonged psychological exploration, but the information is not easily available, even though these things affect me. Why do I have an immediate emotional dislike of noise? Is there some unconscious reaction behind it? How have I come to maintain certain muscle sets in my face that are affected by stress in certain ways?

The outer circle in Figure 4–6 represents basic learnings, conditionings, motor patterns, instincts, reflexes, language categories, and the like, which are so implicit the individual can hardly recognize their existence. This is the level of the hardware, the biological givens, and the basic enculturation processes. The distance of these things from consciousness makes it extremely difficult for him to discover and compensate for their controlling influences: they are, in many ways, the basis of *himself*.

If the stimulus in the middle of Figure 4–6 is a cat, this whole complex machine functions, a machine designed by our culture. We don't "just" see the cat! Our ordinary state of consciousness is a very complex construction indeed, yet Figure 4–6 hardly goes into details at all. So much for the naturalness of our ordinary state of consciousness.

5.

Discrete States of Consciousness

✿✿✿

The terms *state of consciousness* and *altered state of consciousness* have become very popular. As a consequence of popularization, however, the terms are frequently used in such a loose fashion as to mean almost nothing in particular. Many people now use the phrase state of consciousness, for example, to mean simply whatever is on one's mind. So if I pick up a water tumbler and look at it, I am in "water tumbler state of consciousness," and if I now touch my typewriter, I am in "typewriter state of consciousness." Then an altered state of consciousness simply means that what one is thinking about or experiencing now is different from what it was a moment ago.

To rescue the concepts of state of consciousness and altered state of consciousness for more precise scientific use, I introduce the terms and abbreviations *discrete state of consciousness* (d-SoC) and *discrete altered state of consciousness* (d-ASC). I discuss in Chapter 2 the basic theoretical concepts for defining these crucial terms. Here, I first describe certain kinds of experiential data that led to the concepts of discrete states and then go on to a formal definition of d-SoC and d-ASC.

Mapping Experience

Suppose that an individual's experience (and/or behavior and/or physiology) can be adequately described at any given moment if we know all the important dimensions along which experience varies and can assess the exact point along each dimension that an individual occupies or experiences at a given moment. Each dimension may be the level of functioning of a psychological structure or process. We presume that we have a multidimensional map of psychological space and that by knowing exactly where the individual is in that psychological space we have adequately described his experiential reality for that given time. This is a generally accepted theoretical idea, but it is very difficult to apply in practice because many psychological dimensions may be important for understanding an individual's experience at any given moment. We may be able to assess only a small number of them, and/or an individual's position on some of these dimensions may change even as we are assessing the value of others. Nevertheless, the theory is an ideal to be worked toward, and we can assume for purposes of discussion that we can adequately map experience.

To simplify further, let us assume that what is important about an individual's experiences can be mapped on only two dimensions. We can thus draw a graph, like Figure 5–1. Each small circle represents an observation at a single point in time of where a particular individual is in this two-dimensional psychological space. In this example, we have taken a total of twenty-two binary measures at various times.

The first thing that strikes us about this individual is that his experiences seem to fall in three distinct clusters and that there are large gaps between these three distinct clusters. Within each cluster this individual shows a certain amount of variability, but he has not had any experiences at all at points outside the defined clusters. This kind of clustering in the plot of an individual's locations at various times in experiential space is what I mean by *discrete states of consciousness*. Put another way, it means that you can be in a certain region of experiential space and show some degree of movement or variation *within* that space, but to transit out of that space you have to cross a "forbidden zone"[1] where you cannot function and/or cannot have experiences and/or cannot be conscious of having experiences; then you find yourself in a discretely different experiential space. It is

[1] Forbidden zone applies under circumstances of a stable personality structure, and should not be taken too absolutely: personality sometimes changes, and a person sometimes finds himself in an extraordinary situation.

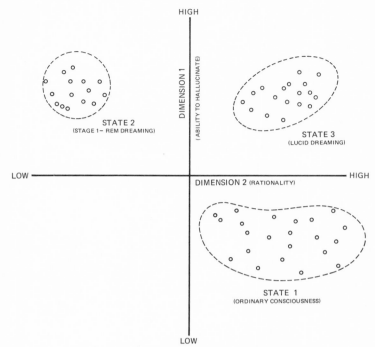

Figure 5–1.   Mapping experiential space at various times.

the quantum principle of physics applied to psychology (see Chapter 18). You can be either here or there, but not in between.

There are transitional periods between some d-SoCs; they are dealt with in more detail later. For now, being in a d-SoC means that you are in one of the three distinct regions of psychological space shown in Figure 5–1.

Now let us concretize this example. Let us call the vertical dimension ability to image or hallucinate, varying from a low of imagining something outside yourself but with nothing corresponding in intensity to a sensory perception, to a high of imagining something with all the qualities of reality, of actual sensory perception. Let us call the horizontal dimension ability to be rational, to think in accordance with the rules of some logic. We are not now concerned with the cultural arbitrariness of logic, but simply take it as a given set of rules. This dimension varies from a low of making many mistakes in the application of this logic, as on days when you feel rather stupid and have a hard time expressing yourself, to a high of following the rules of the logic perfectly, when you feel sharp and your mind works like a precision computer.

We can assign names of known d-SoCs to the three clusters of data points on the graph. *Ordinary consciousness* (for our culture) is shown in the lower right-hand corner. It is characterized by a high degree of rationality and a relatively low degree of imaging ability. We can usually think without making many mistakes in logic, and our imaginings usually contain mild sensory qualities, but they are far less intense than sensory perceptions. Notice again that there is variability *within* the state we call ordinary consciousness. Logic may be more or less accurate, ability to image may vary somewhat, but this all stays in a range that we recognize as ordinary, habitual, or normal.

At the opposite extreme, we have all experienced a region of psychological space where rationality is usually very low indeed, while ability to image is quite high. This is *ordinary nocturnal dreaming,* where we create (image) the entire dream world. It seems sensorily real. Yet we often take considerable liberties with rationality.

The third cluster of data points defines a particularly interesting d-SoC, *lucid dreaming.* This is the special kind of dream named by the Dutch physician Frederick Van Eeden [88 or 115, ch. 8], in which you feel as if you have awakened in terms of mental functioning *within* the dream world: you feel as rational and in control of your mental state as in your ordinary d-SoC, but you are still *experientially located within the dream world.* Here both range of rationality and range of ability to image are at a very high level.

Figure 5–1 deliberately depicts rationality in ordinary nocturnal dreaming as lower than rationality in the ordinary d-SoC. But some nocturnal dreams seem very rational for prolonged periods, not only at the time but by retrospectively applied waking state standards. So the cluster shown for nocturnal dreaming should perhaps be oval and extend into the upper right region of the graph, overlapping with the lucid dreaming cluster. This would have blurred the argument about distinct regions of experiential space, so the graph was not drawn that way. The point is not that there is never any overlap in functioning for a *particular psychological dimension* between two d-SoCs (to the contrary, all the ones we know much about do share many features in common), but that a complete *multidimensional* mapping of the important dimensions of experiential space shows this distinct clustering. While a two-dimensional plot may show apparent identity or overlap between two d-SoCs, a three-dimensional or *N*-dimensional map would show their discreteness. This is important, for d-SoCs are not just quantitative variations on one or more continua (as Figure 5–1 implies), but qualitative, pattern-changing, system-functioning differences.

A d-SoC, then, refers to a particular region of experiential space, as shown in Figure 5–1, and adding the descriptive adjective *altered* simply means that with respect to some state of consciousness (usually the ordinary state) as a baseline, we have made the quantum jump to another region of experiential space, the d-ASC.[2] The quantum jump may be both *quantitative,* in the sense that structures function at higher or lower levels of intensity, and *qualitative,* in the sense that structures in the baseline state may cease to function, previously latent structures may begin to function, and the system pattern may change. To use a computer analogy, going from one d-SoC to a d-ASC is like putting a radically different program into the computer, the mind. The graphic presentation of Figure 5–1 cannot express qualitative changes, but they are at least as important or more important than the quantitative changes.

Figures 5–2 and 5–3 illustrate the qualitative pattern difference between two d-SoCs. Various psychological structures are shown connected by information and energy flows into a pattern in different ways. The latent pattern, the discrete *altered* state of consciousness with respect to the other, is shown in lighter lines on each figure. The two states share some structures/functions in common, yet, their organizations are distinctly different.

Figures 5–2 and 5–3 express what William James [30, p. 298] meant when he wrote:

> Our ordinary waking consciousness . . . is but one special type of consciousness, whilst all about it, parted from it by the

2 I want to emphasize the purely descriptive nature of the adjective *altered*. It means simply "basically different" or "importantly different," without implying that the d-ASC is better or worse than any other d-SoC. The first business of science is accurate description. Valuation cannot be avoided, but must not be confused with description. This is discussed at greater length in Chapter 17.

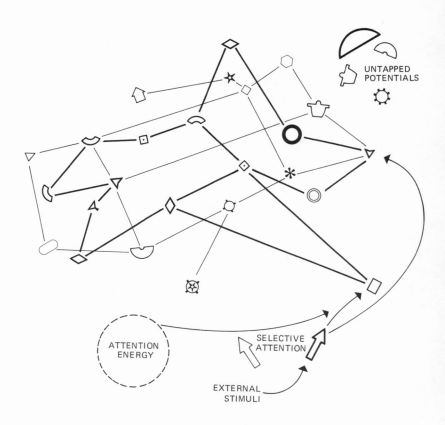

Figure 5–2. Representation of a d-SoC as a pattern of energy/aware-ness flow interrelating various human potentials. Lighter lines show a possible d-ASC pattern.

filmiest of screens, there lie potential forms of consciousness entirely different. We may go through life without suspecting their existence; but apply the requisite stimulus, and at a touch they are all there in all their completeness, definite types of mentality which probably somewhere have their field of ap-plication and adaptation. No account of the universe in its totality can be final which leaves these other forms of con-sciousness quite disregarded. How to regard them is the ques-tion—for they are so discontinuous with ordinary consciousness.

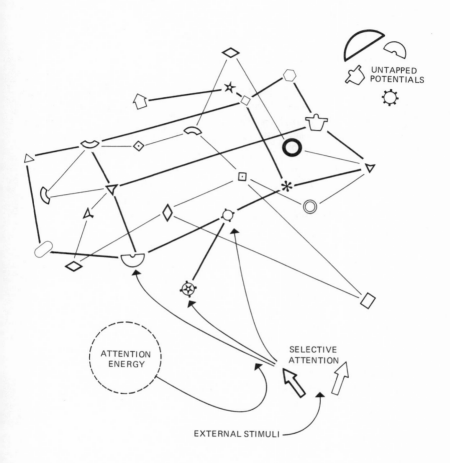

Figure 5–3. Representation of a d-ASC as a reorganization of information and enegy flow pattern and an altered selection of potentials. The b-SoC is shown in lighter lines.

It is important to stress that the pattern differences are the essential defining element of different d-SoCs. Particular psychological functions may be identical for several d-SoCs, but the overall system functioning is quite different. People still speak English whether they are in their ordinary waking state, drunk with alcohol, stoned on marijuana, or dreaming; yet, we would hardly call these states identical because the same language is spoken in all.

Definition of a Discrete State of Consciousness

We can define a d-SoC *for a given individual* as a unique *configuration* or *system* of psychological structures or subsystems. The structures vary in the way they process information, or cope, or affect experiences within varying environments. The structures operative within a d-SoC make up a *system* where the operation of the parts, the psychological structures, interact with each other and stabilize each other's functioning by means of feedback control, so that the *system,* the d-SoC, maintains its overall pattern of functioning in spite of changes in the environment. Thus, the individual parts of the system may vary, but the overall, general configuration of the system remains recognizably the same.

To understand a d-SoC, we must grasp the nature of the parts, the psychological structures/subsystems that compose it, and we must take into account the gestalt properties that arise from the overall system—properties that are not an obvious result of the functioning of the parts. For example, the parts of a car laid out singly on a bench tell me only a little about the nature of the functioning system we call an automobile. Similarly, a list of an individual's traits and skills may tell me little about the pattern that emerges from their organization into a personality, into a "normal" state of consciousness. But to understand adequately either the car or the individual, I have to study the whole functioning system itself.[3]

To illustrate this, let us go back to the question I asked at the beginning of Chapter 2 about whether you are dreaming you are reading this book rather than actually reading it in your ordinary d-SoC. To conclude that what was happening was real (I hope you concluded that!) you may have looked at the functioning of your component structures (my reasoning seems sound, sensory qualities are in the usual range, body image seems right) and decided that since these component structures were operat-

---

[3] A practical limitation on our understanding of d-SoCs is that they must have some reasonable stability over time: we could imagine d-SoCs that would hold a particular pattern for only a second, but this time would be too short for us to make many useful observations. All the d-SoCs about which we have some knowledge last for periods ranging from minutes to hours to a lifetime.

ing in the range you associate with your ordinary d-SoC, that was the condition you were in. Or you may have simply felt the gestalt pattern of your functioning, without bothering to check component functions, and instantly recognized it as your ordinary pattern. Either way, you scanned data on the functioning of yourself as a system and categorized the system's mode of functioning as its ordinary one.

Discreteness of States of Consciousness

Let me make a few further points about the discreteness of different states of consciousness, the quantum gap between them.

First, the concept of d-SoCs, in its commonsense form, did not come from the kind of precise mapping along psychological dimensions that is sketched in Figure 5–1. Rather, its immediate experiential basis is usually gestalt pattern recognition, the feeling that "this condition of my mind feels *radically different* from some other condition, rather than just an extension of it." The experiential mapping is a more precise way of saying this.

Second, for most of the d-SoCs we know something about, there has been little or no mapping of the transition from the baseline state of consciousness (b-SoC) to the altered state. Little has been done, for example, in examining the process by which a person passes from an ordinary d-SoC into the hypnotic state,[4] although for most subjects the distinction between the well-developed hypnotic state and their ordinary state is marked. Similarly, when a person begins to smoke marijuana, there is a period during which he is in an ordinary d-SoC and smoking marijuana; only later is he clearly stoned, in the d-ASC we call marijuana intoxication. Joseph Fridgen and I carried out a preliminary survey asking experienced marijuana users about the transition from one state to the other. We found that users almost never bothered to look at the transition: they were either in a hurry to enter the intoxicated state or in a social situation that did not encourage them to observe what was going on in their minds. Similarly, Berke and Hernton [6] reported that the "buzz" that seems to mark this transitional period is easily overlooked by marijuana users.

So, in general for d-SoCs, we do not know the size and exact

---

[4] Some preliminary psychoanalytic investigations by Gill and Brenman are of interest here [19].

nature of the quantum jump, or indeed, whether it is possible to effect a continuous transition between two regions of experiential space, thus making them extremes of one state of consciousness rather than two discrete states. The important factor of individual differences is discussed in Chapter 9.

Because the science of consciousness is in its infancy, I am forced to mention too frequently those things we do not know. Let me balance that a little by describing a study that has mapped the transition between two d-SoCs—ordinary waking consciousness and stage 2 sleep. Vogel et al [143], using electroencephalographic (EEG) indices of the transition from full awakeness (alpha EEG pattern with occasional rapid eye movement, REMs) to full sleep (stage 2 EEG, no eye movements), awoke subjects at various points in the transition process, asked for reports of mental activity just prior to awakening, and asked routine questions about the degree of contact with the environment the subjects felt they had just before awakening. They classified this experiential data into three ego states. In the *intact ego state,* the content of experience was plausible, fitted consensus reality well, and there was little or no feeling of loss of reality contact. In the *destructuralized ego state,* content was bizarre and reality contact was impaired or lost. In the *restructuralized ego state,* contact with reality was lost but the content was plausible by consensus reality standards.

Figure 5–4 (reprinted from G. Vogel, D. Foulkes, and H. Trosman, *Arch. Gen. Psychiat.,* 1966, *14,* 238–248) shows the frequency of these three ego states or states of consciousness with respect to psychophysiological criteria. The psychophysiological criteria are arranged on the horizontal axis in the order in which transition into sleep ordinarily takes place. You can see that the intact ego state is associated with alpha and REM or alpha and SEM (slow eye movement), the destructuralized ego state mainly with stage 1 EEG, and the restructuralized ego state mainly with stage 2 EEG. But there are exceptions in each case. Indeed, a finer analysis of the data shows that the *psychological* sequence of intact ego→destructuralized ego→restructuralized ego almost always holds in the experiential reports. It is a more solid finding than the association of these ego states with particular physiological stages. Some subjects start the intact→destructuralized→ restructuralized sequence earlier in the EEG sequence than others. This is a timely reminder that the results of equating

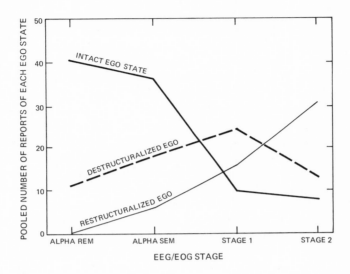

Figure 5–4.   Ego states during sleep onset.

psychological states with physiological indicators can be fal-
lacious. But the main thing to note here is the orderliness of the
transition sequence from one discrete state to another. This kind
of measurement is crude compared with what we need to know,
but it is a good start.

The intact ego state and the restructuralized ego state seem to
correspond to bounded regions of experiential space, d-SoCs, but
it is not clear whether the destructuralized ego state represents a
d-SoC or merely a period of unstable transition between the b-
SoC of the intact state (ordinary consciousness) and the d-ASC
of the restructuralized state (a sleep state) .[5] We need more data
about the condition they have labeled destructuralized before we
can decide whether it meets our criteria for a d-SoC. The later
discussions of induction of a d-ASC, transitional phenomena, and
the observation of internal states clarify the question we are
considering here.

5 We should not equate the restructuralized ego state with ordinary nocturnal dreaming, as this state is usually associated with stage 1 EEG and REMs
later during the night.

We have now defined a d-SoC for a given individual as a unique configuration or system of psychological structures or subsystems, a configuration that maintains its integrity or identity as a recognizable system in spite of variations in input from the environment and in spite of various (small) changes in the subsystems. The system, the d-SoC, maintains its identity because various *stabilization* processes modify subsystem variations so that they do not destroy the integrity of the system. These stabilization processes are discussed in Chapter 6.

In closing this chapter, I want to add a warning about the finality of the discreteness of any particular d-SoC. In Chapter 2 I stated that the particular nature of the basic structures underlying the human mind limits their possible interactions and so forms the basis of d-SoCs. Note carefully, however, that many of the structures we deal with in our consciousness, as constructed in our personal growth, are not ultimate structures but compound ones peculiar to our culture, personality, and belief system. Later chapters, particularly Chapter 9 on individual differences, clarify this. Meanwhile I want to emphasize the pragmatic usefulness of a maxim of John Lilly's [35] as a guide to personal and scientific work in this area: "In the province of the mind, what one believes to be true either is true or becomes true within certain limits, to be found experientially and experimentally. These limits are beliefs to be transcended." Lilly's work comparing the mind to a human biocomputer [34], as well as his autobiographical accounts of his explorations in consciousness [35], are essential reading in this area.

6.

Stabilization of a
State of Consciousness

✿✿

The basic function of a d-SoC is to cope successfully with an (external) environment. A d-SoC is a tool that senses and interprets what the world is and plans and executes strategies for dealing with that changing world. A good tool should not break easily when applied to the job: the system of structures and energies that constitutes a state of consciousness should maintain its integrity in coping with the changing world it was designed for. It would be most unadaptive, for example, if, while you were driving on the freeway, your d-SoC suddenly converted to a d-ASC of great ecstasy that totally shut down your senses! A d-SoC is a *dynamic* system: its components change all the time, but the overall pattern/organization that is its nature is maintained because the possible interactions between the component structures and subsystems are controlled and limited by various stabilization processes.

This chapter describes four major ways of stabilizing a system that constitutes a d-SoC. They are analogous to the ways people control one another. If you want someone to be a good citizen (1) you keep him busy with the activities that constitute being a good citizen, so he has no time or energy for anything else; (2) you reward him for carrying out these activities; (3) you punish him if he engages in undesirable activities; and (4) you try to limit his opportunities for engaging in undesirable activities. The following discussion applies to stabilizing a d-SoC as a whole, but it could also be applied to the stabilization of the individual structures/subsystems within a d-SoC.

Loading Stabilization

The first type of stabilization is ballasting or loading, to use an electrical analogy. In electrical ballasting, you impose a large electrical load on a circuit that draws on the power resources sufficiently so that very high voltages cannot occur; the power supply lacks the capacity to produce them, given the load. Loading in general refers to any activity that draws a large proportion of the energy of the system so that the system does not have excess free energy available. A load may also store energy, giving the system inertia that prevents a sudden slowdown or speedup.

Psychologically, loading means keeping a person's consciousness busy with desired types of activities so that too little (attention/awareness) energy is left over to allow disruption of the system's operation. As Don Juan told Carlos Castaneda [10], people's ordinary, repeated, day-to-day activities keep their energies so bound within a certain pattern that they do not become aware of nonordinary realities.

For example, right now, in your ordinary d-SoC, a number of things act as loading stabilization processes. The stable physical world you constantly deal with, the dependable relationships in it, give you a pattern of input that constantly stimulates you in expected patterns, in ways you are used to. If you push your hand against your chair, the chair feels solid, just as it always has felt. If you push it again, it still feels solid, and so on. You can depend on the lawfulness of the spectrum of experience we call physical reality. But, if the next time you pushed on the chair, your hand passed *through* it, you would be surprised or alarmed. You would begin to suspect that this was not your ordinary d-SoC or find it difficult to maintain your composure, your ordinary d-SoC.

Your body (and your internalized body image) is another source of stabilization by loading. Every morning when you wake up you have sensations from one head, two arms, and two legs. Although the exact relationships of the parts of your body to one another change as do your body's internal feelings, the changes are within a well-learned range. If you suddenly felt half your body starting to disappear, you would question whether you were in your ordinary d-SoC.

Body movement also supplies a type of loading. If you move your body, it has a certain feel to it. The kinesthetic feedback information on the relation of parts of your body and on muscle tensions as you move is within an anticipated range. If your arm suddenly felt three times as heavy as usual when you lifted it, this again would disrupt your ordinary d-SoC. Conversely, if you felt sleepy but did not want to enter the d-ASC of sleep, getting up and moving around would help you stay awake.

A final example of loading concerns the thinking process. You have a constant internal thinking process going on, constant internal chatter, which runs through familiar and habitual associative pathways and keeps you within your ordinary d-SoC. You think the kinds of things that please you; you feel clever as a result of thinking them; feeling clever makes you relax; feeling relaxed makes you feel good; feeling good reminds you that you are clever; and so on. This constant thinking, thinking, thinking loads your system and is extremely important in maintaining your ordinary b-SoC.

The importance of this constant loading of consciousness by thinking in maintaining and stabilizing our ordinary d-SoC cannot be overestimated. A Hindu metaphor for the ordinary d-SoC compares it to a drunken, horny monkey, carousing madly through the treetops, driven by its desires for sex, food, pleasure. The linkages between thought processes and emotional processes addict us to clever thoughts and make it hard to slow or stop the thinking process. Don Juan instructed Castaneda [10] to "not do," cease the constant thinking and doing that maintain ordinary consciousness, and Casteneda found this extraordinarily difficult to accomplish. This experience has been shared by innumerable practitioners of meditation who have found how difficult it is to escape from the incessant chatter of their minds.

Negative Feedback Stabilization

The second type of stabilization is *negative feedback*. Particular structures or subsystems sense when the rate or quality of operation of other subsystems goes beyond certain preset limits, and they then begin a correction process. This correction process may be conscious, as for example, anxiety resulting when your thoughts stray into certain areas you consider taboo. The anxiety then functions to restabilize subsystems within the acceptable range.

You may not be conscious of a particular feedback correction process, however. You may be lost in thought, for example, and suddenly find yourself very alert and listening, although not knowing why. A sound that indicated a potentially threatening event may have occurred very briefly, and while not intense enough to be consciously perceived, it was sufficient to activate a monitoring structure that then sent out correction signals to bring the system of consciousness back within optimal (for dealing with the threat) limits. This kind of negative feedback stabilization essentially measures when a subsystem's or structure's operation is going beyond acceptable limits and initiates an act of correction, reduces the deviation.

Positive Feedback Stabilization

The third stabilization process, positive feedback, consists of structures or subsystems that detect when acceptable activity is going on and then stimulate the emotional reward systems (making us feel good when we do a particular activity) or otherwise strengthen the desired activity. We may or may not be particularly conscious of feeling good, but we like to maintain and repeat the rewarded activity. During the formation of our ordinary d-SoC during childhood, we are greatly rewarded by our parents, peers, and teachers for doing various socially approved things, and because most of our socially approved actions are initiated by socially approved thoughts and feelings, we then internalize this reward system and feel good simply by engaging in the thoughts or actions that were rewarded earlier.

Let us illustrate how negative and positive feedback stabilization can work. Suppose you are driving home late at night and are rather sleepy. Driving carefully was an active program in your ordinary d-SoC, but now, because of fatigue, your mind is drifting toward a hypnagogic state even though you are managing to hold your eyes open. Hypnagogic thoughts are very interesting and your mind starts pursuing them further. Because the integrity of your ordinary d-SoC is now beginning to be disrupted, you do not make an appropriate correction as the car begins to drift over toward the shoulder of the road. You run off the shoulder, narrowly avoiding an accident, and this jars you back to full wakefulness. Learning occurs; a structure is formed. Sometime later the same circumstances occur again, but this time the new structure notes two facts—that your thoughts are becoming interesting in that hypnagogic way *and* that you are driving. Via the Emotion subsystem, the new structure sends a feeling of anxiety or alarm through you that immediately activates various subsystems toward the "physical world survival priority" mode of operating, and so reinstates full consciousness. This is negative feedback stabilization. Then you feel clever at not succumbing to the hypnagogic state. It shows you are a good driver; all sorts of authorities would approve: this constitutes positive feedback for keeping your consciousness within the wakefulness pattern.

Thus, a state of consciousness learns that certain processes indicate that part of its system is going beyond a safe limit of functioning (the error information) and then does something to restore that ordinary range of functioning (feedback control). You may or may not directly experience the feedback process.

Note that the terms *positive* feedback and *negative* feedback, as used here, do not necessarily refer to consciously experienced *good* or *bad* feelings, although such feelings may be experienced and be part of the correction process. Negative feedback refers to a correction process initiated when a structure or system starts to go or has gone beyond acceptable limits, and designed to decrease undesirable deviation. Positive feedback refers to an active reward process that occurs when a structure or subsystem is functioning within acceptable limits and that strengthens functioning within those limits.

Limiting Stabilization

A fourth way of stabilizing a d-SoC, limiting stabilization, consists of interfering with the ability of some subsystems or structures to function in a way that might destabilize the ongoing state of consciousness. It limits the range of possible functioning of certain subsystems.

An example of limiting stabilization is one effect of tranquilizing drugs in blunting emotional responses of any sort, limiting the ability of certain subsystems to produce strong emotions.

Since strong emotions can be important disrupting forces in destabilizing an ongoing state of consciousness, this limiting stabilizes the ongoing state. Sufficient limiting of crucial subsystems would not only stabilize any d-SoC (although at some cost in responsiveness of that d-SoC in coping with the environment), but would prevent transit into a d-ASC that required changes in the limited subsystems either for inducing the d-ASC or for stabilizing the d-ASC if it were attained.

Loading stabilization can, in some instances, be a limiting stabilization, but the two types of stabilization are not identical. Limiting directly affects certain structures or subsystems, while the effect of loading is indirect and operates more by consuming energy than by affecting structures directly.

In a system as multifaceted and complex as a d-SoC, several of each of the four types of stabilization activities may be going on at any given instant. Further, any particular action may be complex enough to constitute more than one kind of stabilization simultaneously. For example, suppose I have taken a drug and for some reason decide I do not want it to affect my consciousness. I begin thinking *intensely* about personal triumphs in my life. This stabilizes my ordinary state of consciousness by loading it, absorbing most of my attention/awareness energy into that activity so that it cannot drift off into thoughts that would help the transition to an altered state. It also acts as positive feedback, making me feel good, and so increasing my desire to continue this kind of activity.

Many stabilizing processes use psychological energy, energy that could be used for other things. Thus there is a cost to stabilizing a d-SoC that must be balanced against the gain that results from the focus obtainable from a stable d-SoC. The question of the optimal degree of stabilization for a given d-SoC when functioning in a given environment is important, although it has not been researched. If there are too few stabilization processes, the d-SoC can be broken down too easily, a circumstance that could be most unadaptive—when driving, for example. If the d-SoC is too stabilized, if too much energy is being consumed in stabilization processes, then that much less energy is available for other purposes. Some of the psychological literature on rigidity as a personality variable might provide a good starting point for investigating optimal stabilization.

A d-SoC, then, is not simply a collection of psychological parts thrown together any old way; it is an integral system because various stabilization processes control the interaction patterns among the structures and subsystems so as to maintain the functional identity of the overall system.

7.

Induction of Altered States: Going to Sleep, Hypnosis, Meditation

✿✿

We have now seen that a d-SoC is a system that is stabilized in multiple ways, so as to maintain its integrity in the face of changing environmental input and changing actions taken in response to the environment. Suppose that the coping function of the particular d-SoC is not appropriate for the existing environmental situation, or that the environment is safe and stable and no particular d-SoC is needed to cope with it, and you want to transit to a d-ASC: what do you do?

This chapter examines the process of inducing a d-ASC in general from the systems approach, and then considers its application to three transitions from ordinary consciousness: to sleep, to hypnosis, and to meditative states.

Inducing a d-ASC: General Principles

The starting point is the baseline state of consciousness (b-SoC), usually the ordinary d-SoC. The b-SoC is an active, stable, overall patterning of psychological functions which, via multiple stabilization relationships (loading, positive and negative feedback, and limiting) among its constituent parts, maintains its identity in spite of environmental changes. I emphasize *multiple* stabilization, for as in any well-engineered complex system, there are many processes maintaining a state of consciousness: it would be too vulnerable to unadaptive disruption if there were only a few.

Inducing the transition to a d-ASC is a three-step process, based on two psychological (and/or physiological) operations. The process is what happens internally; the operations are the particular things you do to yourself, or someone does to you, to make the induction process happen. In the following pages the steps of the process are described sequentially and the operations are described sequentially, but note that the same action may function as both kinds of induction operation simultaneously.

INDUCTION OPERATIONS: DISRUPTION AND PATTERNING

The first induction operation is to disrupt the stabilization of your b-SoC, to interfere with the loading, positive and negative feedback, and limiting processes/structures that keep your psychological structures operating within their ordinary range. Several stabilization processes must be disrupted. If, for example, someone were to clap his hands loudly right now, while you are reading, you would be somewhat startled. Your level of activation would be increased; you might even jump. I doubt, however, that you would enter a d-ASC. Throwing a totally unexpected and intense stimulus into your own mind could cause a momentary shift *within* the pattern of your ordinary d-SoC but not a transition to a d-ASC. If you were drowsy it might totally disrupt one or two stabilization processes for a moment, but since *multiple* stabilization processes are going on, this would not be sufficient to alter your state of consciousness.[1]

So the first operation in inducing a d-ASC is to disrupt enough stabilization processes to a great enough extent that the baseline pattern of consciousness cannot maintain its integrity. If only some of the stabilization processes are disrupted, the remaining undisrupted ones may be sufficient to hold the system together;

1 This particular example is true for your ordinary d-SoC. But if you had been asleep, you might have been awakened as a result of the hand clap. It might have been sufficient in a sleep d-SoC to disrupt stabilization enough to allow a transition back to ordinary waking consciousness. Also, if the expectational context were right, it could cause a transition from your ordinary d-SoC to a d-ASC. The Abbé de Faria, in the early days of hypnosis, "hypnotized" ignorant peasants by leading them through dark passages into a dark room, then suddenly setting off a tray of flash powder while striking a huge gong [38]. This must be one of the most authentic ways of "blowing one's mind."

thus, an induction procedure can be carried out without actually inducing a d-ASC. Unfortunately, some investigators have equated the procedure of induction with the presence of a d-ASC, a methodological fallacy discussed in Chapter 13. Stabilization processes can be disrupted directly when they can be identified, or indirectly by pushing some psychological functions to and beyond their limits of functioning. Particular subsystems, for example, can be disrupted by overloading them with stimuli, depriving them of stimuli, or giving them anomalous stimuli that cannot be processed in habitual ways. The functioning of a subsystem can be disrupted by withdrawing attention/awareness energy or other psychological energy from it, a gentle kind of disruption. If the operation of one subsystem is disrupted, it may alter the operation of a second subsystem via feedback paths, etc.

Drugs can disrupt the functioning of the b-SoC, as can any intense physiological procedure, such as exhaustion or exercise.

The second induction operation is to apply *patterning forces,* stimuli that then push disrupted psychological functioning toward the new pattern of the desired d-ASC. These patterning stimuli may also serve to disrupt the ordinary functioning of the b-SoC insofar as they are incongruent with the functioning of the b-SoC. Thus the same stimuli may serve as both disruptive and patterning forces. For example, viewing a diagram that makes little sense in the baseline state can be a mild disrupting force. But the same diagram, viewed in the altered state, may make sense or be esthetically pleasing and thus may become a mandala for meditation, a patterning force.

STEPS IN THE INDUCTION PROCESS

Figure 7–1 sketches the steps of the induction process. The b-SoC is represented as blocks of various shapes and sizes (representing particular psychological structures) forming a system/construction (the state of consciousness) in a gravitational field (the environment). At the extreme left, a number of psychological structures are assembled into a stable construction, the b-SoC. The detached figures below the base of the construction represent psychological potentials not available in the b-SoC.

Disrupting (and patterning) forces, represented by the arrows, are applied to begin induction. The second figure from the left

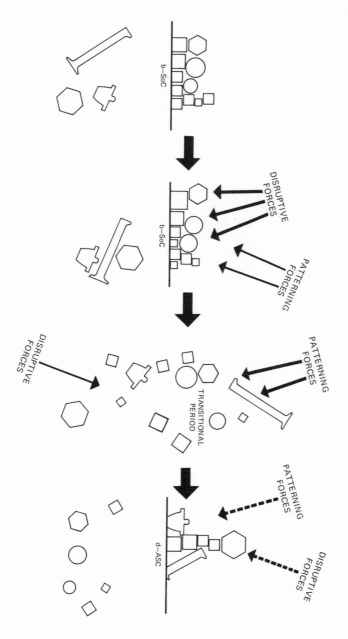

Figure 7–1. Steps in the induction of a d-ASC.

depicts this beginning and represents change *within* the b-SoC. The disruptive (and patterning) forces are being applied, and while the overall construction remains the same, some of the relationships within it have changed. System change has about reached its limit: at the right and left ends of the construction, for example, things are close to falling apart. Particular psychological structures/subsystems have varied as far as they can while still maintaining the overall pattern of the system.[2]

Also shown is the changing relationship of some of the latent potentials outside consciousness, changes we must postulate from this systems approach and our knowledge of the dynamic unconscious, but about which we have little empirical data[3] at present.

If the disrupting forces are successful in finally breaking down the organization of the b-SoC, the second step of the induction process occurs, the construction/state of consciousness comes apart, and a transitional period occurs. In Figure 7–1 this is depicted as the scattering of parts of the construction, without clear-cut relationships to one another or perhaps with momentary dissociated relationships as with the small square, the circle, and the hexagon on the left side of the transition diagram. The disrupting forces are now represented by the light arrow, as they are not as important now that the disruption has actually occurred; the now more important patterning forces are represented by the heavy arrows. The patterning stimuli/forces must now push the isolated psychological structures into a new construction, the third and final step of the processes in which a new, self-stabilized structure, the d-ASC, forms. Some of the psychological structures/functions present in the b-SoC, such as those represented by the squares, trapezoids, circles, and small hexagon, may not be available in this new state of consciousness; other psychological functions not available in the b-SoC have now become available. Some functions available in the b-SoC may be available at the same or at an altered level of functioning in the d-ASC. There is a change in both the selection of human potentials

[2] There is a *depth* or intensity dimension within some b-SoCs (discussed in Chapter 14) . So we could speak of the b-SoC having reached its deepest (or shallowest) extreme.

[3] Psychoanalytical studies [19] of hypnotic induction give us inferential information on such activities: experiential phenomena reported during induction are interpreted as indicators of changes in unconscious forces, drives, and defenses.

used and the manner in which they are constructed into a working system.

Figure 7–1 also indicates that the patterning and disrupting forces may have to continue to be present, perhaps in attenuated form, in order for this new state to be stable. The d-ASC may not have enough internal stabilization at first to hold up against internal or environmental change, and artificial props may be needed. For example, a person may at first have to be hypnotized in a very quiet, supportive environment in order to make the transition into hypnosis, but after he has been hypnotized a few times, the d-ASC is stable enough so that he can remain hypnotized under noisy, chaotic conditions.

In following this example you probably thought of going from your ordinary state to some more exotic d-ASC, but this theoretical sequence applies for transition from any d-SoC to any other d-SoC. Indeed, this is also the *de*induction process, the process of going from a d-ASC back to the b-SoC. Disrupting forces are applied to destabilize the altered state, and patterning forces to reinstate the baseline state; a transitional period ensues, and the baseline state re-forms. Since it is generally much easier to get back into our ordinary state, we usually pay little attention to the deinduction process, although it is just as complex in principle as the induction process.[4]

It may be that some d-SoCs cannot be reached directly from another particular d-SoC; some intermediary d-SoC has to be traversed. The process is like crossing a stream that is too wide to leap over directly: you have to leap onto one or more stepping stones in sequence to get to the other side. Each stepping stone is a stable place in itself, but they are transitional with respect to the beginning and end points of the process. Some of the *jhana* states of Buddhist meditation may be of this nature (see Goleman's chapter in *Transpersonal Psychologies* [128]). This kind of stable transitional *state* should not be confused with the inherently unstable transitional *periods* discussed above, and we should be careful in our use of the words *state* and *period*.

---

[4] We might hypothesize that because the ordinary d-SoC is so tremendously overlearned compared with almost any other d-SoC, whenever there is a transitional period the dominant tendency is to repattern the ordinary d-SoC mode. Sleep would also be likely. Only the presence of special patterning forces allows some d-ASCs to be structured from a transitional state.

Let us now look at examples of three inductions of d-ASCs, all starting from a b-SoC of the ordinary waking state—the process of falling asleep, the induction of hypnosis, and the practice of two kinds of meditation toward the goal of reaching a meditative state. These examples are intended not as final analyses from the systems approach, but simply as illustrations of how the systems approach to states of consciousness deals with the induction of d-ASCs.

Going to Sleep

You begin by lying down in a quiet, dimly lit or dark room. The physical act of lying down, closing the eyes, being in a quiet place, immediately eliminates much of the loading stabilization that helps to maintain your ordinary d-SoC. Since there are far fewer sensory stimuli coming in from the quiet environment, energy is not required for dealing with these stimuli, and some of this psychological energy is freed. Some of it may, for example, go to enhancing imagery. Further, incoming stimuli tend to pattern the kind of psychological energies that maintain your active, waking state; they *activate* you. Without this stimulation, then, certain kinds of psychological energies are no longer generated. When these activation energies are generated, they ordinarily circulate through and further stabilize the waking state by loading it.

Lying down and relaxing eliminate another major source of loading stabilization, the familiar, expected pattern of input from your body. Almost all your kinesthetic receptors for telling you what your body is doing respond primarily to *change*, and when you are relaxed and still for long periods, these receptors stop sending messages into the central nervous system. Your body, in a neural impulse sense, disappears; it is no longer there to pattern consciousness.

You adopt an attitude that there is nothing to accomplish, no goals to be attained, no problems to solve, nothing important to deal with. Your attitude is that there is no normative pattern to hold your consciousness.

It is usually futile to *try* to go to sleep. The active attitude that works so well in doing things *within* your ordinary waking d-SoC does not help here. Taking this passive attitude further withdraws attention/awareness energy from many of your feedback stabilization processes. If there is no norm to hold to, there is no need to monitor for and correct deviations from the norm. This is important for allowing thought processes and other psychological processess to drift into the hypnagogic mode.

So far these attitudes (nothing is important) and physical actions (inactions really, lying still and relaxing) are similar to the start of many other procedures for inducing various d-ASCs. What tips the balance toward inducing the particular d-SoC of sleep are the physiological factors (not well understood, in spite of two decades of intense research on sleep) we call *tiredness,* or need to sleep. These tiredness factors constitute both a further disrupting force for the waking state and a patterning force or forces for shaping the transitional period into the sleep state. Their intensity is important in determining whether the induction is successful: if you are not at all tired, sleep will probably not occur. If you are *very* tired, sleep may occur even if the other disrupting operations (lying down, reducing sensory input, taking a "nothing is important" attitude) have not been carried out.

The study by Vogel and his colleagues of ego states during the transition to sleep, described in Chapter 5, showed how the experiential mapping of consciousness fell into two (or perhaps three) distinct clusters, two (or perhaps three) d-SoCs. For a time after lying down, the subjects retained a feeling of contact with the environment and their thoughts remained plausible by consensus reality standards. This was the intact ego state. The subjects then moved into the destructuralized ego "state," losing contact with the external environment and with their thoughts deviating greatly from consensus reality standards of normality. They regained plausibility of thought in the restructuralized ego state. The destructuralized ego "state" is transitional between the intact ego state and the restructuralized ego state. Whether it constitutes a d-SoC by our definition is not clear from Vogel's data: we do not know whether there was a coherent pattern or just constant change.

Inducing Hypnosis

The procedures for inducing hypnosis are many and varied, but certain steps are common to most of these procedures. The first such step usually involves having you sit or lie comfortably, so you do not have to exert any effort to maintain your bodily position, and telling you not to move and to relax your body as much as possible. This step has a variety of effects. For one thing, if you are somewhat anxious about what is going to happen, your anxiety, which is intimately related to bodily tension, is at least partially relieved if you relax. You limit your ability to feel anxiety. This makes it easier for you to alter your state of consciousness. Also, when your body is in a relaxed position and lying still, many of the kinesthetic receptors adapt out, as in going to sleep. Thus the body as a whole begins to fade out as a conscious experience; this known, patterned stimulation fades and no longer serves as a load and patterning force to help stabilize your b-SoC.

Second, the hypnotist commonly tells you to listen only to his voice and to ignore other thoughts or sensations that come into your mind. Ordinarily you constantly scan the environment to see if important stimuli are present. This constant scanning keeps up a continuous, varied pattern of information and energy exchanges among subsystems, which tends to keep subsystems active in the waking state pattern: as varied perceptions come in, you must decide whether they are important, you must draw on memories from the past in making these decisions, etc. By withdrawing attention/awareness energy from this scanning of the environment, you withdraw a good deal of psychological energy and activity from a number of subsystems: a major loading and patterning process is attenuated.

A third common instruction is that you should not *think about* what the hypnotist is saying, but just listen to it passively. If the hypnotist says your arm is feeling heavy, you are not to think, "He says it's feeling heavy, I wonder if it really will get heavy, I remember it got heavy a long time ago but that's because there was a weight on it; well, I guess I shouldn't be doubting. . . ." In the ordinary d-SoC you constantly think about what is being said to you and what is happening to you, and this maintains a great deal of evaluative and decision-making activity and again activates other subsystems. Thus, this step also slows down the constant thinking that helps to maintain your ordinary d-SoC through loading stabilization.

Fourth, you are frequently told to focus your attention on some particular thing in addition to the hypnotist's voice. Let us take the example of your being asked to look fixedly at some simple object like a candle flame or a bright, shiny disk. This fixation serves to reduce further your scanning of the environment, with the same effects mentioned above, but it has an additional effect. It is unusual for you in your ordinary d-SoC to stare fixedly at one thing. If you do, all sorts of unexpected (to most people) visual effects occur because the retina becomes fatigued. Colored halos start to appear around the object being stared at, shadows appear and disappear, apparent movements occur, parts of the object fade. To the extent that these are not part of your usual experience, they constitute a kind of input that the Input-Processing subsystem (discussed later) is not used to handling, and so they tend to disrupt the normal functioning of this subsystem.

Further, because the hypnotist earlier stated that he has the power to make you have unusual experiences, the fact that you are now having unusual experiences enhances the prestige of the hypnotist and gives you more trust in him. This is a kind of trick: by using physiological effects that you do not realize are the expected result of staring at anything, the hypnotist manages to take credit and so enhances his psychological effectiveness. The importance of this will become even clearer later when we discuss the Sense of Identity subsystem.

Fifth, the hypnotist commonly suggests to you that you are feeling sleepy or drowsy. This elicits a variety of memory associations that help the induction process. Since going to sleep means that your b-SoC breaks down, this suggestion acts as a disruptive force. And since going to sleep is associated with a fading out of your body image, this suggestion enhances the fading of the body image that is already occurring because of the adaptation of kinesthetic receptors to your relaxed, still posture. Further, since going to sleep is a passive activity, the suggestion encourages a sense of passivity on your part and so reinforces the earlier instructions not to think *about* what the hypnotist is saying but simply to accept it. The references to sleep also draw up memories and expectations of your identity fading, so energy is not required to keep evaluating the situation in terms of your personal values.

Sixth, as well as suggesting sleep, the hypnotist often further indicates that this sleep is not quite the same as real sleep because you will still hear him. The hypnotist may not need to suggest this overtly: everyone in our culture knows enough about hypnosis to realize that the subject can still hear the hypnotist. This is a specific patterning force. The suggestions telling you that what is happening is like sleep primarily serve to disrupt your d-SoC, but since the hypnotist does not want you actually to go to sleep, he adds a patterning force to produce a passive sleep*like* state in which communication with the hypnotist is still effective.

Seventh, once you appear passive and relaxed, most hypnotic procedures go on to simple motor suggestions, such as having you hold an arm horizontally out in front of you and telling you it is getting heavy. Motor suggestions like this are relatively easy for most people to experience, and as you begin to respond to these suggestions, the hypnotist's prestige is further enhanced.

This automatic response to suggestion affects your Sense of Identity subsystem. Ordinarily it is your own "voice" inside you that tells you to do a thing that you then do. Now the hypnotist's voice takes over this role, and your sense of self begins to include the hypnotist. The special modulation from this subsystem that constitutes the ego sense (discussed later) is added to the stimuli that would ordinarily be perceived as the voice of an outsider. Psychoanalysts call this the *transference* element of hypnosis, especially when some of the transference involves parental transferences onto the hypnotist. The deliberate or implicit encouragement of identification with the hypnotist's voice is an application of patterning forces.

Success with simple motor suggestions also produces a novel kind of body stimulation: you feel your body moving, but with different qualities than ordinarily. Your arm, for instance, feels exceptionally heavy and seems to move by itself. This kind of datum again does not fit the habitual input-processing patterns, and so tends both to disrupt the stabilization of your d-SoC and to help pattern the hypnotic state.

As you respond well to simple motor suggestions, the hypnotist usually goes on to harder and more impressive motor suggestions and various kinds of cognitive suggestions, and continued success leads to increasing inclusion of the hypnotist within your ego sense.

Finally, we should note that an important factor in understanding the hypnotic induction technique is the subject's implicit expectations of what it is like to be hypnotized and how a hypnotized subject behaves. Shor [59] did a survey showing that among college students there is a fairly good general knowledge of what hypnosis is like, in spite of some misconceptions. So if a subject agrees to be hypnotized and believes that the hypno-

tist can do it, he has implicit expectations that affect his reactions
to the particular things the hypnotist does.

THE HYPNOTIC STATE

If the induction is successful and the neutral hypnotic state is
developed, the result is a d-ASC characterized by a quiet mind
[78]; most of the structures are inactive, many of the psychological
subsystems discussed in Chapter 8 are not actively functioning.
Typically, if a deeply hypnotized subject is asked what he is
thinking about or experiencing, the answer is "Nothing." However, this state is also characterized by greatly enhanced suggestibility, a greater mobility of attention/awareness energy, so when
a particular experience is suggested to the subject he usually
experiences it far more vividly than he could in his ordinary d-SoC,
often to the point of total experiential reality. Thus the hypnotic
state shows a high flexibility of functioning, even though it is relatively quiet between particular functionings. The state is also
characterized by a quality called *rapport,* a functioning of the
Sense of Identity subsystem to include the hypnotist as part of
the subject's own ego.

It is easy to see how the various techniques mentioned above
destabilize the ordinary pattern and operate on various psychological subsystems to push them toward extreme values of functioning. But where is the actual transition? We do not know.
Studies of hypnosis have generally paid little attention to the
transition between hypnosis and waking. Some psychoanalyti-
cally oriented case studies [19] have reported marked transitional effects, but no study has tried to map the exact nature and
extent of the quantum jump.

Much modern research that has tried to determine whether
hypnotic suggestibility is indeed greater than waking suggestibility has committed an important methodological error (discussed
in Chapter 9) : using group data without examining individual
data. Thus, unless every individual makes the transition at exactly the same point on the appropriate measures of psychological subsystem functioning, no transition point would appear in
the group data. Put another way, if there were some one variable
on which the jump was made from the normal state into hypnosis, and one subject jumped from a value of two to six to make
his transition, and a second subject jumped from three to seven,

and a third from four to eight, etc., the group data would show absolute continuity and no evidence for a transitional phase. Superimposing many maps destroys the patterns. The systems approach stresses the importance of examining the transitional period of hypnotic phenomena.

One further idea should be mentioned. Because most or all subsystems in the unprogrammed deep hypnotic state, so-called neutral hypnosis, are idling or relatively inactive, the hypnotic state may be better than the ordinary waking state as a b-SoC with which to compare other states. The ordinary waking state seems an incredibly complex, active, and specialized construction compared with the hypnotic state.

Meditation and Meditative States

Meditation refers to a variety of *techniques* that may or may not induce a d-ASC at a given time.

Meditation techniques are varied, but Naranjo and Ornstein [39] have classified them into three basic types: (1) concentrative meditation, (2) opening-up meditation, and (3) expressive meditation. Here we consider the first two and begin by analyzing a technique common to both before further distinguishing between them.

Most meditation techniques involve, as the initial step, sitting absolutely still in a posture that is not only comfortable, but that involves keeping the head, neck, and spine in a straight vertical line. A small but significant amount of muscular effort is needed to maintain this posture. Like the comfortable position assumed for inducing sleep or hypnosis, the comfortable posture in meditation allows various kinesthetic receptors to adapt out, so the body image generally fades. In contrast with going to sleep, the fact that a slight amount of muscular effort is needed to hold the body in this upright position prevents sleep from occurring for most people. Hypnotic induction procedures can allow the subject to slip in and out of actual sleep, but this is usually quite disruptive in meditative procedures, as the person begins to fall over.

Since much of a person's sense of identity comes from his body image, the fading of the body in a comfortable, steady posture also tends to reduce his sense of identity, thus helping to destablilize his b-SoC and to free energy.

Sitting absolutely still, not acting, also frees energy that would otherwise be automatically absorbed in acting: meditation is a technically simplified situation in this way.

The vertical posture for head, neck, and spine is also of theoretical importance in meditation systems that believe that a latent human potentiality, the Kundalini force, is stored at the base of the spine and may flow upward, activating various other postulated latent potentials, the psychic energy centers or *chakras,* as it rises [128, ch. 6].

Since the meditator is sitting absolutely still, his muscular subsystem similarly has little to do beyond postural maintenance. This further reduces loading stabilization. Thus many sources of activity that maintain ordinary d-SoC fade out when the meditative posture is assumed.

CONCENTRATIVE MEDITATION

Concentrative meditation techniques basically instruct you to put *all* of your attention on some particular thing. This can be an external object that is looked at fixedly or some internal sensation such as the rise and fall of the belly in breathing. As in hypnotic induction, the meditator is told that if his mind wanders away from this focus he is to bring it back gently[5] to this focus, and not allow it to be distracted.

This greatly restricts the variety of input to the system, inhibits thinking about various stimuli that come from scanning the environment, and in general takes attention/awareness energy away from and reduces the activity of the various subsystems of ordinary consciousness.

The meditator fixes his attention on *one* thing, usually an external or internal sensation. This can produce unusual phenomena due to various kinds of receptor fatigue, as in the induction of hypnosis, but most meditation systems stress that these anomalous perceptual phenomena should not be taken as signs of success or be paid any special attention. In Zen Buddhism, for example, there is a teaching story of a student excitedly rushing to his roshi (master) to describe a vision of gods bowing down to him and feelings of ecstasy that occurred during his meditation.

[5] Gently bringing attention back to the concentration focus is important: if you violently bring it back, fight the distractions, this sends large quantities of attention/awareness to them, and so keeps attention/awareness energy circulating through the system generally. This stabilizes the ordinary d-SoC, which involves many flows of attention/awareness energy to a variety of things.

The roshi asks him if he remembered to keep his attention fixed on the rise and fall of his belly in breathing during the vision, as per the meditation instructions, and when the student says no (who would care about the rise and fall of your belly during such a vision?), the roshi reprimands the student for allowing himself to become distracted! Thus while anomalous perceptual phenomena may act as disruptive forces for our ordinary state, they do not attract the same amount of attention in meditation as they do in hypnosis and so may have different effects.[6]

As in any induction technique, the person preparing to meditate has explicit and implicit expectations of what will come about. His explicit expectations stem from his immediately conscious memories of what he knows about meditation and his goal in doing it. His implicit expectations range from the implicit but potentially conscious ones that come from other knowledge about meditation he *could* recall but is not recalling at the moment, to more implicit ones that he has absorbed over a longer time and of which he may not be consciously aware. The more implicit expectations may or may not accord with the teachings of the particular meditative system, for they may have come through personality-induced distortions of teaching situations in the past. The discussion (in Chapter 4) of the construction of ordinary consciousness and how it affects our perception of the world is relevant here.

STATE RESULTING FROM CONCENTRATIVE MEDITATION

Naranjo and Ornstein [39] describe the meditative state[7] of consciousness that can result from concentrative meditation as a discrete state characterized as "voidness," "blankness," or

---

[6] Another important difference is that in hypnosis induction the hypnotist takes credit for these anomalous effects, thus helping to incorporate himself into the subject's own psyche. We have given little attention to the role of the hypnotist as "outsider," for he only becomes effective as he becomes able to control the subject's own attention/awareness energy. The meditator in the Buddhist tradition is seeking to free himself from control by external events or persons, and so does not value particular phenomena.

[7] We speak here of a single state resulting from concentrative meditation because our rudimentary scientific knowledge goes only this far. But we should remember that spiritual disciplines distinguish many states where we see one. In Buddhist terms, for example, eight distinct states of samadhi (concentration) are described, each of which may be a d-SoC (see Chapter 17 and [128]). Whether these are actually useful descriptions of eight d-SoCs or only descriptions of techniques is a question for the developing science of consciousness to research.

"no-thingness." There seems to be a temporary nonfunctioning of all psychological functions. In some sense, difficult to deal with verbally, awareness seems to be maintained, but there is no *object* of awareness. The appearance of this meditative state seems to be sudden and to clearly represent a quantum leap. The practice of meditation quiets down the various subsystems, but there is a sudden transition to this pattern of voidness.

The meditative state may or may not be valued in and of itself, depending on the particular spiritual discipline and its philosophy. What does generally seem to be valued is its after-effect, generally described as a great "freshening" of perception or increase in feelings of aliveness. In terms of the systems approach, a major aftereffect of the concentration-produced meditation state is a decrease in processing and abstracting of sensory input from what occurs in the ordinary d-SoC. Much more raw sensory data are passed to awareness, instead of the highly selected abstractions usually seen, and this produces a great intensification of sensory perception of both the external world and one's own body. This is usually felt as quite joyful. As Wordsworth put it in *Ode on Intimations of Immortality* [147]:

> There was a time when meadow, grove, and stream,
> The earth and every common sight,
>   To me did seem
>   Apparelled in celestial light,
> The glory and the freshness of a dream.

Going on to contrast this with perception in his ordinary d-SoC, he said:

> It is not now as it hath been of yore;—
>   Turn whereso'er I may,
>   By night or day,
> The things which I have seen I now can see no more.

I suspect that if Wordsworth were alive today he would be quite interested in altered states of consciousness.

This is a good place to remind ourselves that a state of consciousness generally has *many* processes stabilizing it. Many of you have had the experience of sitting down and trying to meditate according to some prescription and finding that rather than reaching some desirable d-ASC you only obtained a sore back! Sitting still in the correct posture and trying to do the technique may indeed disrupt *some* of the customary feedback processes that stabilize your b-SoC, but if others are still active, such as continual thinking, no actual shift in state of consciousness will result.

Confusion results when the word *meditation* is used to describe many different things. It is probably too late to prevent sloppy usage, but ideally, the phrase *tried to meditate* means that the meditator attempted to carry out the instructions but was not successful at concentrating or holding the posture. The phrase *did meditate* means the meditator felt he was relatively successful in following the instructions, even though no meditative state developed. The phrase *reached a meditative state* means that the meditator actually did so.

OPENING-UP MEDITATION

Opening-up meditation refers to a variety of techniques whose aim is to help you achieve full sensitivity to and awareness of *whatever* happens to you, to be a *conscious* observer observing what is happening to you without being caught up in your reactions to it. It is a matter of being aware of what is happening without *thinking about* what *is* happening to the exclusion of perceiving what is happening, or becoming identified with re-actions to what is happening. *Vispassana* is a Buddhist meditation of this sort. The word means something like bare attention—bare attention to sensations, feelings, thoughts, and reactions to these things as they occur. The "simple" rule[8] is to notice anything and everything that happens, to neither reject anything as unworthy of attention, nor welcome anything as worthy of more attention than anything else. This includes being aware of "failures," such as thoughts, rather than fighting them.

Opening meditation is usually practiced in the same sort of posture as concentrative meditation, so all the effects of posture on disrupting the b-SoC are similar.

This nonidentification with stimuli prevents attention/aware-ness energy from being caught up in the automatic, habitual processes involved in maintaining the ordinary d-SoC. Thus while awareness remains active, various psychological subsystems tend to drift to lower and lower levels of activity. Traditional accounts indicate that after a high level of success is achieved,

8 "Simple" to say, extremely difficult to do!

there is a sudden shift into a meditative state of consciousness characterized by a great freshening of perception and deautomatization of the subsystem of Input-Processing. This is the meditative state itself, rather than an *after*effect of it, as in concentrative meditation. Almost all psychological energy is present in the awareness function, and there seems to be far less input-processing, so things are perceived more directly.[9] The meditator experiences things as much more intense and clear; whether this means that he perceives the external more *accurately* has not, to my knowledge, been tested.

Although meditation has been a neglected topic of scientific research, this is changing rapidly: the interested reader should see the bibliography on research in this area put out by Timmons and Kamiya [141], as well as the recent updating of that bibliography by Timmons and Kanellakos [142].

This concludes our brief survey of the process of inducing a d-ASC. In some ways it is too simplified: the actual situation in which a person, either by himself or with the help of another, sits down to induce a d-ASC is influenced by many variables that affect our lives, especially those implicit factors stemming from our personal and cultural histories that are so hard for us to see.

One final example to illustrate the importance of these implicit and expectational factors. When phonograph recordings were still something of a novelty, George Estabrooks [16], one of the early researchers in hypnosis, decided to see if hypnosis could be induced by simply recording the verbal procedure on a record and playing it to a group of volunteer subjects. He recorded an induction procedure and got some volunteers from one of the college classes he taught. At the time for the experiment, he put the record on and, to his consternation, found he had brought the wrong record from his office: he was playing a record of Swiss yodeling! Deciding to let it entertain his subjects while he got the right one, he said nothing but left and went to his office.

When he returned, he found one subject was in a deep hypnotic state! The professor had said this record would hypnotize him, the student went into hypnosis.

---

[9] We do not know enough at present to adequately describe how the d-ASC reached from opening meditation, characterized by freshened perception, differs from the feeling of freshened perception occurring within one's ordinary d-SoC as an aftereffect of concentrative meditation.

8.

Subsystems

✿✿

We began this discussion of the systems approach to consciousness by describing the concepts of attention/awareness, energy, and structure. We defined a structure as a basic unit that can be assembled into larger structures or be analyzed into substructures. At present, our scientific knowledge is generally too rudimentary to allow the breakdown of structures into their components. We can, however, describe the assembly of multiple structures into major experiential and experimental divisions—subsystems—of consciousness. Ten such subsystems are described in this chapter. They are convenient conceptual tools for understanding the currently known range of variations in d-ASCs. They do not refer to localized regions of the brain. They are concepts I have developed by classifying the greatly varying experiences and behaviors reported in d-ASCs into clusters of phenomena that seem to hold together, on the basis of both their own internal similarity and other known psychological data.

In their present form, I find these subsystems a useful conceptual tool for organizing the otherwise chaotic masses of data about d-ASCs. I also believe that further thinking can sharpen our ideas about the properties of these subsystems and their possible interactions with each other and allow us to predict d-ASCs in addition to those already known. Making these predictions and testing them should further sharpen our conceptions about the nature of various subsystems, and so further increase our understanding. This is the standard scientific procedure of conceptualizing the data as well as possible, making predictions on that basis, confirming and disproving various predictions, and thus sharpening the conceptual system or modifying it. The socialized repetition of this procedure is the essence of scientific method.

Figure 8–1 sketches ten major subsystems, represented by the labeled ovals, and their major interaction routes. The solid arrows represent major routes of information flow: not all known routes are shown, as this would clutter the diagram. The hatched arrows represent major, known feedback control routes whereby one subsystem has some control over the functioning of another subsystem. The dashed arrows represent information flow routes from the subconscious subsystem to other subsystems, routes that are inferential from the point of view of the ordinary d-SoC. Most of the subsystems are shown feeding information into, or deriving information from, awareness, which is here considered not a subsystem but the basic component of attention/awareness and attention/awareness energy that flows through various systems.

A brief overview of a state of consciousness as a functioning system, as represented in Figure 8–1, can be described as follows. Information from the outside world comes to us through the Exteroception subsystem (classical sense organs), and information from our own bodies comes to us via the Interoception subsystem (kinesthetic and other bodily functioning receptors). Data from both sets of sense organs undergo Input-Processing (filtering, selecting, abstracting), which in turn influences the functioning of Exteroception and Interoception. Input-Processing draws heavily on stored Memory, creates new memories, sends information both directly into awareness and into our subconscious, and stimulates our Sense of Identity and our Emotions. Information we are aware of is in turn affected by our Sense of Identity and Emotions. We subject this information to Evaluation and Decision-Making; and we may act on it, produce some sort of motor output. This Motor Output subsystem produces action in the body that is sensed via Interoception, in a feedback process through the body. The Motor Output also produces effects on the external world that are again sensed by Exteroception, constituting feedback via the external world. Our perception and decision-making are also affected by our Space/Time Sense. Also shown in Figure 8–1 are some latent functions,

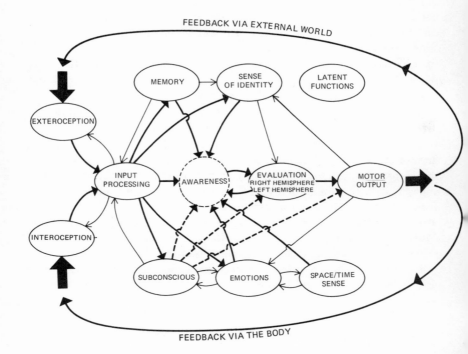

Figure 8–1. Major subsystems of consciousness and principal information flow routes.

which may be tapped in a d-ASC, but are not available in the b-SoC.

In the following pages the basic nature of each subsystem is defined and the range of both quantitative and qualitative alterations that occur in its functioning over the range of various d-ASCs is indicated. Of necessity, these descriptions are somewhat sketchy. One of the major tasks of future research is to fill in the details about each of these subsystems, their changes in d-ASCs, and their interaction with other subsystems.

Exteroception

The subsystem Exteroception includes the classical sense organs for registering changes in the environment: eyes, ears, nose, taste organs, and touch organs.

The exteroceptive organs constitute a model of a whole system of consciousness. First, they are *active* organs. While all of them can respond to stimulation when they are passive, as when a light is suddenly shined in your eye, they normally engage in an active scanning of the environment. Your eyes dart about; you turn your head or perk up your ears to hear sounds more clearly; you reach out to touch things that interest you. Similarly, consciousness can be passively stimulated, but ordinarily it is an active process.

Second, each of the classical exteroceptive sense organs has limited responsiveness. The eye cannot respond to ultraviolet light, the ear cannot pick up sounds above or below certain frequencies, touch cannot respond to exceptionally subtle stimuli. Similarly, any state of consciousness has certain limits to what it can and cannot react.

Third, you have some voluntary control over the input to your exteroceptive sense organs. If you do not want to see something, you can look away or close your eyes; if you do not want to hear something, you can move away from the sound source or put your fingers in your ears. In any state of consciousness, you have some voluntary control over exteroceptive functioning. But the control is limited: if the sound is intense enough, it is difficult not to hear it at all, even with your hands over your ears.

Although many changes in perception of the external environment are reported in d-ASCs, these usually do not represent changes in the exteroceptors themselves, except possibly in some drug-induced d-ASCs. Each of the classical sense organs is a masterpiece of engineering; it is already as sensitive as it can be. Thus its useful sensitivity is not increased, even if a person *experiences* himself as being in more contact with the environment in a d-ASC. As we shall see later, practically all phenomena dealing with feelings of increased contact with the environment are related to changes in the Input-Processing subsystem.

Sometimes when a drug is used to induce a d-ASC there may be some physiological changes in the exteroceptors. LSD, for example, may actually cause pupillary dilation, thus allowing in more light (although one might quarrel whether this is a direct physiological effect or a secondary effect due to the increased attention being paid to the external environment). Similarly, since psychedelic drugs affect neural functioning generally, they may have some direct effects on the neural components of the sense organs themselves, but little is known of this now. So, in terms of present knowledge about d-ASCs, changes in the exteroceptors seem of little importance.

Input to the exteroceptors is usually deliberately manipulated and patterned in the course of attempting to induce a d-ASC. Although most of the important changes resulting from these techniques occur in Input-Processing, some do start with direct effects on the exteroceptors and should be noted.

Input from the environment that, while varying, remains within a learned, anticipated range, acts as a source of loading stabilization. Thus, changing the input to the exteroceptors may interfere with the loading stabilization function and/or inject anomalous input that may destabilize a d-SoC.

A major way of doing this is to reduce or eliminate sensory input. In the induction process for many d-ASCs, there is an attempt to make the environment quiet, to cut down the amount of sensory input a person has to handle. Consider, for example, the techniques of guided imagery [3] or twilight imagery, where, while lying down with closed eyes, a person enters more and more into fantasy. A genuine d-ASC may develop in some cases, as fantasy intensifies, but it is clear that sensory input must usually be kept at a low level to both induce and maintain this d-ASC. I have seen people get into intense experiences through guided imagery techniques, but the simple act of opening the eyes and allowing visual input from the physical world to enter immediately disrupts this state.

Reduction of sensory input to a level as near zero as possible is a potent technique for inducing d-ASCs. In the fifties and early sixties, there were many *sensory deprivation* experiments during which the subject lay comfortably in a dark, quiet room without moving. The findings were interpreted as showing that if the brain did not receive sufficient sensory input, the subject went "crazy." It is now clear [46, 55] that practically all these studies were severely contaminated, as were the contemporary studies of psychedelic drugs, by implicit demand characteristics that account for most of the phenomena produced. If you put a person through a procedure he thinks will make him crazy, in a medical setting, he is likely to act crazy. That tells you something about suggestibility, but little about the effects of reduced sensory input per se. Traditional literature from many spiritual psychologies [128] as well as accounts from people who have been trapped in isolation situations, indicate that sensory deprivation can be a powerful technique in affecting consciousness. But its effect is apparently always patterned by other factors.[1]

Changing the *patterning* of input to the exteroceptors, and the subsequent processing of the information in Input-Processing, can also be a major way of altering consciousness. When the same kind of input is repeated over and over again, so that the exteroceptors become saturated, all sorts of changes take place. For example, if, by means of special apparatus, an image is held absolutely still on the retina of the eye, it soon begins to break up and display all sorts of unusual perceptual changes. Even when we believe we are looking steadily at something, there are actually tiny saccadic movements of the eye that keep the image moving slightly on the retina. Like so many of our receptors, the eye actually responds to slight, continuous change and cannot "see" absolutely steady input.

Overloading the exteroceptors is another way of inducing d-ASCs. The principle is recognized by people who attend rock concerts. Even if they have not taken some drug to help induce a d-ASC, the light show of complex, changing patterns accompanied by exceptionally loud music overloads and fatigues the exteroceptors, blowing their minds.

Interoception

The subsystem Interoception includes the various senses that tell us what is going on inside our bodies—the position of our limbs, the degree of muscle tension, how our limbs are moving, pressure in our intestines, bodily temperature. It is a way of sensing our internal world, as opposed to our external world. Many of the output signals from our interoceptors seem to be permanently excluded from our awareness; many of our sensing systems for governing the function of internal organs seem to have no representation in consciousness, regardless of conditions.

---

[1] Lilly's work [34, 35], in which a mature person uses the ultimate in sensory deprivation (floating in body-temperature water in the quiet and dark) as a tool, *under his own direction,* to explore consciousness, should be consulted by anyone interested in this area. Lilly's use of sensory deprivation as a tool under the subject's own control, rather than as a "treatment," imposed by people who are studying "craziness," is a breakthrough in research in this area. Suffice it to note here that sensory deprivation, by removing a major source of loading stabilization by the exteroceptors, can be a major tool for inducing d-ASCs and deserves much study.

For example, the functioning of our kidneys is regulated, but I know of no one who claims to have a direct experiential feel for what his kidneys are doing. We should, however, be careful about setting any ultimate limits on what aspects of Interoception can *never* reach or be affected by consciousness. The modern technology of biofeedback enables us to focus attention on and to control many bodily processes formerly thought to be completely incapable of voluntary control.

Many other interoceptive signals not normally in our awareness can be put in our awareness by turning our attention/awareness to them. For example, you may not have been thinking of sensations in your belly a moment ago, but now that I mention them and your attention/awareness turns there, you can detect various signals. With practice you might become increasingly sensitive to signals from this area of your body. Thus, as with our exteroceptors, we have some voluntary control over what we will attend to, but this control is limited.

We can also control interoceptive input by doing various things to our bodies. If you have an unpleasant sensation from some part of your body, you can relax, change position, take a deep breath, and change the nature of that signal, presumably by changing whatever is causing it. This is an ability we take for granted and know little about, but it is an important way of affecting interoceptive input. Some techniques for inducing d-ASCs, such as hatha yoga procedures, have a highly sophisticated technology for affecting one's body and how one perceives it. This is the reason biofeedback technology is sometimes said to have the potential to become an "electronic yoga," a way of rapidly learning about various internal conditions and using them to affect consciousness. We are still a long way from attaining this, however.

As is the case with exteroceptors, there is little evidence that actual physiological changes take place in the interoceptors during various d-ASCs, except possibly in some drug-induced d-ASCs. Also as in Exteroception, the learned, anticipated range of constant input from Interoception acts as a source of loading stabilization for maintaining the ordinary d-SoC.

The pattern of input from interoceptors can be subsumed under a useful psychological concept, the *body image*. You not only have a real body whose actual sensations are picked up by the interoceptors, but, in the course of enculturation, you have learned to perceive your own body in learned, patterned ways, just as you have learned to perceive the external world in socially learned ways. The degree to which your body image corresponds to your actual body may vary considerably. My own observations suggest that people's internal images of their bodies can differ amazingly from what an external observer sees.

An individual's body image may be very stable. An intriguing example of this is the *phantom limb* phenomenon. When an arm or a leg is amputated, the patient almost always reports he can still feel the limb, even though he can see and otherwise intellectually know it is not there. Sensations coming in from the severed nerve tracts are nonconsciously organized in the learned, habitual way so that the patient perceives the limb as still there. Most patients soon lose perception of their phantom limbs as they are subjected to considerable social pressure to do so. In some, however, the phantom limb persists in spite of all attempts to unlearn it. The sensations may or may not be painful.

The primary things to note are that the body image can be very rigid and may or may not show much correspondence to the actual body contours and what actually goes on in the body. I am convinced that as Westerners we generally have distorted images of our bodies and poor contact with sensations that go on in them. Since body sensations often represent a thinking about, or data processing of, experience, and a way of expressing emotions, our lack of contact with our actual body sensations puts us out of contact with ourselves. This is considered further in connection with the Subconscious subsystem.

People's experiential reports from d-ASCs indicate that enormous changes can take place in Interoception. The body may seem to get larger or smaller, change in shape, change in internal functioning, change in terms of the relationships of its parts, so that the body may not "work" in the usual fashion. Most of this range of experience probably represents changes in Input-Processing, rather than changes in the interoceptors themselves.

As with Exteroception, changing your body image is a common technique for inducing d-ASCs. Reducing interoceptive input, overloading it, or patterning it in novel ways have all been used. The primary effects are on Input-Processing, but the techniques start by affecting the interoceptors themselves. Let us look at some of these techniques briefly.

Immobilizing the body in a relaxed position is a major way of causing the output from Interoception to fade and, consequently, causing the body image either to fade or to change, since it is no longer stabilized by actual input from the interoceptors. The discussion of the induction of hypnosis, going to sleep, and meditation in Chapter 7 mentions the importance of allowing the interoceptors to adapt out so the input from the body disappears. In sensory deprivation techniques it is important to relax the body and at the same time not move at all. Even a slight movement can stimulate large numbers of interoceptors and reestablish the body image readily.

Overloading interoceptors is an important technique for altering consciousness. A good massage, for instance, or sensory awareness exercises that make you aware of bodily stimuli normally overlooked, have been known to induce d-ASCs. At the opposite end of the continuum from this pleasurable kind of manipulation of Interoception, pain and torture are some of the surest ways of inducing d-ASCs.

Patterning interoceptive input in unusual fashions is another way of inducing d-ASCs. Mudras, gestures of symbolic significance used in yoga, consist of putting the body into certain positions. I suspect that the actual bodily posture has a definite patterning effect on interoceptive input and can affect consciousness if you are sensitive to bodily input. If you are not highly sensitive to input from your own body, the patterning of interoceptive input may occur, but since not much awareness is gained, posture does not pattern attention/awareness energy in a way that would affect consciousness.

Another way of patterning interoceptive input is the altered states of consciousness induction device (ASCID) developed by Masters and Houston [37] on the basis of medieval accounts of the witch's cradle. This is an upright frame into which a person straps himself. The frame is hung from a short rope, so slight motions cause it to rock in erratic patterns. This produces anomalous patterns of input for the occupant to process: some interoceptors tell him he is standing up and therefore needs to exert certain muscular actions to maintain this posture, but other interoceptors tell him he is relaxed and not making these muscular actions. Other interoceptive senses indicate that he is moving and must do things to maintain his balance, but these are in conflict with other interoceptive sensations that he is passive. Since he is not used to such an anomalous, conflicting pattern of stimulation, it can greatly disrupt Input Processing.

Input Processing

Before reaching awareness, all input data, whether interoceptive or exteroceptive, normally goes through various degrees of processing. The Input-Processing subsystem consists of a complex, interlocking series of totally automatic processes that compares incoming data against previously learned material stored in memory, rejects much of the data as irrelevant, selects some of them as important enough to deserve further processing, transforms and abstracts these important data, and passes this abstraction along to awareness. Thus, a major function of Input-Processing is rejection. At any given instant, you are generally bombarded by an enormous quantity of sensory data of all sorts. Most of the data is not important in terms of defined needs, such as your biological survival. Since your ability to handle information and awareness is limited, you would be overwhelmed if all this mass of incoming data came through. Instead, you receive a small abstraction of incoming information that is important by personal and consensus reality standards.

Input-Processing is totally automatic. Look at this thing that is in your hands with the question, "What is it?" in your mind. Immediately you see a book. You did not have the experience of seeing a whitish rectangular object with dark spots on it. You did not further experience these spots as being arranged in lines, and the individual spots as having distinctive characteristics, which you then, by painstaking examination, arranged into words and sentences, and so concluded that this was a book in your hands. No, the recognition of this thing as a book was instantaneous and automatic. To demonstrate how automatic the processing is, look at the book again and try to see it as simply a collection of incoming, assorted stimuli instead of as a book.

Unless you have some unusual abilities, you find it very difficult to see this object as anything but a book.

Numerous psychological studies have focused on the way perception is automated. Many of these studies have mistakenly assumed they were studying the "accuracy" of perception. What they were usually studying was the agreement with consensus reality standards for perceiving things. An immediate, automatic perception of socially defined reality is taken as being "realistic" and as a sign of a "good observer."

Thus, Input-Processing is a learned behavior, probably the most complex a human being has to acquire. Think of the number of connections among stimuli and the number of responses associated with the various stimuli that an infant must learn before he can be said to "think." The task is staggering. The infant must learn to perceive *instantly* and *automatically* all major features of consensus reality as his parents, peers, and teachers do. This means that an immense amount of information must be stored in memory (it does not matter whether it is stored in the Memory subsystem or in a special Input-Processing memory) and be almost instantly available to Input-Processing. Total automation of the process is equated with efficiency: if I have to struggle to identify an object, I feel stupid; but if I recognize it right away, I feel competent and smart.

In relation to the enculturation process, we discussed the fact that a child has more options for his consciousness than a teenager or an adult. This is another way of saying that the automatization of Input-Processing and its efficiency become comprehensive with increasing age, until by the time we are adults almost everything in our world is instantly recognized and dealt with "appropriately." An adult sees things almost exclusively in a culturally approved way and makes culturally approved responses. Rigidity increases with age: that is what Timothy Leary meant when he said, "Don't trust anyone over thirty." The statement is overgeneralized, but it does contain an important psychological truth: older people are liable to be less able to see things differently from the way they have always been accustomed to seeing them.

Numerous psychological studies show variations in Input-Processing that are related to differences within consensus reality. An early study of perception, for example, showed that poor children tend to perceive coins as physically larger than rich children do. People with strong religious values tend to pick up words and other stimuli relating to religion more readily than they do those relating to economics, and vice versa. People with neuroses or psychoses tend to be especially sensitive to certain stimuli that trigger their neurotic structures and to distort perception in ways that fit these neurotic structures. Projective tests, in which the subject is shown a relatively ambiguous stimulus like an ink blot and asked to describe what he sees, are a way of investigating the underlying structures of Input-Processing. If he repeatedly sees a murdered baby in several different ink blots, we might begin to wonder about the way he has dealt with aggression in his life or about his feelings toward his parents.

In terms of the basic concepts of attention/awareness, psychological energy, and structure, Input-Processing represents a large number of structures, each specialized in responding to certain kinds of stimulus patterns. It has a certain amount of psychological energy always available, so that this active set of structures almost always stands between you and your senses. Input-Processing is automatized in the sense that the structures always draw energy of some sort when activated and process information in a relatively fixed way before passing this information on to awareness.

The ubiquity of Input-Processing is a main reason I have elsewhere distinguished consciousness from awareness. Some kind of "pure" awareness may be a basic from which we start, but ordinarily we experience *consciousness,* awareness as it is vastly modified by the machinery of the mind. Here Input-Processing in effect places a number of structures between us and our sensory input, and even our sensory input comes through the Exteroception and Interoception subsystems, which are themselves structures with characteristics of their own. Other subsystems are also structures that modify or pattern basic awareness into consciousness. The systems diagram presented as Figure 8–1 shows awareness in a distinct place, but it really spreads through the various subsystems and so becomes consciousness.

The main function of Input-Processing, then, is abstraction. This subsystem is rather like a vast organization that keeps track of an industry's progress and problems and, through hierarchical chains, passes on only the most abstracted reports to the president of the company.

Input-Processing also generalizes, gives a *familiar* abstracted output to unfamiliar situations that are reasonably close to particular perceptions that have been learned. Thus you recognize this object as a book even though you have never seen this particular book before: it is similar enough to other books to have that label automatically applied to it. This kind of generalization may be greatly affected by dominant needs and emotions: all apples look alike to a hungry man.

Various aspects of Input-Processing can show extremely large changes in various d-ASCs. There are large quantitative changes: that is, the range of continuous changes in various aspects of Input-Processing may be greater or less than in your ordinary d-SoC. Your ability to focus attention on particular percepts, for example, may be quantitatively greater or quantitatively less in various d-ASCs.

There are also many important qualitative changes that may be experienced as entirely new modes of perception. Some of these may be the activation of latent human potentials. Patterns may be seen in ordinarily ambiguous data, making it *obviously* meaningful. An important effect of marijuana intoxication, for example, is the ability to look at normally ambiguous material, such as the grain pattern in a sheet of wood, and see it as an actual picture. New shades of color are reported in various d-ASCs, new qualities to sound. We shall reserve judgment for the moment on whether these are veridical with respect to the actual stimulating objects.

Apparently fixed properties of perceptual organization may change in various d-ASCs as Input-Processing changes. Carlos Castaneda [9] for example, describes how Don Juan taught him how to turn into a crow while he was intoxicated with a hallucinogenic plant: an outstanding aspect of this experience was that his visual field from each eye became split, so that he had two quite different fields, just as if his eyes were on separate sides of his head, instead of the usual overlapping, integrated field.

Illusions and hallucinations, frequently reported in d-ASCs, represent important changes in Input-Processing. The conventional definition of illusion is a misinterpretation of a stimulus that is actually there, as, for example, when on entering a dimly lit room you mistake a coat hanging on a rack for a person. Hallucination is conventionally defined as a vision of something that is not there at all, as, for example, when on entering the same dimly lit room you see a person, even though the room is empty. While it is easy to distinguish these two extremes, there is obviously a continuum between them: there is always a certain amount of random neural firing in your retina, a "something" there.

In a more general sense, we must realize that "misperception" and "what is and is not there" are usually defined in terms of consensus reality. We may hope that our consensus reality has a high degree of accuracy with respect to physical reality, but to assume automatically that it does is to be very parochial. If one person hears a given piece of music as exceptionally beautiful in its melody, and another hears it as quite common, was the first person suffering an illusion, or was he really more perceptive? We must be particularly careful in dealing with many phenomena from d-ASCs that our consensus reality automatically defines as hallucinatory. Should we have so much faith in the conceptual schemes evolved in our ordinary d-SoC that we automatically dismiss anything that does not fit with them? It is bad science to continue to do so.

An illusion, then, is Input-Processing's interpretation of a stimulus in a way that does not match consensus reality standards. Whether the interpretation added by the illusion is a richer and more accurate perception of a stimulus pattern, or a more distorted and less accurate one, varies with individual cases. In terms of d-ASCs we know about, my general impression is that they possess the property of making our perception more accurate in some ways and less accurate in others.

A hallucination is a functioning of Input-Processing whereby stored information is drawn from Memory, worked over by Input-Processing, and passed along to awareness as if it were sensory data. The special label or quality that identifies the source of this vivid image as Memory is missing; the quality that identifies it as a sensory stimulus is present. Depending on the type of d-ASC, a hallucination may completely dominate perception, totally wiping out all sensory input coming through Input-Processing, or may be mixed with processed sensory data. The intensity of the hallucination may be as great as that of ordinary sensory information, even greater, or less.

An interesting dimension of variability of Input-Processing in d-ASCs is the degree to which it can be voluntarily altered. The degree of control may be high or low. I recall participating in some experiments on the effect of psilocybin, a psychedelic like LSD, when I was a graduate student. While intoxicated by the drug, I had to sort through a batch of file cards, each of which contained a statement of various possible symptoms. If I was experiencing the symptom, I was to put the card in the "true" pile, if I was not, in the "false" pile. I quickly found that I could make almost every statement true if I so desired, simply by reading it several times. I would pick up a statement like "My palms are sweating green sweat," think that would be an interesting experience, reread the statement several times, and then look at my hands and see that, sure enough, they were sweating green sweat! I could read a statement like "The top of my head is soft" several times and feel the top of my head become soft! Thus, while intoxicated with psilocybin my degree of voluntary control over Input-Processing became very large, sufficiently to create both illusions and hallucinations by merely focusing attention/awareness energy on the desired outcome.

Another type of variation that can occur in Input-Processing in d-ASCs is the partial or total blocking of input from exteroceptors or interoceptors. The d-ASC of deep hypnosis is an example. One can suggest to a talented, deeply hypnotized subject that he is blind, that he cannot feel pain, that he cannot hear, and *experientially* this will be so. The subject will not respond to a light or to objects shown him, and both during the d-ASC and afterward in his ordinary d-SoC, will swear that he perceived nothing. His eyes are still obviously functioning, and evoked brain responses recorded from the scalp show that input is traveling over the sensory nerves from his eye to his brain, but at the stage of Input-Processing the input is cut off so it does not reach awareness. Similarly, analgesia to pain may be induced in hypnosis and other d-ASCs.

When input is completely blocked in Input-Processing, there may or may not be a substitution of other input. Thus information may be drawn from Memory to substitute a hallucination for the actual blocked information. If, for example, a deeply hypnotized subject is told that he cannot see a particular person who is in the room, he may not simply experience a blank when looking at that person (which sometimes happens), he may actually hallucinate the details of the room behind the person and thus see no anomalous area in his visual field at all.

Another important change in d-ASCs is that, experientially, there may seem to be less Input-Processing, less abstracting, so a person feels more in touch with the raw, unprocessed input from his environment. This is especially striking with the psychedelics and is also reported as an aftereffect of concentrative meditation and as a direct effect of opening-up meditation. I know of no experimental studies that have thoroughly investigated whether one can actually be more aware of raw sensory data, but this is certainly a strong experiential feeling. It is not necessarily true, however. Vivid illusions can be mistaken for raw sensory data or (probably what happens) there can be a mixture of greater perception of raw data and more illusion substituted. Whether there is any particular d-ASC in which the balance is generally toward better perception through less abstracting is unknown at present.

Psychedelic-drug-induced conditions are particularly noteworthy for the experience of feeling in contact with the raw data of perception, and this makes perceptions exceptionally beautiful, vibrant, and alive. By contrast, usual perception in the ordinary d-SoC seems lifeless, abstract, with all the beauty of reality removed to satisfy various needs and blend in with consensus reality.

Also reported in d-ASCs is an experience of feeling more in touch with the actual machinery of Input-Processing, gaining some insight or direct experience of how the abstracting processes work. For example, I was once watching a snowfall through a window at night, with a brilliant white spotlight on the roof illuminating the falling snow. I was in an unusually quiet state of mind (it was too brief for me to decide whether it was a d-ASC), and suddenly I noticed that instead of simply watching *white* snow fall (my usual experience), I was seeing each snowflake glinting and changing with all colors of the spectrum. I felt strongly that an automated Input-Processing activity that makes snow white had temporarily broken down. Afterward, it struck me that this was likely, for white is actually all the colors of the spectrum combined by Exteroception (eyes) and Input-Processing to the sensation of white. Thus a snowflake actually reflects all the colors of the spectrum, and active "doing" (to use Don Juan's term) on the viewer's part is required to turn it into white. There is no light energy of "white" in the physicist's world. Similarly, persons have reported gaining insights into how various automatic processes organize their perception by being able to see the lack of organization of it or by seeing the alternative organizations that occur.

Synesthesia is another radical change in Input-Processing that sometimes takes place in some d-ASCs. Stimulation of one sense is perceived in awareness as though a different sense had been stimulated at the same time. For example, hearing music is accompanied by seeing colored forms. This is the most common and perhaps the most beautiful form of synesthesia, and is sometimes reported with marijuana intoxication.

All techniques for inducing d-ASCs, except drug or physiological effects that act directly on various bodily functions, must work through Input-Processing. That subsystem mediates all communication. Yet it is useful to distinguish between induction techniques that are primarily designed to disrupt stabilization of the b-SoC in some other subsystem without significantly affecting Input-Processing per se, and those that are designed to disrupt Input-Processing directly as a way of destabilizing the b-SoC.

In this latter class is a wide variety of techniques designed to give a person input that is uncanny in terms of the familiar ways of processing input in the b-SoC. The input is uncanny, anomalous in a sense of seeming familiar yet being dissimilar enough in various ways to engender a pronounced feeling of nonfitting. Often the events are associated with an emotional charge or a feeling of significance that makes the fact that they do not fit even more important. Don Juan, for example, in training Carlos Castaneda to attain various d-ASCs would often frighten Castaneda or destabilize his ordinary state to an extraordinary degree by doing something that seemed almost, but not quite, familiar, such as simply acting normally but with subtle differences at various points.

The use of uncanny stimuli is not limited to inducing a d-ASC from an ordinary d-SoC; it can work in reverse. When a person talks about "being brought down" from a valued d-ASC, he means he is presented with stimulation patterns that Input-Processing cannot handle in that d-ASC, so the d-ASC is destabilized, and he returns to his ordinary d-SoC.

Memory

The Memory subsystem is concerned with information storage, with containing residues of past experiences that are drawn upon in the present. Memory is thus a large number of semipermanent changes caused by past experience. We can think of Memory as structures, presumably in the brain (but perhaps also in the body structure), which, when activated, produce certain kinds of information. And we should not assume that there is just one Memory; there is probably a special kind of memory for almost every subsystem.

Conventional psychological views of Memory also often divide memory functioning into short-term or immediate memory, medium-term memory, and long-term memory. Short-term memory is the special memory process that holds information about sensory input and internal processes for a few seconds at the most. Unless it is transferred to a longer-term memory, this information is apparently lost. Thus, as you look at a crowd, searching for a friend's face for a short time, you may remember a lot of details about the crowd. Then you find your friend's face, and the details about the crowd are lost. There is no point in storing them forever. This short-term memory is probably an electrical activity within the brain structure that dies out after a few seconds: no long-term structural changes occur. Once the electrical activity dies out, the information stored in the pattern or in the electrical activity is gone forever.

Medium-term memory is storage of from minutes to a day or so. It probably involves partial structural changes as well as patterns of energy circulation. You can probably recall what you had for breakfast yesterday morning, but in a few days you will not remember the contents of that meal.

Long-term memory involves semipermanent structural changes that allow you to recall things experienced and learned a long time ago.

This division into short-, medium-, and long-term memory is of interest because these kinds of memories may be differentially affected during d-ASCs. At high levels of marijuana intoxication, for example, short-term memory is clearly affected [105], although long-term memory may not be. Thus, a marijuana user often reports forgetting the beginning of a conversation he is engaged in, but he continues to speak English. There is little more we can say about differential effects of various d-ASCs on these three kinds of memory, as they have not yet been adequately studied. They offer a fruitful field for research.

A most important aspect of Memory subsystem functioning in various d-ASCs is the phenomenon of *state-specific memory*. In a number of studies, subjects learned various materials while in d-ASCs, usually drug-induced, and were tested for retention of these materials in a subsequent ordinary d-SoC. Generally, retention was poor. The researchers concluded that things were not stored well in Memory in various d-ASCs. It is now clear that these studies must be reevaluated. Memory is specific. The way in which information is stored, or the kind of Memory it is stored in, is specific to the d-SoC the material was learned in. The material may be stored, but may not transfer to another state. If material is learned in a d-ASC and its retention tested in another d-SoC and found to be poor, the nonretention may indicate either an actual lack of storage of the information or a state-specific memory and lack of transfer. The proper way to test is to reinduce the d-ASC in which the material was learned and see how much material is retained in that state. State-specific memory has been repeatedly demonstrated in animals, although the criterion for the existence of a "state" in such studies is simply that the animals were drugged to a known degree, a criterion not very useful with humans, as explained later.

There is now experimental evidence that for high levels of alcohol intoxication there is definite state-specific memory in humans [21]. It is an experimental demonstration of the old folk idea that if you lose something while very drunk and cannot find it the next day, you may be able to find it if you get very drunk again and then search. Experiential data collected in my study of marijuana users [105] also indicate the existence of state-specific memory, and I have recently received verbal reports that laboratory studies are finding state-specific memory for marijuana intoxication. There also seems to be state-specific memory for the conditions induced by major psychedelic drugs.

State-specific memory can be readily constructed for hypnosis; that is, state-specific memory may not occur naturally for hypnosis, but it can be made to occur. If you tell a hypnotized subject he will remember everything that happened in hypnosis when he comes back to his ordinary state such will be his experience. On the other hand, if you tell a deeply hypnotized subject he will remember nothing of what went on during hypnosis or that he will remember certain aspects of the experience but not others, this will also be the case when he returns to his ordinary state. In any event he will recall the experiences the next time he is hypnotized. This is not a pure case of state-specific memory, however, because amnesia for hypnotic experiences in the waking state can be eliminated by a prearranged cue as well as by reinducing the hypnosis.

Another excellent example of state-specific memory is that occurring in spiritualist mediums. A medium enters a d-ASC in which his ordinary consciousness and sense of identity appear to blank out for a time. He may report wandering in what may be loosely called a dreaming state. Meanwhile, an alleged spirit entity ostensibly possesses him and acts as if it has full consciousness. Upon returning to a normal state, the medium usually has total amnesia regarding the events of the d-ASC. The alleged spirit communicator, however, usually shows perfect continuity of memory from state to state.[2]

I suspect that state-specific Memory subsystems will be discovered for many or most d-ASCs, but the necessary research has not been done. The kinds of state-specific memories may vary in completeness. The ones we know of now—from marijuana intoxication, for example—are characterized by transfer of some information to the ordinary d-SoC but nontransfer of other information, the latter often being the most essential and important aspects of the d-ASC experience.

Ordinarily, when we think of Memory we think of information becoming accessible to awareness, becoming part of consciousness, but we should note that we "remember" many things even though we have no awareness of them. Your current behavior is affected by a multitude of things you have learned in the past but which you are not aware of as *memories*. You walk across the room and your motion is determined by a variety of memories, even though you do not think of them as memories.

Note also that you can remember things you were not initially aware of. When you scan a crowd looking for a friend's face, you

2 The d-ASC or d-ASCs entered into by spiritualist mediums are a promising, but almost totally neglected field of research. Scientists have generally avoided having anything to do with mediums as a result of a priori dismissal of the claims made for survival of bodily death. The few scientists (parapsychologists) who have studied mediums have been concerned with whether the alleged surviving entities can provide evidence that they actually had an earthly existence, and whether this evidence could be explained by other hypotheses than postmortem survival. The nature of the medium's trance state per se is virtually unknown, yet it is clearly one of the most profound d-ASCs known and has tremendous effects on its experiencers. I mention this to alert researchers to an opportunity for learning a great deal with even a small investment of decent effort.

may be consciously aware of hardly any details of other faces, being sensitive only to your friend's. A minute later, when asked to recall something about the crowd, however, you may be able to recall a lot of information about it. For this reason, Figure 8–1 shows a direct information flow arrow from Input-Processing to Memory. We store in Memory not only things that have been in awareness, but also things that were never much in awareness to begin with.

An interesting quality of information retrieved from Memory is that we generally know, at least implicitly, that we are retrieving *memories*. We do not confuse these with sensations or thoughts. Some kind of operating signal or extra informational quality seems to be attached to the memory information itself that says "This is a memory." There is an intriguing analogy for this. In the early days of radio, when a newscast tuned you in to a foreign correspondent, there was an obvious change in the quality of the audio signal, a change that you associated with a foreign correspondent broadcasting over a long distance on short wave. The sound was tinny, the volume faded in and out, there were hisses and crackles. This was a noninformational extra that became so associated in listeners' minds with hearing a real foreign correspondent that many radio stations resorted to the trick of deliberately adding this kind of distortion years later when communication technology had improved so much that the foreign correspondent's voice sounded as if he was actually in the studio. The added distortions made the listeners feel they were indeed hearing a faraway reporter and made the broadcast seem more genuine. Similarly, memory information is usually accompanied by a quality that indentifies it as memory. The quality may be implicit: if you are searching actively for various things in your Memory, you need not remind yourself that you are looking at memories.

This extra informational quality of memory can sometimes be detached from Memory operation per se. It is possible to have a fantasy, for example, with the "this is a memory" quality attached, in which you mistakenly believe you are remembering something instead of just fantasizing it. Or, the quality may be attached in a d-ASC to an incoming sensory perception, triggering the experience of *déjà vu,* the feeling that you have seen this before. Thus you may be touring in a city you have never visited and it all looks very familiar; you are convinced you remember what it is like because of the presence of the "this is a memory" quality.[3]

When information is actually drawn from Memory without the quality "this is a memory" attached, interesting things can happen in various d-ASCs. Hallucinations, for example, are information drawn from Memory without the memory quality attached, but with the quality "This is a perception" attached.

Much of the functioning of the Sense of Identity subsystem (discussed later) occurs via the Memory subsystem. Your sense of who you are is closely related to the possession of certain memories. If the "this is a memory" quality is eliminated from those memories so that they become just data, your sense of identity can be strongly affected.

Other variations of Memory subsystem functioning occur in various d-ASCs. The ease with which desired information can be retrieved from Memory varies so that in some d-ASCs it seems hard to remember what you want, in others it seems easier than usual. The richness of the information retrieved varies in different d-ASCs, so that sometimes you remember only sketchily, and at other times in great detail. The search pattern for retrieving memories also varies. If you have to go through a fairly complex research procedure to find a particular memory, you may end up with the wrong memories or associated memories rather than what you were looking for. If you want to remember an old friend's name, for example, you may fail to recall the name but remember his birthday.

Finally, we should note that a great many things are stored in Memory but not available in the ordinary d-SoC. The emotional charge connected with those memories makes them unacceptable in the ordinary d-SoC, and so defense mechanisms repress or distort our recall of such information. In various d-ASCs the nature of the defense mechanisms may change or their intensity of functioning may alter, allowing the memories to become more or less available.

Subconscious

The Subconscious is usually defined as representing mental processes or phenomena that occur outside conscious awareness

---

[3] Note that while this is probably the cause of most *déjà vu* experiences, some kinds of *déjà vu* may actually represent paranormal experience.

and that ordinarily cannot become conscious. They are part of the mind, but not conscious. How do we know they exist if we cannot be consciously aware of them? We infer their existence: we observe certain aspects of our own and others' functioning that cannot be adequately explained on the basis of our or their immediately available conscious experiences, and we infer that forces or phenomena outside consciousness are affecting it—from behind the scenes, as it were. Thus, from the viewpoint of our ordinary d-SoC, the Subconscious subsystem is a hypothesis, an inferential construct needed to explain conscious behavior. A psychoanalyst, for example, observes that a patient becomes pale and trembles every time he speaks of his brother, yet when questioned about him says they have a good relationship. The psychoanalyst hypothesizes that in the patient's Subconscious there is a good deal of unresolved anxiety and anger toward the brother.

The emphasis here is that subconscious processes occur outside awareness *from the viewpoint of the ordinary d-SoC.* What is subconsciousness from the reference point of the ordinary d-SoC may become conscious in d-ASCs.

I deliberately use the term *sub*conscious rather than the more commonly employed *un*conscious to avoid the strictly psychoanalytic connotations of unconscious mind. The classical, Freudian unconscious (the sexual and aggressive instincts and their sublimations and repressions) is included in the Subconscious subsystem described here. The Subconscious also includes creative processes, the kinds of things we vaguely call intuition and hunches, tender and loving feelings that may be just as inhibited in their expression as sexual and aggressive ones, and other factors influencing conscious behavior. All these things are mysterious and poorly understood by our conscious minds.

Also included as subconscious processes for many of us are the kinds of thinking that are now called right hemisphere modalities of thinking [47]. The type of thinking associated with the right hemisphere seems holistic rather than analytic, atemporal rather than sequential in time, more concerned with patterns than with details. But for many of us in whom intellectual, sequential, rational development has been overstressed and this other mode inhibited or ignored, this right hemisphere thinking is largely subconscious.

D-ASCs may alter the relationship between what is conscious and what is subconscious. Figure 8–2 expresses this idea. In the ordinary d-SoC, it is convenient to think of the conscious part of the mind as the part that is in the full focus of consciousness or is readily available to such consciousness, to think of a preconscious part that is ordinarily not in the full focus of consciousness but can be made so with little effort, and a Subconscious subsystem that is ordinarily completely cut off from conscious awareness even though special techniques, such as psychoanalytic ones, give inferential information about it. I have followed the general psychoanalytic conventions (1) of showing the Subconscious as the largest part of the mind, to indicate that the largest portion of experience and behavior is probably governed by subconscious forces we are not aware of, and (2) of showing the conscious and preconscious parts of the mind as about equal in size. The barrier between conscious and preconscious has many "holes" in it while the Subconscious is relatively inaccessible. For example, if you dislike someone and I ask you to think about why you dislike him, a little thought may show you that the reasons behind your immediate dislike result from a synthesis of the person's appearance and some unpleasant experiences you previously have had with people of that appearance. These reasons might actually be based on deeply buried subconscious feelings that all people of the same sex are rivals for mother's affection, things you ordinarily cannot become aware of without special therapeutic techniques.

Preconscious and subconscious contents may be more or less readily available in a d-ASC, depending on the d-ASC. In d-ASC 1 in Figure 8–2, more of the mind and preconscious material are directly in consciousness and less are in the Subconscious subsystem. This, incidentally, is one of the dangers of experiencing a d-ASC: a person may be overwhelmed by emotionally charged material, normally subconscious, that he is not ready to handle. This can happen with marijuana intoxication or other psychedelic-drug-induced states, as well as with meditative states or hypnosis. In all these states things that are ordinarily preconscious or subconscious may become conscious.

D-ASC 2 illustrates the kind of state in which things that are ordinarily conscious may become preconscious or subconscious. Certain drug-induced states or other d-ASCs that tend toward

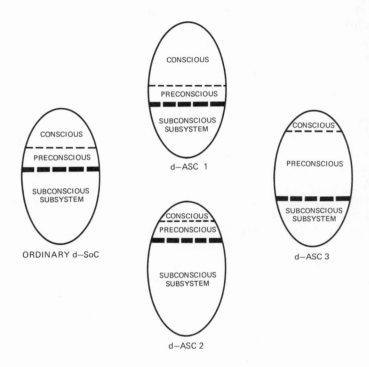

Figure 8–2. Possible changes in relationship among conscious, pre-conscious, and subconscious subsystems.

stupor might fit in this category, where consciousness feels quite restricted and dull, even though the subject's behavior suggests that previously conscious material is still affecting him. The alcoholic blackout state is interesting in this context, for the person seems to behave "normally" in many ways, indicating that much ordinarily conscious knowledge is still present, even though this is a blackout in terms of later recall.

D-ASC 3 represents various d-ASCs in which much subconscious material might become preconscious: it will not necessarily well up by itself, but it is much more readily available than ordinarily. Thus the potential for exploring the mind is greater, but effort must still be exerted. Marijuana intoxication can do this.

In terms of overall system functioning, I have shown a direct information flow arrow from Input-Processing to the Subconscious, and a feedback control arrow from the Subconscious to Input-Processing. Processed input information may reach the Subconscious and have effects even when it does not reach awareness. To use again the example of scanning the crowd, even though you are consciously looking for your friend's face, the impact of another face may trigger subconscious processes because of resemblance to someone emotionally meaningful to you, and may produce later effects on you even though you were not consciously aware of seeing that particular person.

The feedback control arrow from Subconscious to Input-Processing indicates that the Subconscious subsystem may have a major control over perception. Our likes and dislikes, needs and fears, can affect what we see. This kind of selectivity in perception is discussed in relation to the Input-Processing subsystem. I bring it up here to indicate a distinction between relatively permanent, learned selectivities of perception that are inherent in Input-Processing itself, such as ability to recognize words, and selectivities that are more dependent on the current emotional state of the Subconscious subsystem, and so may show more variation from time to time. For example, we have many permanent learnings that are part of Input-Processing and that enable us to distinguish men from women at a glance. But we have sexual needs that peak from time to time, and these may be partially or wholly in the Subconscious subsystem because of cultural repressive pressures. As these repressed needs vary, they affect Input-Processing and change our current perceptions of people of the opposite sex: they can become much more attractive when we are aroused.

We should also briefly note the possibility of the activation of archetypes from the Collective Unconscious during d-ASCs. The terms *archetypes* and *Collective Unconscious* are used in Carl Jung's sense. The Collective Unconscious refers to a large body of biologically inherited psychological structures, most of which remains latent human potentials. Particular structures are archetypes, innate patterns that can emerge and dominate consciousness because of the high psychic energy residing in them if the right stimuli for activation occur. Myths of heroic quests, demons, gods, energies, God, Christ, are held by Jung to be particular archetypes from the Collective Unconscious, which express themselves at various times in human history. It would

take far too much space here to give them adequate consideration; the interested reader should refer to the collected works of
Carl Jung. It should be noted, however, that some d-ASCs frequently facilitate the emergence of archetypes.

Evaluation and Decision-Making

The Evaluation and Decision-Making subsystem refers to those
intellectual, cognitive processes with which we deliberately
evaluate the meaning of things and decide what to do about
them.[4] It is the subsystem constituting our thinking, our prob-
lem-solving, our understanding. It is where we apply a logic to
data presented to us and reach a conclusion as a result of processing the data in accordance with that logic.

Note that a *logic* is a self-contained, arbitrary system. Two and
two do not make four in any "real" sense; they make four
because they have been *defined* that way. That a particular logic
is highly useful in dealing with the physical world should not
blind us to the fact that it is basically an arbitrary, self-contained, assumptive system. Thus, when I define the Evaluation
and Decision-Making subsystem as processing information in
accordance with a logic, I do not intend to give it an ultimate
validity, but just to note that there is an assumptive system,
heavily influenced by culture and personal history, which processes data. In our ordinary d-SoC there may actually be several
different logics applied at various times. I might apply the logic
of calculus to certain kinds of problems in electronics, but not to
problems of interpersonal relationships.

We should also note, as honest self-observation will reveal, that
much of what passes as rationality in our ordinary d-SoC is in
fact rationalization. We want something, so we make up "good"
reasons for having it.

The discussion that follows is confined to intellectual, conscious evaluation and decision-making. Some aspects of this
become automated and go on in the fringes of awareness, but
they are potentially available to full consciousness should we
turn our attention to them. Other subsystems, such as Emotions
and the Subconscious, also evaluate data, classify them as good or

---

[4] Much meaning is automatically supplied by Input-Processing: when you
see a stop sign, you need not consciously evaluate its meaning.

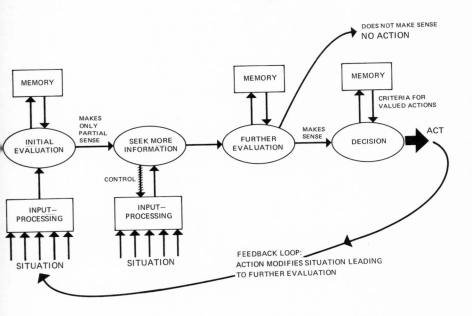

Figure 8–3. Steps in a typical evaluation and decision-making process.

bad, threatening or benign, etc. We are not concerned with these here, however; we shall consider only conscious, intellectual kinds of decision-making and evaluation.

Figure 8–3 illustrates the typical operation of the Evaluation and Decision-Making subsystem for the ordinary d-SoC. The process starts (lower left-hand corner) when you encounter some kind of problem situation in life. The stimuli from this situation, coming in via the Exteroception subsystem, are subjected to a large amount of Input-Processing, and some abstraction of the situation reaches your awareness. Assume this initial abstraction is puzzling: it doesn't make sense to you and you don't know what to do. So the Evaluation and Decision-Making subsystem draws upon information stored in the Memory subsystem in order to evaluate it. Figure 8–3 shows information both coming from Memory and going to Memory to guide the retrieval of memory information, making it selective and relevant. Further assume that, given the presented information and what is available in Memory, the situation still makes only partial sense. You decide to seek more information. Controlling information is sent to Input-Processing to produce more information about the situation, to look at it from another angle. Getting this further information, you again compare it against what you already know, and one of two sequences results. If the situation still does not make sense, and you have no way of getting further information, you may take the option, shown by the upward-slanting arrow, of simply not acting on the situation for the time being. If it does make sense, in accordance with whatever logic you are using, you can then consult your memory for criteria for valued or appropriate kinds of actions, given your understanding of the situation, and then act in that appropriate way. Your action modifies the situation, which changes the data reaching you from the situation through Exteroception and Input-Processing, and the whole process may be repeated. Continuous cycling through this sort of process is what we call thinking and action.

In the ordinary d-SoC, the operation of the Evaluation and Decision-Making subsystem is often hyperactive to the point of constituting noise—noise in the sense that the overinvestment of attention/awareness energy in this process lowers the ability to notice and deal with other sources of relevant information. You cannot hear your senses over the noise of your thoughts. The cycle shown in Figure 8–3 tends to be endless and self-perpetuating. Something happens, you think about it, reach a decision, and act, which changes the situation and makes you reevaluate it. Or you do not act, but thinking about it reminds you of something else, which reminds you of something else, about which you make a decision, which results in action that modifies another situation, which starts more evaluation and association processes. For example, someone on the street asks me for money, which starts me thinking about disinterested charity versus the work ethic ("Why doesn't he get a job? I work for my money. Maybe he is unfortunate, but he could also be too lazy. Maybe I'm being manipulated; I've been manipulated before, etc. etc.") and I'm so involved in this thought process that I do not notice various perceptual cues that would inform me about this person's actual situation and intentions.

Earlier, in discussing the stabilization processes that maintain a state of consciousness I pointed out that this endless thinking process is a major source of loading stabilization in an ordinary d-SoC. It continually reinforces consensus reality, for we tend to think continuously about the things we have been reinforced for thinking about, and it absorbs such a large amount of our attention/awareness energy that we have little of that energy available for other processes. This Evaluation and Decision-Making subsystem activity has an extremely large amount of psychological inertia: if you are not fully convinced of this, I suggest that you put this book down right now and try to turn the system off for five minutes. Don't think of anything, don't evaluate anything for the next five minutes. That also means don't think about not thinking.

Now, unless you are a rare individual indeed, you have seen the difficulty of stopping the activity of your Evaluation and Decision-Making subsystem. This enormous psychological inertia is excellent for maintaining your social membership in consensus reality, but if your personality structure and/or consensus reality is unsatisfactory and/or you wish to explore other d-SoCs besides your ordinary one, this endless activity of the Evaluation and Decision-Making subsystem can be a tremendous liability.

Within the ordinary d-SoC, there is some quantitative variation in the activity of the Evaluation and Decision-Making subsystem. Some days you feel intellectually sharp, and your mind is quick and you solve problems accurately on the first try. Other days your mind seems dull; you fail to grasp things right away, have to think a lot just to understand elementary points, have a hard time putting things together. There is also some variation within the ordinary d-SoC in the overall quantity of thoughts: some days your thoughts seem to race, other days they are a bit slower than normal. There is probably also quantitative variation in the redundancy of thinking, the degree to which you use multiple, overlapping processes to check on your own accuracy. And there is a quantitative variation in the degree to which your logical evaluation is distorted by emotional factors. When you are in a situation that activates conscious and subconscious emotions, your logic borders on pure rationalization; in a less threatening situation your logic may be relatively flawless. But these variations all stay within an expected range that you have come to think of as your ordinary d-SoC.

All the above relatively quantitative variations in the functioning of the Evaluation and Decision-Making subsystem may be exaggerated in various d-ASCs. Your thoughts may seem to race faster than you can comprehend them; the slowing down or accuracy of your logic processes can seem much more extreme than in your ordinary d-SoC. A drunk, for example, may not be able to think through a simple problem, while someone intoxicated on marijuana may have crystal-clear insights into a formerly baffling problem. I cannot be more specific about this, as there has been little quantitative research on it so far. However, experiential reports suggest that the quantitative variations can be large.

Even more interesting are qualitative variations in various d-ASCs. One of these is the substitution of a different logic from one ordinarily used in your b-SoC. Martin Orne [44] has reported some interesting demonstrations. A deeply hypnotized subject is given a suggestion—for example, "The number three no longer makes any sense, the idea of three is a meaningless concept." The subject is then given various arithmetical problems such as two plus one equals what? Depending on subsidiary assumptions the subject makes, he rapidly evolves a new arithmetical logic that does not involve the number three. To the question, "What does two plus one equal?" he answers, "Four." To the question, "Six divided by two equals what?" he answers either, "Two" or "Four," depending on the subsidiary assumptions. Thus a whole new logic can be readily programmed in the d-ASC of hypnosis. Various state-specific logics have been reported for meditative and psychedelic states, but they do not seem communicable in the ordinary d-SoC.

In the ordinary d-SoC, we are intolerant of contradictions in logic; in a d-ASC, tolerance for contradictions may be much higher. Again, an example from hypnosis is illustrative. I once suggested to an extremely susceptible subject, while he was in the hypnotic d-ASC, that mentally he was getting up from his chair, going down the hall and outside the laboratory building. He described this experience to me as it was happening. He experienced himself as being in the yard in back of the laboratory, where he reported seeing a mole come up to the surface from its tunnel. I asked him to catch the mole and hold on to it, and he said he had. Later I had him in his mental journey come back into the laboratory, walk upstairs, reenter the room where we were sitting, and stand in the middle of the floor. I asked him what he saw in the room, and he gave a general overall description of the room, omitting any mention of the chair in which he was sitting. Something like the following dialogue then occurred:

> CT: Is there anyone sitting in the chair?
> S: I am.
> CT: Didn't you just tell me you were standing in the middle of the room?
> S: Yes, I am standing in the middle of the room.
> CT: Do you think it's contradictory to tell me you're standing in the middle of the room and sitting in the chair at the same time?
> S: Yes.
> CT: Does the contradiction bother you?
> S: No.
> CT: Which one of the two selves is your real self?
> S: They are both my real self.

This stumped me until I finally thought of another question.

> CT: Is there any difference at all between the two selves?
> S: Yes, the me standing in the middle of the floor has a mole in his hands.

It is tempting to view this tolerance for contradictions as a deterioration in logic, but remember that contradiction is itself defined in terms of a particular logic, and since logics are self-contained assumptive structures, thinking in a pattern containing contradictions according to one system of logic may not necessarily mean that the thinking is useless or absolutely invalid. Indeed, some investigators have hypothesized that an increased ability to tolerate contradictions is necessary for creative thought. It should also be noted that many people who experience this ability to tolerate contradictions in d-ASCs believe it to be a transcendent, superior quality, not necessarily an inferior one. Sometimes they feel they are using a superior logic. Nevertheless, the ability to tolerate contradictions per se is not necessarily a superior quality.

Since this book is written in ordinary, Western d-SoC logic, there are difficulties in writing about d-ASC logics. New logics can emerge, appropriate to a particular d-ASC. New sets of (implicit) assumptions and rules for handling information in accordance with these assumptions seem to be inherent or learnable in a particular d-ASC. *Within* that particular d-ASC, and in repeated experiences in that d-ASC, these rules may be quite consistent and logical. But writing about this is difficult because new state-specific logics may not seem like logics at all in other d-SoCs. From the viewpoint of some other d-SoC (usually the ordinary one) the logic of a d-ASC may seem absurd. Yet within that d-ASC, the logic is apparent, consistent, and useful. The existence of such state-specific logics is obvious to a number of people who have experienced them in d-ASCs: they have not yet been proved to exist in a way acceptable to ordinary d-SoC evaluation.

The question whether there are state-specific logics or merely inferior, error-ridden logics in d-ASCs is further complicated by the tendency of new experiencers of d-ASCs to overvalue their experiences in those d-ASCs. The experiences are so fascinating and often so emotionally potent in a d-ASC that is new to you that you tend to accept uncritically everything about it. Clearly, the sense of "This is a remarkable, obviously true and wonderful truth" is a parainformational quality, like the quality "This is a memory" discussed earlier, and can attach itself to various contents regardless of their logical truth value. The *feeling* that something is true, no matter how emotionally impressive, is no guarantee of its truth. The final test of whether a state-specific logic exists for a particular d-ASC will involve not only the sequential validation and replication of a logic by an individual experiencer as he reenters a particular d-ASC time after time, but also his ability to communicate that logic to others in that d-ASC and have them independently validate it, a point elaborated later in connection with state-specific sciences.

An exciting finding of recent psychological research is the apparent existence of two discrete modes of cognition associated with the functioning of the left and right cerebral hemispheres, respectively [47]. In the normal person there are a huge number of interconnections via the corpus callosum between these two hemispheres, and on that physiological basis a person should be able to alternate between these two modes of thinking quite readily, choosing whichever is appropriate for a problem. Our culture, however, has greatly overvalued the style of thinking associated with left hemisphere activity—linear, sequential, rational, intellectual, cause-and-effect, analytical thinking. Right hemisphere functioning seems more concerned with pattern recognition, with wholes, with simultaneity rather than sequence, and with bodily functioning. The right hemisphere mode is more an analog mode than a digital mode. Since each mode of evaluation is highly valid *when appropriately applied to a problem it is suited for,* we become limited and less effective if we overvalue one mode and apply it to problems more appropriate to the other mode. In the ordinary d-SoC, especially among Western academics, linear thinking is greatly overvalued, so we exist in an unbalanced, pathological state. The reasoning behind this is complex, and the interested reader should consult Ornstein's *The Psychology of Consciousness* [47] and the sources he draws upon.

Many d-ASC experiences seem to reflect a greatly increased use of the right hemisphere mode of cognition. Experiencers talk of seeing *patterns* in things, of simultaneously and instantaneously grasping *relationships* they cannot ordinarily grasp, of being unable to express these things verbally. The experience is usually reported as pleasant and rewarding and often is valued as a higher or more true form of cognition. Apparently left and right hemisphere functioning is more balanced or there may even be a shift to dominance of right hemisphere functioning. The experience does not lend itself to verbal description, but may be communicable in other ways, as through music or dance. It should be noted as a major shift in the Evaluation and Decision-Making subsystem that can occur in d-ASCs.[5]

In the ordinary d-SoC, constant, repetitive thinking absorbs a great deal of attention/awareness energy and acts as a form of loading stabilization. Since attention/awareness energy is taken away from this left hemisphere type of activity in d-ASCs, and the energy becomes more freely available, psychological functions that are only latent potentials in the ordinary d-SoC may become noticeable. They are made noticeable not only through the availability of attention/awareness energy, but also because the noise of constant thinking is reduced. These new functions may resemble instincts giving us information about situations or,

[5] I do not consider right and left hemisphere modes of functioning to be two d-SoCs themselves, but rather two modes of functioning of the Evaluation and Decision-Making subsystem. The balance can vary in different d-ASCs.

since a right hemisphere mode of functioning may emit some of its output in the form of bodily sensations (a hypothesis of mine that I believe future research will validate), they may enhance sensitivity to such sensations. It is as if in our ordinary d-SoC we are surrounded by a crowd of people talking and shouting continually. If they would all quiet down, we might be able to hear individuals or to hear someone at the edge of the crowd who is saying something important.

Ordinarily Evaluation and Decision-Making activity consists of a sequential progression from one thought to another. You think of something, that draws up a certain association from memory, which you then think about; this draws up another association, etc. In this temporal sequence of the Evaluation and Decision-Making process, the progression from one thought to another, from association to association to association, is probabilistically controlled by the particular structures/programming built up by enculturation and life experience. Thus, if I say the word *red* to you, you are likely to associate some word like *blue, green, yellow,* some color word, rather than *iguana,* or *sixteen-penny nail,* or *railroad track.* The association that occurs to any particular thought is not absolutely determined, but since some associations are highly likely and others highly unlikely, we could, in principle, generally predict a person's train of thinking if we knew the strength of these various associative habits. Thus, much of our ordinary thinking/evaluation runs in predictable paths. These paths of likely associations are a function of the particular consensus reality we were socialized in.

Figure 8–4 diagrams, with the heavy arrows, ordinary thinking processes. Given a certain input stimulus for thought, a certain deduction or conclusion is likely to be reached that will draw highly probable association 1, which will result in certain deductions, which will draw up highly probable memory association 2, and so on until conclusion 1 is reached. The light arrows represent possible branchings not taken because they are weak, improbable, not made highly likely by habits and enculturation.

In various d-ASCs the rules governing the probability of associations change in a systematic and/or random way, and so progress along a chain of thought becomes much less predictable by ordinary d-SoC criteria. This is shown by the lower chain of

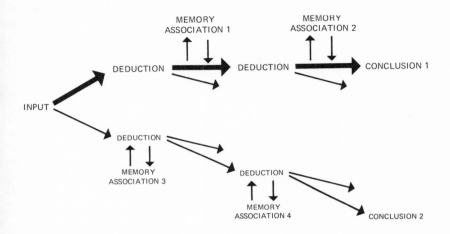

Figure 8–4. Steps and choice-points in associative thinking.

light arrows in Figure 8–4. An unlikely association is made to the same input, which calls up different memory associations, leading to different deductions and further memory associatons, etc., until a quite different conclusion, conclusion 2, is reached. Given the same presented problem in two d-SoCs, two quite different conclusions may result. This is creative, in the sense of being unusual. Whether it is practically useful is another question.

In some of the more stable d-ASCs, like hypnosis or dreaming, I believe the rules for associations may be systematically changed. In d-ASCs induced by powerful psychedelic drugs like LSD (which may not be stable d-ASCs) there may be a relatively random inter- ·ference with the association processes that may still lead to crea- tive conclusions but that may show no lawfulness in and of them- selves.

Note that the Evaluation and Decision-Making subsystem con- trols Input-Processing to some extent in order to find "relevant" data to help solve problems. This can be useful or it can merely reinforce prejudices. Our evaluation of a situation may distort our subsequent perception of it and thus increase our faith in our evaluation, but at the price of distorted perception. In our desire for certainty, we can throw out the reality of the situation.

Emotions

The Emotions subsystem is one which I, as a typical overintellectualized Western academic, feel least qualified to write about. I share the intellectual's distrust of emotions as forces that distort my reasoning and are liable to lead me astray. And yet, like most people, my life and consciousness are strongly controlled by the pursuit of pleasant emotions and the avoidance of unpleasant ones.

Emotions are feelings that can be named but not easily defined. They are feelings that we call grief, fear, joy, surprise, yearning, anger, but that we define inadequately in terms of words: at best we use words to evoke memories of experiences that fit those names.

The Emotions subsystem is, in one sense, the most important subsystem, for it can exert tremendous influence. If you are experiencing the emotion of fear, it may very well control your evaluations and decisions, the memories you draw upon, how you see the world and how you act. Any strong emotion tends to constellate the rest of consciousness about it. Indeed, I think that while mild levels of any emotion can occur within the region of experiential space we call the ordinary d-SoC, most strong levels of feeling may actually constitute d-ASCs. If you talk about feeling mildly angry, somewhat angry, or extremely angry, you can imagine all these things occurring in your ordinary d-SoC. But if you speak of being *enraged,* the word evokes associations of changes in perception (such as "seeing red") and cognition that strongly suggest that somewhere in the anger continuum there was a quantum jump, and a d-ASC of rage developed. The same is true for other strong emotions. I shall not develop the idea further here, as strong emotional states have seldom been studied scientifically as they must be to determine if they actually constitute d-SoCs. The idea holds promise for future research.

Our culture is strongly characterized by poor volitional control over the Emotions subsystem in the ordinary d-SoC. Emotions can change with lightning rapidity; external events can induce them almost automatically. We have accepted this in a despairing way as part of the human condition, ambivalently regarding attempts to control emotions as either virtuous (since all emotions make us lose control, we should suppress them) or artificial (not "genuine"). Techniques from various spiritual disciplines indicate, however, that there can be emotional control that does not involve simple suppression or denial of content of the emotion [128]. Don Juan, for example, stated that since becoming a "man of knowledge" he had transcended ordinary emotions, but could have any one he wished [11]. In d-ASCs, people often report either greatly increased or decreased control over their emotions.

In addition to changes in the degree of control over emotions, the intensity of emotions themselves may also change in d-ASCs. Dissociation from or dis-identification with emotions also occurs: a person reports that an emotion is going on quite strongly within him, yet is not "his": he is not identified with it and so little affected by it.

In some d-ASCs new emotions appear, emotions that are never present in the ordinary d-SoC. These include feelings like serenity, tranquility, and ecstasy. Because we use these words in our ordinary d-SoC we think we understand them, but those who have experienced such emotions in d-ASCs insist that we have only known the palest shadows of them.

Space/Time Sense

Events and experiences happen at a certain time in a certain place. The naive view of this situation is that we simply perceive the spatial and temporal dimensions of real events. A more sophisticated analysis shows that space and time are experiential constructs that we have used to organize sensory stimuli coming to us. Because the organization has been so often successful for dealing with the environment, we have come to believe that we are simply perceiving what is "out there," rather than automatically and implicitly imposing a conceptual framework on what comes in to us. Ornstein [47] illustrates this in considerable detail in his analysis of time perception, showing that psychological time is a construct, as is physical time, and that a simple equation of the two things is misleading. If we bear in mind that our ordinary concepts of space and time are psychological constructs—highly successful theoretical ones, but nonetheless only constructs—then we shall be less inclined to label as distortions the changes in the functioning of the Space/Time subsystem reported in d-ASCs.

In the ordinary d-SoC there is a small amount of variation in

Space/Time sense, but not much. On a dull day time drags somewhat and on an exciting day it goes by quickly, but this range is not large. The dull hour may seem two or three hours long, a walk home when you are tired may seem twice as far, but this is about the maximum quantitative variation for most people in the ordinary d-SoC. Many other aspects of the space/ time framework this subsystem generates are unchanging in the ordinary d-SoC: effects do not precede causes, up and down do not reverse, your body does not shrink or grow larger with respect to the space around it.

Variations in the apparent rate of time flow may be much larger in some d-ASCs than ordinarily. In the d-ASC of marijuana intoxication, for example, a common experience is for an LP record to seem to play for an hour or more. Since an LP record generally plays for about fifteen minutes, this is approximately a fourfold increase in experienced duration. Ornstein [47] believes that a person's estimate of duration is based on the number of events that have taken place in a given period, so as more things are experienced the elapsed time seems longer. Since marijuana intoxication, like many d-ASCs, involves major changes in Input-Processing so that more sensory information is admitted, this experience of increased duration for a single record and for similar events may be due to the fact that a lot more *is* happening experientially in that same period of clock time. The converse effect can also happen in d-ASCs: time seems to speed by at an extraordinary rate. An experience that seems to have lasted a minute or two actually lasted an hour.

A rare but especially intriguing experience reported from some d-ASCs is that the direction of flow of time seems to change. An event from the future happens now; the experiencer may even know it does not belong in the now but will happen later. An effect seems to precede the cause. Our immediate reaction, resulting from our deeply ingrained belief in the total reality of clock time, is that this cannot be "true," and we see the phenomenon as some confusion of time perception or possibly a hallucination.

A rewarding d-ASC experience is an increased focus on the present moment, a greatly increased here-and-nowness. In the ordinary d-SoC, we usually pay little attention to what is actually happening in the present. We live among memories of the past and amid plans, anticipations, and fantasies about the future. The greatly increased sense of being in the here and now experienced in many d-ASCs usually accompanies a feeling of being much more alive, much more in contact with things. Many meditative practices specifically aim for this increased sense of here-and-nowness. Some d-ASCs seem to produce the opposite effect: the size of the present is "narrowed," making it very difficult to grasp the present moment.

The experience of *archetypal time,* the eternal present, is a highly valued and radical alteration in time sense reported in various d-ASCs. Not only is there a great here-and-nowness, a great focus on the present moment, but there is a feeling that the activity or experience of the moment is *exactly* the right thing that belongs in this moment of time. It is a perfect fit with the state of the universe, a basic that springs from one's ultimate nature. Some of my informants in my studies of marijuana intoxication [105] expressed this, in terms of relationships, as no longer being the case of John Smith and Mary Williams walking together in New York City on June 30, 1962, but Man and Woman Dancing Their Pattern Together, as it always has been and always will be.

The experience of archetypal time is similar to, and may be identical with, the experience of *timelessness,* of the feeling that any kind of temporal framework for an experience is meaningless. Experiences simply *are,* they do not seem to take place at a specific time. Samadhi, for example, is described as lasting for an eternity, even though the meditator may be in that d-ASC for only a few seconds. Occasionally in such timeless experiences some part of the mind is perceived as putting a temporal location and duration on the event, but this is seen as meaningless word play that has nothing to do with reality. In some accounts of mystical experiences in d-ASCs, the adjectives *timeless* and *eternal* are used almost interchangeably. Eternity probably did not arise as a concept, but as a word depicting an experience of timelessness, an immediate *experiential reality* rather than a *concept* of infinite temporal duration.

Déjà vu, the French phrase meaning "seen before," is a time experience that occasionally happens in the ordinary d-SoC (it may actually represent a momentary transition into a d-ASC) and happens more frequently in d-ASCs. As an event is unfolding you seem to be *remembering* it, you are convinced it has happened before because it has the quality of a memory. In discussing the Memory subsystem, we speculated that *déjà vu* might sometimes result from a misplacement of the quality "this is a memory" on a current perceptual event. Other types of *déjà vu* experiences may represent an alteration of functioning of the Space/Time subsystem, where the extra informational quality "this is from the past" is added to current perceptual events. The quantitative variations in space perception that occur in the ordinary d-SoC may occur in greatly increased form in d-ASCs. Distances walked, for example, may seem much shorter or much longer than ordinarily. Nor is active movement through space necessary for changes in distance to occur: as you sit and look at something, it may seem to recede into the distance or to come closer. Or it may seem to grow larger or smaller.

Depth is an important quality of spatial experience. A photograph or a painting is usually seen as a two-dimensional, flat representation of what was in reality a three-dimensional scene. Perception of a three-dimensional quality in the two-dimensional painting is attributed to the artist's technical skill. In d-ASCs, the degree of depth in ordinary perceptions may seem to change. Aaronson [88 or 115, ch. 17] notes that in many psychotic states, such as those associated with depression, the world seems flat, the depth dimension seems greatly reduced, while in many valued d-ASCs, such as those induced by psychedelic drugs, the depth dimension seems enhanced, deeper, richer. In some intriguing experiments, Aaronson shows that by artificially altering a hypnotized subject's depth perception through suggestion, to flatter or deeper, he can produce great variations in the subject's moods, and perhaps actually produce d-ASCs by simply changing this basic operation of the Space/Time subsystem.

The ability to see three-dimensional depth in two-dimensional pictures is an interesting phenomenon reported for marijuana intoxication [105]. The technique my main informant reported is to look at a color picture through a pinhole held right at the eye, so your field of vision includes only the picture, not any other elements. If you are highly intoxicated with marijuana, the picture may suddenly become a three-dimensional scene instead of a flat, two-dimensional one.

Another d-ASC-associated spatial change is loss of the spatial framework as a source of orientation. Although there are enormous individual differences, some people always keep their orientation in physical space plotted on a mental map; they generally know what direction they are facing, in what direction various prominent landmarks are located. This kind of orientation to the physical spatial framework may simply fade out, not be perceived in d-ASCs, or it may still be perceptible but become a relatively meaningless rather than an important type of information.

This kind of change can be accompanied by new ways of perceiving space. Lines may become curved instead of straight, for example. Some people report perceiving four or more dimensions in d-ASCs, not as a mathematical construct but as an experiential reality. The difficulties of expressing this in a language evolved from external adaptation to three-dimensional reality are obvious.

We ordinarily think of space as empty, but in d-ASCs space is sometimes perceived as having a more solid quality, as being filled with "vibrations" or "energy," rather than as being empty. Sometimes experiencers believe this to be an actual change in their perception of the space around them; sometimes they perceive it as a projection of internal psychological changes onto their spatial perception.

Our ordinary concept of space is a visual one, related to maps, lines and grids, visual distances, and diagrams. Space may be organized in other ways. Some marijuana smokers, for example, report that space becomes organized in an auditory way when they are listening to sounds or music with their eyes closed. Others report that tactual qualities determine space.

I recall a striking evening I once spent with some friends. One of them had just rented a new house, which none of us had seen. We arrived after dark, were blindfolded before entering the house, and spent the next couple of hours exploring the house by movement and touch alone, with no visual cues at all. The concept that gradually evolved of the space of the house without the usual visual organizing cues was vastly different from the subsequent perception of the space when the blindfolds were removed.

Sense of Identity

We noted earlier that an extra informational "This is a memory" quality is either explicitly or implicitly attached to data coming from the Memory subsystem and that this quality is sometimes attached to nonmemory information in consciousness, producing interesting phenomena. The primary function of the Sense of Identity subsystem is to attach a "This is me" quality to certain aspects of experience, to certain information in consciousness, and thus to create the sense of an ego. Presumably semipermanent structures exist incorporating criteria for what the "This is me" quality should be attached to. However, the functioning of the Sense of Identity subsystem varies so greatly, even in the ordinary d-SoC, that I emphasize the extra informational aspects of the "This is me" quality rather than the structures underlying it.

Any item of information to which the "This is me" quality is attached acquires considerable extra potency and so may arouse strong emotions and otherwise control attention/awareness energy. If I say to you, "The face of someone you don't know, a Mr. Johnson, is ugly and revolting," this information probably will not be very important to you. But if I say to you, *"Your* face is ugly and revolting," that is a different story! But why do you react so strongly to the latter sentence? True, under some circumstances such a statement might preface more aggressive action, against which you want to defend yourself, but often such a remark prefaces no more than additional words of the same sort; yet, you react to those words as if to actual physical attack.[6] Adding the ego quality to information *radically* alters the way that information is treated by the system of consciousness as a whole.

At any given time only some of the contents of awareness are modulated by the ego quality. As I sit writing and pause to glance around the room, I see a large number of objects; they become the contents of my consciousness, but they are not *me.* The ego quality has not been added to them. Much of our experience is just information; it does not have a special ego quality added.

Another major function of the Sense of Identity subsystem is the exact opposite of its usual function: a *denial* of the sense of self to certain structures. Because certain of our personal charac-

[6] The old childhood rhyme, "Sticks and stones will break my bones/ But names will never hurt me!/Call me this, and call me that/And call yourself a dirty rat!" must be looked upon as a morale-builder, or perhaps an admonition that we adults *should* heed, but certainly not as a statement of truth. We are terribly hurt by names and words and what people think of us—often much more hurt than by sticks and stones. People have "chosen" to die in a burning house rather than run out of it naked.

teristics and mind structures are considered undesirable and/or evoke unpleasant emotions in us, we create blocks and defenses against perceiving them as parts of ourselves. Many of these interdicted structures are culturally determined, many are specific products of personal developmental history and are not widely shared in the culture. So we deny that we have certain characteristics or we project them on to others: *I* am not quarrelsome, *he* is!

I mention this function only in passing, in spite of its enormous importance, for it leads into the vast realm of psychopathology, and is beyond the scope of this book.

The functioning of the Sense of Identity subsystem is highly variable in the ordinary d-SoC, much more variable than we are ordinarily aware. There are many transient identifications, many short-term modulations of particular information, by the ego feeling. When you read a good novel or see a good movie and empathize with one of the characters, you are adding the ego sense to the information about that character. Empathy is the ability to take in information about another's experiences and treat it as if it were your own. However, a person's degree of control over, and self-awareness of, empathy is highly variable. Lack of control over ability to identify with particular things can cause psychological difficulties. For example, if a shopkeeper treats you brusquely, you may feel hurt and upset about it all day long, even though you know intellectually that he is a brusque person who treats everyone that way. Your ego sense was attached to that particular information and is difficult to detach. Thus, various kinds of stimulus patterns can catch the ego sense and are difficult to disentangle.

To illustrate the high variability of functioning of the Sense of Identity subsystem, consider how it can be invested in possessions. Suppose you are in New York City, having a "sophisticated" discussion with a friend about the breakdown of social values and the consequent rebellion by young people. Through the window you see some teenagers across the street trashing a car, and, with detachment, you point out to your friend that these unfortunate teenagers are what they are because their parents could not transmit values they lacked themselves. Then you notice it is *your* car they are trashing, and your feelings of sympathy for those poor teenagers vanish rather quickly!

Each person has a number of relatively permanent identifications, well-defined experiential and behavioral repertoires that he thinks of as himself. His role in society gives him several of these: he may be a salesman in one situation, a father in another, a lover in another, a patient in another, an outraged citizen in another. Often these various roles demand behaviors and values that are contradictory, but because he identifies strongly with each role at the time he assumes it, he does not think of his other roles, and experiences little conscious conflict. For example, a concentration camp guard who brutalizes his prisoners all day may be known as a loving and doting father at home. This ability to compartmentalize roles is one of the greatest human dilemmas.

Some roles are situation-specific. Others are so pervasive that they continue to function in situations for which they are not appropriate. For example, if you take your job concerns home with you or to a party where other kinds of experiences and behavior are desired and expected, you have overidentified with a particular role.

One of a person's most constant, semipermanent identifications is with his body, more precisely, with his body image, the abstract of the data from his body as mediated through the Exteroception, Interoception, and Input-Processing subsystems. This body image he identifies with may or may not have much actual resemblance to his physical body as other people see it. The degree of identification with the body may vary from time to time. When I am ill I am very aware of my physical body and its centrality in my consciousness; when I am healthy and happy I am aware of my body more as a source of pleasure, or I forget it as I become involved in various tasks.

On the basis of this mass of transient and semipermanent identifications, with various degrees of compartmentalization, each of us believes in something he calls his ego or self. He may assume that this self is a property of his soul and will live forever. He may vigorously defend this self against slights or other attacks. But what is this ego, this "real" self?

This difficult question has long plagued philosophers and psychologists. I am intrigued by the Buddhist view that asks you to search your experience to find the basic, permanent parts of it that constitute the essence of your ego. When you do this, you find it hard to identify anything as being, finally, *you.* You may discern certain long-term constancies in your values, connected sets of memories, but none of these qualifies as an ultimate self. The Buddhist view is that you have no ultimate self, thus you need not defend it. Since it is the ego that suffers, realization that ego is an illusion is supposed to end suffering.

In terms of the systems approach, we can characterize ego as a continuity and consistency of functioning to which we attach special importance, but which does not have the reality of a solid *thing* somewhere, which is only a *pattern* of operation that disappears under close scrutiny. I believe that this view is congruent with the enormous changes that can occur in the sense of self in various d-ASCs. The ego or self is thus a certain kind of extra informational modulation attached to other contents of consciousness. It is not a solid sort of thing, even though there must be some semipermanent structures containing the information criteria for controlling the functioning of this subsystem. A change in the pattern of functioning changes the ego.

Reports from d-ASCs indicate that the sense of ego can be disengaged from a wide variety of kinds of information and situations to which it is normally attached. Memories, for example, may come into your consciousness unaccompanied by the feeling that this is *your* memory, as just information pulled from memory. This can be therapeutically useful for recovering information about traumatic events from a patient who is unable to handle the emotional charge on the events. The sense of ego can also be detached from the body, so that you are associated simply with *a* body rather than *your* body. Reaction to pain, for instance, can be altered this way. You may feel a stimulus as just as painful as ordinarily, but you do not get upset about it because *you* are not being injured. Situations that evoke particular roles may not evoke such roles in d-ASCs. For example, all the necessary stimulus elements may be present for automatically invoking the role of teacher, but in the d-ASC the role does not appear. The sense of ego can be detached from possessions and responsibilities, and even from actions, so that things you do seem not to be *your* actions for which *you* are responsible, but just actions.

Sometimes the sense of ego is detached from several or all of the above concepts so that you feel entirely egoless for a while. There is experience, but none of it is "possessed" by *you* in any special ego sense.

The converse effect can also occur in d-ASCs: the sense of ego may be added to things it is not ordinarily attached to. A situation, for example, may call for a certain role that is not important to you ordinarily but which you come to identify with strongly.

This detachment and addition of the ego sense that accompanies d-ASCs may result in actions that are later regretted when the ordinary d-SoC returns. In our culture, the classic case is the person who behaves while drunk as he would never behave sober. A certain amount of social tolerance exists for drunken behavior, so while some people have profound regrets on realizing what they did, others are able to compartmentalize these experiences and not be particularly bothered by them.

These large shifts in ego sense in d-ASCs may later modify the ordinary d-SoC functioning of the Sense of Identity subsystem. When things you firmly identify with in the ordinary d-SoC are experienced in a d-ASC as detached from you, your conviction of their permanence is undermined and remains so when you resume your ordinary d-SoC. You are then receptive to other possibilities.

Since attachment of the sense of ego to certain information greatly increases the power of that information, these large shifts in Sense of Identity subsystem functioning can have profound consequences. For example, if the sense of ego is used to modulate most information about another person, you may feel united with that person. The usual ego-object dichotomy is broken. If your sense of being an ego separate from other things is greatly reduced or temporarily abolished in a d-ASC, you may feel much closer to another person because there is no *you* to be separate from *him*. The other may be a perceived, real person or a concept or belief. Who or what this other is is very important. If he is a religiously respected person, a saint, or god, you may have a mystical experience in which you feel identified with something greater than yourself.

It is important to note, however, that the expansive or contractive change in the Sense of Identity subsystem that allows identification with something greater than/or outside oneself can have negative consequences and can be used to manipulate others. Group procedures at some religious meetings or political rallies, such as the Nazis held, illustrate how an intense emotional state can be generated which disrupts the stabilization of the ordinary d-SoC and leaves it vulnerable to psychological pressure to identify with the cause being promoted. Whether the cause is that of the Nazi party or of Christian salvation, the method is manipulation, playing on a subject's ignorance to disrupt his d-SoC and then reprogramming him.

These negative aspects should be emphasized, for too many people who have had good experiences in d-ASCs tend to think d-ASCs are inherently good. Consider, therefore, one more example, that of the *berserkers.* The English word *berserk,* meaning "violently running amuck, killing and slaying at random," comes from the Scandinavian word *berserker,* referring to groups in medieval times who took a psychedelic drug in order to become better killers. Tradition has it that these Vikings, to whom raiding and killing was a respectable way of life, ingested *Amanita muscaria,* a mushroom with psychedelic properties, under ritual conditions (patterning forces) to induce a day-long d-ASC in which they became exceptionally ferocious killers and fighters, carried away by rage and lust, supposedly impervious to pain, and possessed of extra strength. Such a d-ASC experience hardly creates "flower children."

Additionally we should note that the semiconstancy of the consensus reality we live in imposes a fair degree of consistency on the kinds of experiences and contents of consciousness to which the Sense of Identity subsystem attaches the ego quality. Every morning you awaken with an apparently identical body; people call you by the same name; they have relatively fixed expectations of you; they reward you for fulfilling those expectations; you are usually surrounded by a fair number of possessions that reinforce your sense of identity. As long as these consensus reality conditions remain relatively constant, you can easily believe in the constancy of your ego. But if these props for your Sense of Identity are changed, as they sometimes are deliberately as a way of destabilizing the b-SoC in preparation for inducing a d-ASC, your sense of ego can change radically. An example familiar to some readers is induction into the army: you are stripped of personal possessions, including clothes; all your ordinary social roles are gone; your name is replaced by a number or a rank; and you are "reeducated" to be a good soldier. Induction into the army and induction into a d-ASC have much in common, but because the army is a well-known subset of consensus reality it is not considered odd, as hypnosis or dreaming are.

Finally, because of its enormous ability to control emotional and attention/awareness energy, the Sense of Identity subsystem can at times constellate the entire structure of consciousness about particular identity patterns, just as can archetypes (in the Jungian sense) arising from the Collective Unconscious can.

Motor Output

The Motor Output subsystem consists of those structures by which we physically affect the external world and our own bodies. In terms of conscious awareness, these structures are primarily the skeletal, voluntary musculature. If I take a minute out from writing to pet my cat, I am using my Motor Output subsystem with full awareness. The Motor Output subsystem elements that primarily affect our own bodies are glandular secretions and other internal, biological processes. These latter, involuntary effectors are controllable not directly, but through intermediates. I cannot directly increase the amount of adrenaline in my bloodstream, for example, but if I make myself angry and wave my fists and shout and holler, I will almost certainly increase the amount of adrenaline secreted.

Two kinds of inputs control Motor Output: input from the Evaluation and Decision-Making subsystem, conscious decisions to do or not to do something, and input from a series of controlling signals that bypasses the Evaluation and Decision-Making subsystem. The latter includes reflexes (jumping at a sudden sound, for example), emotional reactions, and direct control of Motor Output from the Subconscious subsystem. Subconscious control in the ordinary d-SoC includes qualities added to otherwise conscious gestures that reflect nonconscious mental processes: you may state, for example, that a certain person does not make you angry, but an observer notices that your fists clench whenever this person is mentioned.[7]

---

[7] In relation to subconscious control of movement, Gurdjieff [24] put forth an idea about body movement that is interesting because it parallels the idea of discrete states of consciousness on a body level. He states that any person has only a set number of postures and gestures that he uses of his own will. The number varies from person to person, perhaps as low as fifty, perhaps as high as several hundred. A person moves rapidly, almost jerks, from one preferred posture to another. If he is forcibly stopped in between discrete postures, he is uncomfortable, even if it is not a physical strain. Since the functioning of consciousness seems to be strongly affected by body postures and strains, these "discrete states of posture" (d-SoPs) are important to study.

Motor Output operates with almost constant feedback control. By monitoring the environment with the Exteroception subsystem and the body with the Interoception subsystem, you constantly check on the effect of your physical actions and on whether these are desirable and make adjustments accordingly.[8] Many voluntary movements are quite unconscious in terms of their details. You decide to lift your arm, yet you have little awareness of the individual muscle actions that allow you to do so. In d-ASCs, greatly increased awareness of particular aspects of the Motor Output subsystem are sometimes reported. Greatly decreased awareness has also been reported: actions that are ordinarily subject to conscious awareness, via feedback from the interoceptors, are done with no awareness at all. During my first experience with a psychedelic drug, mescaline, I told my body to walk down to the end of the hall. Then my awareness became completely absorbed in various internal events. After what seemed a very long time, I was surprised to notice that my body had walked down the hall and obligingly stopped at the end, with no conscious participation or awareness on my part. To some extent this occurs in an ordinary d-SoC, especially with well-learned actions, but the effect can be much more striking in a d-ASC. We should distinguish lack of sensory awareness of body actions from awareness of them but without the sense of ego added. The latter also creates a different relationship with motor actions.

Deautomatization of motor actions is another sort of altered awareness of motor output that can occur in a d-ASC. Either you become unusually aware of components of automatized actions normally inaccessible to consciousness or you have deliberately to will each of these component actions to take place because the whole automated action will not occur by itself.

Gurdjieff used this as a basis for his "Halt" exercise. Pupils agreed to freeze instantly whenever the command "Halt!" was given. The exercise was intended to show the pupils some of their limitations, among other things. Gurdjieff claims it is a dangerous exercise unless used by someone with an exceptional knowledge of the human body. The idea suggests interesting research possibilities. More information can be found in Ouspensky [48].

8 Conscious control over aspects of bodily functioning long considered to be automatic, not susceptible to voluntary control, is now a major research area under the rubric of *biofeedback*. The interested reader can find the most important researches reprinted each year in *Biofeedback and Self-Control*, an annual published by Aldine Publishing Company, Chicago.

D-ASC-related changes in the way the body is experienced via the Exteroception subsystem and in awareness of functioning of the Motor Output subsystem can alter the *operating characteristics* of voluntary action. You may have to perform a different kind of action internally in order to produce the same kind of voluntary action. Carlos Castaneda [9] gives a striking example of this in a drug-induced d-ASC. His body was completely paralyzed from the "little smoke" in terms of his ordinary way of controlling it. Doing all the things he ordinarily did to move produced zero response. But if he simply willed movement in a certain way, his body responded.

Changes in the awareness of the functioning of the Motor Output subsystem may include feelings of greatly increased strength or skill, or of greatly decreased strength or skill. Often these feelings do not correspond with performance: you may feel exceptionally weak or unsure of your skill, and yet perform in a basically ordinary fashion. Or you may feel exceptionally strong, but show no actual increase in performance. The potential for a true increment in strength in d-ASCs is real, however, because in the ordinary d-SoC you seldom use your musculature to its full strength. Safety mechanisms prevent you from fully exerting yourself and possibly damaging yourself. For example, some muscles are strong enough to break your own bones if they were maximally exerted. In various d-ASCs, especially when strong emotions are involved, these safety mechanisms may be temporarily bypassed, allowing greater strength, at the risk of damage.

In a d-ASC the Subconscious subsystem may control the Motor Output subsystem or parts of it. For example, if a hypnotist suggests to a subject that his arm is moving up and down by itself, the arm will do so and the subject will experience the arm moving *by itself,* without his conscious volition. If a hypnotist suggests automatic writing, the subject's hand will write complex material, with as much skill as in ordinary writing, without any conscious awareness by the subject of what he is going to write and without any feeling of volitional control over the action. This kind of disassociated motor action can also sometimes occur in the ordinary d-SoC, where it may represent the action of a disassociated d-ASC.

This ends our survey of the main subsystems of states of consciousness. It is only a survey, pointing out the major variations. Much literature already exists from which more specific information about various subsystems can be gleaned, and much research remains to be done to clarify our concepts of particular subsystems. Particularly we need to know exactly how each subsystem changes for each specific d-ASC.

So we must know our parts better, although I emphasize again that it is just as important to know how these parts are put into the functioning whole that constitutes a system, a d-SoC.

9.

Individual Differences

✿✪✿

Inadequate recognition of individual differences is a methodological deficiency that has seriously slowed psychological research. Lip service is paid to individual differences, but in reality they are largely ignored. Psychologists, caught up in the all-too-human struggle for prestige, ape the methods of the physical sciences, in which individual differences are not of great significance and the search is for general fundamental laws. I believe this failure to recognize individual differences is the rock on which psychology's early attempts to establish itself as an introspective discipline foundered. Following the lead of the tremendously successful physical scientists, the early psychologists searched for general laws of the mind, and when their data turned out to be contradictory, they quarreled with each other over who was right, not realizing they were all right, and so wasted their energies. They tried to abstract too much too soon before coming to terms with the experiential subject matter.

We psychologists all too often do the same thing today, albeit in a more sophisticated form. Consider, for example, the procedure described in Chapter 5 for mapping a person's location in experiential space. Suppose that in the course of an experiment we measure two variables, X and Y, in a group of subjects. To concretize the example, we can define X as the degree of analgesia (insensitivity to pain) the subject can show and Y as the intensity of the subject's imagery. Tempted by the convenience

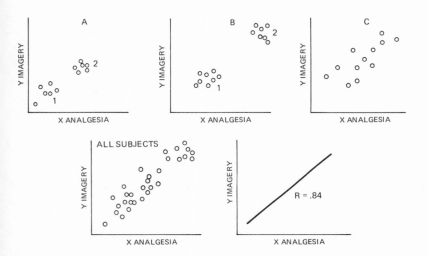

Figure 9–1. Problems arising when individual differences are ignored. Charts A, B, and C are experiential mappings of the sort done in Figure 5–1. The other two charts are summary charts, as explained in the text.

and "scientificness" of a nearby computer, we feed our group data into a prepackaged analysis program and get the printout in the lower right-hand chart of Figure 9–1—a straight line fitted to the data and indicating a highly significant (thus publishable) correlation coefficient between variables X and Y. It looks as if ability to experience analgesia is linearly related to intensity of imagery, that in this region of experiential space there is a straight-road connection: if you do whatever is needed to enhance imagery, you automatically increase analgesia.

If we distrust such great abstraction of the data, we can ask the computer to print out a scatter plot of the raw data, the actual position of each subject instead of the abstraction for all subjects. This new printout (lower left-hand chart of Figure 9–1) apparently reassures us that the fitted curve and correlation coefficient are adequate ways of presenting and understanding our results. The straight road is somewhat broad, but still basically straight. More imagery goes with more analgesia.

We have extracted a principle (more imagery leads to more

analgesia) from group data that is based on one pair of observations from each subject. Suppose, however, that we actually go back to our subjects and test some of them repeatedly, obtain samples over time, an experiential mapping, of their simultaneous abilities to experience analgesia and imagery. Then we find that our subjects actually fall into three distinct types, as shown in the upper charts of Figure 9–1. Type A shows either a low degree of both analgesia and imagery or a fair degree of analgesia and imagery, but no other combinations. Type B shows a low to fair degree of analgesia and imagery or a very high degree of analgesia and imagery, but no other combinations. Type C shows a high variability of degree of analgesia and imagery, a much wider range of combinations.

For subjects of type C, the conclusion, drawn from the group data, of a linear relationship between intensity of imagery and intensity of analgesia, is valid. But how many type C subjects are included in our group? Subjects of types A and B, on the other hand, do *not* show a linear relationship between analgesia and imagery. There is no straight road, only some islands of experience. For type A subjects, analgesia and imagery cluster together at low levels or at moderate levels of functioning, but show no clear *linear* relationship within either cluster. For type B subjects, analgesia and imagery cluster at low to moderate or at very high levels, and again show no clear linear relationship within either clustering. Indeed, subjects of types A and B show the clustering used in Chapter 5 to define the concept of multiple d-SoCs, while subjects of type C seem to function in only a single d-SoC.

Thus the conclusion drawn from the grouped data about relations between analgesia and imagery in this region of experiential space turns out to apply only to some people and to misrepresent what others experience. Indeed, the error may be more profound: people may be only of the A and B types, but combining their results as subjects when some are in one part of experiential space and some in another gives us a set of numbers that spans the whole range. This leads us to the straight-road or linear relationship concept, even though that concept actually represents no one's experience.

It is hard to realize the full impact of individual differences because of the deep implicitness of the assumption that we all share a common d-SoC. Since we are members of a common culture, this is *generally* true, but the more I come to know other individuals and get a feeling for the way their minds work, the more I am convinced that this general truth, the label *ordinary* d-SoC, conceals enormous individual differences. If I clearly understood the way your mind works in its ordinary d-SoC, and if you understood the same about me, we would both be amazed. Yet because we speak a common language, which stresses external rather than internal events, we are seldom aware of these differences.

Psychologically, each of us assumes that his own mind is an example of a "normal" mind and then projects his own experiences onto other people, unaware of how much projecting he is doing. For example, most of us have imagery in our ordinary d-SoC that is unstable and not very vivid, so that trying to visualize something really steadily and intensely is impossible. Some people report that in d-ASCs their imagery is much more intense and controllable, steady. Yet the inventor Nikola Tesla had such intense, controllable imagery in his ordinary d-SoC. When Tesla designed a machine, he did it in his head, without using physical drawings: nevertheless, he could instruct a dozen different machinists how to make each separate part, to the nearest ten-thousandth of an inch, and the completed machine would fit together perfectly. Tesla is also reported to have tested wear on his machines through imagery. He designed the machine by visualization, put the imaged parts together into a complete machine, started it running in his mind, forgot about it, resurrected the image thousands of hours later, mentally dismantled the machine, and inspected the parts for wear to see what needed reinforcement or redesign [43]. Regardless of how one evaluates the accuracy of such imagery, Tesla's procedure is a good example of what for most of us is exotic imagery associated with d-ASCs, but what was for him the imagery of his "ordinary" d-SoC.

On those occasions when we do recognize great differences in the mental functioning of others, we are tempted to label the differences weird or abnormal or pathological. Such blanket labels are not useful. What are the specific advantages and disadvantages under what circumstances for each individual difference or pattern?

This tendency to project implicitly the workings of one's own mind pattern as a standard for the workings of all minds can have interesting scientific results. For example, controversy rages in the literature on hypnosis over whether the concept of a d-SoC is necessary to explain hypnosis, or whether the hypnotic "state" is in fact continuous with the ordinary "state," is simply a case of certain psychological functions, such as suggestibility and role-playing involvement, being pushed to higher levels of activity than they are under ordinary conditions. A chief proponent of this latter view, Theodore X. Barber [4], can produce most of the classical hypnotic phenomena in himself without doing anything special. He can anesthetize his hand or produce mild hallucinations without experiencing a breakdown of his ordinary consciousness, a transitional period from one d-SoC to another, or anything else special.[1] The phenomena included in his ordinary d-SoC encompass a range that, for another person, must be attained by unusual means. How much does this affect his theorizing? How much does anyone's individual psychology affect his thinking about how other minds work? Again consider Figure 9–1. Whereas A and B type people may have two d-SoCs, one that we call their ordinary d-SoC and a second called their hypnotic state, the ordinary range of consciousness of type C people includes both these regions. Thus it may be more accurate to say that what has been called hypnosis, to stick with this example, is indeed merely an extension of the ordinary range of functioning for *some* people, but for other people it is a d-ASC.

I cannot emphasize too strongly that the mapping of experience and the use of the concept of d-SoCs *must first be done on an individual basis. Only* then, *if* regions of great similarity are found to exist across individuals, can common names that apply across individuals be legitimately coined.

This idealistic statement does not reflect the way our concepts actually evolved. The very existence of names like dreaming state or hypnotic state indicates that there appears to be a fair degree of commonality among a fair number of individuals. Though I often speak as if this commonality were true, its veracity cannot be precisely evaluated at the present stage of our knowledge, and

---

[1] As discussed in Chapter 12, some individuals may transit so rapidly and easily between d-SoCs that they do not notice the transitions and so mistakenly believe they experience only one d-SoC. This case is ordinarily difficult to distinguish from that of actual continuity through a wide region of experiential space.

the concept is clearly misleading at times. Several d-ASCs may be hidden within common names like hypnosis or dreaming.

In addition to the large individual differences that may exist among people we think are all in the same d-SoC, there are important individual differences among people's abilities to transit from one d-SoC to another. In discussing stabilization processes, I mentioned that some people seem overstabilized and others understabilized. The former may be able to experience only a few d-SoCs, while the latter may transit often and effortlessly into d-ASCs. Understabilized people may undergo breakdown of the ordinary d-SoC and be unable to form a new d-ASC, unable to organize consciousness into a stable coping form. Some types of schizophrenia may represent this understabilized mode of consciousness.

Besides the sheer number of simultaneous and reinforcing stabilization processes, the degree of voluntary control over them is important. To the extent that your stabilization processes are too powerful or too implicit to be altered at will, you are stuck in one mode of consciousness. These dimensions of stabilization, control, and ability to transit from one d-SoC to another are important ones that must be the focus of future research, as we know almost nothing about them now.

10.

Using Drugs to Induce
Altered States

✿✿✿

Serious misunderstandings occur when an external technique that *might* induce a d-ASC is equated with that altered state itself. This error is particularly seductive in regard to psychoactive or psychedelic drugs, for we tend automatically to accept the pharmacological paradigm that the specific chemical nature of the drug interacts with the chemical and physical structure of the nervous system in a lawfully determined way, invariably producing certain results. This view may be mostly true at a neurological or hormonal level, but is misleading at the level of consciousness. Within this paradigm, observed variability in human reactions is seen as the "perverseness" of psychological idiosyncrasies interfering with basic physiological reactions, and is averaged out by treating it as "error variance." While this pharmacological paradigm seems usefully valid for a variety of simple drugs, such as barbiturates that induce drowsiness and sleep, it is inadequate and misleading for the psychedelic drugs, such as marijuana or LSD.

Nondrug Factors

Figure 10–1 depicts a model of the effects of drugs on consciousness that I developed when I was beginning to study marijuana intoxication [103, 105]. In addition to the physiological effects that constitute disrupting and patterning forces impinging

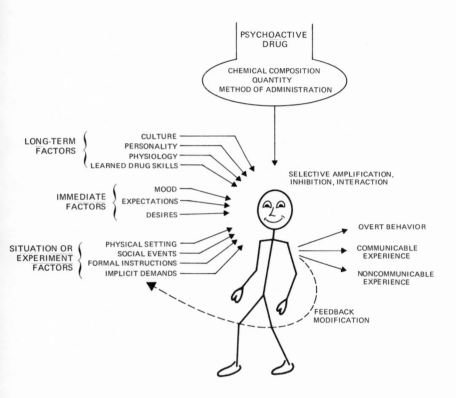

Figure 10–1.   Factors affecting reactions to a psychoactive drug.

on the subject (upper right portion of the figure), there are a large number of psychological disrupting and patterning forces that are, in many cases, more important than the physiological effects in determining whether a d-ASC will occur and what the content of that altered state will be. Thus while it is useful to know what psychoactive drug a subject has taken, the quantity of the drug, and the method of administration, such information may be relatively unimportant. Without some knowledge of the psychological factors, accurate prediction of the subject's behavioral and experiential reactions may be very difficult.

These nondrug factors can be classified in three groups: long-term factors, immediate factors, and factors related to the setting in which the drug is used.

Long-term factors include (1) the culture the subject was raised in and all the effects that has had in terms of structuring his ordinary d-SoC, and providing specific expectations about the drug; (2) the personality of the subject; (3) possible specific physiological vulnerabilities he may have to the drug; and (4) his learned drug skills—whether he has taken this drug many times before, and learned to enhance desired reactions and inhibit undesired reactions, or is naive with respect to this drug, so that most of his energy will be needed to cope with the (often stressful) effects of the novelty.

Immediate factors are (5) the subject's mood when he takes the drug, since this mood may be amplified or inhibited; (6) the subject's expectations about the experience; and (7) whether these expectations are the same as what he *desires* to experience.

Factors related to the situation or experimental setting in which the drug is taken include (8) the physical setting and its effect on the subject; (9) the social setting and its effect—the kinds of people who are with the subject and how they interact with him (a frightened person present, for example, may communicate his fright sufficiently to make the effect of the drug quite anxiety-provoking) ; (10) in the case of an experiment, the formal instructions given to the subject and how he reacts to and interprets them; and (11) the *demand characteristics* [45, 55], the *implicit* instructions, and how they affect the subject (for example, if the experimenter tells the subject the drug is relatively harmless, but asks him to sign a comprehensive medical release form, the total message communicated belies the statement that this is a relatively harmless drug) .

Further, the subject or user is not just a passive recipient of all these forces, reacting mechanically. He may selectively enhance the action of some and inhibit others. If the social situation is "bringing you down," you can leave. If you feel unsettled and unsure of your control, you can choose to use only a small amount of the drug. If certain aspects of the situation are unsettling, you can try not to focus attention on them but on more pleasant or useful aspects of the situation. This aspect is indicated by the feedback arrow in Figure 10–1.

Since, as discussed earlier, a person's control of his attention and energy is limited, to some extent he is at the mercy of the various factors diagrammed in Figure 10–1. In the experimental situation particularly, the subject usually has **no control at all** over most of these factors and so is at their mercy. This is important because so much of our scientific knowledge in this area is based on *experimental* studies of drugs—studies that might be assumed to be the most dependable. Unfortunately, a close reading of the experimental literature on drugs suggests that most experimenters were not only unaware of the importance of the psychological factors diagrammed in Figure 10–1, and so failed to report them, but usually set up the experiment in a way that maximized the probability of bad trips, of anxiety-filled, unpleasant reactions.

This situation is summarized in Table 10–1. The values of drug and psychological factors listed in the rightmost column are those that increase the probability of a bad trip; those in the third left column, a good trip. Knowing that the values of some of these factors are in one or the other direction has little predictive value at the present stage of our knowledge, but knowing that most of them are in one direction allows fair prediction. I infer (sometimes from the published description per se, sometimes from reading between the lines or talking to former subjects) that in the more than one thousand scientific experiments on drug-induced d-ASCs reported in the literature that most experiments had most of the determining factors in the bad trip direction. Thus most of our scientific knowledge about drug effects is badly confused with effects of coping with the stress of a bad trip.

Physiological and Psychological Effects

Given this cautionary note on the complexity of using drugs to induce d-ASCs, a few general things can be said about drug-induced states in terms of the systems approach.

Particular drugs may specifically affect the neurological bases of various psychological structures/subsystems, exciting or activating some of these structures/subsystems, suppressing or slowing the activity of other structures/subsystems, altering or distorting the mode of information-processing within some structures/subsystems. Psychological processes in relatively unaffected structures/subsystems may, however, compensate for changes in affected subsystems and/or maintain sufficient stabilization processes so that the d-SoC does not break down. The drug may both disrupt and pattern on a *physiological* level, but not necessarily induce a d-ASC. Remember that a d-SoC is *multiply* stabilized.

Table 10–1
Values of Variables for Maximizing Probability of Good or Bad Trip

	Variables	Good Trip Likely	Bad Trip Likely
Drug factors	Quality	Pure, known	Unknown drug or unknown degree of (harmful) adulterants
	Quantity	Known accurately, adjusted to individual's desire	Unknown, beyond individual's control
Long-term factors	Culture	Acceptance, belief in benefits	Rejection, belief in detrimental effects
	Personality	Stable, open, secure	Unstable, rigid, neurotic, or psychotic
	Physiology	Healthy	Specific adverse vulnerability to drug
	Learned drug skills	Wide experience gained under supportive conditions	Little or no experience or preparation, unpleasant past experience
Immediate factors	Mood	Happy, calm, relaxed, or euphoric	Depressed, overexcited, repressing significant emotions

Experiment or situation factors		
Expectations	Pleasure, insight, known eventualities	Danger, harm, manipulation, unknown eventualities
Desires	General pleasure, specific user-accepted goals	Aimlessness, (repressed) desires to harm or degrade self for secondary gains
Physical setting	Pleasant and esthetically interesting by user's standards	Cold, impersonal, "medical," "psychiatric," "hospital," "scientific"
Social events	Friendly, nonmanipulative interactions overall	Depersonalization or manipulation of the user, hostility
Formal instructions	Clear, understandable, creating trust and purpose	Ambiguous, dishonest, creating mistrust
Implicit demands	Congruent with explicit communications, supportive	Contradictory to explicit communications and/or reinforcing other negative variables

Reprinted from C. Tart, *On Being Stoned: A Psychological Study of Marijuana Intoxication*, Palo Alto, Calif., Science & Behavior Books, 1971, by permission of Science & Behavior Books.

When physiological effects occur in various structures/subsystems, their *interpretation* by the subject determines much of his (multilevel) reaction and whether a d-ASC results. Changing the interpretation of a sensation alters its importance and the degree of attention/awareness energy it attracts. For example, if you consider a tingling sensation in your limbs "just" a dull feeling from "tiredness," you handle it differently than if you interpret it to mean that you are getting high, that the drug is beginning to work.

An excellent example comes from marijuana use. Most marijuana smokers have to *learn* how to achieve the d-ASC we refer to as marijuana intoxication or being stoned. Typically, the first few times a person smokes marijuana, he feels an occasional isolated effect like tingling, but the overall pattern of his consciousness stays quite ordinary and he usually wonders why others make so much fuss about a drug that has so little effect. With the assistance of more experienced drug users, who suggest he focus his attention on certain kinds of happenings or try to have certain specified kinds of experiences, additional psychological factors, patterning and disrupting forces, are brought to bear to disrupt the ordinary d-SoC and pattern the d-ASC. Often the transition takes place quite suddenly, and the smoker finds that he is now stoned. This is a good illustration of how the physiological action of the marijuana disrupts many of the ordinary feedback stabilization processes of the ordinary d-SoC, but too few to destabilize and alter the d-SoC.

The fact that a naive user can smoke enormous amounts of marijuana the first several times without getting stoned, and then easily get stoned with a tenth as much drug once he has learned how, is paradoxical to pharmacologists. They call it the *reverse tolerance effect*. This effect is not at all puzzling in terms of the systems approach. It simply means that the physiological disrupting and patterning effects of the drug per se are generally not sufficient to destabilize the b-SoC. Once the user knows how to deploy his attention/awareness properly, however, this deployment needs only a small boost from the physiological effects of the drug to finally destabilize the b-SoC and pattern the d-ASC—being stoned.

Indeed, the placebo response of getting stoned on marijuana from which the THC (tetrahydrocannabinol, the main and perhaps only active ingredient) has been extracted may not illustrate the idea that some people are hypersuggestible so much as the fact that psychological factors are the main components of the d-ASC associated with marijuana use.

We should also note that it is a common experience for marijuana users [105] to say they can come down at will, that if they find themselves in a situation they feel unable to cope with adequately while in the d-ASC of marijuana intoxication, they can deliberately suppress most or all the effects and temporarily return almost instantly to the ordinary d-SoC. By psychological methods alone they can disrupt the altered state and pattern their ordinary state into existence: yet the same amount of THC is still circulating in their bloodstreams.

A third and quite striking example of the importance of psychological factors in determining whether a drug produces a d-ASC comes from a review by Snyder [60] of the attempts to use marijuana in medicine in the nineteenth century:

> It is striking that so many of these medical reports fail to mention any intoxicating properties of the drug. Rarely, if ever, is there any indication that patients—hundreds of thousands must have received cannabis in Europe in the nineteenth century—were "stoned," or changed their attitudes toward work, love, their fellow men, or their homelands. . . . When people see their doctor about a specific malady they expect a specific treatment and do not anticipate being "turned on."

Apparently, then, unless you have the right kinds of expectations and a "little help from your friends," it is unlikely that marijuana will produce a d-ASC. Equating the inhalation of marijuana with the existence of a d-ASC is a tricky business.

This should not be interpreted to mean that marijuana is a weak drug, however. Some people fail to respond to large doses of far more powerful drugs like LSD.

Major Psychedelic Drugs

The results of using the very powerful drugs, like LSD, mescaline, or psilocybin, are extremely variable. Almost everyone who takes these more powerful psychedelic drugs experiences a disruption of his ordinary d-SoC. The *primary effect* of the powerful psychedelic drugs is to disrupt the stabilization processes of the ordinary d-SoC so that d-SoC breaks down. But, while there is a great deal of commonality of experience among marijuana users (at least in our cultural setting) [105], so that it is useful to speak of the "marijuana state" as a distinctive d-ASC across users, the variability of experience with the powerful psychedelics is so great that there seems to be no particular d-ASC *necessarily* produced by them. Rather, a highly unstable condition develops characterized by transient formations of patterns that constitute d-ASCs. The temporary association of scattered functions in the third part of Figure 7–1 illustrates this. There is a continuous transition between various kinds of unstable conditions. The colloquial phrase *tripping* is appropriate: one is continually going somewhere, but never arriving.[1]

While this is probably true for most experiences with powerful psychedelics in our culture, it is not universally true. Carlos Castaneda's accounts of his work with Don Juan [9–12] indicate that Castaneda's initial reactions to psychedelic drugs were of this tripping sort. But Don Juan was not interested in having him trip. Among other things, Don Juan tried to train Casteneda to *stabilize* the effects of the psychedelic drugs so that he could get into particular d-ASCs suited to particular kinds of tasks at various times. Thus, the addition of further psychological patterning forces to the primarily disruptive forces caused by psychedelic drugs enables development of d-ASCs with particularly interesting properties.

Meanwhile, we should avoid terms like "the LSD state." We should not believe that the statement, "X took LSD" (or any powerful psychedelic drug), tells us much about what happened to X's consciousness. Indeed, a statement like "subjects were administered 1.25 micrograms of LSD per kilogram of body weight," commonly found in the experimental literature, is especially misleading because it seems so precise. It must be replaced by statements like "subject number 2 was administered such and such a dose of LSD, which then produced a d-ASC of type X, while subject number 3 did not enter a d-ASC with the same dose of LSD."

---

1 Alternatively, this variability can be interpreted as indicating very rapid transitions from one d-SoC of a few seconds' duration to another, to another, etc., but as discussed earlier, a d-SoC cannot be readily studied unless it lasts for a while.

I want to emphasize that I am in no way downgrading the potential value of psychedelic drug experiences simply because they probably seldom become stable d-ASCs in our culture. When used under the right circumstances by individuals who have been prepared, psychedelic drug experiences can be very valuable. Perhaps the most basic value is simply the total, experiential demonstration that other modes of awareness exist, that the ordinary d-SoC is only one of the many possible ways of structuring the mind. Specific insights into a person's ordinary self, which are valuable for therapy and growth, can also occur, and data and ideas about the nature of the mind can be obtained. This book is not the place to discuss the growth and therapeutic use of psychedelics: the interested reader should consult several chapters in *Altered States of Consciousness* [88 or 115].

I I.

Observation of Internal States

✿✿✿

Observation of internal events is often unreliable and difficult. Focusing on external behavior or physiological changes is useful, but experiential data are primary in d-SoCs. We must develop a more precise language for communicating about such data.

Observing oneself means that the overall system must observe itself. Thus, in the conservative view of the mind self-observation is inherently limited, for the part cannot comprehend the whole and the characteristics of the parts affect their observation. In the radical view, however, in which awareness is partially or wholly independent of brain structure, the possibility exists of an Observer much more independent of the structure.

Introspection, the observation of one's own mental processes, and the subsequent communication of these observations to others have long been major problems in psychology. To build a general scientific understanding requires starting from a general agreement on what are the facts, what are the basic observations across individuals on which the science can be founded. Individuals have published interesting and often beautiful accounts of their own mental processes in the psychological literature, but analysis of these accounts demonstrates little agreement among them and little agreement among the analyzers that the accounts are *precise* descriptions of observable mental processes. Striving for precise understanding is an important goal of science.

One reaction to this has been behaviorism, which ignores mental processes and declares that external behavior, which can be observed more easily and reliably, is the subject matter of psychology. Many psychologists still accept the behavioristic position and define psychology as the study of behavior rather than the study of the mind. That way is certainly easier. One hundred percent agreement among observers is possible, at least for simple behaviors. For example, in testing for susceptibility to hypnosis with the Stanford Hypnotic Susceptibility Scale [144], the examiner suggests to the subject that his arm is feeling heavier and heavier and will drop because of the increased weight. The hypnotists and observers present can easily agree on whether the subject's arm moves down at least twelve inches within thirty seconds after the end of the suggestion.

Behaviorism is an extremely valuable tool for studying simple behaviors, determining what affects them, and learning how to control them. But it has not been able to deal well with complex and important human experiences, such as happiness, love, religious feelings, purposes. The behavioristic approach is of particularly limited value in dealing with d-ASCs because almost all the interesting and important d-ASC phenomena are completely internal. A behavioristic approach to the study of a major psychedelic drug like LSD, for example, would lead to the conclusion that LSD is a sedative or tranquilizer, since the behavior most frequently produced is sitting still and doing nothing!

If we are to understand d-SoCs, introspection must become an important technique in psychology in spite of the difficulties of its application. I have primarily used peoples' reports of their internal experiences in developing the systems approach, even though these reports are undoubtedly affected by a variety of biases, limitations, and inadequacies, for such reports are the most relevant data for studying d-SoCs.

I believe psychology's historical rejection of introspection was premature: in the search for general laws of the mind, too much was attempted too soon. Mental phenomena are the most complex phenomena of all. The physical sciences, by comparison, deal with easy subject matter. We can be encouraged by the fact that many spiritual psychologies [128] have developed elaborate vocabularies for describing internal experiences. I do not understand these psychologies well enough to evaluate the validity of these vocabularies, but it is encouraging that others, working over long periods, have at least developed such vocabularies. The

English language is well suited for making reliable discriminations among everyday external objects, but it is not a good language for precise work with physical reality. The physical sciences have developed specialized mathematical languages for such work that are esoteric indeed to the man in the street. Sanskrit, on the other hand, has many presumably precise words for internal events and states that do not translate well into English. There are over twenty words in Sanskrit, for example, which are translated to mean "consciousness" in English, but which carry different shades of meaning in the original. Development of a more precise vocabulary is essential to progress in understanding consciousness and d-SoCs. If you say you feel "vibrations" in a d-ASC, what *precisely* do you mean?

The Observer

In science the word *observation* usually refers to scrutiny of the external environment, and the observer is taken for granted. If the observer is recognized as possessing inherent characteristics that limit his adequacy to observe, these specific characteristics are compensated for, as by instrumentally aiding the senses or adding some constant to the observations; again the observer is taken for granted. In dealing with the microworld, the particle level in physics, the observer cannot be taken for granted, for the process of observation alters the phenomena being observed. Similarly, when experiential data are used to understand states of consciousness, the observation process cannot be taken for granted.

For the system to observe itself, attention/awareness must activate structures that are capable of observing processes going on in other structures. Two ways of doing this seem possible, which we shall discuss as pure cases, even though they may actually be mixed. The first way is to see the system breaking down into two semiindependent systems, one of which constitutes the observer and the other the system to be observed. I notice, for example, that I am rubbing my left foot as I write and that this action seems irrelevant to the points I want to make. A moment ago I was absorbed in the thinking involved in the writing and in rubbing my foot, but some part of me then stepped back for a moment, under the impetus to find an example to illustrate the current point, and noticed that I was rubbing my foot. The "I" who observed that I was rubbing my foot is my ordinary self, my personality, my ordinary d-SoC. The major part of my system held together, but temporarily singled out a small, connected part of itself to be observed. Since I am still my ordinary self, all my characteristics enter into the observation. There is no objectivity to my own observation of myself. My ordinary self, for example, is always concerned with whether what I am doing is useful toward attaining my short-term and long-term goals; thus the judgment was automatically made that the rubbing of the foot was a useless waste of energy. Having immediately classified foot-rubbing as useless, I had no further interest in observing it more clearly, seeing what it was like. The observation is mixed with evaluation; most ordinary observation is of this nature.

By contrast, many meditative disciplines take the view that attention/awareness can achieve a high degree or even complete independence from the structures that constitute a person's ordinary d-SoC and personality, that a person possesses (or can develop) an Observer that is highly objective with respect to the ordinary personality because it is an Observer that is essentially pure attention/awareness, that has no judgmental characteristics of its own. If the Observer had been active, I might have observed that I was rubbing my foot, but there would have been no structure immediately activated that passed judgment on this action. Judgment, after all, means relatively permanent characteristics coded in structure to make comparisons against. The Observer would simply have noted whatever was happening without judging it.

The existence of the Observer or Witness is a reality to many people, especially those who have attempted to develop such an Observer by practicing meditative disciplines, and I shall treat it as an experiential reality.

The question of its ultimate reality is difficult. If one starts from the conservative view of the mind, where awareness is no more than a product of the nervous system and brain, the degree of independence or objectivity of the Observer can only be relative. The Observer may be a semi-independent system with fewer characteristics than the overall system of consciousness as a whole, but it is dependent on the operation of neurologically based structures and so is ultimately limited and shaped by them; it is also programmed to some extent in the enculturation process. Hilgard [26] has found the concept of such a partially dissociated Observer useful in understanding hypnotic analgesia. In the radical view of the mind, awareness is (or can become) different from the brain and nervous system. Here partial to total independence of, and objectivity with respect to, the mind/brain can be attained by the Observer. The ultimate degree of this objectivity then depends on whether awareness per se, whatever its ultimate nature is, has properties that limit it.

It is not always easy to make this clear distinction between the observer and the Observer. Many times, for example, when I am attempting to function as an Observer, I Observe myself doing certain things, but this Observation immediately activates some aspect of the structure of my ordinary personality, which then acts as an observer connected with various value judgments that are immediately activated. I pass from the function of Observing from outside the system to observing from inside the system, from what feels like relatively objective Observation to judgmental observation by my conscience or superego.

Some meditative disciplines, as in the vipassana meditation discussed earlier, strive to enable their practitioners to maintain the Observer for long periods, possibly permanently. The matter becomes rather complex, however, because a major job for the Observer is to Observe the actions of the observer: having Observed yourself doing some action, you then Observe your conscience become activated, rather than becoming completely caught up in the conscience observation and losing the Observer function. Such self-Observation provides much data for understanding the structure of one's own consciousness. For a comprehensive discussion of this method of understanding, I refer the reader to Riordan's and Goleman's chapter in *Transpersonal Psychologies* [128].

Self-Observation During Transition Periods

The distinction between these two kinds of observers is important in considering the transition period between two d-SoCs. If we ask questions about what phenomena are experienced during the transition period, we must ask who is going to make these experiential observations for us. Since the ordinary observer *is* the structure, then the radical destructuring necessary for transition into a d-ASC eliminates the ability to observe. At worst, if there is total destructuring we can expect no direct experiential observation of the transitional period, perhaps only a feeling of blankness. Such blackouts are often reported.

Yet people do report transitional experiences. Destructuring of the b-SoC may not be total, certain parts of it may hold together as subsystems through the transition period, partial observations may be made by these subsystems, and such observations are recoverable on return to the b-SoC or in the d-ASC. But the observations are necessarily limited and incomplete, since they come from a partially incapacitated observer.

Now consider the role of the Observer, *if* it is well developed in a particular person, during the transition from one d-SoC to another. Because the Observer is either not at all based in particular structures, only partially based in particular structures, or based in structures that are not part of the b-SoC undergoing destructuring, it should be able to observe transitional phenomena. Exactly this sort of phenomenal report has come from reporters who feel they have a fairly well-developed Observer. They believe this Observer can make essentially continuous observations not only within a particular d-SoC but during the transition among two or more d-SoCs.

For example, Evans-Wentz [17] describes the following Tibetan yogic exercise for comprehending the nature of dreaming:

> That which hath been called "the initial comprehending of the dream," refereth to resolving to maintain unbroken continuity of consciousness throughout both the waking-state and the dream-state . . . sleep on the right side, as a lion doth. With the thumb and ring-finger of the right hand press the pulsation of the throat-arteries; stop the nostrils with the fingers (of the left hand) ; and let the saliva collect in the throat.

Evans-Wentz comments:

> As a result of these methods, the *yogin* enjoys as vivid consciousness in the dream-state as in the waking-state; and in passing from one state to another experiences no break in the continuity of memory.

I can say no more about the nature of the Observer here because we know so little about it in our Western scientific tradition. However, I think it is extremely important to find out to what extent the Observer's apparent objectivity is a reality and to what extent a fiction. Insofar as it is a reality, it offers an objectivity and a possible escape from cultural consensus reality conditionings that are highly important.

I must, however, caution the reader against taking this discussion of the Observer too concretely. I am using words to describe a certain kind of experience, but the words are not the experience. As Korzybski said: "The map is not the territory." Unfortunately, we not only habitually mistake the map for the territory, we *prefer* the map to the territory—it is so much clearer! I find it difficult to express the concept of Observing, and words can do no more than create analogies that point to aspects of your own experience. The term *Observer* is a way of referring to an important aspect of experience, a *process,* but we must not become too attached to the concept of one "thing" separate from and observing another "thing."

I 2.

Identity States

✿✿✿

Self-observation, observation of others, and psychoanalytic data indicate that various stimuli can produce marked reorganizations of ego functioning very rapidly, even though these all remain within the consensus reality definitions of "normal" consciousness. These *identity states* are much like d-SoCs and can be studied in the systems approach framework. They are hard to observe in ordinary life because of the ease and rapidity of transition, their emotional charge, and other reasons. The isolation of knowledge and experience in various identity states is responsible for much of the psychopathology of everyday life.

Definition of Identity States

The concept of d-SoCs comes to us in commonsense form, as well as in terms of my initial research interests, from people's experiences of *radically* altered states of consciousness—states like drunkenness, dreaming, marijuana intoxication, certain meditative states. These represent such radical shifts in the patterning, the system properties of consciousness, that most people experiencing them are *forced* to notice that the state of their consciousness is quite different, even if they are poor observers. A person need not have developed an Observer in order to notice such a change in his state of consciousness: so many things are so clearly different that the observation is forced on him.

Although this is the origin and the main focus of the concept of d-SoCs, the systems approach is applicable to important variations occurring within the overall pattern we call the ordinary d-SoC, variations that can be termed *identity states*. My own self-observation and much scattered psychological data, particularly data gathered in the course of psychoanalytic investigations, indicate that as different situations impinge on a person and activate different emotional drives, distinct changes in the organization of his ego can take place. Certain drives become inhibited or activated, and the whole constellation of psychological functioning alters its configuration around them.

The most cogent formulation of these data into a comprehensive picture is that of the Armenian philosopher and spiritual teacher, George Gurdjieff. The following selection from Ouspensky's report of Gurdjieff's early lectures [48, pp. 59–60] expresses Gurdjieff's idea that we have many "I's," many little egos:

> "One of man's important mistakes," he said, "one which must be remembered, is his illusion in regard to his I.
>
> "Man such as we know him, the 'man-machine,' the man who cannot 'do,' and with whom and through whom everything 'happens,' cannot have a permanent and single I. His I changes as quickly as his thoughts, feelings, and moods, and he makes a profound mistake in considering himself always one and the same person; in reality he is *always a different person,* not the one he was a moment ago.
>
> "*Man has no permanent and unchangeable I.* Every thought, every mood, every desire, every sensation, says 'I.' And in each case it seems to be taken for granted that this I belongs to the *Whole,* to the whole man, and that a thought, a desire, or an aversion is expressed by this Whole. In actual fact there is no foundation whatever for this assumption. Man's every thought and desire appears and lives quite separately and independently of the Whole. And the Whole never expresses itself, for the simple reason that it exists, as such, only physically as a thing, and in the abstract as a concept. Man has no individual I. But there are, instead, hundreds and thousands of separate small I's, very often entirely unknown to one another, never coming into contact, or, on the contrary, hostile to each other, mutually exclusive and incompatible. Each minute, each moment, man is saying or thinking 'I.' And each time his I is different. Just now it was a thought, now it is a desire, now a

sensation, now another thought, and so on, endlessly. *Man is a plurality.* Man's name is legion.

"The alternation of I's, their continual obvious struggle for supremacy, is controlled by accidental external influences. Warmth, sunshine, fine weather, immediately call up a whole group of I's. Cold, fog, rain, call up another group of I's, other associations, other feelings, other actions. There is nothing in man able to control this change of I's, chiefly because man does not notice, or know of it; he lives always in the last I. Some I's, of course, are stronger than others. But it is not their own conscious strength; they have been created by the strength of accidents or mechanical external stimuli. Education, imitation, reading, the hypnotism of religion, caste, and traditions, or the glamour of new slogans, create very strong I's in man's personality, which dominate whole series of other, weaker, I's. But their strength is the strength of the 'rolls'[1] in the centers. "And all I's making up a man's personality have the same origin as these 'rolls'; they are the results of external influences; and both are set in motion and controlled by fresh external influences.

"Man has no individuality. He has no single, big I. Man is divided into a multiplicity of small I's.

"And each separate small I is able to call itself by the name of the Whole, to act in the name of the Whole, to agree or disagree, to give promises, to make decisions, with which another I or the Whole will have to deal. This explains why people so often make decisions and so seldom carry them out. A man decides to get up early beginning from the following day. One I, or a group of I's, decide this. But getting up is the business of another I who entirely disagrees with the decision and may even know absolutely nothing about it. Of course the man will again go on sleeping in the morning and in the evening he will again decide to get up early. In some cases this may assume very unpleasant consequences for a man. A small accidental I may promise something, not to itself, but to someone else at a certain moment simply out of vanity or for amusement. Then it disappears, but the man, that is, the whole combination of other I's who are quite innocent of this, may have to pay for it all his life. It is the tragedy of the human being that any small I has the right to sign checks and promissory notes and the man, that is, the Whole, has to meet them.

[1] The analogy is to old phonograph rolls: we would say "programs" with a computer analogy today [C. T.].

People's whole lives often consist in paying off the promissory notes of small accidental I's."

Gurdjieff's concept of these rapidly alternating I's is similar to the systems approach concept of d-SoCs. If we call each I an *identity state,* then each (1) has an overall pattern of functioning, a gestalt, which gives it a system identity and distinguishes it from other identity states; (2) is composed of structures/subsystems, psychological functions, skills, memories; (3) possesses unique properties not present in other identity states; (4) presumably has some stabilizing processes, although apparently fewer than the ordinary d-SoC as a whole, since identity states can change so rapidly; (5) functions as a tool for coping with the world, with varying degrees of effectiveness; and (6) requires an induction process to transit from one identity state to another, a requisite stimulus to bring on a new identity state.

These alterations in functioning that I call identity states can thus be usefully studied with the systems approach to consciousness. Yet they are almost never identified as d-SoCs in ordinary people, for several reasons.

First, each person has a large repertoire of these identity states and transits between one and another of them extremely readily, practically instantly. Thus, no *obvious* lapses or transitional phenomena occur that would make him likely to notice the transitions.

Second, all these identity states share much psychological functioning in common, such as speaking English, responding to the same proper name, wearing the same sets of clothes. These many common properties make differences difficult to notice.

Third, all a person's ordinarily used identity states share in his culturally defined consensus reality. Although certain aspects of reality are emphasized by particular identity states, the culture as a whole implicitly allows a wide variety of identity states in its definitions of "normal" consciousness and consensus reality. Within the cultural consensus reality, for example, there are well-understood concepts, perceptions, and allowed behaviors associated with being angry, being sad, feeling sexual desire, being afraid.

Fourth, a person's *identification* is ordinarily very high, complete, with each of these identity states. He projects the feeling of

"I" onto it (the Sense of Identity subsystem function discussed in Chapter 8). This, coupled with the culturally instilled need to believe that he is a single personality, causes him to gloss over distinctions. Thus he says, *"I* am angry," *"I* am sad," rather than, "A state of sadness has organized mental functioning differently from a state of anger." The culture also reinforces a person for behaving as if he were a unity.

Fifth, identity states are *driven* by needs, fears, attachments, defensive maneuvers, coping mechanisms, and this highly charged quality of an identity state makes it unlikely that the person involved will be engaged in self-observation.

Sixth, many identity states have, as a central focus, emotional needs and drives that are socially unacceptable or only partially acceptable. Given the fact that people need to feel accepted, an individual may have many important reasons for *not* noticing that he has discrete identity states. Thus, when he is in a socially "normal" identity state, being a good person, he may be unable to be aware of a different identity state that sometimes occurs in which he hates his best friend. The two states are incompatible, so automatized defense mechanisms (Gurdjieff calls them *buffers*) prevent him from being aware of the one identity state while in the other. This is, in systems approach terminology, state-specific knowledge. Ordinarily, special psychotherapeutic techniques are required to make a person aware of these contradictory feelings and identity states within himself. Meditative practices designed to create the Observer also facilitate this sort of knowledge.

The development of an Observer can allow a person considerable access to observing different identity states. An outside observer can often clearly infer different identity states, but a person who has not developed the Observer function well may never notice his own many transitions from one identity state to another. Thus ordinary consciousness, or what society values as "normal" consciousness, may actually consist of a large number of d-SoCs, identity states. But the overall similarities between these identity states and the difficulty of observing them, for the reasons discussed above, lead us to think of ordinary consciousness as a relatively unitary state.

Gurdjieff sees the rapid, unnoticed transitions between identity states, and their relative isolation from one another, as the major cause of the psychopathology of everyday life. I agree with him, and believe this topic deserves intensive psychological research.

Functions of Identity States

An identity state, like a d-SoC, has coping functions. The culture a person is born into actively inhibits some of his human potentials, as well as developing some. Thus, even in the most smoothly functioning cultures, there is bound to be some disharmony, some conflict between a person's emerging and potential self and the demands placed on him to which he *must* conform in one way or another if he is to survive in that social environment. The psychopathology of everyday life is abundantly obvious and has been amply documented by psychological studies.

At the fringes of consciousness, then, there is a vast unknown, not simply of relatively neutral potentials that never developed, but of emotionally and cognitively frightening things, conflicts that were never resolved, experiences that did not fit consensus reality, feelings that were never expressed, problems that were never faced. Immersion in consensus reality in the ordinary d-SoC is a protection from this potentially frightening and overwhelming unknown; it is the safe, cultivated clearing in the dark, unexplored forest of the mind.

An identity state is a specialized version of the ordinary d-SoC, a structure acceptable to consensus reality (ignoring obviously pathological identity states). The extrainformational "This is me" quality from the Sense of Identity subsystem added to certain contents/structures constellates the energies of consciousness around them and produces an identity, a role[2] that a person is partially or completely identified with for the time. The identity "eats energy."

A particular identity state thus acts as loading stabilization for the ordinary d-SoC; it absorbs much available energy that might otherwise activate unknown and perhaps implicitly feared contents that are not acceptable. When you "know" who you are, when you take on an identity state, then you immediately have

---

[2] I use the term *role* to indicate that a person consciously knows he is acting a part that is not really him, and the term *identity state* to mean he has become the part. Clearly, the degree of identification can vary rapidly.

criteria for dealing with various situations. If I am a "father" in this moment I know that certain things are expected and desired of me and I can cope well within that framework with situations involving my children. If the situation changes and I now become a "professor," then I have a new set of rules on how to cope with situations involving people who have identified with the roles of "students."

Some of a person's most important problems arise when he is in an identity state that is not really suited to the situation: my children are unhappy when I am a professor when they want a father, and I am not comfortable when my students want me to be like a father when I think the role of professor is more appropriate.

Being caught in a situation in which one has no ready role to use and identify with is unusual. For most people such situations can be highly confusing or frightening, since they do not know how to think or act. They can become susceptible to any authority who offers ready-made roles/solutions in such situations. If the country is "going to hell" and nobody seems to have any answer, it may feel much better to be a "patriot" and blame "traitors" than to live with your confusion. On the other hand, lack of an immediately available role can offer a unique opportunity to temporarily escape from the tyranny of roles.

Once a person has identified with a role, the resulting identity state stabilizes his d-SoC not only through loading stabilization, but through the other three stabilization processes discussed in Chapter 6. When he is coping successfully and thus feeling good in a particular identity state, this constitutes positive feedback stabilization; he tends to engage in more thoughts and actions that expand and strengthen the identity state. If the fear of having no identity is strong and/or the rewards from a particular identity state are high, this can hinder escape from that identity state. Consider how many successful businessmen work themselves to death, not knowing how to stop being businessmen for even short periods, or how many men die within a few years of retiring, not having their work identity to sustain them.

Success from being in a particular identity state encourages a person to avoid or suppress thoughts and actions that tend to disrupt that state: this is negative feedback stabilization. A "good soldier" is obtaining valuable information about enemy troop movements—information that may save the lives of his buddies—

by torturing a native child: he actively suppresses his own identity state of a "father" in order to function effectively in his "soldier" identity.

Being in a particular identity state also functions as limiting stabilization. The identity leads to selective perception to make perceptions congruent with the reigning identity state. Certain kinds of perceptions that might activate other identity states are repressed. The tortured child is perceived as an "enemy agent," not as a "child." This keeps emotional and attention/awareness energy out of empathic processes that, if activated, would undermine and disrupt the "soldier" identity.

Identity states, then, are both tools for coping with the environment and ways of avoiding the unknown. The degree to which they serve mainly one or the other function probably varies tremendously from individual to individual and identity to identity. Some people are terribly afraid of anything outside the few narrow identities they always function in: by staying in one or the other of those identity states constantly, they never feel the fear of the unknown. Others have less fear of the unknown, but find the rewards from functioning in a few identity states are so high that they have no real need or interest to go outside them. The latter type probably characterizes a stable, well-integrated society, with most citizens quite content in socially accepted identity states.

For discussion of *radically* altered discrete states like hypnosis or drunkenness, the concept of the ordinary d-SoC as relatively unitary is useful. As the systems approach becomes more articulated, however, we shall have to deal with these identity states that exist within the boundaries of the ordinary d-SoC and that probably also function within the boundaries of various d-ASCs.

In this book, I continue to use the terms *discrete state of consciousness* and *discrete altered state of consciousness* to refer to the rather radical alterations like hypnosis or drunkenness that gave rise to the concept in the first place. I use the phrase *identity state* to indicate the more subtle division.

13.

Strategies in Using
the Systems Approach

✿✿✿

The systems approach generates a number of strategies for studying states of consciousness. Some of these are unique consequences of using a systems approach, some are just good-sense strategies that could come from other approaches. Many of these methodological strategies have been touched on in previous chapters; some are brought out in later chapters. Here I bring together most of these methodological points and introduce some new ones.

The Constructed Nature of Consciousness

Realizing that the ordinary d-SoC is not natural and given, but *constructed* according to semiarbitrary cultural constraints, gives us the freedom to ask some basic questions that might not otherwise occur to us. And it should make us more cautious about labeling other states as "pathological" and other cultures as "primitive." The Australian bushmen, for example, are almost universally considered one of the world's most primitive cultures because of their nomadic life and their paucity of material possessions. Yet Pearce [49] argues that, from another point of view, these people are among the most sophisticated in the world, for they have organized their entire culture around achieving a certain d-ASC, which they refer to as the experience of "Dream Time." Our bias toward material possessions, however, makes us unable to see this.

Recognizing the semiarbitrary nature of the system of the ordinary d-SoC that has been constructed in our culture should make us especially aware of the implicit assumptions built into it, assumptions we so take for granted that it never occurs to us to question them. In *Transpersonal Psychologies* [128], nine expert practitioners of various spiritual disciplines wrote about their disciplines not as religions, but as psychologies. In the course of editing these contributions, I was increasingly struck by the way certain assumptions are made in various spiritual psychologies that are different from or contrary to those made in Western psychology. As a result, I wrote a chapter outlining several dozen assumptions that have become implicit for Western psychologists and that, by virtue of being implicit, have great control over us.

I have found that when asked what some of these assumptions are, I have great difficulty recalling them: I have to go back and look at what I wrote! Although my study of systems that make different assumptions brought these implicit assumptions to mind, they have already sunk back to the implicit level. We should not underestimate the power of culturally given assumptions in controlling us, and we cannot overestimate the importance of trying to come to grips with them.

We should also recognize that the enculturation process, discussed earlier, ties the reward and punishment subsystems to the maintenance and defense of ordinary consensus reality. We are afraid of experiencing d-ASCs that are foreign to us and this fear strengthens our tendency to classify them as abnormal or pathological and to avoid them. It also further strengthens our resolve to deal with all reality from the point of view of the ordinary d-SoC, using only the tool or coping function of the ordinary d-SoC. But since the ordinary d-SoC is a limited tool, good for some things but not for others, we invariably distort parts of reality. The tendency to ignore or fight what we do not consider valuable and to distort our perceptions to make them fit is good for maintaining a cohesive social system, but poor for promoting scientific enquiry. A possible solution is the proposal for establishing state-specific sciences, discussed in Chapter 16.

The Importance of Awareness

The systems approach stresses the importance of attention/awareness as an activating energy within any d-SoC. Yet if we ask what awareness is or how we direct it and so call it attention, we cannot supply satisfactory answers.

We may deal with this problem simply by taking basic awareness for granted, as we are forced to do at this level of development of the systems approach, and work with it even though we do not know what it is. After all, we do not really know what gravity is in any ultimate sense, but we can measure what it does and from that information develop, for example, a science of ballistics. We can learn much about d-SoCs in the systems approach if we just take basic awareness and attention/awareness energy for granted, but we must eventually focus on questions about the nature of awareness. We will have to consider the conservative and radical views of the mind to determine whether awareness is simply the product of brain and nervous system functioning or whether it is something more.

System Qualities

The systems approach emphasizes that even though a d-SoC is made up of components, the overall system has gestalt qualities that cannot be predicted from knowledge of the components alone. Thus, while investigation of the components, the subsystems and structures, is important, such investigative emphasis must be balanced by studies of the overall system's functioning. We must become familiar with the pattern of the overall system's functioning so we can avoid wasting energy on researching components that turn out to be relatively unimportant in the overall system. We might, for example, avoid spending excessive research effort and money, as is now being done, on investigating physiological effects of marijuana, since examination of the overall nature of marijuana intoxication, as we have seen, indicates that psychological factors are at least as important as the drug factor in determining the nature of the d-ASC produced.

The systems approach also emphasizes the need to examine the system's functioning under the conditions in which it was designed to function. We are not yet sure what, if anything, d-ASCs are particularly designed for, what particular function they have. We must find this out. On the other hand, we should try not to waste effort studying d-ASCs under conditions they were clearly not designed for. For example, conducting studies that show a slight decrement in arithmetical skills under marijuana intoxication is of some interest, but since no record exists of anyone using marijuana in order to solve arithmetical problems, such studies are somewhat irrelevant. This emphasizes a point made earlier: that it is generally useless to characterize any d-ASC as "better" or "worse" than any other d-SoC. The question should always be, "Better or worse for what particular task?" All d-ASCs we know of seem to be associated with improved functioning for certain kinds of tasks and worsened functioning for others.[1] An important research aim, then, is to find out what d-ASCs are optimal for particular tasks and how to train people to enter efficiently into that d-ASC when they need to perform that task. This runs counter to a strong, implicit assumption in our culture that the ordinary d-SoC is the best one for all tasks; that assumption is highly questionable when it is made explicit. Remember that in any d-SoC there is a limited selection from the full range of human potential. While some of these latent human potentials may be developable in the ordinary d-SoC, some are more available in a d-ASC. Insofar as we consider some of these potentials valuable, we must learn what d-SoCs they are operable in and how to train them for good functioning within those d-SoCs.

This last point is not an academic issue: enormous numbers of people are now personally experimenting with d-ASCs to attain some of these potentials. While much gain will undoubtedly come out of this personal experimentation, we should also expect much loss.

Individual Differences

As we have seen, what for one individual is a d-ASC may, for another individual, be merely part of the region of his ordinary d-SoC, one continuous experiential space. By following the common experimental procedure of using group data rather than data from individual subjects, we can (see Chapter 9) get the impression of continuity (one d-SoC) when two or more d-SoCs actually occurred within the experimental procedure. We should indeed search for general laws of the mind that hold across

[1] Objectivity is hard to maintain here, for functions that are improved in a particular d-SoC may not be valued functions for the culture of the investigator. The first thing we can do is be *explicit* about our value judgments, rather than pretending we do not make them.

individuals, but we must beware of enunciating such laws prematurely without first understanding the behavior and experiences of the individuals within our experiments.

Recognizing the importance of individual differences has many applications outside the laboratory. If a friend tries some spiritual technique and has a marvelous experience as a result, and you try the same technique with no result, there is not necessarily something wrong with you. Rather, because of differences in the structures of your ordinary d-SoCs, that particular technique mobilizes attention/awareness energy in an effective way to produce a certain experience for him, but is not an effective technique for you.

Operationalism, Relevant and Irrelevant

Operationalism is a way of rigorously defining some concept by describing the actual operations required to produce it. Thus an operational definition of the concept of "nailing" is defined by the operations (1) pick up a hammer in your right hand; (2) pick up a nail in your left hand; (3) put the point of the nail on a wood surface and hold the nail perpendicular to the wood surface; (4) strike the head of the nail with the hammer and then lift the hammer again; and (5) repeat step 4 until the head of the nail is flush with the surface of the wood. An operational definition is a precise definition, allowing total reproducibility.

Some claim that whatever cannot be defined operationally is not a legitimate subject for scientific investigation. That is silly. No one can precisely specify all the steps necessary to experience "being in love," but that is hardly justification for ignoring the state of being in love as an important human situation worthy of study. A further problem is that in psychology, operationalism implicitly means *physical* operationalism, specifying the overt, physically observable steps in a process in order to define it. In the search for an objectivity like that of the physical sciences, psychologists emphasize aspects of their discipline that can be physically measured, but often at the cost of irrelevant studies.

An example is the equating of the hypnotic state, the d-ASC of hypnosis, with the performance of the hypnotic induction procedure. The hypnotic state is a psychological construct or, if induction has been successful, an experiential reality to the hypnotized person. It is not defined by external measurements. There are no obvious behavioral manifestations that clearly indicate hypnosis has occurred and no known physiological changes that invariably accompany hypnosis. The hypnotic procedure, on the other hand, the words that the hypnotist says aloud, is highly amenable to physical measurement. An investigator can film the hypnotic procedure, tape-record the hypnotist's voice, measure the sound intensity of the hypnotist's voice, and accumulate a variety of precise, reproducible physical measurements. But that investigator makes a serious mistake if he then describes the responses of the "hypnotized subject" and means by "hypnotized subject" the person to whom the hypnotist said the words. The fact that the hypnotist performs the procedure does not guarantee that the subject enters the d-ASC of hypnosis. As discussed earlier, a person's b-SoC is multiply stabilized, and no single induction procedure or combination of induction procedures will, with certainty, destabilize the ordinary state and produce a particular d-ASC.

I stress that the concept of the d-SoC is a psychological, experiential construct. Thus, the ultimate criterion for determining whether a person is in a d-ASC is a map of his experiences that shows him to be in a region of psychological space we have termed a d-ASC. The external performance of an induction technique is not the same as achievement of the desired d-ASC. A hypnotic induction procedure does not necessarily induce hypnosis; lying down in bed does not necessarily induce sleeping or dreaming; performing a meditation exercise does not necessarily induce a meditative state.

When an induction procedure is physiological, as when a drug is used, the temptation to equate the induction procedure with the altered state is especially great. But the two are not the same, even in this case. As discussed in Chapter 10, smoking marijuana does not necessarily cause a transition out of the b-SoC. Nor, as is shown in Chapter 14, is knowledge of the dose of the drug an adequate specification of depth.

We do need to describe techniques in detail in our reports of d-ASCs, but we must also specify the degree to which these techniques were actually *effective* in altering a subject's state of consciousness, *and we must specify this for each individual subject.* In practice, physiological criteria may be sometimes so highly correlated with experiential reports indicating a d-ASC that those criteria can be considered an indicator that the d-ASC has occurred. This is the case with stage 1 REM dreaming. Behavioral criteria may be similarly correlated with experiential data, though I am not sure any such criteria are well correlated at present. But the primary criterion is an actual assessment of the kind of experiential space the subject is in that indicates the induction procedure was effective.

Operationalism, then, which uses external, physical, and behavioral criteria, is inadequate for dealing with many of the most important phenomena of d-ASCs. Most of the phenomena that define d-ASCs are internal and may never show obvious behavioral or physiological[2] manifestations.

Ultimately we need an *experiential operationalism*, a set of statements such as (1) if you stop all evaluation processes for at least three minutes, (2) and you concurrently invest no attention/awareness energy into the Interoception subsystem for perceiving the body, (3) so that all perception of the body fades out, then (4) you will experience a mental phenomenon of such and such a type. Our present language is not well suited to this, as discussed earlier, so we are a long way from a good experiential operationalism. The level of precision of understanding and communication that an experiential operationalism will bring is very high; nevertheless, we should not overvalue operationalism and abandon hope of understanding a phenomenon we cannot define operationally.

Predictive Capabilities of the Systems Approach

In Chapter 8 I briefly describe some basic subsystems we can recognize in terms of current knowledge. We can now see how the systems approach can be used to make testable predictions about d-SoCs.

The basic predictive operation is cyclical. The first step is to observe the properties of structures/subsystems as well as you can from the current state of knowledge. You ask questions in terms of what you already know. Then you take the second step of organizing the observations to make better theoretical models of the structures/subsystems you have observed. The third step is to

---

[2] I refer to present-day levels of physiological measurement: in principle, if we could measure the microstructures of the brain finely enough, we could distinguish d-ASCs that are presently not distinguishable from scalp recordings of brain activity.

predict, on the basis of the models, how the structures/subsystems can and cannot interact with each other under various conditions. Fourth, you test these predictions by looking for or attempting to create d-SoCs that fit or do not fit these improved structure/subsystem models and seeing how well the models work. This takes you back to the first step, starting the cycle again, further altering or refining your models, etc.

The systems approach provides a conceptual framework for organizing knowledge about states of consciousness and a process for continually improving knowledge about the structures/subsystems. The ten subsystems sketched in Chapter 8 are crude concepts at this stage of our knowledge and should eventually be replaced with more precise concepts about the exact nature of a larger number of more basic subsystems and about their possibilities for interaction to form systems.

I have given little thought so far to making predictions based on the present state of the systems approach. The far more urgent need at this current, chaotic stage of the new science of consciousness is to organize the mass of unrelated data we have into manageable form. I believe that most of the data now available can be usefully organized in the systems approach and that to do so will be a clear step forward. The *precise* fitting of the available mass of data into this approach will, however, take years of work.

One obvious prediction of the systems theory is that because the differing properties of structures restrict their interaction, there is a definite limit to the number of stable d-SoCs. Ignoring enculturation, we can say that the number is large but limited by the biological/neurological/psychical endowment of man in general, by humanness. The number of possible states for a particular individual is even smaller because enculturation further limits the qualities of structures.

My systems approach to consciousness appears to differ from Lilly's approach [34, 35] to consciousness as a human biocomputer. I predict that only certain configurations can occur and constitute stable states of consciousness, d-SoCs. Lilly's model seems to treat the mind as a general-purpose computer, capable of being programmed in any way one can conceive of: "In the province of the mind, what one believes to be true either is true or becomes true within certain limits." Personal conversations between Lilly and I suggest that our positions actually do not differ that much. The phrase "within certain limits" is important here. I agree entirely with Lilly's belief that what we currently *believe* to be the limits, the "basic" structures limiting the mind are probably mostly arbitrary, programmed structures peculiar to our culture and personal history. It is the discovery of the really basic structures behind these arbitrary cultural/personal ones that will tell us about the basic nature of the human mind. The earlier discussion of individual differences is highly relevant here, for it can be applied across cultures: two regions of experiential space that are d-SoCs for many or all individuals in a particular culture may be simply parts of one larger region of experiential space for many or all individuals in another culture.

I stress again, however, that our need today, and the primary value of the systems approach, is useful organization of data and guidance in asking questions, not prediction. Prediction and hypothesis-testing will come into their own in a few years as our understanding of structures/subsystems sharpens.

Stability and Growth

Implicit in the act of mapping an individual's psychological experiences is the assumption of a reasonable degree of stability of the individual's structure and functioning over time. The work necessary to obtain a map would be wasted if the map had to be changed before it had been used.

Ordinarily we assume that an individual's personality or ordinary d-SoC is reasonably stable over quite long periods, generally over a lifetime once his basic personality has been formed by late adolescence. Exceptions to this assumption occur when individuals are exposed to severe, abnormal conditions, such as disasters, which may radically alter parts of their personality structure, or to psychotherapy and related psychological growth techniques. Although the personality change following psychotherapy is often rather small, leaving the former map of the individual's personality relatively useful, it is sometimes quite large.

The validity of assuming this kind of stability in relation to research on d-SoCs is questionable. The people who are most interested in experiencing d-ASCs are dissatisfied with the ordinary d-SoC and so may be actively trying to change it. But studies confined to people not very interested in d-ASCs (so-called naive subjects) may be dealing with an unusual group who are afraid of d-ASCs. Stability of the b-SoC or of repeatedly induced d-ASCs is something to be *assessed,* not assumed. This is particularly true for a person's early experiences with a d-ASC, where he is learning how to function in the d-ASC with each new occurrence. In my study of the experiences of marijuana intoxication [103, 105], I deliberately excluded users who had had less than a dozen experiences of being stoned on marijuana. The experience of these naive users would have mainly reflected learning to cope with a new state, rather than the common, stable characteristics of the d-ASC of being stoned.

An individual may eventually learn to merge two d-SoCs into one. The merger may be a matter of transferring some state-specific experiences and potentials back into the ordinary state, so that eventually most or many state-specific experiences are available in the ordinary state. The ordinary state, in turn, undergoes certain changes in its configuration. Or, growth or therapeutic work at the extremes of functioning of two d-SoCs may gradually bring the two closer until experiences are possible all through the former "forbidden region."

Pseudomerging of two d-SoCs may also be possible. As an individual more and more frequently makes the transition between the two states, he may automate the transition process to the point where he no longer has any awareness of it, and/or efficient routes through the transition process are so thoroughly learned that the transition takes almost no time or effort. Then, unless the individual or an observer was examining his whole pattern of functioning, his state of consciousness might appear to be single simply because transitions were not noticed. This latter case would be like the rapid, automated transitions between identity states within the ordinary state of consciousness.

Since a greater number of human potentials are available in two states than in one, such merging or learning of rapid transitions can be seen as growth. Whether the individual or his culture sees it as growth depends on cultural valuations of the added potentials and the individual's own intelligence in actual utilization of the two states. The availability of more potentials does not guarantee their wise or adaptive use.

Sequential Strategies in Studying d-SoCs

The sequential strategies for investigating d-SoCs that follow from the systems approach are outlined below. These strategies are idealistic and subject to modification in practice.

First, the general experiential, behavioral or physiological components of a rough concept of a particular d-ASC are mapped. The data may come from informal interviews with a number of people who have experienced that state, from personal experience with it, or from a fairly detailed survey of many peoples' experiences in that d-ASC. This exercise supplies a feeling for the overall territory and its main features.

Then the experiential space of various individuals is mapped to determine whether their experiences show the distinctive clusterings and patternings that constitute d-SoCs. This step overlaps somewhat with the first, for the investigator assumes or has data to indicate a distinctness about the d-ASC for at least some individuals as a start of his interest.

For individuals who show this discreteness, the third step of more detailed individual investigation is carried out. For those who do not, studies are begun across individuals to ascertain why some show various discrete states and others do not: in addition to recognizing the existence of individual differences, the researcher must find out why they exist and what function they serve.

The third step is to map the various d-SoCs of particular individuals *in detail*. What are the main features of each state? What induction procedures produce the state? What deinduction procedures cause a person to transit out of it? What are the limits of stability of the state? What uses, advantages does the state have? What disadvantages or dangers? How is the depth measured? What are the convenient marker phenomena to rapidly measure depth?

With this background, the investigator can profitably ask questions about interindividual similarities of the various discrete states. Are they really enough alike across individuals to warrant a common state name? If so, does this relate mainly to cultural background similarities of the individuals studied or to some more fundamental aspect of the nature of the human mind?

Finally, even more detailed studies can be done on the nature of particular discrete states and the structures/subsystems comprising them. This sort of investigation should come at a late stage to avoid premature reductionism: we must not repeat psychology's early mistake of trying to find the universal Laws of the Mind before we have good *empirical* maps of the territory.

14.

The Depth Dimension of a
State of Consciousness

✦✦

I indicated earlier that we can define a d-SoC as a clustering of psychological functioning in a (multidimensional) region of experiential space. Nevertheless, there may be movement or variation *within* that particular cluster, a quantitative variation in aspects of experience and psychological functioning. Although the overall system pattern maintains its identity, variations occur within it, and these variations are related to what we call the *depth* or intensity of a state of consciousness. For example, we talk about the ordinary d-SoC as being more or less clear; we speak of someone as being lightly or deeply hypnotized, slightly or very drunk, somewhat or very stoned on marijuana.

While any d-SoC can vary in many ways within its cluster, often one way predominates. We call this principal dimension the depth dimension. Information about variation along this dimension tells us a lot about variations along related dimensions.

The concept of depth is much like the concept of a d-SoC. It can simply be a convenient way of describing orderly change in the relationships within a d-SoC, or, developed further, it can be a theoretical explanation of changes in the underlying subsystems' action in the d-SoC, a hypothesis that enables predictions about things not yet observed about that d-SoC. For example, the concept of depth or level of alcohol intoxication may, on a descriptive level, be simply an observational statement that increasing intensity of intoxication is associated with increasing numbers of errors in some kind of performance task. On a theoretical level, however, depth of intoxication can be understood as changes in some fundamental brain structures, changes that have widespread effects on a variety of experiences and behaviors.

In terms of the systems approach, changes in the depth of a d-SoC result from quantitative changes in the operation of structures/subsystems within the particular pattern of subsystem operation that makes up the d-SoC. I emphasize *quantitative* because these are "more or less" changes, not changes of kind. Earlier investigators have sometimes used the term *depth* to include qualitative changes, changes in kinds of experiences. In the systems approach only minor qualitative changes are included as part of depth changes, changes small enough to not alter the major pattern of consciousness.

This is a good place to repeat that both d-SoCs and depth are *concepts* whose function is to help us understand experience; they are not ultimate realities. A d-SoC consists of radical, *qualitative* changes in patterning; depth consists of *quantitative* or *minor qualitative* changes within a discrete pattern. Someday we may reach a stage of knowledge where the exact boundary between the two concepts become indistinct, but we have not yet arrived there. The major d-SoCs we know much about today differ from one another the way boats, cars, trains, and planes differ; depths are more like the miles per hour measurements within each of these modes of transportation.

Relation of Depth to Intensity

Assuming that we have some convenient and valid way to measure a person's location on the depth dimension for a given d-SoC, how might different kinds of effects and their intensity relate to depth? Figures 14–1 through 14–5 illustrate some of the possible relations between depth and the intensity of various experiences or observable effects. The intensity of each effect is plotted on the vertical scale; the horizontal scale represents the depth dimension. The effects might be intensities of experiences, behaviors, or physiological indices.

An effect of type A (Figure 14–1) is present in the ordinary d-SoC at a low or zero level and as the d-ASC deepens, at some threshold the effect starts to become more intense. Then it

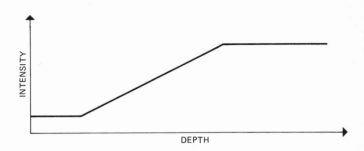

Figure 14–1.   The type A rise-and-plateau effect.

reaches some maximum level of intensity and stays there, even though depth increases. This rise-and-plateau effect is often found with marijuana intoxication. The feeling that time is slowing down, for example, does not become manifest until a moderately great depth of intoxication is reached; then it starts to manifest itself, steadily gets stronger (time seems to slow even more), and finally plateaus at a maximum level, even if the person feels more intoxicated later [105].

An effect of type B (Figure 14–2) does not become manifest until a certain threshold depth is reached; then it manifests itself and increases in intensity with increasing depth, as does type A. But, after stabilizing at some maximum value for a while, the

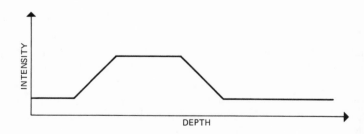

Figure 14–2.   The type B rise-plateau-and-fall effect.

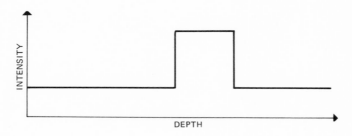

Figure 14–3.   The type C step-rise-and-fall effect.

effect begins to decrease and finally disappears with further increases in depth. This rise-and-plateau-and-fall effect occurs, for example, during marijuana intoxication. When a person is mildly intoxicated, he begins to find reading easier than usual. This feeling increases for a while, but as medium levels of intoxication are reached, the feeling of finding it easier to read lessens and finally disappears, to be replaced with a feeling of finding it difficult to read [105].

An effect of type C (Figure 14–3) does not become manifest until a certain depth is reached in the d-SoC. Then it manifests itself completely over a certain range, without variation in its own intensity and disappears beyond that range. This step-rise-and-fall effect is the extreme case of the rise-plateau-and-fall effect. It can easily be missed in studying a d-SoC if the subject does not remain at that depth for a while. Indeed, some d-SoCs may consist entirely of type C effects. Most ordinary dreaming, for example, is seldom considered to have a depth dimension. Type C effects may actually be rare or may simply not have been noticed. An example of one is given later in this chapter, in connection with the case of William.

An effect of type D (Figure 14–4) begins to manifest itself mildly at the lowest depth level, as soon as the d-ASC is entered, and increases steadily in intensity all through the depth dimension. This linear increase effect is commonly (but probably erroneously) assumed to be typical of most d-ASCs. Examples of type D effects from marijuana intoxication are the feeling that

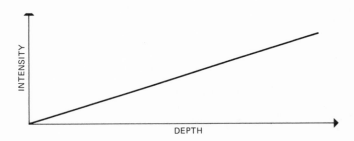

Figure 14–4. The type D linear increase effect.

sensations become more vivid and take on new qualities, the
feeling of becoming more tolerant of contradictions, the difficulty
in playing ordinary social games. All these begin to become
manifest as soon as the subject starts to feel stoned and increase
in intensity the more stoned he gets [105].

Various curvilinear variations of this effect can occur.

An effect of type E (Figure 14–5) is manifested strongly in the
ordinary d-SoC and is not changed up to a certain depth in the d-
ASC. But then it begins to decrease in intensity with increasing
depth or, as shown in this example, returns more or less intensely
at a greater depth, perhaps in a step-rise-and-plateau effect. An

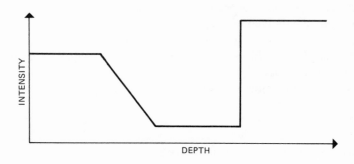

Figure 14–5. The type E effect, illustrating complex relationships to
depth, here a plateau-decrease-plateau-step/increase.

example is the feeling that one can describe one's experiences while in a d-ASC: description is easy at first, gradually becomes less adequate, finally is quite inadequate but at greater depth becomes adequate again. As an example, Erickson [25] describes a stuporous state occurring in some of his very deeply hypnotized subjects, but as hypnosis becomes even deeper they are able to function again.

There are, of course, many more complex ways that various experiences in d-ASCs can relate to depth, but the above are sufficient to illustrate the more common types.

The depth-intensity relationships depicted in Figures 14–1 through 14–5 are based on some assumed a priori measure of depth. The concept of depth, however, can be utilized without assuming an a priori measure. To do this, we begin empirically from scratch by arbitrarily defining any one varying effect we can conveniently measure as the depth dimension. We then let it vary throughout its range in the d-SoC, measure every other effect over this range of variation, and plot them against our arbitrarily defined depth dimension. For marijuana intoxication, for example, we might take a subject's ratings of how unusually intense his sensory experience is, and for a given rating of this, measure and/or have him rate a variety of other effects. Then we change the intensity to which his sensory experience is altered (by drugs or by psychological means), remeasure the other effects, etc. The map or graphical plot obtained of how the different effects relate to each other *is* the depth dimension. We need no longer define one particular effect as "depth." We have arrived at a good descriptive concept of depth by empirical mapping without having had to know what it was before we could start.

In doing this, we are lucky if we happen to start with an effect of type D as the initial index of depth. Since we are used to thinking in linear ways, plotting everything against an effect that changes linearly will produce a map we can understand fairly easily.

Depth obtained in the above way is a purely descriptive concept. It helps us summarize and relate our observations, but it will probably not allow us to predict things we have not yet observed. If, however, we view the effects and their changes as manifestations or alterations in the subsystems and structures that make up the d-SoC, depth becomes a scientific hypothesis. We should then be able to predict things other than those we have measured and test these predictions.[1]

Self-Reports of Depth

The feeling of varying depth is one often described as directly experienced in a d-ASC. A person often has an immediate feel for how intense the d-ASC is. He may remark, for example, that the marijuana he smoked must have been awfully potent because he feels intensely stoned or that his meditative state is more profound than usual.

Even if a person does not spontaneously comment about the depth of his d-ASC, if asked he often gives an extremely useful estimate—"extremely useful" in the sense that the estimate can be an excellent predictor of other aspects of the experience or of his behavior.

The fact that people do estimate the depths of their d-ASCs prompted me to do extensive investigations of self-report scales of depth, and I have found such scales very useful for measuring the intensity of the hypnotic state [114] and of marijuana intoxication [105, 139]. Charles Honorton has found that similar state reports relate well to the degree of alpha rhythm and muscle tension subjects show in learning to control their brain waves [28], and to the amount of extrasensory perception they show [27, 29]. This material is somewhat technical for the general reader and I shall not detail it here; I refer my colleagues to the above sources, for this research has convinced me that self-reporting of the depth of a d-ASC is probably the best measure of depth currently available, certainly better than such parameters as drug dose.

A detailed example of self-report scaling of the depth of hypnosis is presented below. It illustrates the idea of depth and the way a common language is established between experiencer and investigator and provides some information about deep hypnosis and its possible transition into another d-ASC entirely.[2]

---

[1] The researcher planning work with self-report depth scales should note some other precautions outlined in my chapter in Fromm and Shor's book [114.]

[2] Much of the following account is drawn from my chapter in Fromm and Shor [114].

THE EXTENDED NORTH CAROLINA SCALE

The Extended North Carolina Scale has been used in a large number of experiments in my laboratory, primarily where experienced hypnotic subjects are used repeatedly in various experiments. It is similar to the North Carolina Scale [61, 63, 80] with the addition that subjects are told that there is really no "top" to the scale, that it is possible for them to go considerably deeper into hypnosis than the defined points. The exact instructions for the scale are:

> We are interested in the ways in which the intensity or depth of your hypnotic state may vary from time to time. It has been our experience that we can get quite accurate reports of hypnotic depth or intensity by teaching you a way of scaling it and getting your first impressions whenever we ask you about your hypnotic state.
>
> Basically, whenever I ask, "State?" a number will flash into your mind, and I want you to call it out to me right away. This number will represent the depth of your hypnotic state at the time. This number will flash into your mind and you'll call it out automatically, without any effort on your part. You won't have to think about what this number *should* be, or try to reason it out; you'll just call out the first number that comes to mind whenever I ask, "State?" If, of course, you then think the number is very inaccurate for some reason, I'd like you to tell me so, but people rarely feel the number is not accurate, even though they are sometimes surprised by it.
>
> Getting these depth numbers is very important, because every person is unique in his reactions while hypnotized. Some people react at different speeds than others; some react to a particular hypnotic experience by going deeper into hypnosis, others sometimes find the depth of their hypnotic state decreased by the same experience. Thus by getting these state reports from you every so often I can tell whether to go a little faster or slower, where to put emphasis in the suggestions I use to guide you, etc. These depth reports are not always what I expect, but it's more important for me to know where you really are than just assume you're there because I've been talking that way!
>
> Now here is the numerical scale you are to use. I'll give you various highlights that identify different degrees of hypnosis

on the scale, but you can report any point on the scale when asked for your state.

Zero is your normal, waking state.

From *1* to *12* is a state in which you feel relaxed and detached, more so as the numbers increase toward *12*; in this range you can experience such hypnotic phenomena as your arm rising up or feeling heavy or moved by a force.

When you reach a depth of *20* or greater you feel very definitely hypnotized, and you can experience great changes in your feeling of your body, such as your hand getting numb if I suggest it.

By the time you reach a depth of *25* or greater you can have strong inner experiences such as dreams or dreamlike experiences.

At a depth of *30* or greater you can temporarily forget everything that happened in the hypnosis if I suggest it. Many other experiences are possible at this depth and greater, such as regressing into the past and reliving some experience, experiencing tastes and smells I might suggest, or not experiencing real stimuli if I tell you not to sense them. There are hardly any hypnotic phenomena you can't experience at least fairly well, and most extremely well, at this depth. At *30* and beyond your mind is very quiet and still when I'm not directing your attention to something, and you probably don't hear anything except my voice or other sounds I might direct your attention to.

You have reached at least *30* in earlier sessions, and it is a sufficient depth to be able to learn all the skills needed in this experiment, but it is very likely that you will go deeper than *30* in these studies.

By the time you have reached a depth of *40* or greater you have reached a *very* deep hypnotic state in which your mind is perfectly still and at peace if I'm not directing your attention to something. Whatever I do suggest to you at this depth and beyond is *perfectly real*, a total, real, all-absorbing experience at the time, as real as anything in life. You can experience *anything* I suggest at *40* and beyond.

I'm not going to define the depths beyond this, for little is known about them; if you go deeper than *40*, and I hope you do, I'll ask you about the experiences that go with these greater depths so we may learn more about deep hypnosis.[3]

---

[3] In some of my earlier work with the North Carolina Scale, *50* was defined as a state so profound that the subject's mind became sluggish, but this definition was dropped here.

Remember now that increasing numbers up from zero indicate an increasing degree of hypnotic depth, from the starting point of ordinary wakefulness up to a state in which you can experience anything in hypnosis with complete realism. Your quick answers whenever I ask, "State?" will be my guide to the depth of your hypnotic state, and help me guide you more effectively. Always call out the *first* number that pops into your mind loudly and clearly. Whenever I ask, "State?" a number on the scale will instantly come into mind and you call it out.

These instructions for the scale are usually read to the subject after he is hypnotized, and he is asked whether he comprehends them. Also, the instructions are briefly reread to the subject every half-dozen hypnotic sessions or so to refresh his memory of them.

The overall attitude in working with subjects in my laboratory on a prolonged basis is to treat them as explorers or colleagues working with the investigators, rather than as subjects who are being manipulated for purposes alien to them.

WILLIAM: DEEP HYPNOSIS AND BEYOND

William, a twenty-year-old male college student, is extremely intelligent, academically successful, and well adjusted. His only previous experience with hypnosis was some brief work with a psychiatrist cousin to teach him how to relax. In a screening session with the Harvard Group Scale of Hypnotic Susceptibility, he scored 11 out of a possible 12. On a questionnaire he reported that he almost always recalled dreaming, that such dreaming was vivid and elaborate, and that he had kept a dream diary at times in the past. William reported that he had sleeptalked rather frequently as a child but did so only occasionally now. He had never sleepwalked. On individual testing with the Stanford Hypnotic Susceptibility Scale [145], he scored 12 out of a possible 12. He then had two training sessions, described elsewhere [136], designed to explore and maximize his hypnotic responsiveness in various areas. In the first of these special training sessions, he was taught the Extended North Carolina Scale. He then took Forms I and II of the Stanford Profile Scale of Hypnotic Susceptibility [146] and scored 26 and 27 on Forms I and II, respectively, out of a possible maximum of 27 on each.

Over the course of the next eight months, William participated in a variety of experiments in my laboratory, which served to further increase his hypnotic experience and make him well adapted to functioning in the laboratory setting; he had ten sessions of training for operant control of the EEG alpha rhythm [94], four experimental sessions in various aspects of hypnosis, and eight evening sessions in which he was hypnotized and given posthypnotic suggestions to carry out in his subsequent sleep in the laboratory, such as dreaming about a suggested topic [136], incorporating auditory stimuli into his dreams, and talking during his sleep. Thus, by the time William participated in the deep hypnosis experiment described here, he was familiar with the lab and had been hypnotized there 18 times. The deepest depth report given in any of these sessions was 60, and he usually gave reports between 40 and 50.

In the experimental session reported below, I explained to William that the purpose of the session was to find out what hypnosis meant to him personally. Specifically, he was informally interviewed for about an hour to determine what he usually experienced under hypnosis, other than his reactions to specifically suggested phenomena, and, if possible, what depth level, according to the Extended North Carolina Scale, he was at when he experienced these particular things. I then hypnotized him and at each 10-point interval on a depth continuum I asked William to remain at that depth and describe whatever it was he was experiencing. No particular probing was done except for phenomena already mentioned by William; the emphasis was on his individual hypnotic experience. William also agreed to attempt to go much deeper than he ever had gone before.

The session was quite rewarding. Although William had never gone beyond 60 before, he went to 90, reporting at 10-point intervals on the Extended North Carolina Scale, and also briefly went from 90 to 130. These values beyond 40 had not, of course, been defined by me: they were the result of his own definition. Or, according to William's report, they were simply numbers that came to his mind when he was asked for his state. Despite repeated questioning by me and despite the fact that the subject was quite verbal and extremely good at describing his experiences, his only comment on how he measured his hypnotic depth was that when I asked him for a state report a number popped into his mind, he said it, and that was it. He had no idea how these numbers were generated, nor did he "understand" them, but he assumed they meant something since he had been told in

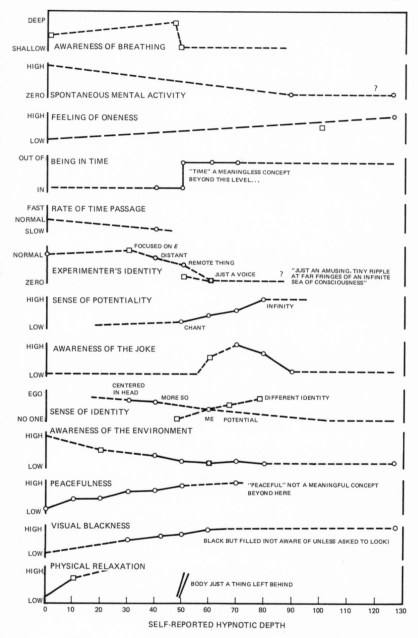

Figure 14-6.   Self-report of hypnotic experience.

the original Extended North Carolina Scale instructions that they would.

The results of both his preinduction interview about his general experience of hypnosis and the particular hypnotic session have been condensed into the graph shown in Figure 14–6 (Reprinted from C. Tart, *J. Transpersonal Psychol.*, 1970, 2, 27–40, by permission of the American Transpersonal Association).

William felt that his particular experience during this exploration was typical of his general experience with hypnosis. Various phenomena are plotted, each with its own ordinate of intensity. Circles indicate reports obtained during this particular hypnotic session, triangles are reports obtained during the interview preceding this session about all his hypnotic experiences to date. Not every phenomenon was assessed on every 10-point interval on the depth scale, so curves are shown as dotted where data points are missing. The following discussion indicates some of the phenomena of extremely deep hypnotic states and illustrates some of the theoretically possible relationships of effects to hypnotic depth discussed earlier.

The first effect, "physical relaxation," is not plotted beyond 20. According to William his relaxation increases markedly as he is hypnotized and quickly reaches a value of extremely relaxed. However, he reports that after a depth of 50 it does not make sense to ask him about physical relaxation because he is no longer identified with his body; his body is "just a thing, something I've left behind." One does not rate the relaxation of things.

The second experiential effect is of a "blackness" of the visual field. His visual field becomes quite black and formless as he goes into hypnosis. Nevertheless, it continues to become somehow blacker[4] in a roughly linear increase up to about 60. At this point he says the field continues to become blacker as he goes deeper, but it is in some sense "filled," there is a sense that there is some kind of form (s) filling his visual field even though he is not perceiving any particular forms. Beyond 60 he is not particularly aware of any visual sensation unless his attention is drawn to it by the experimenter.

---

[4] William insists that this progression is not going from gray to darker gray to black because his visual field is black to begin with, even though it gets "blacker." He recognizes the paradox of this statement, but considers it the best description he can give.

The third effect, a feeling of "peacefulness," also increases linearly from the beginning of the hypnotic state through approximately 60. William reports that he is extremely peaceful at this point. Beyond 60, he says, that peacefulness is not a meaningful concept, as was the case with physical relaxation. As described later in connection with the plots of William's identity, there is no longer a self to be peaceful or not peaceful beyond this point.

The fourth plotted effect is William's degree of "awareness of his environment," primarily the small sounds in the experimental room and the temperature and air currents in it. His awareness of the environment falls off rapidly and roughly linearly, and at about 50 reaches a point where he reports that he is not at all aware of the environment (with the exception of the hypnotist's voice). His awareness of the environment then stays at zero throughout the rest of the plotted continuum.

The fifth effect, labeled "sense of identity," is a little more complex. In the light stages of hypnosis William is fully aware of his ordinary identity and body image, but as he reaches a depth of about 30 he reports that his identity is "more centered in his head," is dominated by feelings of his head and his mind. This feeling continues to increase, plotted as a decrease of his ordinary identity, and then his ordinary identity continues to decrease until around 80 or 90 he feels that his ordinary identity is completely in abeyance: "William" no longer exists. On the other hand, starting from about 50 he begins to sense another identity, and this continually increased up through about 80, the last point plotted for this phenomenon. This identity is one of *potential*—he doesn't feel identified as any specific person or thing but only as the steadily increasing *potential to be anything or anyone.*

The sixth phenomenon, labeled "awareness of the joke," is even more difficult to explain. This phenomenon manifests at about 50, reaches a maximum at about 70, then fades in intensity and is completely gone at 90. The "joke" is that William should engage in strange activities like deep hypnosis, meditation, or taking drugs in order to alter his d-SoC; some "higher" aspect of his self is amused by all this activity, and William himself becomes aware of this amusement. Most people who have had several psychedelic drug sessions will recognize this as an effect that often occurs as the drug is beginning to take hold.

The next effect, labeled "sense of potentiality," starts off at a zero level but at around 50 first manifests itself as an awareness of some sort of chant or humming sound identified with the feeling that more and more experience is potentially available.[5] The specific form of the chant is lost but this sense of potentiality increases linearly from this point, until around 80 William feels that an infinite range of experience is potentially available, so this phenomenon levels off.

The eighth effect, "experimenter's identity," at first increases as the subject goes down to about 30 in hypnosis; that is, he becomes more and more aware of the experimenter. The experimenter then seems to become more and more distant and remote, and finally the experimenter possesses no identity, he is just a voice, and at the very deep levels he is "just an amusing, tiny ripple at the far fringes of an infinite sea of consciousness." There is a slight discrepancy at 50 between William's actual experience and his estimate of what he generally experienced.

The ninth effect, "rate of time passage," indicates that William feels time passing more and more slowly in a linear fashion as he goes down to about 40. This effect is no longer plotted, for as the next effect, "being in time," shows, William feels that time suddenly ceases to be a meaningful concept for him: at 50 he is no longer in time, his experiences are somehow timeless, they do not have a duration or a place, an order in the scheme of things.[6]

The next effect, labeled "feeling of oneness," increases linearly throughout the depth range plotted. Here William reports feeling more and more at one with the universe, although he does not ordinarily feel this. The effect is plotted as being very low in his ordinary waking state.

The next effect is "spontaneous mental activity," how much conscious mental activity goes on that is not related to specific suggestions by the hypnotist to do something or to experience something. In the ordinary waking state this is quite high: recall the Hindu metaphor that describes the ordinary mind as being like a sexually aroused and drunken monkey, constantly hopping

---

5 The chant William reported may be related to the Hindu concept of the sacred syllable *Om*, supposedly a basic sound of the universe that a man can "hear" as mind becomes more universally attuned [13].

6 Priestley [53] discusses such experiences of being in and out of time quite extensively.

about and chattering. This spontaneous mental activity goes steadily down until it reaches an essentially zero level at about 90 and stays there through the rest of the depth range plotted. I have discussed such a decrease in spontaneous mental activity for hypnosis elsewhere [78].

The final effect plotted is William's "awareness of his own breathing." He feels that his breathing tends to become steadily deeper as he becomes more deeply hypnotized, but at 50 there is a sudden change in his perceived breathing: it becomes extremely shallow, almost imperceptible, and stays that way through the rest of the hypnotic state. It is not known whether an objective measure of respiration would show any changes at this point; William did not actually stop breathing.

Considering the above phenomena as a report of a well-trained observer, we can make a number of comments. First it should be clear that William has an exceptional ability for hypnosis; he appears to have gone far deeper than the usual range of phenomena conventionally labeled "deep hypnosis." As the Extended North Carolina Scale was defined for him, 30 was the level ordinarily defined as deep hypnosis (amnesia, positive and negative hallucinations as defining phenomena), and 40 would be the approximate limit reported by many of the highly hypnotizable subjects I have worked with in the laboratory. Yet William reported a maximum depth of 130 which, if one assumes reasonable validity and linearity for the scale, may be one of the deepest hypnotic states on record. This ability to go so deep may partially stem from his previous experience with meditation and psychedelic drugs. Further, William is exceptionally verbal and able to describe his experiences well. In the past, Erickson's [33, pp. 70–112] exceptionally good subjects have reached a "stuporous" state, which may have reflected an inability to conceptualize and verbalize their experiences. Thus William's hypnotic experiences are illustrative of a potential range of hypnotic phenomena, but are not typical.

Second, the expected nonlinearity and noncontinuity of possible effects (and subsystem operation, insofar as effects may be taken as indicators of subsystem operation) are apparent in William's data. In the ordinary range of light to deep hypnosis (roughly 0–40), most effects are linear, but "experimenter's identity" is curvilinear, and "physical relaxation" is noncontinuous, and becomes a meaningless variable halfway through this range.

Considering the entire depth range plotted, some effects show step functions ("awareness of breathing," "being in time"), rapid increases and decreases from zero ("awareness of the joke"), plateauing after an initial linear increase or decrease ("experimenter's identity," "sense of potentiality," "awareness of the environment," "visual blackness"), or disappearance by becoming meaningless ("peacefulness," "physical relaxation"). If, in the course of investigation, one used the intensity of *one* phenomenon as an index of hypnotic depth, confusing results would be obtained if it were not linear and continuous. The value of a multiphenomenal approach is apparent.

Third, the large number of step changes or fairly rapid changes in the 50–70 range raises the question, in view of the definition of d-SoCs, of whether we are still dealing with "deep hypnosis" beyond the depth of approximately 70. These rapid changes may represent a transition from the gestalt configuration we call hypnosis to a new configuration, a new d-SoC.

This research with William is a prototype of the research strategy recommended in Chapter 13 for working with d-SoCs—detailed mapping of a single individual's experiential space to see if certain clusterings emerge that constitute d-SoCs. This particular example is an imperfect prototype, however, because the systems approach was not clear in my mind when I did this research with William. I was expecting continuity of experience in one state, the hypnotic state, so I did not sample enough data points to determine whether there was a clear discontinuity showing William transiting from one d-SoC to another. Thus the changes plotted in Figure 14–6 are a rough sort of plot, consistent with the systems approach, but not done precisely enough.

Note also that there is little mapping of the very light region of hypnosis and consequently no data on the transition from the ordinary d-SoC to hypnosis.

At its maximum level (assuming that the 70–130 range represents depth continuum for the new d-SoC), the state has the following phenomenological characteristics: (1) no awareness of the physical body; (2) no awareness of any discrete "thing" or sensation, but only awareness of a flux of potentiality; (3) no awareness of the real world environment, with the one exception of the (depersonalized) voice of the experimenter as "an amusing tiny ripple at the far fringes of an infinite sea of consciousness"; (4) a sense of being beyond, outside of time; and (5) a sense of the identity "William" being totally in abeyance, and identity being simply potentiality.

States of this type have not been dealt with in Western scientific literature to any great extent, but sound similar to Eastern descriptions of consciousness of the Void, a d-SoC in which time, space, and ego are supposedly transcended, leaving pure awareness of the primal nothingness from which all manifested creation comes [22, 51]. Writers who have described the Void insist that the experience cannot be described in words, so the above description and comparison with William's experience is rough, to say the least. Thus William's data are not only of interest in terms of hypnotic depth and the transition from one d-SoC to another, but raise the possibility of using hypnotic states to induce and/or model mystical states.[7]

The resemblance between William's description of his state and classic descriptions of Void consciousness suggests the question, Who is reporting to me, the experimenter? If William's personality is in abeyance, if he has no awareness of his physical body, who is talking?

The concept of dissociation may supply an answer. Some structures/subsystems may form a (semi-) independent entity from the rest of the system, so that more than one d-SoC can exist simultaneously in one individual. Thus, some aspects of William are structured into a d-SoC I loosely call Void consciousness; other aspects are structured/patterned into a kind of consciousness that can (at least partially) observe what the Void consciousness part is doing, can understand my questions, and can reply to me. Is this the Observer discussed in Chapter 11, or a dissociated series of subsystems forming a d-SoC, or what? Grappling with this sort of question forces confrontation with some basic issues about the nature of consciousness.

William's data illustrate some of the practical aspects of studying the depth of a d-SoC, particularly hypnosis. Using the individual subject as a unit, a set of interrelationships of various phenomena with respect to hypnotic depth has been found; self-reported depth has ordered observed phenomena in a useful and theoretically important manner. Further research will study this same sort of procedure in other subjects, repeat sessions with some

---

[7] Aaronson [1] has reported direct hypnotic induction of the Void experience through specific suggestion.

subjects to study consistency, and make initial intersubject comparisons to determine which depth-phenomenology relationships are general and which represent idiosyncratic qualities of subjects. General relationships of phenomena with depth may be found and/or several classes of subjects may be found and/or several d-SoCs may be identified that have in the past all been indiscriminately termed "hypnosis."

Finally, it should be stressed that the case of William is presented to illustrate the *potential* of self-reporting of hypnotic depth. The effects of subtle factors in my laboratory, demand characteristics, and William's uniqueness must be assessed in the course of replication and extension of this work by others to establish how much of this potential holds up and becomes practically and theoretically useful.

15.

State-Specific Communication

✿✿✿

"According to the general opinion of the uninitiated,"
mused Nasrudin, as he walked along the road, "dervishes are
mad. According to the sages, however, they are the true masters
of the world. I would like to test one, and myself, to make
sure."

Then he saw a tall figure, robed like an Akldan dervish—
reputed to be exceptionally enlightened men—coming towards
him.

"Friend," said the Mulla, "I want to perform an experiment, to test your powers of psychic penetration, and also my
sanity."

"Proceed," said the Akldan.

Nasrudin made a sudden sweeping motion with his arm,
then clenched his fist. "What have I in my hand?"

"A horse, chariot, and driver," said the Akldan immediately.

"That's no real test," —Nasrudin was petulant—"because you
saw me pick them up." [57, p. 79]

In d-ASCs people often claim to have exceptional and important insights about themselves or about the nature of the world
that they are unable to communicate to the rest of us owing to
the ineffability of the experience, the inadequacy of language, or
the "lowness" of the ordinary d-SoC that makes us incapable of
understanding "higher" things. The general scientific opinion,
however, is that communicative ability deteriorates in various d-

ASCs, such as drug-induced or mystical states. This opinion is usually based on the observation that the experimenter/observer has difficulty understanding what the person in the d-ASC is talking about; his comments make no sense by ordinary consensus reality standards.

I suspect that sometimes this judgment is based on fear, on the semiconscious recognition that what a person in a d-ASC is saying may be all too true, but somehow unacceptable. I recall the time when a friend of mine was having a psychotic breakdown: it struck me that half the things he said were clearly crazy, in the sense of being unrelated to the social situation around him and reflecting only his own internal processes, but the other half of the things he said were such penetrating, often unflattering, observations about what other people were really feeling and doing that they were threatening to most of us. Bennett [5] makes the same observation, noting that after his wife had a cerebral hemorrhage she seemed to lose all the usual social inhibitions and said directly what she felt. This was extremely threatening to most people and was regarded as senile dementia or insanity; yet to a few who were not personally threatened by her observations, her comments were extremely penetrating. If you label someone as crazy, you need not listen to him.

How can we decide in an objective fashion whether someone in a d-ASC is able to communicate more or less clearly? Perhaps this is the wrong question. I propose that, for at least some d-ASCs, there are significant alterations in the manner in which a person communicates. Changes in various subsystems, especially the Evaluation and Decision-Making subsystem, produce a new logic, so that the grammar of communication, including the nonverbal aspects of expression, constitutes a different *kind* of language, one that may be just as effective in communicating with someone else *in the same d-ASC* as ordinary communication is in the ordinary d-SoC. We must consider this possibility in an objective manner, but be careful not implicitly to equate "objectivity" with the standards of only one d-SoC.

For a given d-ASC, then, how can we determine whether there is deterioration, improvement, or simply alteration in communication ability, or a complex combination of all three? More specifically, we must ask this question with respect to communication *across* d-SoCs—about communication between two persons in different d-SoCs as well as about communication between two persons in the same d-SoC. In regard to the last two situations, only theorizing is possible, for all published research deals only with the restricted situation of an experimental subject in a d-ASC and the experimenter/observer in his ordinary d-SoC.

If the grammar of communication is altered in a d-ASC, then clearly a judge in an ordinary d-SoC cannot distinguish between the hypotheses of deterioration and of alteration in the communicative style of a person in a d-ASC. The specialized argot of a subcultural group may sound, to an outside observer, like the talk of schizophrenics. A person familiar with that subculture, on the other hand, finds the communications exchanged among the group perfectly meaningful, perhaps extraordinarily rich. In this example, contextual clues may make the outsider suspect this is a subcultural argot, but if the group is in an institutional setting and is labeled "schizophrenic," he may readily conclude that its speech has indeed deteriorated, without bothering to study the matter further.

To judge adequately whether communicative patterns have altered (and possibly improved) rather than deteriorated, the judge must function in the same d-ASC as the communicator. Experienced marijuana smokers, for example, claim they can subtly communicate all sorts of things—especially humor—to each other while intoxicated [105]. The degree to which an observer in a different d-SoC—for example, his ordinary d-SoC— can understand the same communication is interesting, but not a valid measure of the adequacy of the communication within the d-ASC. And, as explained in earlier chapters, identification of a person as being in a particular d-ASC must be based not just on the fact that he has undergone an induction procedure (for example, taken a drug) but on actual mapping of his location in experiential space.

Suppose the judge is in the same d-ASC as the subjects in the study, and reports that their communication is rich and meaningful, not at all deteriorated. How do we know that the judge's mental processes themselves are not deteriorated and that he is not just enjoying the *illusion* of understanding, rather than prosaically judging the subjects' communication? The question leads to general problems of measuring the accuracy and adequacy of communication, an area I know little about. All the work in this area has been done with respect to ordinary d-SoC communication, but I believe the techniques can be applied to this question of adequacy of communication in d-ASCs. I shall try to show this by describing one technique for rating ordinary d-SoC communication with which I am familiar that could be readily applied to judging d-ASC communication.

It is the Cloze technique [140]. It measures, simultaneously, how well a written or verbal communication is both phrased (encoded) and how well it is understood by a receiver or judge. From a written message or a transcript of a spoken message, every fifth word is deleted. Judges then guess what the deleted words are, and the total number of words correct is a measure of the accuracy and meaningfulness of the communication. If a judge understands the communicator well, he can fill in a high proportion of the words correctly; if he does not understand him well he gets very few correct. This technique works because ordinary language is fairly redundant, so the overall context of the message allows excellent guesses about missing words. This technique can be applied to communications between subjects as judged both by a judge in the same d-ASC, thus testing adequacy of communication within the d-ASC, and by a judge in a different d-SoC, thus measuring transfer across states. We think of the different d-SoC as being the ordinary state, but other d-SoCs are possible, and we can eventually use this technique for a cross-comparison across all d-SoCs we know of and produce important information about both communication and the nature of various d-SoCs.

Two problems arise in applying the Cloze technique to investigating communications in d-ASCs. One is that a particular d-ASC may be associated with a switch to more nonverbal components of communication. This difficulty could probably be remedied by making videotapes of the procedure, and systematically deleting every fifth second, and letting the judges fill in the gap. The second problem is that communication in a d-ASC may be as adequate, but less redundant, a circumstance that would artificially lower the scores on the Cloze test without adequately testing the communication. I leave this problem as a challenge to others.

Another important methodological factor is the degree of adaptation to functioning in a particular d-ASC. I am sure techniques of the Cloze type would show deterioration in communication within d-ASCs for subjects who are relatively naive in functioning in those d-ASCs. Subjects have to adapt to the novelty of a d-ASC; they may even need specific practice in learning to communicate within it. The potential for an altered style of communication, state-specific communication, may be present and need to be developed, rather than being available immediately upon entering the d-ASC. I do not imply simply that people learn to compensate for the deterioration associated with a d-ASC, but rather that they learn the altered style of communication inherent in or more natural to that particular d-ASC.

In Chapter 16, in which I propose the creation of state-specific sciences, I assume that communication within some d-ASCs is adequate: this is a necessary foundation for the creation of state-specific sciences. In making this assumption, I depend primarily on experiential observations by people in d-ASCs. Objective verification with the Cloze technique or similar techniques is a necessary underpinning for this. As state-specific sciences are developed, on the other hand, techniques for evaluating the adequacy of communication may be developed within particular states that can be agreed upon as "scientific" techniques within that state, even though they do not necessarily make sense in the ordinary d-SoC.

Another interesting question concerns transfer of communicative ability after the termination of a d-ASC to the ordinary (or any other) d-SoC. Experienced marijuana smokers, for example, claim that they can understand a subject intoxicated on marijuana even when they are not intoxicated themselves because of partial transfer of state-specific knowledge to the ordinary d-SoC. We need to study the validity of this phenomenon.

In earlier chapters I avoid talking about "higher" states of consciousness, as the first job of science is description, not evaluation. Here, however, I want to speculate on what one relatively objective definition of the adjective *higher*, applied to a d-SoC, could mean with respect to communication. If we consider that understanding many communications from other people is more valuable than understanding few of their communications, then a higher d-SoC is one in which communications from a variety of d-ASCs are adequately understood; a lower d-SoC is one in which understanding is limited, perhaps to the particular lower d-SoC itself.

16.

State-Specific Sciences

✿✿✿

In previous chapters I argue that the ordinary (or any) d-SoC is a semi*arbitrary* construction, a specialized tool, useful for some things but not for others. A consequence of this is that science is specialized, because it is a one-d-SoC science. *As a method of learning* science has been applied only in a limited way because it has been used in only one of many possible d-SoCs. This chapter works out the consequences of this idea in detail and proposes that if we are to understand d-ASCs adequately, as well as ourselves as human beings, we must develop *state-specific sciences.*[1]

Disaffection with Science

Blackburn [7] recently noted that many of our most talented young people are "turned off" from science: as a solution, he proposed that we recognize the validity of a more sensuous-intuitive approach to nature, treating it as complementary to the classical intellectual approach.

I have seen the same rejection of science by many of the brightest students in California, and the problem is indeed seri-

---

1 I originally presented the proposal for state-specific sciences in an article in *Science* [119.] Most of it is reprinted here with the permission of the American Association for the Advancement of Science. I have updated the text and terminology to fit the rest of this book.

ous. Blackburn's analysis is valid, but not deep enough. A more fundamental source of alienation is the widespread experience of d-ASCs by the young, coupled with the almost total rejection by the scientific establishment of the knowledge gained during the experiencing of d-ASCs. Blackburn himself exemplifies this rejection when he says: "Perhaps science has much to learn along this line from the disciplines, *as distinct from the content,* of Oriental religions" (my italics).

To illustrate, a 1971 Gallup poll [41] indicated that approximately half of American college students have tried marijuana and that a large number of them use it fairly regularly. They do this at the risk of having their careers ruined and going to jail for several years. Why? Conventional research on the nature of marijuana intoxication tells us that the primary effects are a slight increase in heart rate, reddening of the eyes, some difficulty with memory, and small decrements in performance on complex psychomotor tests.

Would you risk going to jail to experience these?

A young marijuana smoker who hears a scientist or physician refer to these findings as the basic nature of marijuana intoxication will simply sneer and have his antiscientific attitude further reinforced. It is clear to him that the scientist has no real understanding of what marijuana intoxication is all about (see [105] for a comprehensive description of this d-ASC).

More formally, an increasingly significant number of people are experimenting with d-ASCs in themselves and finding the experiences thus gained of extreme importance in their philosophy and style of life. The conflict between experiences in these d-ASCs and the attitudes and intellectual-emotional systems that have evolved in the ordinary d-SoC is a major factor behind the increased alienation of many people from conventional science. Experiences of ecstasy, mystical union, other dimensions, rapture, beauty, space-and-time transcendence, and transpersonal knowledge, all common in d-ASCs, are simply not treated adequately in conventional scientific approaches. These experiences will not go away if we crack down more on psychedelic drugs, for immense numbers of people now practice various nondrug techniques for producing d-ASCs, such as meditation [39] and yoga.

My purpose here is to show that it is possible to investigate and work with the important phenomena of d-ASCs in a manner that is perfectly compatible with the essence of scientific method. The conflict discussed above is not necessary.

States of Consciousness

To review briefly, a d-ASC is defined as a qualitative alteration in the overall pattern of mental functioning, such that the experiencer feels his consciousness is radically different from the way it functions ordinarily. A d-SoC is defined not in terms of any particular content of consciousness or specific behavior or physiological change, but in terms of the overall patterning of psychological functioning.

An analogy with computer functioning can clarify this definition. A computer has a complex program of many subroutines. If we reprogram it quite differently, the same sorts of input data may be handled in quite different ways; we can predict little from our knowledge of the old program about the effects of varying the input, even though old and new programs have some subroutines in common. The new program with its input-output interactions must be studied in and of itself. A d-ASC is analogous to a temporary change in the program of a computer.

The d-ASCs experienced by almost all ordinary people are dreaming states and the hypnagogic and hypnopompic states, the transitional states between sleeping and waking. Many others experience another d-ASC, alcohol intoxication.

The relatively new (to our culture) d-ASCs that are now having such an impact are those produced by marijuana, more powerful psychedelic drugs such as LSD, meditative states, so-called possession states, and autohypnotic states.[2]

States of Consciousness and Paradigms

It is useful to compare this concept of a d-SoC, a qualitatively distinct organization of the pattern of mental functioning, with Kuhn's [32] concept of paradigms in science. A paradigm is an intellectual achievement that underlies normal science and attracts and guides the work of an enduring number of adherents in their scientific activity. It is a "super" theory, a formulation wide enough in scope to affect the organization of most or all of the

---

[2] Note that a d-SoC is defined by the stable parameters of the *pattern* that constitute it, not by the particular technique of inducing that pattern.

major known phenomena of its field. Yet it is sufficiently open-ended that there still remain important problems to be solved within that framework. Examples of important paradigms in the history of science have been Copernican astronomy and Newtonian dynamics.

Because of their tremendous success, paradigms undergo a change which, in principle, ordinary scientific theories do not undergo. An ordinary scientific theory is always subject to further questioning and testing as it is extended. A paradigm becomes an *implicit* framework for most scientists working within it; it is the natural way of looking at things and doing things. It does not seriously occur to the adherents of a paradigm to question it (we may ignore, for the moment, the occurrence of scientific revolutions). Theories become referred to as *laws:* people talk of the law of gravity, not the theory of gravity, for example.

A paradigm serves to concentrate the attention of a researcher on sensible problem areas and to prevent him from wasting his time on what might be trivia. On the other hand, by implicitly defining some lines of research as trivial or nonsensical, a paradigm acts as a blinder. Kuhn has discussed this blinding function as a key factor in the lack of effective communications during paradigm clashes.

The concept of a paradigm and a d-SoC are quite similar. Both constitute complex, interlocking sets of rules and theories that enable a person to interact with and interpret experiences within an environment. In both cases, the rules are largely implicit. They are not recognized as tentative working hypotheses; they operate automatically and the person feels he is doing the obvious or natural thing.

Paradigm Clash Between Straight and Hip

Human beings become emotionally attached to the things that give them success and pleasure, and a scientist making important progress within a particular paradigm becomes emotionally attached to it. When data that make no sense in terms of the (implicit) paradigm are brought to his attention, the usual result is not a reevaluation of the paradigm, but a rejection or misperception of the data. This rejection seems rational to others sharing that paradigm and irrational or rationalizing to those committed to a different paradigm.

The conflict now existing between those who have experienced certain d-ASCs (whose ranks include many young scientists) and those who have not is a paradigmatic conflict. For example, a subject takes LSD and tells his investigator, "You and I, we are all one, there are no separate selves." The investigator reports that his subject showed a "confused sense of identity and distorted thinking process." The subject is reporting what is obvious to him; the investigator is reporting what is obvious to him. The investigator's (implicit) paradigm, based on his scientific training, his cultural background, and his normal d-SoC, indicates that a literal interpretation of the subject's statement cannot be true and therefore the statement must be interpreted as mental dysfunction on the part of the subject. The subject, his paradigms radically changed for the moment by being in a d-ASC, not only reports what is obviously true to him, but perceives the investigator as showing mental dysfunction because he is incapable of perceiving the obvious!

Historically, paradigm clashes have been characterized by bitter emotional antagonisms and total rejection of the opponent. Currently we see the same sort of process: the respectable psychiatrist, who would not take any of those "psychotomimetic" drugs himself or experience that crazy meditation process, carries out research to show that drug-takers and those who practice meditation are escapists. The drug-taker or meditator views the same investigator as narrow-minded, prejudiced, and repressive, and as a result drops out of the university. Communication between the two factions is almost nil.

Must the experiencers of d-ASCs continue to see the scientists as concentrating on the irrelevant, and scientists see the experiencers as confused[3] or mentally ill? Or can science deal adequately with the experiences of these people? The thesis I present is that we can deal with the important aspects of d-ASCs using the essence of scientific method, even though a variety of nonessentials, unfortunately identified with current science, hinder such an effort.

---

[3] States of confusion and impaired functioning may certainly be aspects of some drug-induced d-ASCs for some people, but are not of primary interest here.

The Nature of Knowledge

Science deals with knowledge. Knowledge may be defined as an immediately given experiential feeling of congruence between two different kinds of experience, a matching. One set of experiences may be regarded as perceptions of the external world, of others, of oneself; the second set may be regarded as a theory, a scheme, a system of understanding. The feeling of congruence is something immediately given in experience, although many refinements have been worked out for judging degrees of congruence.

All knowledge, then, is basically experiential knowledge. Even my knowledge of the physical world can be reduced to this: given certain sets of experiences, which I (by assumption) attribute to activation of my sensory apparatus by the external world, I can compare them with purely internal experiences (memories, previous knowledge) and predict with a high degree of reliability other kinds of experiences, which I again attribute to the external world.

Because science has been highly successful in dealing with the physical world, it has been historically associated with a philosophy of physicalism, the belief that reality is all reducible to certain kinds of physical entities. The vast majority of phenomena of d-ASCs have no known physical manifestations: thus to physicalistic philosophy they are epiphenomena, not worthy of study. But since science deals with knowledge, it need not restrict itself to physical kinds of knowledge.

The Essence of Scientific Method

As satisfying as the *feeling* of knowing can be, we are often wrong: what seems like congruence at first, later does not match or has no generality. Man has learned that his reasoning is often faulty, his observations often incomplete or mistaken, and that emotional or other nonconscious factors can seriously distort both reasoning and observational processes. His reliance on authorities, "rationality," or "elegance," are no sure criteria for achieving truth. The development of scientific method may be seen as a determined effort to systematize the process of acquiring knowledge in such a way as to minimize the pitfalls of observation and reasoning.

There are four basic rules of scientific method to which an

investigator is committed: (1) good observation, (2) the public nature of observation, (3) the necessity to theorize logically, and (4) the testing of theory by observable consequences. These constitute the scientific enterprise. I consider below the wider application of each rule to d-ASCs and indicate how unnecessary physicalistic restrictions may be dropped. I also show that all these commitments or rules can be accommodated in the development of state-specific sciences.

OBSERVATION

The scientist is committed to observe as well as possible the phenomena of interest and to search constantly for better ways of making these observations. But his paradigmatic commitments, his d-SoCs, make him likely to observe certain parts of reality and to ignore or observe with error certain other parts of it.

Many of the most important phenomena of d-ASCs have been observed poorly or not at all because of the physicalistic labeling of them as epiphenomena, so that they have been called "subjective," "ephemeral," "unreliable," or "unscientific." Observations of internal processes are probably much more difficult than those of external physical processes, because of their inherently greater complexity. The essence of science, however, is to observe what there is to be observed, whether or not it is difficult.

Furthermore, most of what is known about the phenomena of d-ASCs has been obtained from untrained people, almost none of whom have shared the scientist's commitment to constantly re-examine observations in greater and greater detail. This does not imply that internal phenomena are inherently unobservable or unstable; we are comparing the first observations of internal phenomena with observations of physical sciences that have undergone centuries of refinement.

We must consider one other problem of observation. One of the traditional idols of science, the "detached observer," has no place in dealing with many internal phenomena of d-SoCs. Not only are the observer's perceptions selective, he may also affect the things he observes. We must try to understand the characteristics of each individual observer in order to compensate for them.

A recognition of the unreality of the detached observer in the psychological sciences is becoming widespread, under the topics of experimenter bias [55] and demand characteristics [45]. A similar recognition long ago occurred in physics when it was realized that the observed was altered by the process of observation at subatomic levels. When we deal with d-ASCs where the observer is the experiencer of the d-ASC, this factor is of paramount importance. Not knowing the characteristics of the observer can also confound the process of consensual validation.

PUBLIC NATURE OF OBSERVATION

Observations must be public in that they must be replicable by any *properly trained* observer. The *experienced* conditions that led to the report of certain experiences must be described in sufficient detail that others can duplicate them and consequently have *experiences* that meet criteria of identicality. That someone else may set up similar conditions but not have the same experiences proves that the original investigator gave an incorrect description of the conditions and observations, or that he was not aware of certain essential aspects of the conditions.

The physicalistic accretion to this rule of consensual validation is that, physical data being the only "real" data, internal phenomena must be reduced to physiological or behavioral data to become reliable or they will be ignored entirely. I believe most physical observations to be much more readily replicable by any trained observer because they are inherently simpler phenomena than internal ones. In principle, however, consensual validation of internal phenomena by a trained observer is possible.

The emphasis on public observations in science has had a misleading quality insofar as it implies that any intelligent man can replicate a scientist's observations. This may have been true early in the history of science, but nowadays only the trained observer can replicate many observations. I cannot go into a modern physicist's laboratory and confirm his observations. Indeed, his talk of what he has found in his experiments (physicists seem to talk about innumerable invisible entities) would probably seem mystical to me, just as descriptions of internal states sound mystical to those with a background in the physical sciences.[4]

---

[4] The degree to which a science can seem incomprehensible, even ridiculous, to someone not specializing in it never ceases to astound me. I have always thought I had a good general background in science. So much so that, for

Given the high complexity of the phenomena associated with d-ASCs, the need for replication by trained observers is exceptionally important. Since it generally takes four to ten years of intensive training to produce a scientist in any of the conventional disciplines, we should not be surprised that there has been little reliability of observations by untrained observers of d-ASC phenomena.

Further, for the state-specific sciences I propose, we cannot specify the requirements that constitute adequate training. These can only be determined after considerable trial and error. We should also recognize that very few people may complete the training successfully. Some people do not have the necessary innate characteristics to become physicists, and some probably do not have the innate characteristics to become scientific investigators of meditative states.

Public observation, then, always refers to a limited, specially trained public. It is only by basic agreement among those specially trained people that data become accepted as a foundation for the development of a science. That laymen cannot replicate the observations is of little relevance.

A second problem in consensual validation arises from a phenomenon predicted by my concept of d-ASCs, but not yet empirically investigated: *state-specific communication*. Given that a d-ASC is an overall qualitative and quantitative shift in the complex functioning of consciousness, producing new logics and perceptions (which constitute a paradigm shift), it is quite reasonable to hypothesize that communication may take a different pattern. For two observers, both of whom, we assume, are fluent in communicating with each other in a given d-SoC, communication about some new observations may seem adequate or may be improved or deteriorated in specific ways. To an outside observer, an observer in a different d-SoC, the communication between these two observers may seem deteriorated.

Practically all investigations of communication by persons in d-

example, I was able to appreciate some of the in-group humor in an article I read in *Science* some years ago about *quarks*. Quarks? Yes, quarks. To me, the article was obviously a put-on, about how physicists were hunting for particles no one had ever seen, called quarks. Much of the humor was too technical for me to understand, but I was pleased that a staid journal like *Science* could unbend enough to publish humor. Of course, it was not humor. Physicists are very serious about quarks, even though no one has ever detected one with certainty (at least not yet, despite an awful lot of research).

ASCs have resulted in reports of deterioration of communication abilities. In designing their studies, however, these investigators have not taken into account the fact that the pattern of communication may have changed. If I am listening to two people speaking in English, and they suddenly begin to intersperse words and phrases in Polish, I, as an outside (non-Polish-speaking) observer, note a gross deterioration in communication. Adequacy of communication between people in the same d-SoC and across d-SoCs must be empirically determined. This is discussed in Chapter 15.

Thus consensual validation may be restricted by the fact that only observers in the same d-ASC are able to communicate adequately to each other. Someone in a different d-SoC, say normal consciousness, might find their communication incomprehensible.[5]

THEORIZING

A scientist may theorize about his observations as much as he wishes, but the theory he develops must consistently account for all he has observed and should have a logical structure that other scientists can comprehend (but not necessarily accept).

The requirement to theorize logically and consistently with the data is not as simple as it looks, however. Any logic consists of a basic set of assumptions and a set of rules for manipulating information based on these assumptions. Change the assumptions, or change the rules, and there may be entirely different outcomes from the same data. A paradigm, too, is a logic: it has certain assumptions and rules for working within these assumptions. By changing the paradigm, altering the d-SoC, the nature of theory-building may change radically. Thus a person in d-SoC 2 might come to very different conclusions about the nature of the same events that he observed in d-SoC 1. An investigator in d-SoC 1 can comment on the comprehensibility of the second person's ideas from the point of view (paradigm) of d-SoC 1, but can say nothing about their inherent validity. A scientist who could enter either d-SoC 1 or d-SoC 2, however, could evaluate the comprehensibility of the other's theory and the adherence of

---

[5] A state-specific scientist might find his own work somewhat incomprehensible when he was not in his work d-ASC because of the phenomenon of *state-specific memory*. Not enough of his work would transfer to his ordinary d-SoC to make it comprehensible, even though it would again make perfect sense when he was again in the d-ASC in which he did his scientific work.

that theory to the rules and logic of d-SoC 2. Thus, scientists trained to work in the same d-SoC can check on the logical validity of each other's theorizing. So we can have inter-observer validation of the state-specific logic underlying theorizing in various d-SoCs.

OBSERVABLE CONSEQUENCES

Any theory a scientist develops must have observable consequences, it must be possible to make predictions that can be verified by observation. If such verification is not obtained, the theory must be considered invalid, regardless of its elegance, logic or other appeal.

Ordinarily we think of *empirical validation,* validation in terms of testable consequences that produce physical effects, but this is misleading. Any effect, whether interpreted as physical or nonphysical, is ultimately an experience in the observer's mind. All that is essentially required to validate a theory is that it predict that when a certain experience (observed condition) has occurred, another (predicted) kind of experience will follow, under specified experiential conditions. Thus a perfectly scientific theory may be based on data that have no physical existence.

State-Specific Sciences

We tend to envision the practice of science like this: centered around interest in some particular range of subject matter, a small number of highly selected, talented, and rigorously trained people spend considerable time making detailed observations on the subject matter of interest. They may or may not have special places (laboratories) or instruments or methods to assist them in making finer observations. They speak to one another in a special language that they feel conveys precisely the important facts of their field. Using this language, they confirm and extend each other's knowledge of certain data basic to the field. They theorize about their basic data and construct elaborate systems. They validate these by recourse to further observation. These trained people all have a long-term commitment to the constant refinement of observation and extension of theory. Their activity is frequently incomprehensible to laymen.

This general description is equally applicable to a variety of sciences or areas that could become sciences, whether we called such areas biology, physics, chemistry, psychology, understanding of mystical states, or drug-induced enhancement of cognitive processes. The particulars of research look different, but the basic scientific method is the same.

I propose the creation of various state-specific sciences. If such sciences can be created we will have a group of highly skilled, dedicated, and trained practitioners able to achieve certain d-SoCs, and able to agree with one another that they have attained a common state. While in that d-SoC, they can investigate other areas of interest—totally internal phenomena of that given state, the interaction of that state with external physical reality, or people in other d-SoCs.

The fact that the experimenter can function skillfully in the d-SoC itself for a state-specific science does not necessarily mean he must always be the subject. While he may often be the subject, observer, and experimenter simultaneously, it is quite possible for him to collect data from experimental manipulations of other subjects in the d-SoC, and either be in that d-SoC himself at the time of data collection or be in that d-SoC himself for data reduction and theorizing.

Examples of some observations made and theorizing done by a scientist in a specific d-ASC would illustrate the nature of a proposed state-specific science. But this is not possible because no state-specific sciences have yet been established.[6] Also, any example that would make good sense to the readers of this chapter (who are, presumably, all in an ordinary d-SoC) would not really illustrate the uniqueness of a state-specific science. If it did make sense, it would be an example of a problem that could be approached adequately from both the d-ASC and our ordinary d-SoC, and thus it would be too easy to see the entire problem in terms of accepted scientific procedures for our ordinary d-SoC and miss the point about the necessity for developing state-specific sciences.

State-Specific Sciences and Religion

Some aspects of organized religion appear to resemble state-specific sciences. There are techniques that allow the believer to

---

[6] "Ordinary consciousness science" is not a good example of a pure state-specific science because many important discoveries have occurred during d-ASCs such as reverie, dreaming, and meditative states.

enter a d-ASC and then have religious experiences in that d-ASC that are proof of his religious belief. People who have had such experiences usually describe them as *ineffable,* not fully comprehensible in an ordinary d-SoC. Conversions at revival meetings are the most common examples of religious experiences occurring in d-ASCs induced by an intensely emotional atmosphere.

The esoteric training systems of some religions seem to have even more resemblance to state-specific sciences. Often there are devoted specialists, complex techniques, and repeated experiencing of the d-ASCs in order to further religious knowledge.

Nevertheless, the proposed state-specific sciences are not simply religion in a new guise. The use of d-ASCs in religion *may* involve the kind of commitment to searching for truth that is needed for developing a state-specific science, but practically all the religions we know can mainly be defined as state-specific *technologies,* operated in the service of a priori belief systems. The experiencers of d-ASCs in most religious contexts have already been thoroughly indoctrinated in a particular belief system. This belief system may then mold the content of the d-ASCs to create specific experiences that reinforce or validate the belief system.

The crucial distinction between a religion utilizing d-ASCs and a state-specific science is the commitment of the scientist to reexamine constantly his own belief system and to question the "obvious," in spite of its intellectual or emotional appeal to him. Investigators of d-ASCs will certainly encounter an immense variety of phenomena labeled religious experience or mystical revelation during the development of state-specific sciences, but they must remain committed to examining these phenomena more carefully, sharing their observations and techniques with colleagues, and subjecting the beliefs (hypotheses, theories) that result from such experiences to the requirement of leading to testable predictions. In practice, because we are aware of the immense emotional power of mystical experiences, this is a difficult task, but it is one that must be undertaken by disciplined investigators if we are to understand various d-ASCs.[7]

---

[7] The idea of state-specific knowledge, introduced earlier, casts some light on an aspect of organized religions, the "dryness" of theology. Consider the feeling so many, both inside and outside organized religion, have had, that theology is intellectual hair-splitting, an activity irrelevant to what religion is all about. I believe this is true in many cases, and the reason is that the essence of much religion is state-specific knowledge, knowledge that can really be known only in a d-ASC. The original founders of the religion

Relationship Between State-Specific Sciences

Any (state-specific) science may be considered as consisting of two parts: observations and theories. The observations are what can be experienced relatively directly; the theories are the *inferences* about what nonobservable factors account for the observations. For example, the phenomenon of synesthesia (seeing colors as a result of hearing sounds) is a theoretical proposition for me in my ordinary d-SoC: I do not experience it and can only generate theories about what other people report about it. If I were under the influence of a psychedelic drug such as LSD or marijuana [105], I could probably experience synesthesia directly, and my descriptions of the experience would become data.

Figure 16–1 (reprinted from C. Tart, *Science,* 1972, *176* 1203–1210, by permission of the American Association for the Advancement of Science) demonstrates some possible relationships between three state-specific sciences. State-specific sciences 1 and 2 show considerable overlap.

The area labeled O_1O_2 permits direct observation in both sciences. Area T_1T_2 permits theoretical inferences about common subject matter from the two perspectives. In area O_1T_2, by contrast, the theoretical propositions of state-specific science 2 are matters of direct observation for the scientist in d-SoC 1, and vice versa for the area T_1O_2. State-specific science 3 consists of a body of observation and theory exclusive to that science and has no overlap with the two other sciences: it does not confirm, contradict, or complement them.

It would be naively reductionistic to say that the work in one

---

know certain things in a d-ASC, they talk about them in the ordinary d-SoC. They realize the words are a poor reflection of the direct experiential knowledge, but the words are all they have to talk with. As the generations pass, more and more theologians who have no direct knowledge of what the words are about discuss the meaning of the words at greater and greater length, and the divergence of the words from the original state-specific knowledge becomes greater and greater.

There are warnings in some religious literature [128] not to take the words literally, to use them only as pointers of the direction experience must go, but our culture is so fascinated with words that we seldom heed such warnings.

So perhaps ideas like "we are all one" or "love pervades the entire universe" cannot be adequately comprehended in the ordinary d-SoC, no matter how hard we try, although they may appropriately affect our thoughts and actions in the ordinary d-SoC if we have *first* experienced them, understood them, in the appropriate d-ASC.

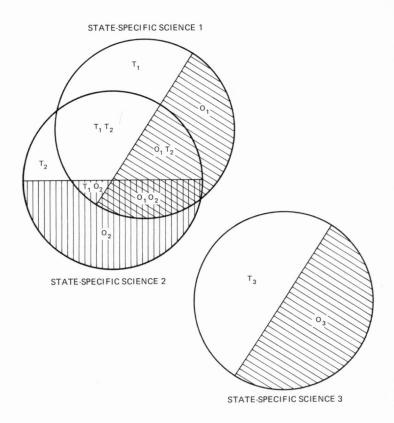

Figure 16–1. Possible relationships among three state-specific sciences.

state-specific science *validates* or *invalidates* the work in a second state-specific science; I prefer to say that two different state-specific sciences, where they overlap, provide quite different points of view with respect to certain kinds of theories and data, and thus *complement*[8] each other. The proposed creation of state-specific sciences neither validates nor invalidates the activ-

[8] The term *complement* is used in a technical sense here, as it is in physics, meaning that each of two explanatory systems deals well with overlapping data areas, but neither disproves the other and neither can be incorporated into some more comprehensive theoretical system as a special case. For example, the electron can be treated adequately as a wave or as a particle. The wave theory handles some kinds of data better than the particle theory, and vice versa.

ities of normal consciousness sciences. The possibility of developing certain state-specific sciences means only that certain kinds of phenomena may be handled more adequately within these potential new sciences.

Interrelationships more complex than those illustrated in Fig. 16–1 are possible.

The possibility of stimulating interactions between different state-specific sciences is very real. Creative breakthroughs in normal consciousness sciences have frequently been made by scientists temporarily in a d-ASC [18]. In such instances, the scientists concerned saw quite different views of their problems and performed different kinds of reasoning, conscious or nonconscious, which led to results that could be tested within their normal consciousness science.

A current example of such interaction is the finding that in Zen meditation (a highly developed discipline in Japan) there are physiological correlates of meditative experiences, such as decreased frequency of alpha-rhythm, which can also be produced by means of instrumentally aided feedback-learning techniques [23]. This finding may elucidate some of the processes peculiar to each discipline.

Individual Differences

A widespread and misleading assumption that hinders the development of state-specific sciences and confuses their interrelationships is the assumption that because two people are "normal" (not certified insane), their ordinary d-SoCs are essentially the same. In reality I suspect that there are enormous differences between the d-SoCs of some normal people. Because societies train people to behave and communicate along socially approved lines, these differences are obscured.

For example, some people think in images, others in words. Some can voluntarily anesthetize parts of their body, most cannot. Some recall past events by imaging the scene and looking at the relevant details; others use complex verbal processes with no images.

This means that person A may be able to observe certain kinds of experiential data that person B cannot experience in his ordinary d-SoC, no matter how hard B tries. There may be several consequences. Person B may think A is insane, too imaginative, or a liar, or he may feel inferior to A. Person A may also feel himself odd, if he takes B as a standard of normality.

B may be able to enter a d-ASC and there experience the sorts of things A has reported to him. A realm of knowledge that is ordinary for A is then specific for a d-ASC for B. Similarly, some of the experiences of B in his d-ASC may not be available for direct observation by A in his ordinary d-SoC.

The phenomenon of synesthesia can again serve as an example. Some individuals possess this ability in their ordinary d-SoC, most do not. Yet 56 percent of a sample of experienced marijuana users experienced synesthesia at least occasionally [105] while in the drug-induced d-ASC.

Thus bits of knowledge that are specific for a d-ASC for one individual may be part of ordinary consciousness for another. Arguments over the usefulness of the concept of states of consciousness may reflect differences in the structure of the ordinary d-SoC of various investigators, as we discussed in Chapter 9.

Another important source of individual differences, little understood at present, is the degree to which an individual can first make an observation or form a concept in one d-SoC and then reexperience or comprehend it in another d-SoC. Many items of information that were state-specific when observed initially may be learned and somehow transferred (fully or partially) to another d-SoC. Differences across individuals, various combinations of d-SoCs, and types of experience are probably enormous.

I have outlined only the complexities created by individual differences in normal d-SoCs and have used the normal d-SoC as a baseline for comparison with d-ASCs, but it is evident that every d-SoC must eventually be compared against every other d-SoC.

Problems, Pitfalls, and Personal Perils

If we use the practical experience of Western man with d-ASCs as a guide, the development of state-specific sciences will be beset by a number of difficulties. These difficulties will be of two kinds: general methodological problems stemming from the inherent nature of some d-ASCs, and those concerned with personal perils to the investigator.

STATE-RELATED PROBLEMS

The first important problem in the proposed development of state-specific sciences is the "obvious" perception of truth. In many d-ASCs, one's experience is that one is obviously and lucidly experiencing truth directly, without question. An immediate result of this may be an extinction of the desire for further questioning. Further, this experience of "obvious" truth, while not necessarily preventing the investigator from further examining his data, may not arouse his desire for consensual validation. Since one of the greatest strengths of science is its insistence on consensual validation of basic data, this can be a serious drawback. Investigators attempting to develop state-specific sciences must learn to distrust the obvious.

A second major problem in developing state-specific sciences is that in some d-ASCs one's abilities to visualize and imagine are immensely enhanced, so that whatever one imagines seems perfectly real. Thus one can imagine that something is being observed and experience it as datum. If the scientist can conjure up anything he wishes, how can he ever get at truth?

One approach to this problem is to consider any such vivid imaginings as potential effects: they are data in the sense that what can be vividly imagined in a d-SoC is important to know. It may be that not everything can be imagined with equal facility and relationships between what can be imagined may show a lawful pattern.

Another approach is to realize that this problem is not unique to d-ASCs. One can have illusions and misperceptions in the ordinary d-SoC. Before the rise of modern physical science, all sorts of things were imagined about the nature of the physical world that could not be directly refuted. The same techniques that eliminated these illusions in the physical sciences can also eliminate them in state-specific sciences dealing with nonphysical data. All observations must be subjected to consensual validation and all their theoretical consequences must be examined. Those that do not show consistent patterns and cannot be replicated can be distinguished from those phenomena that do show general lawfulness across individuals.

The effects of this enhanced vividness of imagination in some d-ASCs will be complicated further by two other problems: experimenter bias [45, 55] and the fact that one person's illusion in a given d-ASC can sometimes be communicated to another person in the same d-ASC so that a false consensual validation results. Again, the only long-term solution is the requirement that predictions based on concepts arising from various experiences be verified experientially.

A third major problem is that state-specific sciences probably cannot be developed for all d-ASCs: some d-ASCs may depend on or result from genuine deterioration of observational and reasoning abilities or from a deterioration of volition. But the development of each state-specific science should result from trial and error, and not from a priori decisions based on reasoning in the ordinary d-SoC that would rule out attempts to develop a science for some particular state.

A fourth major problem is that of ineffability. Some experiences are ineffable in the sense that (1) a person may experience them, but be unable to express or conceptualize them adequately to himself; (2) while a person may be able to conceptualize an experience to himself he may not be able to communicate it adequately to anyone else. Certain phenomena of the first type may simply be inaccessible to scientific investigation. Phenomena of the second type may be accessible to scientific investigation only insofar as we are willing to recognize that a science, in the sense of following most of the basic rules, may exist only for a single person. Since such a solitary science lacks all the advantages gained by consensual validation, we cannot expect it to have as much power and rigor as conventional scientific endeavor.

Many phenomena that are now considered ineffable may not be so in reality. Their apparent ineffability may be a function of general lack of experience with d-ASCs and the lack of an adequate language for communicating about d-ASC phenomena. In most well-developed languages the major part of the vocabulary was developed primarily in adaptation to survival in the physical world.[9]

Finally, various phenomena of d-ASCs may be too complex for

---

[9] Note too that we are a hyperverbal culture, so *ineffable* essentially means not communicable in *words*. But there are other forms of communication. Riding a bicycle or swimming are both ineffable, in the sense that I have never seen a good verbal description of either, but they can be taught. Ornstein [47] presents convincing data that the right hemisphere of the brain specializes in nonverbal functioning, and argues that many of the seemingly exotic techniques of Eastern spiritual disciplines are actually ways of communicating and teaching in the nonverbal mode.

human beings to understand. The phenomena may depend on or be affected by so many variables that we can never understand them. In the history of science, however, many phenomena that appeared too complex at first eventually became comprehensible.

PERSONAL PERILS

The personal perils an investigator faces in attempting to develop a state-specific science are of two kinds: those associated with reactions colloquially called a bad trip and a good trip.

Bad trips, in which an extremely unpleasant emotional reaction is experienced in a d-ASC, and from which there are possible long-term adverse consequences on personal adjustment, often occur because upbringing has not prepared us to undergo radical alterations in our ordinary d-SoC. We depend on stability, we fear the unknown, and we develop personal rigidities and various kinds of personal and social taboos. It is traditional in our society to consider d-ASCs as signs of insanity; d-ASCs therefore can cause great fear in those who experience them.

In many d-ASCs, defenses against unacceptable personal impulses become partially or wholly ineffective, so that the person feels flooded with traumatic material he cannot handle. All these things result in fear and avoidance of d-ASCs, and make it difficult or impossible for some individuals to function in a d-ASC in a way that is consistent with the development of state-specific science. Maslow [36] discusses these as pathologies of cognition that seriously interfere with the scientific enterprise in general, as well as ordinary life. In principle, adequate selection and training can minimize these hazards for at least some people.

Good trips may also endanger an investigator. A trip may produce experiences so rewarding that they interfere with the scientific activity of the investigator. The perception of "obvious" truth and its effect of eliminating the need for further investigation or consensual validation have already been mentioned. Another peril comes from the ability to imagine or create vivid experiences. They may be so highly rewarding that the investigator does not follow the rule of investigating the obvious regardless of his personal satisfaction with results. Similarly, his attachment to good feelings, ecstasy, and the like, and his refusal to consider alternative conceptualizations of these, can stifle the progress of investigation.

These personal perils emphasize the necessity of developing

adequate training programs for scientists who wish to develop state-specific sciences. Although such a training program is difficult to envision, it is evident that much conventional scientific training is contrary to what is needed to develop a state-specific science, because it tends to produce rigidity and avoidance of personal involvement with subject matter, rather than open-mindedness and flexibility. Much of the training program must be devoted to the scientist's understanding of himself so that the (unconscious) effects of his personal biases are minimized during his investigations of a d-ASC.

There are scientists who, after becoming personally involved with d-ASCs, have subsequently become poor scientists or have experienced personal psychological crises. It is premature, however, to conclude that such unfortunate consequences cannot be avoided by proper training and discipline. In the early history of the physical sciences many scientists were fanatics who were nonobjective about their investigations. Not all experiencers of d-ASCs develop pathology as a result: indeed, many seem to become considerably more mature. Given the current social climate, we hear of the failures, but not the successes. Only from actual attempts to develop state-specific sciences can we determine the actual d-SoCs that are suitable for development and the kinds of people best suited to such work.[10]

Prospects

I believe that an examination of human history and our current situation provides the strongest argument for the need to develop state-specific sciences. Throughout history man has been influenced by the spiritual and mystical factors expressed (usually in watered-down form) in the religions that attract the masses. Spiritual and mystical experiences are primary phenomena of various d-ASCs: because of such experiences, untold numbers of both the noblest and most horrible acts of which men are capable have been committed. Yet in all the time that Western science has existed, no concerted attempt has been made to understand these d-ASC phenomena in scientific terms.

10 The d-ASCs resulting from very dangerous drugs may be scientifically interesting, but the risk may be too high to warrant developing state-specific sciences for them. The personal and social issues involved in evaluating this kind of risk are beyond the scope of this book.

Many hoped that religions were simply a form of superstition that would be left behind in our "rational" age. Not only has this hope failed, but our own understanding of the nature of reasoning now makes it clear that it can never be fulfilled. Reason is a *tool,* a tool that is wielded in the service of assumptions, beliefs and needs that are not themselves subject to reason. The irrational, or better, the *a*rational, will not disappear from the human situation. Our immense success in the development of the physical sciences has not been particularly successful in formulating better philosophies of life or increasing our real knowledge of ourselves. The sciences we have developed to date are not very human sciences. They tell us *how* to do things, but give us no scientific insights on questions of *what* to do, what *not* to do, or *why* to do things.

The youth of today and mature scientists are turning to meditation, Oriental religions, and personal use of psychedelic drugs in increasing numbers. The phenomena encountered in these d-ASCs provide more satisfaction and are more relevant to the formulation of philosophies of life and decisions about appropriate ways of living, than "pure reason" [40]. My own impressions are that large numbers of scientists are now personally exploring d-ASCs, but few have begun to connect this personal exploration with their scientific activities.

It is difficult to predict the chances of developing state-specific sciences. Our knowledge is still too diffuse and dependent on the normal d-SoC. Yet I think it is probable that state-specific sciences can be developed for such d-ASCs as autohypnosis, meditative states, lucid dreaming, marijuana intoxication, LSD intoxication, self-remembering, reverie, and biofeedback-induced states [88 or 115]. In all these d-ASCs, volition seems to be retained, so that the observer can indeed carry out experiments on himself or others or both. Some d-ASCs, in which the volition to experiment during the state may disappear, but in which some experimentation can be carried out if special conditions are prepared before the state is entered, are alcohol intoxication, ordinary dreaming, hypnagogic and hypnopompic states, and high dreams [88 or 115]. It is not clear whether other d-ASCs are suitable for developing state-specific sciences or whether mental deterioration is too great. Such questions can only be answered by experiment.

I have nothing against religious and mystical groups. Yet I suspect that the vast majority of them have developed compelling belief systems rather than state-specific sciences. Will scientific method be extended to the development of state-specific sciences to improve our human situation? Or will the immense power of d-ASCs be left in the hands of many cults and sects?

17.

Higher States of Consciousness

✿✿✿

A common reaction to the proposal for creating state-specific sciences is that the project is not necessary, that there is already a superior d-SoC for understanding things. Orthodox scientists [122] aver that the ordinary, "normal" d-SoC is the best, most rational d-SoC possible, so we need only continue the scientific research already begun in that state to ultimately find answers to all our questions. On the other hand, some people who have experienced d-ASCs believe that there are *higher* d-SoCs in which Truth can be directly known so we need not develop sciences in these d-SoCs, only experience them: ultimately we can experience states of enlightenment in which all that is worth knowing or attaining is known and attained.

However, the feeling of being in direct contact with the Truth is no guarantee that such contact has actually been achieved. Such feelings are a part of being human, but such "certain truths," when acted upon, often turn out to be false. They do not work. A primary rule of science is that you must test your understandings against the observable area of reality/experience to which they apply: if observed experience does not tally with the prediction of your truth/theory/understanding, then your truth/theory/understanding is false or needs revision. Scientifically, we cannot broadly assume that any particular d-SoC is higher, in the sense of supplying more insight into truth; we must study and test the various aspects of various d-SoCs in detail. Since a principal task of science is reliable, detailed *description,* it seems preferable to discard the idea of higher states altogether at this stage and concentrate on description.

Yet since experiencers of d-ASCs often describe them as higher or lower states, we should, to be adequately descriptive, examine more closely the idea of higher states.

What does a person mean when he says, "I'm high" or "I'm in a higher state of consciousness"?

On its simplest level, the statement "I'm high" simply means that I feel better now than I did under some other condition. If I had a bad toothache a few minutes ago, and now the pain has stopped, I can say that now I'm high. I feel much better than before. If I am neurotic in my ordinary d-SoC and suffer constant tensions, fears, and anxieties, and I get drunk and feel good, again I can say I'm high by comparison. To reverse this, if I become frightened or feel sick when I am drunk, I can use the phrase "I'm high" to describe my ordinary d-SoC in which I do not feel frightened or sick.

If, then, we clearly describe the reference state and the way in which the current state differs from it, the statement "I'm high" is a useful relative description. Unfortunately, people usually employ the phrase without any clear description of the reference state or the specific way in which the current condition differs from it. Add to this the great individual differences in ordinary d-SoCs, and the degree to which the common language of consensus reality glosses over these differences, and you can see that "I'm high" is usually an ambiguous phrase indicating only that I feel better than in some other, unknown condition. Perhaps I am in a state of fear and anxiety now and that is better than the terror I experienced a few minutes ago, or perhaps I feel blissfully at one with the whole cosmos.

Higher and Lower d-SoCs

There is a more specific use of the adjectives *higher* and *lower,* where the user envisions some absolute ordering of d-SoCs on a value scale. Thus higher and lower become much more specific, less relative, terms. Five such value scales are discussed below. None are scientific scales in the sense of being subjected to prolonged and precise scrutiny by groups of scientists; no such scales exist at this stage of our knowledge.

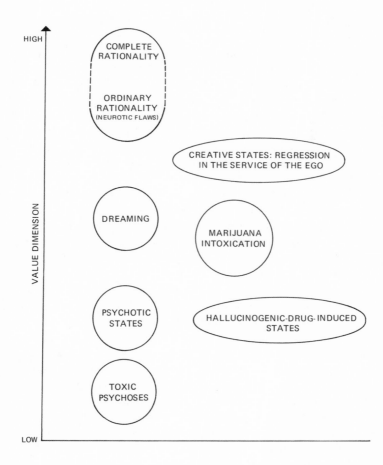

Figure 17–1. Orthodox Western, largely implicit valuation of various states.

The first value scale is depicted in Figure 17–1. It is the value-scaling of d-SoCs implicitly held by most Western intellectuals. I stress that it is held implicitly: it is conveyed along with the general value system of our society in the enculturation process, without need for a teacher to say explicitly, "Complete rationality is our goal and anything less than that is an inferior, lower state of consciousness."

The primary value in this scheme is rationality, adherence to the logic and values our culture believes are true. The scheme recognizes that the ordinary state is occasionally neurotic, in that rationality is often replaced by rationalization of processes based on unconscious drives and emotions. If only we could be cured of these occasional neurotic flaws, it is reasoned, we could be completely rational (although we do not like "completely rational" to being equated with being computerlike). Dreaming is a lower d-SoC because there are many logical flaws in it and the dreamer is out of touch with (consensus) reality. Psychotic states[1] are even lower in these ways, and toxic psychoses (states induced by major poisonings) are usually the most irrational and out-of-touch states of all.

Some ambivalent recognition is given to the value of creative states, so they are shown between ordinary rationality and dreaming. Most intellectuals consider such creative states the province of artists or fringe intellectuals, not themselves, and, since these states are associated with emotionality, they are viewed ambivalently. Marijuana intoxication is generally valued about the same as dreaming: it is irrational and out of touch, but probably not too harmful. Psychedelic-drug-induced changes in consciousness are considered more dangerous and out of touch, like psychoses.

This ordering of these conditions and d-SoCs is not scientific for it has never been made explicit and subjected to detailed examination to determine how well it orders reality. Further, its implicitness under ordinary circumstances makes it a barrier to better understanding. When a value system or a set of assumptions is implicit, you do not know you have it, so you do not question its value. You automatically perceive and think in terms of the value/assumption system. For example, anything said by a person labeled "psychotic" *must* be viewed as a sign of his craziness, not to be taken at face value. Patients are crazy; the doctors are sane.

Many individuals have valuations of d-SoCs somewhat different from the scheme shown in Figure 17–1, of course, but this generally represents the d-SoC valuation system of most intellectuals, doctors, psychiatrists, psychologists, and scientists—the people thought to be authorities in these matters.

A quite different valuing of d-SoCs is held by many people we

---

[1] I use "state" very loosely in this chapter, for we do not know whether all of these value-ordered "states" are stable d-SoCs.

can call hip. As is true of the orthodox ordering, there are important individual exceptions, but the scheme fits many people, especially the young. If you are a parent whose valuation system is orthodox, you may well have experienced some bitter arguments with your sons or daughters whose valuation system is hip.

In this system (Figure 17–2) the highest states are mystical

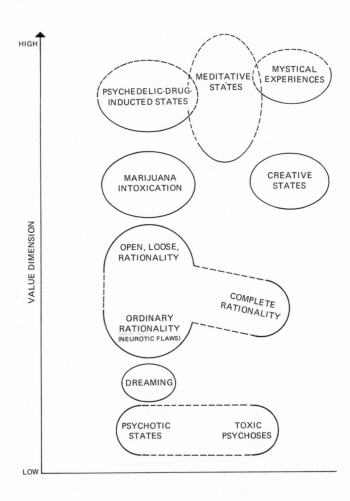

Figure 17–2. The "hip" valuation of various states.

experiences, often experienced in conjunction with psychedelic-drug-induced states or meditative states. Creative states and marijuana intoxication are next in value, and some of the experiences of the higher states can be achieved in them, albeit at reduced intensity. Then comes an open or loose rationality, an ordinary d-SoC in which, because you recall (at least partially) experiences of higher d-ASCs, you do not take too seriously the apparent rationality of your culture's consensus reality. You can function well enough in an ordinary d-SoC, but you do not value that d-SoC as highly as do those who have no other reference experiences of higher states.

Ordinary, neurotically flawed rationality is the next lower state. A state of complete rationality is valued somewhere between open and ordinary rationality, a reflection of existing suspicion of a totally unemotional, computerlike state. Dreaming is generally considered somewhat lower than ordinary rationality, although it is recognized that some dreams can be inspired; psychoses and toxic psychoses are at the bottom of the value continuum. As with dreaming, there is recognition that psychotic states can sometimes be very high, however.

Which of these two value continua is true? Which is more useful?

Neither. In neither have details about each state and the performance potential with respect to *specific tasks* in each state been clarified.

Can you argue that the orthodox ordering is more workable for surviving in consensus reality? What about those other adherents to the relatively high state of ordinary rationality who order napalm dropped on children to protect them from——— (fill in your favorite -ism) ? Can you argue that the hip ordering is better for realizing oneself? What about all the starving children in countries like India, where mystical states have long been considered the highest by cultural norms? Or the near total failure rate of communes of American young people who accept the hip value ordering?

I offer no answers to these questions. Indeed, the questions and examples I have chosen are designed to illustrate how poor our understanding is at present. Higher or lower *for what specific thing?* That is the question we must keep constantly in mind.

Three Explicit Orderings

Three systems for value-ordering d-SoCs are described below to illustrate that explicit and detailed orderings are possible. Two are from the Buddhist tradition and one from the Arica tradition. While none of these is scientific, each is capable of being cast as a scientific theory and tested.

Figure 17–3 presents an ordering of nine d-SoCs that are all higher than ordinary consciousness. These are d-SoCs[2] to be obtained sequentially in seeking enlightenment through a path of concentrative meditation in Buddhism.

The underlying value dimension here might be called freedom. The Buddha taught that the ordinary state is one of suffering and entrapment in the forms and delusions of our own minds. The root cause of this suffering is attachment, the (automatized) desire to prolong pleasure and avoid pain. The journey along the Path of Concentration starts when the meditator tries to focus attention on some particular object of concentration. As he progresses, his concentration becomes more subtle and powerful and he eventually moves from formed experiences (all form has the seeds of illusion in it) to a series of formless states, culminating in the eighth *jhana,* where there is neither perception nor nonperception of anything.

Figure 17–4 illustrates another succession of higher states within the Buddhist framework. Here the technique involves not one-pointed, successively refined concentration, but successively refined states of insight into the ultimate nature of one's own mind. Starting from either the state of Access Concentration (where ability to focus is quite high) or the state of Bare Insight (proficiency in noticing internal experiences), the meditator becomes increasingly able to observe the phenomena of the mind, and to see their inherently unsatisfactory character. The ultimate goal is a state called *nirodh,* which is beyond awareness itself. *Nirodh* is the ultimate accomplishment in this particular version of Buddhism, higher than the eighth *jhana* on the Path of Concentration. The reader interested in more detail about these

---

[2] We do not know enough about these states in scientific terms to be sure whether they represent nine d-SoCs with the quantum jump between each or a smaller number of d-SoCs, some of whose distinctions actually are differences in depth within a d-SoC. For purposes of discussion here, however, we will assume these *jhana* states, and the states described in Figures 17–4 and 17–5, are all d-SoCs.

States of Consciousness

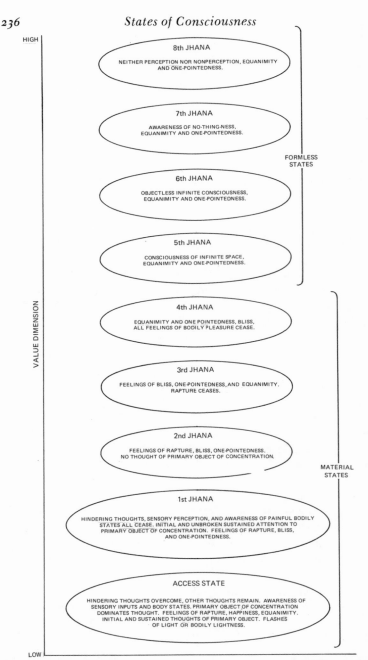

Figure 17–3. Higher states of consciousness on the Buddhist Path of Concentration.

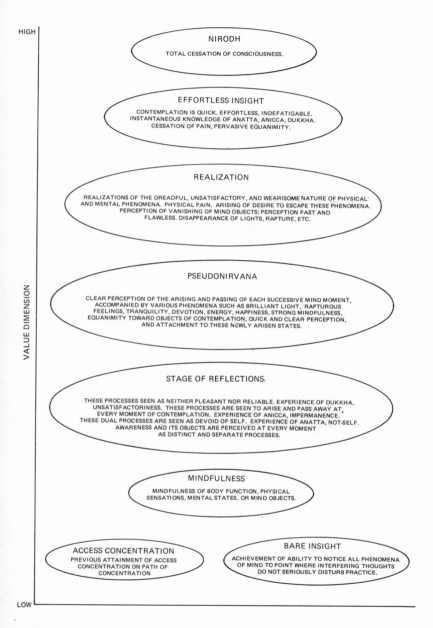

HIGH

VALUE DIMENSION

NIRODH

TOTAL CESSATION OF CONSCIOUSNESS.

EFFORTLESS INSIGHT

CONTEMPLATION IS QUICK, EFFORTLESS, INDEFATIGABLE.
INSTANTANEOUS KNOWLEDGE OF ANATTA, ANICCA, DUKKHA.
CESSATION OF PAIN, PERVASIVE EQUANIMITY.

REALIZATION

REALIZATIONS OF THE DREADFUL, UNSATISFACTORY, AND WEARISOME NATURE OF PHYSICAL
AND MENTAL PHENOMENA. PHYSICAL PAIN. ARISING OF DESIRE TO ESCAPE THESE PHENOMENA.
PERCEPTION OF VANISHING OF MIND OBJECTS; PERCEPTION FAST AND
FLAWLESS. DISAPPEARANCE OF LIGHTS, RAPTURE, ETC.

PSEUDONIRVANA

CLEAR PERCEPTION OF THE ARISING AND PASSING OF EACH SUCCESSIVE MIND MOMENT,
ACCOMPANIED BY VARIOUS PHENOMENA SUCH AS BRILLIANT LIGHT, RAPTUROUS
FEELINGS, TRANQUILITY, DEVOTION, ENERGY, HAPPINESS, STRONG MINDFULNESS,
EQUANIMITY TOWARD OBJECTS OF CONTEMPLATION, QUICK AND CLEAR PERCEPTION,
AND ATTACHMENT TO THESE NEWLY ARISEN STATES.

STAGE OF REFLECTIONS

THESE PROCESSES SEEN AS NEITHER PLEASANT NOR RELIABLE. EXPERIENCE OF DUKKHA,
UNSATISFACTORINESS. THESE PROCESSES ARE SEEN TO ARISE AND PASS AWAY AT
EVERY MOMENT OF CONTEMPLATION. EXPERIENCE OF ANICCA, IMPERMANENCE.
THESE DUAL PROCESSES ARE SEEN AS DEVOID OF SELF. EXPERIENCE OF ANATTA, NOT-SELF.
AWARENESS AND ITS OBJECTS ARE PERCEIVED AT EVERY MOMENT
AS DISTINCT AND SEPARATE PROCESSES.

MINDFULNESS

MINDFULNESS OF BODY FUNCTION, PHYSICAL
SENSATIONS, MENTAL STATES, OR MIND OBJECTS.

ACCESS CONCENTRATION

PREVIOUS ATTAINMENT OF ACCESS
CONCENTRATION ON PATH OF
CONCENTRATION

BARE INSIGHT

ACHIEVEMENT OF ABILITY TO NOTICE ALL PHENOMENA
OF MIND TO POINT WHERE INTERFERING THOUGHTS
DO NOT SERIOUSLY DISTURB PRACTICE.

LOW

Figure 17–4. Higher states of consciousness on the Buddhist Path of
Insight.

Buddhist orderings should consult Daniel Goleman's chapter in *Transpersonal Psychologies* [128].

The third ordering (Figure 17–5) is John Lilly's conceptualization of the system taught by Oscar Icazo in Arica, Chile. More background is available in the chapter by John Lilly and Joseph Harts in *Transpersonal Psychologies* [128], as well as in Lilly's *Center of the Cyclone* [35].

In the Arica ordering the value dimension is one of freedom and of which psychic center dominates consciousness. The numerical designation of each state indicates the number of cosmic laws supposedly governing that state, as expounded by Gurdjieff (see Kathy Riordan's chapter on Gurdjieff in *Transpersonal Psychologies* [128] and Ouspensky [48], with a plus sign indicating positive valuation of that state. For example, in the +3 state only three laws govern; a person is less free in the +6 state, where six laws govern. A minus sign indicates negative emotions. Thus the ordinary d-SoC, the −24 state, is a neurotic one of pain, guilt, fear, and other negative emotions. The −24 state is also under 96 laws, making it less free, as the number of governing laws doubles at each lower level.

Lilly notes that this ordering of highness does not hold for all possible tasks in this scheme. The +12 state and higher, for instance, involve a progressive loss of contact with external reality and so become lower states if one has to perform some external task like driving a car or eating.

Now, is the +24 state higher or lower than the sixth *jhana?* Is the state of realization on the Path of Insight higher or lower than the +3 state? Which state in these three orderings is best for coping with the world food shortage? For understanding an artist's message? For dying?

Arguing a particular answer to any one of these or similar questions involves first fully understanding the system that defines one state, and then fully understanding the system that defines the other state. We must grasp the many implicit assumptions that underlie the world-view of each system. If we do not, we waste our time using common words that carry dissimilar implicit assumptions. When we understand the world-views behind these systems, we still must examine how well each system orders the experience/realities of its own practitioners and how well it orders and explains experiences by nonpractitioners.

What, then, is a higher state of consciousness? It is something

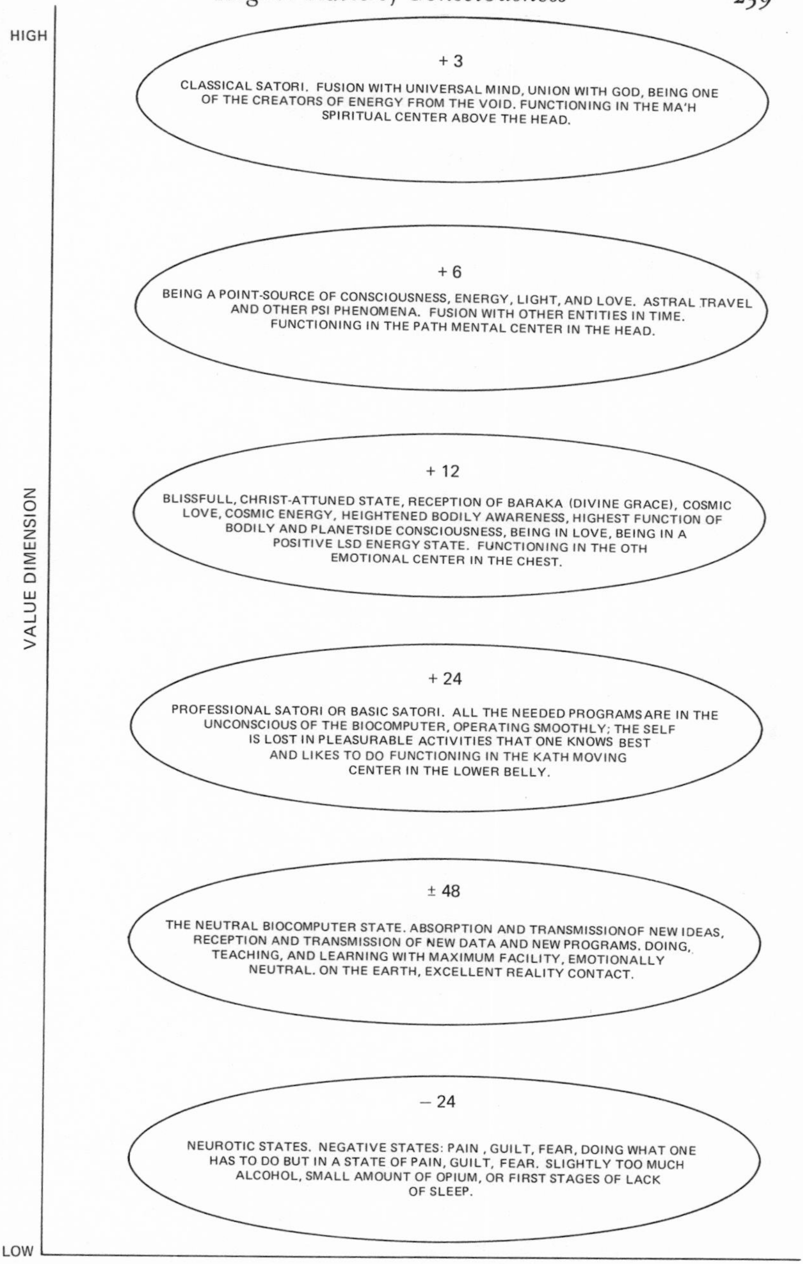

HIGH

VALUE DIMENSION

> **+ 3**
>
> CLASSICAL SATORI. FUSION WITH UNIVERSAL MIND, UNION WITH GOD, BEING ONE OF THE CREATORS OF ENERGY FROM THE VOID. FUNCTIONING IN THE MA'H SPIRITUAL CENTER ABOVE THE HEAD.

> **+ 6**
>
> BEING A POINT-SOURCE OF CONSCIOUSNESS, ENERGY, LIGHT, AND LOVE. ASTRAL TRAVEL AND OTHER PSI PHENOMENA. FUSION WITH OTHER ENTITIES IN TIME. FUNCTIONING IN THE PATH MENTAL CENTER IN THE HEAD.

> **+ 12**
>
> BLISSFULL, CHRIST-ATTUNED STATE, RECEPTION OF BARAKA (DIVINE GRACE), COSMIC LOVE, COSMIC ENERGY, HEIGHTENED BODILY AWARENESS, HIGHEST FUNCTION OF BODILY AND PLANETSIDE CONSCIOUSNESS, BEING IN LOVE, BEING IN A POSITIVE LSD ENERGY STATE. FUNCTIONING IN THE OTH EMOTIONAL CENTER IN THE CHEST.

> **+ 24**
>
> PROFESSIONAL SATORI OR BASIC SATORI. ALL THE NEEDED PROGRAMS ARE IN THE UNCONSCIOUS OF THE BIOCOMPUTER, OPERATING SMOOTHLY; THE SELF IS LOST IN PLEASURABLE ACTIVITIES THAT ONE KNOWS BEST AND LIKES TO DO FUNCTIONING IN THE KATH MOVING CENTER IN THE LOWER BELLY.

> **± 48**
>
> THE NEUTRAL BIOCOMPUTER STATE. ABSORPTION AND TRANSMISSION OF NEW IDEAS, RECEPTION AND TRANSMISSION OF NEW DATA AND NEW PROGRAMS. DOING, TEACHING, AND LEARNING WITH MAXIMUM FACILITY, EMOTIONALLY NEUTRAL. ON THE EARTH, EXCELLENT REALITY CONTACT.

> **− 24**
>
> NEUROTIC STATES. NEGATIVE STATES: PAIN , GUILT, FEAR, DOING WHAT ONE HAS TO DO BUT IN A STATE OF PAIN, GUILT, FEAR. SLIGHTLY TOO MUCH ALCOHOL, SMALL AMOUNT OF OPIUM, OR FIRST STAGES OF LACK OF SLEEP.

LOW

Figure 17–5.   Higher states of consciousness in the Arica system. Some still lower states are not shown.

many of us long for; it is something some of us have put into our value ordering systems; it is a reality that exists under various sets of circumstances. But it is not something we can handle well scientifically, at least not at this stage of our knowledge. But we can begin by making our system of valuing states explicit.

Section II: Speculation

18.

As Above, So Below:
Five Basic Principles Underlying Physics and Psychology

✿✿

I consider the material in this chapter speculative and thus appropriate for introducing this section on speculation about consciousness. The ideas presented are not basic to the applications of the systems approach to the investigation of states of consciousness but are extensions of the approach that intrigue me. They are speculative also in that I am by no means a physicist and do not really understand mathematics, the language in which so much of physics is expressed. I intend this chapter primarily as a stimulus to prompt both physicists and psychologists to think further about some of the ideas expressed here.[1]

Most psychologists accept the idea that reality is ultimately *material*, composed basically of matter and energy operating within the physical framework of space and time. This is a useful set of intellectual constructs for dealing with experiences, but

1 In the spring of 1973, my colleagues at the Institute for the Study of Human Consciousness and I heard an exceptionally lucid presentation by Dean Brown, Stanford Research Institute, of the basic principles of physics, general principles that seem to emerge repeatedly in all areas of physics and that may represent fundamental principles underlying the universe. Brown suggested that these same principles may have parallels in the study of the mind, although he did not expound on this idea. The suggestion took firm root in my mind and has resulted in this chapter. I am also indebted to Andrew Dienes for helping me to understand and express some of the physics ideas in this chapter.

most psychologists think of it as an understanding of reality rather than a philosophy. Psychologists who implicitly or explicitly accept this position (which means most psychologists) thus in effect define psychology as a derivative science, one dealing with phenomena much removed from the ultimate bases of reality. A corollary is that to be really "scientific" (to be fashionable in terms of the prevailing physicalistic philosophy), psychology must ultimately reduce psychological data to physical data.

Figure 18–1 depicts the world-view of philosophical physicalism. The ultimate structures or components of reality (top) are subatomic particles. When I was a high school student, only a few such particles were known and many scientists thought that electrons, protons, and neutrons were the basics whose arrangement in patterns accounted for the way the world was. Now literally hundreds of subatomic particles have been "discovered." The word is enclosed in quotation marks because, of course, no one has actually ever seen a subatomic particle. They are assumed to exist because their presence enables sensible interpretation of various kinds of instrumental readings. Thus modern physicists picture the universe as composed of hundreds of subatomic particles being influenced by three basic types of forces: (1) the nuclear binding forces, which operate only at the extremely tiny distances inside atomic nuclei; (2) the so-called weak forces, which determine particle interaction at extremely close distances; and (3) electromagnetic forces. These forces act on the subatomic particles within a matrix of space and time, which is still largely taken for granted as simply being "space" and "time." Physics, then, is the study of this most basic level of reality.

From this most basic level this world-view builds toward life and consciousness. From subatomic particles, it moves to atoms, primarily influenced by electromagnetic forces and studied by physics and chemistry. From atoms it moves to molecules, primarily governed by chemical forces (which are electromagnetic forces) and studied most appropriately by chemistry. Next come large molecules, which to some extent are self-sustaining, hold their molecular configuration in spite of fairly large changes in their environment. Some of these cross the mysterious dividing line into the simplest forms of life, complex molecular assemblies capable of sustaining themselves and reproducing themselves in spite of environmental changes. Chemical, electromagnetic, and

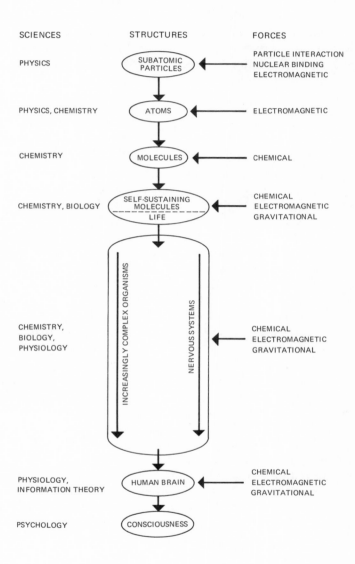

Figure 18–1. Levels of reality according to the physicalistic world-view.

now gravitational forces affect things at this level, and chemistry and biology are the sciences for studying them.

Next comes the evolutionary chain of increasingly complex organisms, which soon develop specialized nervous systems, which themselves increase greatly in complexity. Chemical, electromagnetic, and gravitational forces are active here, and chemistry, biology, and physiology are the important sciences for studying them.

The human brain is considered the epitome of development of nervous systems. I suspect that this is an unduly egocentric view, for animals such as dolphins and whales certainly have larger brains than man. But, perhaps because they do not build weapons to attack each other or us, practically no one seriously considers the idea that they may be as intelligent as we—the notable exception is John Lilly [34]. The human brain is also affected by chemical, electromagnetic, and gravitational forces. Physiology and probably information theory are appropriate sciences for dealing with the human brain.

Finally, there is consciousness, thought of as a by-product or property of the human brain, and psychology is the science for studying it. The forces affecting consciousness are not shown because, in terms of the physicalistic philosophy, social or psychological forces are derivative, not the "real" forces that actually control the universe.

This is the conservative or orthodox view of the mind discussed briefly at the beginning of this book. It does not really explain what consciousness *is,* but, citing good evidence that physically affecting the brain alters consciousness, asks no further questions and simply believes that consciousness itself is a product of brain functioning. The consequence of this view is that for an *ultimate* explanation of consciousness, the phenomena of consciousness must be reduced to those of brain functioning; brain functioning must be reduced to basic properties of nervous systems, which must be reduced to basic properties of live molecules, which in turn must be reduced to properties of molecules per se, which must be reduced to properties of atoms, which must finally be reduced to properties of subatomic particles.

In practice, of course, this would be extremely tedious. Certain relatively simple phenomena can be reduced one or two levels, but if I want to predict what you are next going to do, the amount of information I must deal with, starting with the knowledge of subatomic particles and various forces and building all the way up to consciousness, is simply impossible to handle.

There is no doubt that reductionism to more basic physical levels has been extremely useful in the physical sciences; and, to a certain extent, reductionism to simpler psychological events has been useful in psychology. Finding the physiological bases of psychological events or perhaps more accurately, the physiological parallels or interactions with psychological events, has also been useful. But, by and large, the attempt to reduce psychological events to physiological events is neither the only nor the best activity for psychology.

In the radical view of the mind, discussed earlier, a person's belief about the nature of reality may actually alter the reality, not just his interpretation of it. A fundamental part of the radical view is that basic awareness may have an independently real status itself, rather than being just a derivative of physical processes.

Figure 18–2 shows the scheme I propose for understanding human consciousness. Human consciousness is shown as the result of the interaction of six dimensions, each one just as real in some ultimate sense as any of the others. The dimensions are matter, energy, space, time, awareness, and an unknown factor that may be life itself. Science, guided by a physicalistic, reductionistic philosophy, investigates finer and finer levels of the matter and energy dimensions, within a certain space-time framework; but these dimensions constitute only two of the six or more dimensions that must be examined for full understanding of human consciousness.

I have added space and time as two independent dimensions more on intuition than on a basis I can cogently argue. We tend to assume that space is some uniform thing that is just there and that time is some uniform thing that is just passing. But experiences in d-ASCs (see discussion of the Space/Time subsystem, in Chapter 8) indicate that there may be other kinds of spaces and other kinds of times. I predict that some day our procedure of simply taking space and time for granted as unitary phenomena will seem quite crude.

In the systems approach, awareness is given a real and separate status. Recall the distinction between awareness and consciousness. *Awareness* is that basic, obviously there but hard-to-define

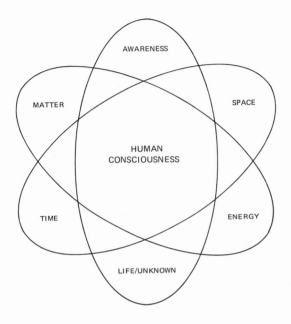

Figure 18-2. The underlying, interacting dimensions from which human consciousness arises.

property that makes us cognizant of things; *consciousness* is awareness as it is modified by and embedded in the structure of the mind. Consciousness is awareness transformed by the brain-body machine so that awareness loses some of its own innate properties, gains certain properties from the structure (probably largely brain structure) it merges with (or arises from in the conservative view), and leads to certain gestalt properties that cannot be predicted from a knowledge of either. The unknown factor dimension is added to remind us of our ignorance and because I feel intuitively that symmetry is called for in this diagram.

The first phrase of this chapter's title, "As Above, So Below," expresses my hypothesis that there is a uniform set of basic laws running the universe. I speculate that whatever fundamental principles or laws run the universe manifest themselves similarly in one area we call psychology and in another we call physics.

The idea can be extended to other areas also, but I am not expert enough to do so. Thus the laws of physics, as we currently understand them, are manifestations (of an unknown degree of directness) of the basic principles running the universe; laws and principles affecting consciousness are manifestations (of an unknown degree of directness) of these same principles. Neither manifestation may be any more basic than the other. If this hypothesis is correct, parallels to the five basic principles that seem to underlie physics should be clearly discernible in the psychological area.

First Principle: Duality

Physics distinguishes between a pure energy state and a matter state, with both energy and matter operating within the framework of space and time. A convenient abbreviation for this quaternity is MEST (matter, energy, space, time). The first principle is that whenever pure energy is converted into matter, it generally (universally?) creates a pair of particles whose properties are, in some important way, opposite. An electron and a positron may be created, for example, with opposite electrical charges, or a pair of particles may be created that spin in opposite directions. Conversely, the proper interaction of a pair of such opposite particles results in their annihilation as particles and their transformation back into pure energy. Thus the transformation of energy into matter is generally done in a dualistic manner. The principle seems so general that whenever a new particle is discovered, its exact opposite is looked for as a matter of course.

Assuming that a resulting duality in a transition from an energy state to a matter state is a general universal principle, a parallel manifestation at the psychological level is seen in a phenomenon encountered in some d-ASCs, the mystical experience of *unity*. This is a direct experience of a condition of consciousness in which all duality is transcended. In contrast to ordinary existence in a world dominated by opposites, there is no up and down, good and evil, creator and created, I and thou; everything is oneness. Our language, of course, cannot express this experience adequately. The experience of what may have been consciousness of the Void (Chapter 14) in William's ultra-deep hypnotic state may be an example of this kind. In Buddhist literature, the highest kind of samadhi, reached by successive refinements of concentration, is described as a state in which there is neither perception nor nonperception [20]. This state of consciousness seems analogous to the condition of pure, undifferentiated energy.

But we do not live in such a state of consciousness. Few people ever attain it, and even to them it is a transient experience, though of supreme importance. All the spiritual systems [128] that have this realization of a transcendence of duality as an *experiential* basis teach that in the ordinary d-SoC (and in many d-ASCs) duality is a basic principle governing the manifestation of consciousness. Thus pleasure cannot exist without pain, hope cannot exist without despair, courage cannot exist without fear, up cannot exist without down. The state of mystical unity, of Void consciousness, seems to be the experience of pure awareness, transcending all opposites, like the pure energy state, while *consciousness,* the condition of awareness deeply intermeshed with and modified by the structures of the mind and brain, is a realm of duality, the analog of the matter state. This seems to be a manifestation of the principle of duality in the psychological realm.

It is an exotic example, as most of us lack an experiential basis for understanding it. When we deal with human consciousness we do not deal with undifferentiated energy manifesting as two opposite particles, the simple, primary phenomena with which physics deals, but with complex, interacting systems made up of untold numbers of more elementary systems constituting the structures of the mind and brain, activated by awareness and energies to constitute a state of consciousness. This hypercomplex construction, consciousness (as opposed to pure awareness), is the experiential area with which we are most familiar. As we shall see in considering the other basic principles, the fact that our ordinary psychological experience is almost always with the complex, ongoing structure of human consciousness makes it difficult to see how these basic principles, derived for ideally simplified situations, can be applied precisely.

Second Principle: Quantum Law, the Law of Discreteness

The quantum principle in physics states that because of the nature of certain physical systems, most obviously that of the atom, certain transitions from one energy configuration to another can occur only in a complete, all-or-none jump. In an atom, for example, an electron can be in one or another precise energy state, but cannot occupy an energy level intermediate between these two. It must go from one to the other, given the requisite energy to bring this about, in an all-or-none fashion. Thus there is one state, a forbidden zone, and then a second state. There may be a third state, a fourth state, and so on, but the transition is always all-or-none. When dealing with macroscopic objects or systems that are made up of large numbers of the more elementary components governed by quantum laws, the aggregate, the macroscopic system, may seem to show continuity over wide ranges of intermediate values, but this is a statistical illusion from a gross level of observation. For example, an aggregate made up of units, many of which are in a quantum state that we can call two, and many of which are in a quantum state that we can call three, can have an *average* value anywhere between two and three, depending on the relative distribution of the quantum units.

I see the quantum principle, as stated in physics, as a particular manifestation of a more general principle that various components of the universe have a "shape" or "structure" or "energy configuration." On a familiar, macroscopic level, for example, water can be in three distinct states, a solid (ice), a liquid (ordinary water), or a gas (steam). There can be mechanical mixtures of the three states, as of water droplets falling or floating in the air, but the solid, liquid, and gas states are quite distinct.

The application to consciousness of this general principle, that various components of reality have properties *that therefore determine the way they can interact with other units,* is outlined in Chapter 2. To recapitulate briefly, a d-SoC is a system or a pattern or an overall configuration of many psychological subsystems or structures. Each subsystem shows variations within itself within certain limits, but maintains its overall identity as a subsystem. Since identity means properties, this limits the number of possible ways a stable system can be built up from the subsystems and thus limits the number of d-SoCs possible for a human being.

The induction of a d-ASC involves the application of disrupting forces to the b-SoC to push one or more subsystems beyond their stable limits and/or to disrupt the feedback loops between subsystems that stabilize the b-SoC. When enough feedback loops have been disrupted and/or enough subsystems pushed beyond their stable, ordinary ranges of functioning, the overall organization of the b-SoC breaks down, and a transitional period of varying duration occurs, with the subsystems having only transient, unstable relationships to each other. Then, with the application of appropriate patterning forces, the subsystems are reassembled in a new configuration that is stable and that we call the d-ASC.

This process constitutes a kind of quantum jump, albeit not the neat quantum jump of an electron from one discrete energy state to another in an atom. We are dealing with highly composite, complex structures, and even when such structures are made up of units that operate on quantum principles, the aggregate may show various degrees of continuity. Recall the earlier discussion of individual differences. For certain individuals, the transition from a b-SoC to a d-ASC definitely shows a quantum jump, with no consciousness during the transition period. The system properties of the d-ASC are quite different from those of the b-SoC.

The quantum jump from one d-SoC to a d-ASC may be a leap along what we can conceive of as a continuum or it may be the emergence of a totally new function or pattern of functioning.

The d-ASCs of which we now have some scientific knowledge occur in human beings who have been thoroughly conditioned by enculturation processes, so the quantum jumps we have seen in investigating various d-ASCs may largely represent the results of semiarbitrary cultural conditioning. That is, in a particular culture you might have to be either straight or stoned, but in another culture you may be able to be a little of each simultaneously. However, we can postulate as a general principle that the various subsystems and structures that make up the human mind cannot be put together in just any arbitrary way: each structure has properties of its own that restrict its possible interaction with other structures into a larger structure or system. Insofar as we can learn to study the mind beyond the semiarbitrary cultural conditionings of consciousness, the study of d-ASCs may eventually tell us something about the fundamental properties of the human mind and the way in which the overall system of consciousness can thus be structured, what its basic states and forbidden zones are.

Third Principle: Relativity

In nonmathematical terms the relativity principle in physics is that there is no such thing as a *neutral* observer. Rather, any observer exists within a particular MEST framework, and this framework affects his observations.

This is more profound than saying that an observer's sense organs affect his observations. We realize, for example, that we do not naturally know how the world looks in the ultraviolet spectrum of light, but we can build instruments to make a translation for us. What is here being said is that the observer *is an inherent part* of the MEST framework, and this gives the observer himself characteristics, over and above what can be compensated for by special instruments, which affect his observations of things outside himself.

The principle of relativity applies in a variety of ways in psychological work, even though most psychologists have not seriously accepted it. Indeed, it applies to you and me in our everyday lives, even though we do not always accept it. At one level, each human being, functioning in his ordinary d-SoC (or in a d-ASC) , shows selective perception, selective thinking, selective action that in turn controls his perceptions. Because of his particular culture and the consensus reality to which his ordinary d-SoC has adapted him, plus his personal idiosyncrasies, he (1) is more prone to observe certain things; (2) is unlikely to observe other kinds of things at all; and (3) may have a great many transformations and distortions of what he does sense before it reaches his consciousness. This all happens unconsciously, automatically, and smoothly in the normally functioning adult. For example, the Christian missionary of the 1800s "saw" sin in the form of public display of "lust" in a native village, when the natives would have said they were only giving polite approval to the dancers.

This kind of relativity is becoming recognized in psychology under the topics of experimenter bias and the implicit demand characteristics of experiments. An experimenter's desire to prove the hypothesis he believes in not only can influence how he perceives his data, but also can subtly influence his subjects to cooperate in ways that will erroneously "prove" his hypothesis. Your beliefs about the nature of things around you can influence the way you see things and subtly influence others to uphold your view of reality.

In addition to this culturally and individually conditioned relativity, the fact that each person is human and therefore born with certain basic properties in his nervous system, sensory receptors, and perhaps in the nature of the awareness that enters into or comes from the operation of his nervous system, equips him with built-in biases for seeing the universe in certain kinds of ways and not other ways. This applies not only to the external universe perceived through his senses or with instrumental aids, but to his observations of his own internal experiences.

It is amazing how little recognized this idea is. The old concept of the "neutral observer," common in nineteenth century physics but now long abandoned by physicists, is alive and well within the ranks of psychologists, implicitly guiding almost all experiments. A wiser course is *always* to assume that an observer or experimenter has biases and selectivities in the way he perceives, evaluates, and acts, even when these are not obvious.

D-ASCs are of particular interest here. The ordinary d-SoC is a complex system incorporating various selectivities for perceiving the outside world and our own internal experiences, and functioning as a tool for coping with our external and internal worlds. Transiting to a d-ASC constitutes a qualitative as well as a quantitative restructuring of the system, which may be looked at as a new set of filters, biases, and tools for the observer/theorizer. By observing both the external and internal worlds from a variety of d-SoCs, rather than only one, we can develop a number of state-specific sciences within various d-ASCs. This enables a complementary series of views of the external and internal universes, which may partially compensate for the limits of the view found in any one d-SoC. I emphasize *partially* compensate, because no matter how many different d-SoCs we observe from, we are still human, and that probably implies ultimate limits on what we can do. We have not begun to approach these ultimate limits.

Note again that the idea that we must obtain complementary (I use this term in the sense it is used in physics) views of the universe from various d-SoCs, in order to get as full a view of it as possible, collides with an implicit and pervasive assumption that the ordinary d-SoC is the optimal, most logical state of consciousness and thus the one in which ultimate understandings will occur. This powerful and implicit bias, a product of enculturation, seriously hinders our thinking. We should always be open to the possibility that there is some "higher" d-SoC of which all other d-SoCs can be seen as fully comprehensible subsets: perhaps this is what enlightenment means in some ultimate sense. The ordinary d-SoC, with all its culturally conditioned limitations, is an unlikely candidate for this high degree.

The last two basic principles of physics do not have obvious parallels in known psychological functioning because the complexity of the human mind precludes such simple analogies. It is interesting, however, to consider them and assume that they ought to be manifest in the psychological realm if they are true. In this way, we can alert ourselves to look for parallels.

Fourth Principle: Conservation

The basic expression of the principle of conservation in physics is that in any reaction nothing is lost. The sum total of what goes in is the sum total of what goes out, even if there are transformations in form. This was originally thought of as the conservation of mass: the amount of matter that went into a chemical reaction was exactly equal to the amount of matter that came out of it. Because of various theoretical prospective changes, as well as the development of extremely precise measurement techniques, this definition was seen to be too simple and the principle was rephrased in terms of the conservation of the sum of mass and energy. Thus mass can be traded for energy, for example, but the sum is still the same. Modifications of the exact quantities are put into this equivalence equation in various physical situations, but the basic principle that what goes in equals what comes out holds generally through physics.

I do not see the obvious application of this to conscious experiences that we know of, because we almost never have simple, straightforward actions of consciousness that allow this kind of input-output comparison. Even apparently simple psychological reactions may consist of many separate steps that are perceived dimly or not at all due to automatization [14]. Also, experience at almost all times involves several things going on in rapid succession or even apparently simultaneously, and we know that important unconscious reactions can occur simultaneously with conscious ones. Thus we may have conscious experiences that seem to deplete or use up psychological energy or create psychological experience (the equivalent of mass?), and other kinds of experiences that seem to increase energy, but we do not know how to assess or measure these in a clear enough way to begin to measure what goes in and what goes out and see whether they are equivalent. We may be able to develop indirect indicators of unconscious reactions or make unconscious reactions more conscious by means of therapeutic or self-observational techniques.

Fifth Principle: Law of Least Action

The physical expression of this principle is that nature is economical: when a process can occur in several alternate ways, the one requiring the least expenditure of energy is the one used. Apparent exceptions generally turn out to conform to the principle and to have seemed exceptional because they were viewed in isolation: when considered as part of a larger system, the principle of least action is, in fact, followed.

An initial glance at psychological experience seems to show many contradictions to this. We do all sorts of things every day in ways that, even to our own perception, are certainly not the most economical ways. An observer may detect even more wasted energy. Suppose I carry a book from here into the next room. If I observe the action carefully, I will probably find that I have not used my body in a way that requires a minimal expenditure of energy to move the book from here to there. The complicating factor in trying to apply the fifth principle to psychology is the human propensity for doing several things simultaneously, many of them not in consciousness or even available to consciousness. So while carrying the book from this room to the next I may also be thinking about what to write in this chapter and using "body English" as part of my thinking process. I may also be semiconsciously trying to improve my posture, semiconsciously trying not to waste bodily energy, and perhaps unconsciously rebelling against the need to try and improve myself so much of the time, and so deliberately wasting some energy, either bodily or psychological energy, in order to express my "freedom."

A claim made in many spiritual writings, supported by some

experiential data from various d-ASCs, is that, with effort, we can become more and more conscious of exactly what we are doing. Whether we can become conscious of everything we are doing psychologically at a given moment is unknown. Thus it is unclear whether we can ever be in a position adequately to assess whether the law of least action applies to psychological phenomena. But it may be profitable to postulate that the fifth principle does apply and then proceed to look for manifestations.

In the history of science it has often been fruitful to postulate some principle as true before there is good evidence for it, and then to examine the subject matter of the particular science with the postulate in mind. It may be profitable to follow this plan for the fourth and fifth principles. They may be true; if they are not, the need to develop more precise ways of measuring many psychological phenomena simultaneously in order to test the truth of the principles will be a major advance in itself.

As above, so below?

19.

Ordinary Consciousness as a State of Illusion

✿✿✿

A belief common to almost all spiritual disciplines is that the human being is ordinarily in a state of consciousness described by such words as illusion, waking dreaming, waking hypnosis, ignorance, maya (Indian), or samsara (Buddhist). The realization of this unsatisfactory nature of one's ordinary d-SoC serves as the impetus for purifying it and/or attaining d-ASCs that are considered clearer and more valuable. This chapter considers the nature of samsara[1] (illusion) from the viewpoint of a Western psychologist. This interpretation does not represent a full understanding of the concept of samsara or related concepts, but is simply a way of expressing it that should be useful to other Westerners. This understanding flows partly from the systems approach developed in previous chapters.

Consciousness, as we ordinarily know it in the West, is not pure awareness but rather awareness as it is embodied in the psychological structure of the mind or the brain. Ordinary experience is of neither pure awareness nor pure psychological structure, but of awareness embedded in and modified by the structure of the mind/brain, and of the structure of the mind/

---

[1] I use the Buddhist term samsara in a general sense to indicate a d-SoC (ordinary or nonordinary) dominated by illusion, as detailed throughout this chapter, rather than in a technically strict Buddhist sense. I express my appreciation to Tarthong Tulku, Rinpoche, for helping me understand the Buddhist view.

brain embedded in and modified by awareness. These two components, awareness and psychological structure, constitute a gestalt, an overall interacting, dynamic system that makes up consciousness.

To most orthodox Western psychologists, awareness is a by-product of the brain. This primarily reflects a commitment to certain physicalistic concepts rather than any real understanding of what awareness is. In most spiritual disciplines, awareness is considered to exist, or have potential to exist, independently of brain structure [128].

Let us now take a Western, psychological look at how ordinary consciousness can be a state of illusion, samsara. Figure 19–1 represents the psychological processes of a person we shall call Sam at six succeeding instants of time, labeled T_1 through T_6. The vertical axis represents stimuli from the external world received in the six succeeding instants of time; the horizontal axis represents internal, psychological processes occurring through these six succeeding instants of time. The ovals represent the main psychological contents that are in the focus of consciousness, what Sam is mainly conscious of, where almost all the attention/awareness (energy) is. The arrows represent information flow; labels along the arrows indicate the nature of that information flow. The small circles containing the letter *A* represent internal psychological associations provoked by the external stimuli or by other internal associations: they are structures, the machinery of the mind.

Figure 19–1 is a flow diagram of what happens in Sam's mind, how information comes in to him and how this information is reacted to. Some of the effects are deliberately exaggerated to make points, so Sam appears psychotic in a rather paranoid way. As is discussed later, this example is not really so very different from our own ordinary consciousness.

In terms of the external world, a stranger walks up to Sam and says, *"Hi, my name is Bill."* For simplicity, we assume that this is all that happens of consequence in the external world, even though in everyday life such a message is usually accompanied by other messages expressed in gestures and bodily postures, modified by the setting in which they occur, etc. But the *defined* reality here is that the stranger says, *"Hi, my name is Bill."* This utterance occupies the first five sequential units of time.

At time T_1 the oval contains the label *Primary Meaning*, indicating that the focus of conscious awareness is the word *Hi*.

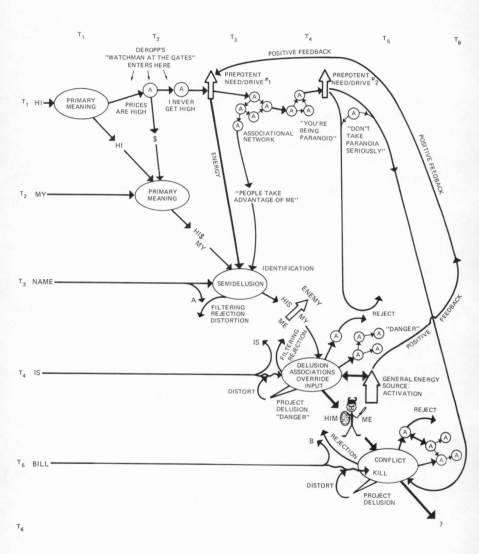

Figure 19–1. Development of samsaric consciousness.

Although this is shown as a simple perception, it is not a simple act. The word *Hi* would be a meaningless pattern of sounds except for the fact that Sam has already learned to understand the English language and thus perceives not only the sound qualities of the word *Hi*, but also its agreed-upon meaning. Already we are dealing not only with awareness per se, but with relatively permanent psychological structures that automatically give conventional meaning to language. Sam is an enculturated person.

The straightforward perception of the meaning of this word in its agreed-upon form is an instance of clear or relatively enlightened consciousness *within the given consensus reality*. Someone says *Hi* to you and you understand that this is a greeting synonymous with words like *hello* and *greetings*.

We can hypothesize that a relatively clear state of mind in the period T_1 through T_5 consists of the following. At each instant in time, the stimulus word being received is clearly perceived in the primary focus of consciousness with its agreed-upon meaning, and there is a sufficient memory continuity across these instants of time to understand the sequence. Information from each previous moment of consciousness is passed clearly on to the next, so that the meaning of the overall *sequence* of words is understood. For example, at time T_2 not only is the word *my* perceived clearly but the word *Hi* has been passed on internally from time T_1 as a memory, so Sam perceives that the sequence is *Hi, my*. Similarly by time T_5, there is primary perception of the agreed-upon meaning of the word *Bill*, coupled with a clear memory of *Hi, my name is* from the preceding four instants of time. This simple message of the speaker is thus perceived for exactly what it is.

Figure 19–1, however, shows a much more complex process than this clear perception of primary stimulus information. My own psychological observations have convinced me that this more complex process takes place all the time, and the straightforward, relatively clear perception described above is a rarity, especially for any prolonged period of time. So, let us look at this diagram of samsara in detail.

Again, we start with the primary meaning reception of the word *Hi* at time T_1. At time T_2, however, not only is there a primary, undistorted reception of the word *my*, but internally an association has taken place to the word *Hi*. This association is that PRICES ARE HIGH. This is deliberately an illogical (by consensus reality standards) association, based on the sound of the word and involving some departure from the primary meaning of the word *Hi* used as a greeting. In spite of our culture's veneration of logic, most of our psychological processes are not logical.

(Ignore the label DEROPP'S "WATCHMAN AT THE GATE" ENTERS HERE for the time being.)

The association PRICES ARE HIGH is not obviously pathological or nonadaptive at this point. Since prices on so many commodities have risen greatly, it is a likely association to hearing the word *Hi*, even though it does not strictly follow from the context of the actual stimulus situation. The pathology begins, the mechanism of samsara begins operating, in the fact that this association is not made in the full focus of consciousness but on the fringes of or even outside consciousness. Most attention/awareness energy is focused on the perception of *my* and the memory of *Hi*, so they are perceived clearly, but some attention/awareness energy, too little for clear consciousness, started "leaking" at T_1 and activated an association structure. The primary focus of consciousness at time T_2 is on the stimulus word *my*. The association PRICES ARE HIGH, operating on the fringes of consciousness, is shown as sending some informational content or feeling about money in general into the primary focus of consciousness at time T_2, but it is secondary content, with too little energy to be clear.

If associational activities decay or die out at this simple level, the state of samsara will not occur. But psychological processes that operate outside the clear focus of consciousness tend to get out of hand, acting much the same as implicit assumptions in a logic: as long as an assumption is implicit you are totally controlled by it as it does not occur to you to question it.

Let us assume that the association PRICES ARE HIGH triggers a further association during time T_2 because of the word HIGH, and this is an association of the sort I NEVER GET HIGH. This second association then connects up at time T_3 with emotionally charged concerns of Sam's, represented by the arrow as PREPOTENT NEED/DRIVE #1. Given the particular personality and concerns of this person (he worries because he never gets high), this is a constant, dynamically meaningful preoccupation with him and carries much psychical energy. In colloquial terms, Sam has had "one of his buttons pushed," even though there was no "good" reason for it to be pushed. Uncontrolled attention/awareness energy activated a structure to which other psychological/emotional energy was connected. Now we begin to deal not just with simple information but with information that is emotionally important. In this particular example, this information is activating and has a negative, depressed quality. At time T_3, when this prepotent need is activated, psychical energy flows into the main focus of consciousness. Also, the activation of this prepotent need/drive activates, by habit, a particular chain of associations centered around the idea that PEOPLE TAKE ADVANTAGE OF ME. This kind of associational content also begins to flow into the main focus of consciousness at time T_3.

Now let us look closely at time T_3 in terms of the primary focus of consciousness. In terms of how we have defined relatively clear functioning of this system of consciousness, the information *Hi, my* should be and is being delivered from the previous moment of consciousness at time T_2 to provide continuity. However, the relatively irrelevant association of money and the price of things, represented by the dollar sign, is also being delivered *as if it were primary meaning,* coming from the preceding primary focus of consciousness, even though it actually represents associational meaning that has slipped in. Because it was not clearly perceived as an *association* in the first place, it gets mixed up with the primary perceptions as memory transfers it from T_2 to T_3. A general activation energy of negative tone is flowing in from the prepotent need that is active at this time as well as the associational contents that PEOPLE TAKE ADVANTAGE OF ME. Because of the highly charged energy that goes with these associational contents, the primary focus of consciousness at time T_3 is labeled semidelusion; the primary focus of Sam's consciousness now begins to center around associational material while under the mistaken impression that it is centering around actual information coming in from the world. By identification with this associational material and the prepotent need activated, Sam begins to live in his associations, in a kind of (day) dream rather than in a clear perception of the world.

Psychologists are well aware of the phenomenon known as *perceptual defense,* of the selectivity of perception, of the fact that we more readily see what we want to see, tend not to see what we do not want to see, and/or distort what we do perceive into what we would like to perceive. What we would "like to" perceive may often seem unpleasant, yet it has secondary advantages insofar as it is supportive of the ego structure.

To indicate distortion of perception, a partial misperception of the actual stimulus is shown (the word *name* at time T_3) in that the *a* gets dropped out of *name* as it enters primary consciousness. While much of the original stimulus gets through and provides materials (in this case the other letters) for later processing, some of it drops out. This process of filtering perceptions, rejecting some things, distorting others, is a major characteristic of samsara. We tend to perceive selectively those elements of situations that support our preexisting beliefs and feelings.

Having reached a state of semidelusion, we now see that instead of the real information *Hi, my name,* a distorted mixture is being transmitted, consisting of some of the actual information that came in plus some of the associations and emotional energy that have come via the associations. Some fragments of stimuli coming in are being distorted to fit in with the beginnings of delusion brought about by the prepotent need and associational chains. Thus the *S* quality of the dollar sign $ becomes more an *S,* and the *Hi* turns into a *HIS,* and the *my* then becomes opposed to the HIS in a classic dichotomy. The letters *m* and *e* from *name* now stand in isolation, affected by the emotional charge of the dichotomy HIS and *my,* so it becomes HIS and ME. Because of the intensity added by the flow of energy at time T_3, all the components of stimuli may be arranged to spell the word ENEMY, further reinforcing the HIS-*my* dichotomy. Elements of the situation are automatically reworked by the Input-Processing subsystem to fit the emerging theme of consciousness.

Thus at time T_4 the primary focus of consciousness may be considered fully delusional in the sense that the internal, charged processes, the associational and emotional processes, distort perception so greatly that we can truly speak of Sam as being deluded or out of contact with the world. We now not only have selective perception in the sense of filtering and rejection, shown as the fourth stimulus word *is* being totally rejected here, but we now begin to get the psychological process known as *projection,* where internal processes become so strong that they are projected onto the environment and wrongly perceived as actual perceptions. Internal processes and memories are fed back into Input-Processing and reemerge in awareness with the quality of perception added. In this case the feelings about the conflict between

HIS and *my* and about ENEMY and about PEOPLE TAKE ADVANTAGE OF ME now begin to be experienced as stimuli coming in from the environment, rather than as internal associations. Other associational chains dealing with DANGER are triggered by this process, including one, discussed later, that keeps out competing associations that do not fit in with the delusional scheme.

By the time the stage of projection of delusions with the negative content of ENEMY and PEOPLE TAKE ADVANTAGE OF ME is reached, we tap into Sam's general energy sources and get an overall activation. It is not only that he has some specific need to think that people take advantage of him, he has now become so convinced that someone is actually taking advantage of him that he gets generally activated, generally uptight, in order to deal with this danger! This general up-tightness not only pours a great deal of energy into the specific focus of consciousness, it also acts as positive feedback, reinforcing the prepotent need to blame others for not getting high that started the whole chain in the first place. The fact that Sam now clearly feels himself getting up-tight as this general energy flows into him acts as a justification for the need to worry about people taking advantage of him in the first place, further reinforcing the whole delusion. He would not feel so up-tight unless something were wrong, would he?

Thus by time T_5, when the real stimulus is simply the name *Bill*, Sam's primary conscious awareness is more a picture of a dangerous warrior attacking, with the whole dichotomy of HIM versus ME in the fore. This is not a simple "cognitive" content, but is charged with energy and emotion, as represented by the spikes on his shield and helmet. Further rejection and distortion of actual input occur to enhance the delusional system. This is shown as the *B* being rejected from *Bill* and the internal processes adding a K, so that Sam in a real sense *hears* this stranger say the word KILL. This again is projection of a delusion that is mistaken for actual sensory input.

The same DANGER associational chains triggered off in time T_4 continue to be triggered off. A pair of associational chains that were separate are shown linked up to represent a tendency for the delusion to further draw together internal structures and so consolidate itself.

Now at this point we would certainly be tempted to say that

Sam is a paranoid psychotic, so out of touch with reality that he should be institutionalized (unless his particular culture values that sort of thing and instead makes him president). But this might not actually be true in social terms: there might be such strong, built-in inhibitions in the structure of his mind against *expressing* hostility, and/or such strong conditionings to act nicely, that Sam would make some sort of socially appropriate response even though he was internally seething with fear and anger and hatred.

At this point Sam is clearly in a state that can well be called samsara or waking dream.

The fact that conditioned inhibitions may keep a person from acting in a socially inappropriate way should remind us that this process is not an exaggeration that has no application to you and me. Some of our own processes may be just as distorted and intense. Although processes have been intensified to a paranoid, psychotic level in this illustration to make points clearer, my own studies of psychological data, plus my own observation of myself, have convinced me that this is the basic nature of much of our ordinary consciousness.

The presentation of samsara so far has been oversimplified by assuming there is only *one* prepotent need or drive that motivates us. Most of us have many such drives. Let us add a second drive to produce a state of conflict and further show the nature of samsara. Suppose after the activation of the prepotent need to blame others at time T_3, these associations themselves activate further associations to the effect YOU'RE BEING PARANOID, and this in turn activates a need not to be paranoid. This latter need might arise from a healthy understanding of oneself, or it might arise from the same kind of mechanical, social conditioning that governs the rest of the process. We need not consider the source of this need at the moment, but can simply say that it activates some further associations on the order of DON'T TAKE PARANOIA SERIOUSLY, along with energy from the second prepotent need.

Figure 19–1 shows these associations of not taking paranoia seriously trying to affect the primary content of consciousness in time T_4, but, because Sam is already in a highly delusional state and his consciousness is completely filled with highly energetic paranoid associations, this conflicting associational message cannot influence his consciousness. The particular route by which it tries to enter is blocked by the associations triggered off by the primary, delusional consciousness. There is no conscious conflict.[2]

The same association DON'T TAKE PARANOIA SERIOUSLY continues to be put out at time T_5 and, by coming into the focus of consciousness by a different route, actually gains some awareness. There is now a conflict situation: Sam "knows" that this very dangerous person may be threatening to kill him, and another part of him is saying that he is being paranoid and should not take this kind of paranoia seriously.

Time T_6 is shown as a question mark because we do not know what the resolution of this conflict will be. If the bulk of energy and contents of consciousness are taken up by the paranoid delusion, the thought DON'T TAKE PARANOIA SERIOUSLY may simply be wiped out or repressed for lack of energy to compete with the delusion.

This, then, is a picture of samsara in six consecutive instants of time. The process, of course, does not stop with six instants of time; it continues through one's lifetime. The consensus reality in which a person lives limits the reality that impinges on him: the physical world is generally known; people generally act toward him in "normal" ways. The internalization of consensus reality he learned during enculturation, his "normal" d-SoC, matches the socially maintained consensus reality. So culturally valued experiences continue to happen to him. This is shown schematically in Figure 19–2.

The horizontal axis represents the flow of time, bringing an ever-changing succession of events, people, interactions, things. The wheel rolling along the axis of time is you. The culturally conditioned selectivity of your perceptions and logics and actions is like a set of selective filters around the periphery of the wheel. If the right filter is activated (perceptual readiness) when a corresponding event occurs, you perceive, experience, and react to it in accordance with your ordinary d-SoC structure (which includes your personality structure). If the current interplay of your prepotent needs and associated structures does not produce

---

[2] Note an implicit, quantitative assumption here that in the competition of two processes, whichever has the greater energy (both attention/awareness energy and other kinds of energies) wins, subject to modification by the particulars of the structures involved. Certain structures may use energy more effectively than others. This line of thought needs development.

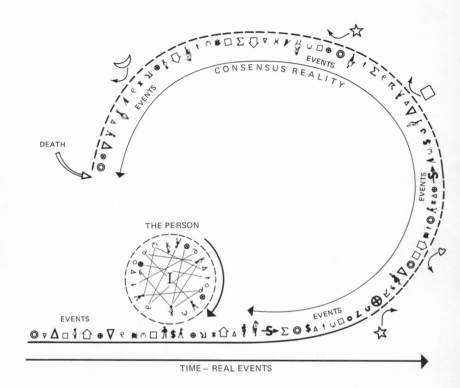

Figure 19–2. The wheel of an individual's life rolling through consensus reality.

a perceptual readiness to notice and respond to the way reality is stimulating you at the moment, you may not perceive an event at all, or perceive it in distorted form, as in the example of what can happen to *"Hi, my name is Bill."* In terms of Figure 19–2, you have the appropriate perceptual category built in, but the dynamic configuration of your mind, the position of that category on the wheel, is not right.

Some kinds of experiences are actively blocked by enculturation, not simply passively neglected: these are represented by a pair of bars between some categories within the wheel and the rim of the wheel. You will *not* experience certain kinds of things, even if they are happening, unless you are subjected to drastic pressures, internal or external.

Similar structures inside the wheel are shown as intercon-
nected. Recall from the earlier discussion of loading and other
kinds of stabilization that attention/awareness energy is constantly flowing back and forth, around and around in familiar,
habitual paths. This means that much of the variety and richness
of life is filtered out. An actual event, triggering off a certain
category of experience, activating a certain structure, is rapidly
lost as the internal processes connected with that structure and
its associated structures and prepotent needs take over the energy
of the system. Thus, the word *Hi* triggers such processes in our
hypothetical person, Sam, as do similar words like HIGH whenever they occur. His dynamically interacting, energy-consuming
network of structures and needs insulates him from the real
world.

Similarly, if your cultural conditioning has not given you any
categories as part of the Input-Processing subsystem to recognize
certain events, you may simply not perceive them. Thus real
events are shown on the time axis that have no corresponding
categories in the person; so the wheel of your life rolls over these
events hardly noticing them, perhaps with only a moment of
puzzlement before your more "important" internal needs and
preoccupations cause you to dismiss the unusual.

Figure 19–2 depicts cracks in the continuum, following Pearce's
analogy of looking for cracks—ways out—in the cosmic egg of your
culture. A crack may be a totally uncanny event, something for
which you have no conditioned categories, a chance to *see* in
don Juan's sense. If you experience such an event, though, the
cultural pressures, both from others and from the enculturated
structures built up within you, will probably force you to forget
it, to explain away its significance. If you experience something
everybody knows cannot happen, you must be crazy; but if you
do not tell anyone and forget about it yourself, you will be okay.

Shah [56, pp. 21–23] records a Sufi story, *"When the Waters
Were Changed,"* that illustrates this:

> Once upon a time Khidr, the Teacher of Moses, called upon
> mankind with a warning. At a certain date, he said, all the
> water in the world which had not been specially hoarded,
> would disappear. It would then be renewed, with different
> water, which would drive men mad.
>
> Only one man listened to the meaning of this advice. He

collected water and went to a secure place where he stored it, and waited for the water to change its character.

On the appointed date the streams stopped running, the wells went dry, and the man who had listened, seeing this happening, went to his retreat and drank his preserved water.

When he saw, from his security, the waterfalls again beginning to flow, this man descended among the other sons of men. He found that they were thinking and talking in an entirely different way from before; yet they had no memory of what had happened, nor of having been warned. When he tried to talk to them, he realized that they thought he was mad, and they showed hostility or compassion, not understanding.

At first he drank none of the new water, but went back to his concealment, to draw on his supplies, every day. Finally, however, he took the decision to drink the new water because he could not bear the loneliness of living, behaving and thinking in a different way from everyone else. He drank the new water, and became like the rest. Then he forgot all about his own store of special water, and his fellows began to look upon him as a madman who had miraculously been restored to sanity.

Finally, in Figure 19–2 time's arrow is shown as turned back upon itself to form a closed loop. This illustrates the conservative character of culture, the social pressure to keep things within the known. Events from outside the consensus reality are shown as deflected from entering it. This does not mean that no change is tolerated; it indicates that while outward forms of some things may change there is immense resistance to radical change. Fundamental assumptions of the consensus reality are strongly defended.

Fortunately we do make contact with reality at times. There are forces for real change in culture so the conservative forces do not always succeed. I have great faith in science as a unique force for constantly questioning the limits of consensus reality (at least in the long run), for deliberately looking for cracks in the cosmic egg that open onto vast new vistas. But, far more than we would like to admit, our lives can be mainly or completely tightly bounded wheels, rolling mechanically along the track of consensus reality.

This is a brief sketch of the way one's whole lifetime in a "normal" d-SoC can be a state of samsara. I cannot yet write more about it. I recommend Pearce's book, *Exploring the Crack in the Cosmic Egg* [50], for a brilliant analysis of the way our culture can trap us in its consensus reality, *even when we believe we are rebelling.*

20.

Ways Out of Illusion

✿✿

The discussion in Chapter 19 involves a value judgment that should be made more explicit: being in clear contact with external reality is good; being in poor contact with it is bad. This statement should not be overgeneralized: there is nothing wrong, for example, with *deliberately* becoming absorbed in a good movie and deliberately igorning those aspects of reality that are inconsistent with enjoying the movie. It is undesirable, on the other hand, to believe you are in good contact with reality when you are not.

I think most readers will have difficulty accepting Chapter 19 on more than an intellectual level. In some of our bad moments we may be unhappy with the ordinary d-SoC, but generally we seem pleased. Feeling happy is a function of a viable culture. If the culture is to survive, the majority of its members must feel contented with what they are doing and feel they are carrying out a meaningful function in life. Whether we generally feel happy or not, however, my personal observations and understanding of much of the research findings of modern psychology have convinced me that the analysis of ordinary consciousness as samsara is basically true. The present chapter is based on the assumption that it is true and is concerned with ways out of a state of illusion. It is not a guide to "enlightenment," for that is both inappropriate in the context of the present volume and beyond the reach of my competence.

Why, then, would you or I or anyone want to escape from the samsaric state that is our ordinary state of consciousness? The exact answer varies for every individual, but in general there is a mixture of cultural, personal, and growth/curiosity reasons.

A major function of a culture is to provide a consensus reality that not only deals adequately with the physical world about it but also produces a psychologically satisfactory life for the majority of its members. Each of us needs to feel that he belongs and that his life has meaning in terms of some valued, larger scheme of things. So every society has a mythos, a set of explicit and implicit beliefs and myths about the nature of reality and the society's place in it, that makes the activities of the people in that society meaningful. The mythos that has sustained our society for so long, largely the Judeo-Christian ethic, is no longer a very satisfactory mythos for many people. Similarly, the rationalism or scientism or materialism that tried to replace the religious mythos of our society has also turned out to be unsatisfactory for a large number of people. So we are faced with disruptions and conflicts in our society as people search consciously or unconsciously for more satisfying values. Our wheels of life, to continue the analogy of Figure 19–2, are not rolling along smoothly through our consensus reality. There are too many flat spots on the wheel that produce unpleasant jolts, and too many pieces of broken glass and potholes in the road of our consensus reality. So the ride is no longer comfortable.

Personal reasons for desiring a way out may involve initial poor enculturation, so we don't fit in well, knowledge of other cultural systems that seem advantageous in certain ways, and/or hope that a more satisfactory substitute can be found for our faulty culture. Various kinds of personal discontent make it difficult or impossible for an individual to find meaning in his life within the consensus reality of the culture. If he acts out these discontents, he may be classified as neurotic or psychotic, as a criminal, or as a rebel, depending on his particular style. If he acts out in a way that capitalizes on widespread cultural discontent, he may be seen as a reformer or pioneer. Or, he may outwardly conform to the mores of contemporary society but be inwardly alienated.

Finally, a person may want to escape for what I call growth/curiosity reasons, a healthy curiosity or desire to know. He may be able to tolerate the limitations and dissatisfactions of the culture around him and cope satisfactorily with it, and yet really want to know what lies outside that consensus reality, what other possibilities exist. He may see the limitations of the current world-view and want to know what world-views could replace it or whether it can be modified.

I emphasize scientific curiosity in this book, the desire to understand coupled with the realization that science is an excellent tool for gaining understanding. But even those of us who seek larger scientific understanding are also motivated by cultural and personal forces.

Are There Ways Out?

A major intellectual theme in the Western world lately has been that there are no ways out. Seeing the irrationality and horror, the samsaric nature of much of the world about us, some philosophers have concluded that this simply *is* human nature and that the best we can hope to do is tolerate it in existential despair or try, without much hope, to do the best we can. Indeed, a person can use such despair as a prop for the ego by priding himself on his "realism" and courage in facing such a dismal situation. While I respect these philosophies of despair for their honest recognition that there is no *easy* way out, I am of an optimistic nature myself and cannot accept despair as an end goal.

More importantly, my studies of people's experiences in various d-ASCs have convinced me that people can and do have vital, living experiences that *are* ways out. People have what Maslow [36] called *peak experiences* of openness, freedom, and belonging in which they feel they transcend, at least temporarily, the samsaric condition of ordinary consciousness. It can be argued that these experiences are just other illusions, that there is no freedom. But the belief that a way out does not exist may be just as illusory.

When the search for a way out is triggered by discontent with the ordinary d-SoC, a common reaction is to blame your discontent on some particular aspect of yourself or your society and look for ready-made solutions. There are thousands of leaders and groups who have ready-made solutions to sell you or give you—a multitude of -isms and -ologies. Give yourself to Jesus, join this commune, join political party X and remake the world, support the revolution, the truth is now revealed through yogi Z, eat your way to enlightenment with organic foods, find health and happiness with a low-cholesterol (or a high-cholesterol) diet, live in foreign country K where nobody hassles you. This is not meant to imply a blanket criticism of all communities, political and social ideas, or spiritual systems: indeed, in *Transpersonal Psychologies* [128] I attempt to promote the psychologies inherent in spiritual disciplines because of their great value. Most of the -isms and -ologies being offered contain valuable techniques for personal growth, ideas and techniques that *can* help you get out. But, when your motive for escape stems from a momentary discomfort with your present consensus reality, from a feeling that your wheel of life has too many flat spots and is hitting too many bumps, you may be seeking not radical change in your *self* as the root cause of your problems, but simply a more satisfactory belief system, a rounder wheel, and a nicely protected consensus reality that has no bumps. Any tool for personal or spiritual growth that humanity has ever devised can be perverted from its original function and used for simply making a person feel comfortable. Too often, a person is not really interested in looking more directly at reality, he simply wants his current samsaric wheel of life, the structures of his mind, overhauled or replaced with a new set that provides many good feelings and hardly any bad feelings.

Figure 20–1 is a revision of Figure 19–1, used to illustrate the concept of samsara. The content of the associational chains that are activated is altered, and the tone of the emotional energies is changed from negative to positive, and so the person's experience is positive. The labels on the figure make it self-explanatory. Still, all that happens in reality is that a stranger walks up and says, *"Hi, my name is Bill."* But this time the person, who we can call Sara, becomes extremely happy as a result and feels very good about herself. Yet she is as much in a state of illusion, samsara, as she was before. She has a set of internal structures, internal machinery, that make her feel good, but she is no more in touch with reality than before.

D-ASCs as Ways Out

Since the ordinary d-SoC is the creator and maintainer of consensus reality on a personal level, and since the sharing of similar, ordinary, "normal" d-SoCs by others is the maintainer of

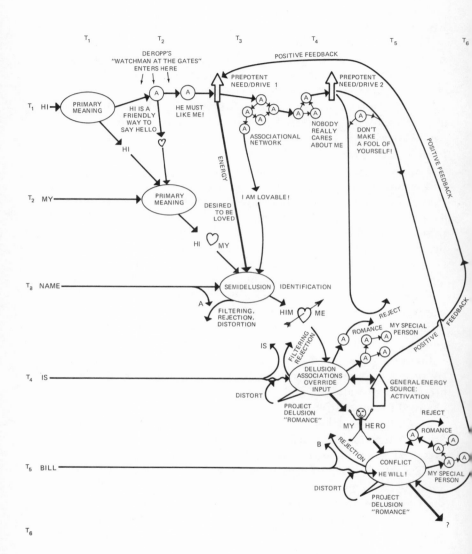

Figure 20-1. Development of samsaric consciousness with positive rather than negative emotional tone. As in Figure 19-1, internal processes soon overwhelm perception and are mistaken for perception.

the consensus reality on a social level, one way out of samsara is to enter a d-ASC, spend as much time there as possible, and get all your friends into that d-ASC too. You would choose a d-ASC or d-ASCs you valued, where you felt "high." To many people today the solution to the discomforts of current reality seems to be to get high and stay high.

Many of us are currently fascinated with the possibilities of being happy or solving our problems by entering into various d-ASCs, using chemical or nonchemical means. We have not yet learned to estimate realistically the costs of this route. We know the costs of chronic alcohol use, but seem willing to tolerate them. We do not know the costs of other d-ASCs very well. Consensus realities can exist and be created in various d-ASCs. The explanation of ordinary consciousness as samsara may well apply in d-ASCs such as drunkenness or marijuana intoxication. In other d-ASCs, such as meditative states, samsaric illusion may be less common, but this has not yet been shown scientifically.

We tend to get into what John Lilly [35] calls "overvaluation spaces"; we tend to be carried away by the contrast between our experience of the d-ASC and the ordinary d-SoC, and so overvalue the d-ASC. I think this is largely a function of novelty or need motivated blindness. Especially if we have taken a risk, such as using illegal drugs, to attain a d-ASC, we have a need to convince ourselves that the experience was worthwhile.

Further discussion of the costs of various d-ASCs seems to me premature. The immense amount of cultural hysteria and propaganda in this area gives us distorted and mostly false views of what the costs are, and we must work through this and build up some scientific knowledge before we can talk adequately about costs and benefits of d-ASCs.

The values of experiencing and working in d-ASCs *can* be exceptionally high. But, as is true of all the many tools that have been devised for human growth, a d-ASC's value depends on how well it is used. Experiencing a d-ASC carries no guarantee of personal betterment. Achieving a valuable d-ASC experience depends on what we want, how deeply and sincerely we want it, what conflicting desires we have, how much insight we have into ourselves, and how well prepared we are to make use of what we get in the d-ASC. There is a saying in many spiritual traditions: "He who tastes, knows." The process is not that automatic. A truer saying is: "He who tastes has an *opportunity* to know."

In the d-ASCs we know much about scientifically, the experiencer can be in a samsaric condition, involved in a personal or a consensus reality that is cut off from reality, even though its *style* is different, interesting, or productive of greater happiness than the ordinary d-SoC.

Techniques exist, however, that are intended to free a person's awareness from the dominance of the structure, of the machinery that has been culturally programmed into him. In terms of the radical view of awareness, whatever basic awareness ultimately is, there are techniques that at least produce the *experience* of freeing awareness partially or wholly from the continual dominance of structure, of moving toward a freer, more wide-ranging awareness rather than a consciousness that is primarily a function of the automated structure pattern of consensus reality. Let us consider the general categories into which these techniques fall, remembering that any discussion of their ultimate usefulness is beyond current science.

The first step in using any of these techniques is to recognize that there is a problem. Assume, therefore, that an individual, through self-observation, has acquired enough experiential knowledge of his samsaric condition to know that he needs to and wants to do something. Although there are many religious definitions of what a clear or higher state of consciousness is, we can define a clear*er* condition of consciousness simply as one in which external reality is recognized more for what it is, less distorted by internal processes.

Discriminative Awareness

One way to begin to escape from the samsaric condition is to pay enough directed attention to your mental processes so that you can distinguish between primary perception coming in from the external world and associational reaction to it. We tend to assume that we do this naturally, but I believe it is rare. This may be done by understanding how your associational structures are built and how they generally operate, thus distinguishing associational reactions on a content basis, and/or by getting a general experiential "feel" for a quality that distinguishes associational reactions. If you can keep your primary perception and your reactions to it clearly distinguished in your consciousness, you are less likely to project your reactions to stimuli onto the environment and others or to distort incoming perception to make your perceptions consistent with internal reactions. I have found, from both personal observation and indications in the psychological literature, that making this discrimination, putting a fairly high degree of awareness on the *beginnings* of the associational process, tends to undercut their ability to automatically stimulate other associational chains and thus activate emotions. You need not *do* anything in particular to the association, just be clearly aware that it is an associational reaction. The situation is analogous to being on your good behavior when you know others are watching, whether or not those others are doing anything in particular to influence your behavior.

A Watchman at the Gate

If you refer to Figures 19–1 and 20–1, you will notice the label, DEROPP'S "WATCHMAN AT THE GATE" ENTERS HERE. The analogy taken from DeRopp's book [15], is to a watchman at the city gate (the senses) who knows that certain slums in the city of the mind have outbursts of rioting when certain mischievous characters (stimulus patterns) are allowed into the city. The watchman scrutinizes each traveler who comes up and does not admit those he knows will cause rioting. If you have a good understanding of your associational and reaction patterns, your prepotent needs, and the particular kinds of stimuli that set them off, you can maintain an attentive watchfulness on your primary perception. When you realize that an incoming stimulus is the sort that will trigger an undesirable reaction, you can inhibit the reaction. It is easier to become self-conscious, and thus remove some of the energy from incoming stimuli *before* they have activated associational chains and prepotent needs, than to stop the reactions once they have been activated.

To a certain extent the practice of discriminative awareness, described above, performs this function. Setting up the watchman, however, provides a more specialized discrimination, paying special attention to certain troublesome kinds of stimuli and taking more active measures when undesirable stimuli are perceived. The watchman robs the reaction of its power early enough to prevent it from gaining any appreciable momentum;

discriminative awareness allows the reaction to tap into various prepotent needs, even though the continuous observation of it lessens identification and so takes away some of its power.

Nonattachment

A classical technique in the spiritual psychologies for escaping from samsara is the cultivation of nonattachment, learning to "look neutrally" on *whatever* happens, learning to pay full attention to stimuli and reactions but not to identify with them. The identification process, the quality added by the operation of the Sense of Identity subsystem discussed in Chapter 8, adds a great deal of energy to any psychological process. Without it, these processes have less energy and therefore make less mischief.

Vipassana meditation is a specific practice of nonattachment performed in the technically restricted meditative setting. Recall that the instructions (Chapter 7) are to pay attention to whatever happens, but not to try to make anything in particular happen or to try to prevent anything in particular from happening. The idea is neither to welcome nor reject any particular stimulus or experience. This is quite different from the ordinary stance toward events, where a person seeks out and tries to prolong pleasant ones and attempts to avoid or terminate unpleasant ones. Meditation, as Naranjo [39] points out, is a technically simplified situation: a person removes himself from the bustle of the world to make learning easier. But it is also designed to teach nonattachment so the practice can be transferred to everyday life.

If one is successful in practicing nonattachment, the machinery of the mind runs when stimulated, but does not automatically grab attention/awareness so readily; reactions and perceptions do not become indiscriminately fused together; and attention/awareness energy remains available for volitional use.

There are two clear ways in which the practice of nonattachment can be flawed. Often a person believes that he is unaffected by certain things, that he just is not interested in them or that they do not bother him This apparent indifference, however, actually comes from an active inhibitory process that takes place outside the focus of awareness. So he is really up-tight even if he does not feel it. Self-observation and/or feedback from others is a corrective for this. Effective growth practices can thus promote unhappiness and upset by breaking through an inhibitory layer before being able to work on the disturbances themselves.

The other flaw is that while nonattachment may free a person from the habitual loss of attention/awareness energy to the machinery of the mind, the machinery is still there. He no longer automatically identifies with the machinery; it no longer forcibly grabs his attention/awareness, but the machinery itself, while dormant, has not been dismantled. What happens if he is put in totally new circumstances in which he has not practiced nonattachment?

Recall that once the machinery of the mind is activated, it grabs attention/awareness energy, and after this, control may be difficult or impossible. Totally new circumstances may activate the previously inactive structures in novel ways so that they cannot be stopped. A person may be unaware that the machinery has begun operating, so it can grab his attention/awareness energy and plunge him into a samsaric state again. This appears to have happened, for example, to some Indian yogis who began living in the West. Their practice of nonattachment as a principal discipline in India had enabled them to achieve a special serenity of mind, but this was under particular cultural circumstances. As one example, yogis and holy men are treated as nonsexual beings in India. Thus women may worship them, but in a completely nonsexual way. When they come to the West and are besieged in a sexual way by beautiful young girls, the yogis, lacking practice in handling this, are subject to strongly activated samsaric mechanisms.

Dismantling Structures

The above techniques are *mindfulness* techniques, involving an increase in awareness of what is happening and how one is reacting to it, usually with some discipline, such as nonattachment, practiced in conjunction with this increased awareness. To some extent, these mindfulness techniques can actually dismantle some of the structures of the mind. This happens in two ways. First, some structures seem to need to operate in the dark; they cannot continue to operate when one is fully conscious of what is happening. Thus, insight into the nature of a structure results in its partial or full dissolution. Second, some structures and combinations of structures seem to need to be activated periodically to maintain their integrity. By practices like the watchman at the gate or nonattachment, which do not allow energy to flow freely into them, they are starved and gradually lose their integrity. Gurdjieff's [48] technique of self-observation, for example, involves paying full attention to one's reactions without making any attempt to change them. Many people practicing self-observation have had the experience of watching an undesirable reaction occur repeatedly, then weakly and later not at all, even though the requisite stimulus occurs.

Many structures and subsystems are an intimate part of a person's enculturated personality, however, and are not only highly resistant to change by insight, but may be incapable of being perceived well at all. They are so connected to prepotent needs and defense mechanisms that they cannot be observed clearly, or else they are so implicit that they are outside awareness. They are never observed, so observation and mindfulness techniques do not work.

Here is where Western-developed psychotherapy becomes exceptionally valuable. Through feedback and pressure provided by others, whether a single therapist or a group, ordinarily invisible aspects of a person's self may be so surcharged with emotional energy that he is *forced* to confront them, and this insight may change them. If insight alone is not sufficient, a variety of techniques are available, ranging from operant-conditioning to guided imagery techniques [3], which can deliberately change specific structures.

Western-style psychotherapy is limited because it is likely to be used not on structures that are basic to the samsaric condition, but only on structures that produce experiences and behaviors that are not acceptable in the particular consensus reality. Thus many psychotherapists are not growth agents in a general sense, but rather work to readjust a deviant person to the consensus reality of his culture. This is not a conscious manipulation on the part of these psychotherapists, but simply a reflection of the power and implicitness of their own enculturation processes. Psychotherapy can be a subversive tool in some practitioners' hands, for some of the assumptions of the consensus reality can be questioned in it, and the patient can grow beyond his culture in some ways. All too often, however, the implicit assumptions are not even questioned.

In stating that most patients do not learn to go beyond consensus reality, I do not want to imply that they should learn to behave in a way that is clearly at odds with consensus reality. To behave in "crazy" ways is no sure sign of escape from samsara. Knowing how to use effectively the consensus reality in which one lives is essential for survival. In terms of cultural, personal, and scientific goals of transcending samasaric limitations of the ordinary state, however, we should be aware of the limits of conventional psychotherapy.

I suspect, as Naranjo [39] has suggested, that the synthesis of the psychotherapy techniques of the West and the spiritual disciplines of the East will form one of the most powerful tools for understanding ourselves that has ever existed. The various kinds of mindfulness and nonattachment techniques are the ultimate tools because of their generality, but there may be some psychological structures in the personality that have so much energy, are so implicit, or are so heavily defended that they must be dealt with by using specific psychotherapeutic techniques to dismantle them.

How Far Can We Go?

If we assume, for the purpose of this discussion, the (at least partial) validity of the radical view of the mind, then what are the limits to human consciousness and awareness? Figure 20–2 presents some speculation along this line.

Consider reality as divided into two realms: MEST, the physical world, of which we know many of the basic laws and are discovering more, and the realm of awareness, whose basic laws are essentially unknown to us at this time. The ordinary d-SoC, then, is the gestalt product of awareness and structure, determined and limited by whatever laws inherently govern each realm, and yet is also an emergent synthesis not fully predictable from the laws of either realm.

In some ways the composite system is even more limited, for both the MEST structure and awareness have been further restricted in the enculturation process. Thus the ordinary d-SoC is capable of considerable expansion: we can change existing structures and build new ones, and we can cultivate the ability to control awareness more freely within these structures and to pay attention to things other than what the culture has defined as important.

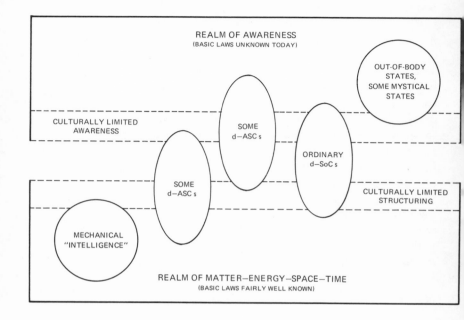

Figure 20–2.   Consciousness and awareness-MEST interaction.

Judging from experiential reports, some d-ASCs seem to be much less mechanical, much less controlled by structures and allowing more free range of awareness. This is represented in Figure 20–2 by the oval just to the left of the ordinary d-SoC penetrating more into the realm of awareness and less into the realm of MEST. Similarly, experiential reports from some d-ASCs—those caused by sedatives, for example—suggest that there is less awareness and far more mechanicalness, that consciousness is far more restricted by structure than ordinarily. Thus another oval, further to the left, is shown as more into the MEST realm and less into the awareness realm. The extreme case of this, of course, is mechanical intelligence, the computer, which (as far as we know) has no awareness at all but processes information in a totally mechanical way, a way totally controlled by the laws of the MEST realm. Present computers are also partially limited by cultural structuring; it only occurs to us to program them to do certain "sensible" things, giving them a range that is probably less than their total capability.

Up to this point the discussion is still compatible with the orthodox view of the mind, which sees awareness as a function of the brain. The circle to the far right in Figure 20–2, however, is compatible only with the radical view that awareness can operate partially or totally independently of the brain structure. In some mystical experiences, and in states called out-of-the-body experiences, people report existing at space/time locations different from that of their physical bodies, or being outside of space/time altogether. I believe that parapsychological data require us to consider this kind of statement as more than interesting experiential data, as possibly being valid rather than simply being nonsense. The reader interested in the implications of parapsychology for the study of consciousness should consult other writings of mine [128, 129, 131]. Let me note here that to the extent that this may be true, awareness may potentially become partially or wholly free of the patterning influence of MEST structure.

An awareness of how structures and systems of structures tend automatically to grab attention/awareness and other psychological energies makes it easy to form a picture of structure as bad and to see d-SoCs that are less involved with structure as automatically better or higher. This is a mistake. Structures perform valuable functions as well as confining ones. A d-SoC is not just a way of limiting awareness; it is also a way of *focusing* attention/awareness and other psychological energies to make effective *tools,* to enable us to cope in particular ways.

I have observed people in d-ASCs where they seem less caught in structures, more inclined toward the unstructured awareness dimension of mind. My impression is that it was both a gain and a loss: new insights were gained, but there was often an inability to hold to anything and change it in a desired direction. Certainly there are times when not attempting to change anything, just observing, is the best course, but the ability to move between activity and passivity *as appropriate* is optimal. The structures of d-SoCs aid us by restricting awareness and facilitating focusing. Perhaps as meditative and similar exercises teach us to control attention/awareness more precisely, we may have less need for structures.

As a scientist, I have tried to keep the speculation in these last three chapters compatible with the scientific world-view and the scientific method as I know them. I have often drawn on data not generally accepted in orthodox scientific circles, but they are data that I would be willing to argue are good enough to deserve closer examination. Because I have set myself that restriction in writing this book, I now end speculation on how far human awareness might be able to go, for to continue would take me further from my scientific data base than I am comfortable in going at this time.

Let me conclude with what may seem a curious observation: Western psychology has collected an immense amount of data supporting the concept in the first place. We have studied some aspects of samsara in far more detail than the Eastern traditions that originated the concept of samsara. Yet almost no psychologists apply this idea to themselves! They apply all this knowledge of human compulsiveness and mechanicalness to other people, who are labeled "abnormal" or "neurotic," and assume that their own states of consciousness are basically logical and clear. Western psychology now has a challenge to recognize this detailed evidence that our "normal" state is a state of samsara and to apply the immense power of science and our other spiritual traditions, East and West, to the search for a way out.

Bibliography

1. Aaronson, B. The Hypnotic Induction of the Void. Paper presented to American Society of Clinical Hypnosis, San Francisco, 1969.
2. Annis, R., and Frost, B. Human visual ecology and orientation anisotropies in acuity. *Science,* 1974, *182,* 729–731.
3. Assagioli, R. *Psychosynthesis: A Manual of Principles and Techniques.* New York: Hobbs & Dorman, 1965.
4. Barber, T. Suggested ("Hypnotic") Behavior: The Trance Paradigm Versus an Alternative Paradigm. In E. Fromm and R. Shor (eds.). *Hypnosis: Research Developments and Perspectives.* Chicago: Aldine/Atherton, 1972, pp. 115–183.
5. Bennett, J. *Witness.* Tucson, Ariz.: Omen Press, 1974.
6. Berke, J., and Hernton, C. *The Cannabis Experience.* London: Peter Owen, 1974.
7. Blackburn, T. Sensuous-intellectual complementarity in science. *Science,* 1971, *172,* 1003–1007.
8. Bohr, N. *Essays, 1958–1962, on Atomic Physics and Human Knowledge.* New York: Wiley, 1963.
9. Castaneda, C. *The Teachings of Don Juan: A Yaqui Way of Knowledge.* Berkeley: University of California Press, 1968.
10. ———. *A Separate Reality: Further Conversations with Don Juan.* New York: Simon & Schuster, 1971.
11. ———. *Journey to Ixtlan: The Lessons of Don Juan.* New York: Simon & Schuster, 1973.
12. ———. *Tales of Power.* New York: Simon & Schuster, 1974.
13. Danielou, A. The influence of sound phenomena on human consciousness. *Psychedelic Rev.,* 1966, No. 7, 20–26.
14. Deikman, A. De-automatization and the mystic experience. *Psychiatry,* 1966, *29,* 329–343.
15. DeRopp, R. *The Master Game.* New York: Delacorte Press, 1968.
16. Estabrooks, G. *Hypnotism.* New York: Dutton, 1943.
17. Evans-Wentz, W. *Tibetan Yoga and Secret Doctrines.* London: Oxford University Press, 1967.
18. Ghiselin, B. *The Creative Process.* New York: New American Library, 1952.
19. Gill, M., and Brenman, M. *Hypnosis and Related States: Psychoana-*

lytic Studies in Regression. New York: International Universities Press, 1959.

20. Goleman, D. The Buddha on meditation and states of consciousness. I. *J. Transpersonal Psychol.,* 1972, *4* (1) 1–44. Reprinted in C. Tart (ed.) . *Transpersonal Psychologies.* New York: Harper & Row, 1975.

21. Goodwin, D., and Powell, B. Alcohol and recall: State-dependent effects in man. *Science,* 1969, *163,* 1358–1360.

22. Govinda, A. *Foundations of Tibetan Mysticism.* New York: Dutton, 1960.

23. Green, E., Green, A., and Walters, E. Voluntary control of internal states: Psychological and physiological. *J. Transpersonal Psychol.,* 1970, *2* (1) , 1–26.

24. Gurdjieff, G. *Views from the Real World.* New York: Dutton, 1973.

25. Haley, J. (ed.) . *Advanced Techniques of Hypnosis and Therapy: Selected Papers of Milton H. Erickson, M. D.* New York: Grune & Stratton, 1967.

26. Hilgard, E. A neodissociation interpretation of pain reduction in hypnosis. *Psychol. Rev.,* 1973, *80,* 396–411.

27. Honorton, C. Feedback-augmented EEG alpha, shifts in subjective state, and ESP card-guessing performance. *J. Am. Soc. Psych. Res.,* 1971, *65,* 308–323.

28. ———. Shifts in subjective state associated with feedback-augmented EEG alpha. *Psychophysiology,* 1972, *9,* 269–270.

29. ———. Shifts in subjective state and ESP under conditions of partial sensory deprivation. *J. Am. Soc. Psych. Res.,* 1973, *67,* 191–196.

30. James, W. *The Varieties of Religious Experience.* New York: Longmans, 1935, p. 298.

31. Keynes, G. (ed.) . *Blake: Complete Writings.* London: Oxford University Press, 1966.

32. Kuhn, T. *The Structure of Scientific Revolutions.* Chicago: University of Chicago Press, 1962.

33. LeCron, L. (ed.) . *Experimental Hypnosis.* New York: Macmillan, 1956.

34. Lilly, J. *Programming and Metaprogramming in the Human Biocomputer.* Miami, Fl.: Communication Research Institute, 1967. Reprinted by Whole Earth Catalog, Menlo Park, Calif., 1971.

35. ———. *The Center of the Cyclone.* New York: Julian Press, 1972.

36. Maslow, A. *Toward a Psychology of Being.* Princeton: Van Nostrand, 1962.

37. Masters, R., and Houston, J. *The Altered States of Consciousness Induction Device: Some Possible Uses in Research and Psychotherapy.* Pomona, N.Y.: Foundation for Mind Research, 1971.

38. Moll, A. *Hypnotism*. New York: Scribner, 1902.

39. Naranjo, C., and Ornstein, R. *On the Psychology of Meditation*. New York: Viking, 1971.

40. Needleman, J. *The New Religions*. New York: Doubleday, 1970.

41. *Newsweek, 25,* January 1971, p. 52.

42. Nicoll, M. *Psychological Commentaries on the Teachings of Gurdjieff and Ouspensky*. London: Stuart & Watkins, 1970.

43. O'Neill, J. *Prodigal Genius: The Life of Nikola Tesla*. New York: Washburn, 1944.

44. Orne, M. The nature of hypnosis: Artifact and essence. *J. Abnorm. Soc. Psychol.,* 1959, *58*, 277–299.

45. ———. On the social psychology of the psychological experiment: With particular reference to demand characteristics and their implications. *Am. Psychologist,* 1962, *17*, 776–783.

46. ———, and Scheibe, K. The contributions of nondeprivation factors in the production of sensory deprivation effects: The psychology of the "panic button." *J. Abnorm. Soc. Psychol.,* 1964, *68*, 3–12.

47. Ornstein, R. *The Psychology of Consciousness*. New York: Viking, 1972.

48. Ouspensky, P. *In Search of the Miraculous*. New York: Harcourt, 1949.

49. Pearce, J. *The Crack in the Cosmic Egg*. New York: Simon & Schuster, 1973.

50. ———. *Exploring the Crack in the Cosmic Egg*. New York: Julian Press, 1974.

51. Phillips, B. (ed.). *The Essentials of Zen Buddhism: An Anthology of the Writings of Daisetz T. Suzuki*. London: Rider, 1963, pp. 31–32.

52. Pribram, K. *Languages of the Brain: Experimental Paradoxes and Principles in Neurophysiology*. Englewood Cliffs, N. J.: Prentice-Hall, 1971.

53. Priestley, J. *Man and Time*. New York: Doubleday, 1964.

54. Rolf, I. Structural integration: Gravity, an unexplored factor in a more human use of human beings. *J. Inst. Comp. Stud. Hist., Philos., Sci.,* 1963, *1*.

55. Rosenthal, R. *Experimenter Effects in Behavioral Research*. New York: Appleton, 1966.

56. Shah, I. *Tales of the Dervishes*. London: Jonathan Cape, 1967.

57. ———. *The Pleasantries of the Incredible Mulla Nasrudin*. New York: Dutton, 1968.

58. ———. *Tales of the Dervishes*. New York: Dutton, 1970.

59. Shor, R. The accuracy of estimating the relative difficulty of typical

hypnotic phenomena. *Int. J. Clin. Exp. Hypnosis,* 1964, *12,* 191–201.

60. Snyder, S. *Uses of Marijuana.* New York: Oxford University Press, 1971.

61. Tart, C. A Comparison of Suggested Dreams Occurring in Hypnosis and Sleep. Unpublished MA thesis, University of North Carolina, 1962.

62. ———. Frequency of dream recall and some personality measures. *J. Consult. Psychol.,* 1962, *26,* 467–470.

63. ———. Hypnotic depth and basal skin resistance. *Int. J. Clin. Exp. Hypnosis,* 1963, *11,* 81–92.

64. ———. Physiological correlates of psi cognition. *Int. J. Parapsychol.,* 1963, *5,* 375–386.

65. ———. A possible "psychic" dream, with some speculations on the nature of such dreams. *J. Am. Soc. Psych. Res.,* 1963, *42,* 283–298.

66. ———. The influence of the experimental situation in hypnosis and dream research: A case report. *Am. J. Clin. Hypnosis,* 1964, *7,* 163–170.

67. ———. A comparison of suggested dreams occurring in hypnosis and sleep. *Int. J. Clin. Exp. Hypnosis,* 1964, *12,* 263–289.

68. ———. The hypnotic dream: Methodological problems and a review of the literature. *Psychol. Bull.,* 1965, *63,* 87–99.

69. ———. Application of instrumentation to the investigation of "haunting" and "poltergeist" cases. *J. Am. Soc. Psych. Res.,* 1965, *59,* 190–201.

70. ———. Toward the experimental control of dreaming: A review of the literature. *Psychol. Bull.,* 1965, *64,* 81–92. Reprinted in W. Webb (ed.) . *Sleep: An Experimental Approach.* New York: Macmillan, 1968, pp. 131–144. Also reprinted in C. Tart (ed.) . *Altered States of Consciousness: A Book of Readings.* New York: Wiley, 1969, pp. 133–144.

71. ———. An inexpensive masking noise generator: Monaural or stereo. *Psychophysiology,* 1965, *2,* 170–172.

72. ———. Models for the explanation of extrasensory perception. *Int. J. Neuropsychiat.,* 1966, *2,* 488–504.

73. ———. Card guessing tests: Learning paradigm or extinction paradigm. *J. Am. Soc. Psych. Res.,* 1966, *60,* 46–55.

74. ———. Some effects of posthypnotic suggestion on the process of dreaming. *Int. J. Clin. Exp. Hypnosis,* 1966, *14,* 30–46.

75. ———. ESPATESTER: An automatic testing device for parapsychological research. *J. Am. Soc. Psych. Res.,* 1966, *60,* 256–269.

76. ———. Types of hypnotic dreams and their relation to hypnotic depth. *J. Abnorm. Psychol.,* 1966, *71,* 377–382.

77. ———. Review of S. Smith, *The Enigma of Out-of-the-Body Travel.* *Theta,* 1966, *13,* 2–3.
78. ———. Spontaneous Thought and Imagery in the Hypnotic State: Psychophysiological Correlates. Paper presented to American Psychological Association, New York, 1966.
79. ———. Patterns of basal skin resistance during sleep. *Psychophysiology,* 1967, *4,* 35–39.
80. ———. The control of nocturnal dreaming by means of posthypnotic suggestion. *Int. J. Parapsychol.,* 1967, *9,* 184–189.
81. ———. A second psychophysiological study of out-of-the-body experiences in a gifted subject. *Int. J. Parapsychol.,* 1967, *9,* 251–258.
82. ———. Psychedelic experiences associated with a novel hypnotic procedure, mutual hypnosis. *Am. J. Clin. Hypnosis,* 1967, *10,* 65–78. Reprinted in C. Tart (ed.) . *Altered States of Consciousness: A Book of Readings.* New York: Wiley, 1969, pp. 291–308.
83. ———. Random output selector for the laboratory. *Psychophysiology,* 1967, *3,* 430–434.
84. ———. A psychophysiological study of out-of-the-body experiences in a selected subject. *J. Am. Soc. Psych. Res.,* 1968, *62,* 3–27.
85. ———. Ethics and psychedelic drugs. *Am. Psychologist,* 1968, *23,* 455–456.
86. ———. Hypnosis, Psychedelics, and Psi: Conceptual Models. In R. Cavanna and M. Ullman (eds.) . *Psi and Altered States of Consciousness.* New York: Garrett Press, 1968, pp. 24–41.
87. ———. Two token object studies with the "psychic," Peter Hurkos. *J. Am. Soc. Psych. Res.,* 1968, *62,* 143–157.
88. ———. *Altered States of Consciousness: A Book of Readings.* New York: Wiley, 1969.
89. ———. Review of C. Green, *Out-of-the-Body Experiences. Theta,* 1969, *25,* 3–4.
90. ———. The "High" Dream: A New State of Consciousness. In C. Tart (ed.) . *Altered States of Consciousness: A Book of Readings.* New York: Wiley, 1969, pp. 169–174. Reprinted in *J. Am. Soc. Psychosom. Dent. Med.,* 1969, *16,* 15–22.
91. ———. Approaches to the study of hypnotic dreams. *Percept. Mot. Skills,* 1969, *28,* 864.
92. ———. The posthypnotic dream: Nature of the effect and individual differences. *Psychophysiology,* 1969, *6,* 268.
93. ———. Influencing Dream Content: Discussion of Witkin's Paper. In M. Kramer (ed.) . *Dream Psychology and the New Biology of Sleep.* Springfield, Ill.: Thomas, 1969, pp. 344–360.
94. ———. Three studies of EEG alpha feedback. *Biofeedback Soc. Proc.,* 1969, Part 3, 14–19.

95. ———. A further psychophysiological study of out-of-the-body experiences in a gifted subject. *Proc. Parapsychol. Assoc.*, 1969, *6*, 43–44.

96. ———. Self-report scales of hypnotic depth. *Int. J. Clin. Exp. Hypnosis*, 1970, *18*, 105–125.

97. ———. Did I Really Fly? Some Methodological Notes on the Investigation of Altered States of Consciousness and Psi Phenomena. In R. Cavanna (ed.) . *Psi Favorable States of Consciousness: Proceedings of an International Conference on Methodology in Psi Research*. New York: Parapsychology Foundation, 1970, pp. 3–10.

98. ———. Increases in hypnotizability resulting from a prolonged program for enhancing personal growth. *J. Abnorm. Psychol.*, 1970, *75*, 260–266.

99. ———. Marijuana intoxication: Reported effects on sleep. *Psychophysiology*, 1970, *7*, 348.

100. ———. Review of Celia Green, *Lucid Dreams and Out-of-the-Body Experiences. J. Am. Soc. Psych. Res.*, 1970, *64*, 219–227.

101. ———. Transpersonal potentialities of deep hypnosis. *J. Transpersonal Psychol.*, 1970, *2*, 27–40. Reprinted in J. White (ed.) . *The Highest State of Consciousness*. New York: Doubleday Anchor, 1972, pp. 344–351.

102. ———. Waking from sleep at a preselected time. *J. Am. Soc. Psychosom. Dent. Med.*, 1970, *17*, 3–16.

103. ———. Marijuana intoxication: Common experiences. *Nature*, 1970, *226*, 701–704. Reprinted in *The Pot Report*. New York: Award Books, 1972. Also reprinted in E. Goode (ed.) . *Marijuana*, 2nd ed. Chicago: Aldine/Atherton, 1972. Also reprinted in R. Evans and R. Rozelle (eds.) . *Social Psychology in Life*, 2nd ed. 1973. Also reprinted in B. Ekstrand and L. Bourne (eds.) . *Principles and Meanings in Psychology*. New York: Dryden Press, 1974, pp. 351–354.

104. ———. A Theoretical Model for States of Consciousness. Paper presented at Menninger Foundation Conference on Voluntary Control of Internal States, Council Grove, Kansas, 1970.

105. ———. *On Being Stoned: A Psychological Study of Marijuana Intoxication*. Palo Alto, Calif.: Science & Behavior Books, 1971.

106. ———. Introduction to R. Monroe, *Journeys Out of the Body*. New York: Doubleday, 1971, pp. 1–17.

107. ———. Work with marijuana. II. Sensations. *Psychol. Today*, 1971, *4*, (12) , 41–45, 66–68.

108. ———. Review of R. Ornstein and C. Naranjo, *The Psychology of Meditation*. In *The Last Whole Earth Catalog*, New York, Random House, 1971, 423.

109. ———. Review of R. Monroe, *Journeys Out of the Body. The Last Whole Earth Catalog*, New York, Random House, 1971, 415.

110. ———. Review of D. Cohen, Current research on the frequency of dream recall. *Psychol. Bull.*, 1970, *73*, 433–440. *UCLA Brain Information Service Sleep Bulletin*, 1971, No. 82, 8.

111. ———. ESP and pot. *Psychic*, 1971, *3*, (2), 26–30.

112. ———. Scientific foundations for the study of altered states of consciousness. *J. Transpersonal Psychol.*, 1972, *3* (2), 93–124.

113. ———. A psychologist's experience with transcendental meditation. *J. Transpersonal Psychol.*, 1972, *3* (2), 135–140.

114. ———. Measuring the Depth of an Altered State of Consciousness, with Particular Reference to Self-Report Scales of Hypnotic Depth. In E. Fromm and R. Shor (eds.), *Hypnosis: Research Developments and Perspectives.* Chicago: Aldine/Atherton, 1972, pp. 445–477.

115. ———. *Altered States of Consciousness.* 2nd. ed., revised. New York: Doubleday Anchor, 1972.

116. ———. Sleep EEG study of out-of-the-body experiences. *Psychophysiology*, 1972.

117. ———. Concerning the scientific study of the human aura. *J. Am. Soc. Psych. Res.*, 1972, *46*, 1–21.

118. ———. La ciena y el alma humana. (Science and the human soul.) *Tribuna Medica*, 1972, *9* (425), 12.

119. ———. States of consciousness and state-specific sciences. *Science*, 1972, *176*, 1203–1210. Reprinted in R. Ornstein (ed.). *The Nature of Human Consciousness.* San Francisco: Freeman, 1973, pp. 41–60. Also reprinted in B. Ekstrand and L. Bourne (eds.). *Principles and Meanings of Psychology.* New York: Dryden Press, 1974, pp. 320–329. Also reprinted in J. Wheatley and H. Edge (eds.). *Philosophical Dimension of Parapsychology.* Springfield, Ill.: Thomas, 1974.

120. ———. The Changing Scientific Attitude in Psychology. In C. Muses and A. Young (eds.). *Consciousness and Reality: The Human Pivot Point.* New York: Outerbridge & Lazard, 1972, pp. 73–88.

121. ———. States of Consciousness. In L. Bourne and B. Ekstrand (eds.). *Human Action: An Introduction to Psychology.* New York: Dryden Press, 1973, pp. 247–279.

122. ———. State-specific Sciences. *Science*, 1973, *180*, 1006–1008.

123. ———. Let's pretend to be rational: Review of Bloomquist's *Marijuana: The Second Trip. Contemp. Psychol.* 1973, *18*, 171–172.

124. ———. Parapsychology. *Science*, 1973, *182*, 222.

125. ———. Preliminary Notes on the Nature of Psi Processes. In

R. Ornstein (ed.). *The Nature of Human Consciousness*. San Francisco: Freeman, 1973, pp. 468–492.

126. ———. On the Nature of Altered States of Consciousness, with Special Reference to Parapsychological Phenomena. In W. Roll, R. Morris, and J. Morris (eds.). *Research in Parapsychology*, 1973. Metuchen, N. J.: Scarecrow Press, 1974, pp. 163–218.

127. ———. Some Methodological Problems in Research on Out-of-the-Body Experiences. In W. Roll, R. Morris, and J. Morris (eds.). *Research in Parapsychology, 1973*. Metuchen, N. J.: Scarecrow Press, 1974, pp. 116–120.

128. ———. (ed.). *Transpersonal Psychologies*. New York: Harper & Row, 1975.

129. ———. Out-of-the-Body Experiences. In E. Mitchell and J. White (eds.). *Psychic Exploration*. New York: Putnam, 1974, pp. 349–374.

130. ———. Out-of-the-Body Experiences. In T. X. Barber et al (eds.). *Alterations in Awareness and Human Potentialities, 1973 Annual*. New York: Psychological Dimensions, 1974.

131. ———. *Studies of Extrasensory Perception*. New York: Dutton, in press.

132. ———. *Studies of States of Consciousness*. New York: Dutton, in press.

133. ———, Boisen, M., Lopez, V., and Maddock, R. Some studies of psychokinesis with a spinning silver coin. *J. Soc. Psych. Res.*, 1972, *46*, 143–153.

134. ———, Cooper, L., Banford, S., and Schubot, S. A further attempt to modify hypnotic susceptibility through repeated individualized experience. *Int. J. Clin. Exp. Hypnosis*, 1967, *15*, 118–124.

135. ———, and Creighton, J. The Bridge Mountain Community: An evolving pattern for human growth. *J. Humanistic Psychol.*, 1966, *6*, 54–67.

136. ———, and Dick, L. Conscious control of dreaming. I. The posthypnotic dream. *J. Abnorm. Psychol.*, 1970, *76*, 304–315.

137. ———, and Fadiman, J. The case of the yellow wheat field: A dream-state explanation of a broadcast telepathic dream. *Psychoanal. Rev.*, 1974–75, *61*, 607–618.

138. ———, and Hilgard, E. Responsiveness to suggestions under "hypnosis" and "waking-imagination" conditions: A methodological observation. *Int. J. Clin. Exp. Hypnosis*, 1966, 14, 247–256.

139. ———, and Kvetensky, E. Marijuana intoxication: Feasibility of experiential scaling of depth. *J. Altered States of Consciousness*, 1973, *1*, 15–21.

140. Taylor, W. "Cloze procedure": A new tool for measuring readability. *Journalism Quart.*, 1953, *30*, 415–433.
141. Timmons, B., and Kamiya, J. The psychology and physiology of meditation and related phenomena: A bibliography. *J. Transpersonal Psychol.*, 1970, *2*, 41–59.
142. Timmons, B., and Kanellakos, D. The psychology and physiology of meditation and related phenomena: Bibliography II. *J. Transpersonal Psychol.*, 1974, *6*, 32–38.
143. Vogel, G., Foulkes D., and Trosman, H. Ego functions and dreaming during sleep onset. *Arch. Gen. Psychiat.*, 1966, *14*, 238–248. Reprinted in C. Tart (ed.). *Altered States of Consciousness: A Book of Readings.* New York: Wiley, 1969, pp. 75–92.
144. Weitzenhoffer, A., and Hilgard, E. *Stanford Hypnotic Susceptibility Scale, Forms A and B.* Palo Alto, Calif.: Consulting Psychologists Press, 1959.
145. Weitzenhoffer, A., and Hilgard, E. *Stanford Hypnotic Susceptibility Scale, Form C.* Palo Alto, Calif.: Consulting Psychologists Press, 1962.
146. Weitzenhoffer, A., and Hilgard, E. *Stanford Profile Scales of Hypnotic Susceptibility, Forms I and II.* Palo Alto, Calif.: Consulting Psychologists Press, 1963.
147. Wordsworth, W. Ode on Intimations of Immortality. In H. Darbishire (ed.), *Poems in Two Volumes of 1807.* Oxford: Clarendon Press, 1952, pp. 321–332.

Index